SEQUEL
AN IAN SPERLING SAGA: THE TOUR CONTINUES

Sequel

An Ian Sperling Saga:

The Tour Continues

K. Adrian Zonneville

Mumford House Publishing

Dedication

This book is dedicated to those who love. Who believe love heals, love is patient, love is kind, and love can last a lifetime. To my parents for gifting me the love of the written word. To David Spero for believing in me. To those who have supported my meager efforts in writing. To my children, Katie and Adrienne who grew up without a father because he was busy on the road. To Greta and Harper who lay by my side while I write. But mostly to my wife who has supported my dreams, my endeavors, my love of writing, performing, and the road. She has been my inspiration and one true love.

Acknowledgments

Without the support of those who believe, none of this is possible. To create, to fill a blank page with words, to find the melody and lyric out of silence, to paint the world as we hope it will be, to capture that one perfect moment in a photograph, to inspire, to find the beauty in all things, these are the people who are the future and give hope. To my children, Kathryn and Adrienne, their significant others, Rich and Michael, and my brand-new eleven-year-old granddaughter, my Lexi, this book is for you and your future.

Cover art, design, and brilliance Janet Sipl

Edited by Linda Wike Calkins

To Tom Misuraca for being Tom for so long

This is Important;

Reprise, but no less true

Caution!!! For those of you about to embark on this journey please understand this is a work of pure fiction, it is meant to be a humorous glimpse of the music biz and fame. The concept was suggested by my friend, David Spero, as a whacky look at his participation in the rock and roll game. Any of the characters or names you think you recognize are figments of my and your imagination. This is not meant to represent anyone in any way except as I see musicians and artists in my own little peanut brain. This is not a brilliant work of fiction such as Steinbeck, Hemingway, Tolstoy, Chekhov, or Sulu would write. It is a B Movie you sneak in to see with a twelve pack and a few friends at the local Drive-in. None of the events chronicled in this book happened outside my cranium, though...that doesn't mean they won't!

From The Mouths Of Babes

Fate lay by the pool of the ever-rippling waters of humanity. She'd gaze from time to time, as people traveled along the path she had laid out for them. Helios slowed his team of horses so he could observe her naked body prone on the soft grass to assure she was not burning. He knew she loved to bask in his glory and he loved allowing her to do just that.

Fame paced on the other side of the pool. Of all the gods that had ever godded in the history of mankind, Fame was the most fickle and jealous. There is a saying among humans that Hephaestus, the god of creativity was the most jealous. Writers, musicians, actors, and performers had claimed such throughout time, but he didn't hold a candle to Fame. If she loved you, she loved you, but if she turned against you because she didn't get her due, it was the end of the line. Ask James Dean, Marilyn Monroe, Jimi Hendrix, Jim Morrison, Kirk Cobain, Amy Winehouse or hundreds of others who tried to turn their back on her. She would not be denied.

And here she was focused on the neer-do-well, nothing of a human speck on the wall, this Ian Sperling, whose only claim to her, was that he facilitated her connection with talented people. Most of them now wishing only the barest brush with her, not to drink her in like bold, dark red wine, just a sip, and that more than satisfied. Where were the egomaniacs of old? Where were those who would sell their mothers, their children, themselves for a meager taste of her wares? She wanted her worship and she wanted it now!

This Sperling ignored her. When every other human in history wooed her with a passion usually reserved for a human lover. He could not care less. Where others would throw themselves on a pyre and immolate themselves for her, he avoided her like a plague. He stuck in her throat like a fingernail chewed off and swallowed, catching just past the larynx.

"Are you still pouting about the one that got away?" chided the naked Goddess Fate, basking in the glory of Helios chariot and his admiration.

"Fuck him!" Fame plopped her perfect derriere on a plot of soft grass and stuck her toes in the cool waters of life. "I have millions of humans chasing me as we speak. I can pick and choose whom I want to love. I have no need for one who is too stupid, too blind, too..."

"Still ignoring you, is he?" Fate couldn't help it, taunting the goddess was too much fun to ignore.

"Yes!" Her sob almost touched Fate's heart but stopped as it froze in place. "I just don't understand why."

"You are pathetic. You said yourself you could have the pick of the litter and here you are whining and moaning over one solitary human who just doesn't seem interested." Fate laughed long and hard and without the slightest trace of compassion. Gods and goddesses alike found compassion a nonessential commodity. "You would lose yourself over the affections of 'one speck of a human' who doesn't know you exist. It is to laugh!" She gave the pond a playful kick upsetting the futures of a few thousand poor souls.

"There are millions of others who worship me!" Pouted Fame. "and this one will see that, he will become jealous, but by then it will be too late. He will beg and plead, get down on his knees, look in my eyes and say pretty please, I love you, I want you, I need you, but it will be too late!" and the proclamation was made.

Questions Without Answers

"Why can't people be honest with each other?" he asked to the empty barstools and booths. His words like muffled explosions coming from a distance, detonating quietly, pieces of words and sentence wedging into the cracked, splintered wood of the once painted walls like shrapnel from tattered library books. The residue from fifty years of smokers now dead, gone, and buried, stunk the air. He looked at his reflection in the filthy dust covered mirror behind bottles too busy for dust to settle. He should've shaved, but why? To impress the other drunks that hung around this dive! He'd call them alcoholics but they were a work in progress. They'd have to try harder and lose more dignity to earn the honorific.

She'd asked him that same question years before and he still didn't have an answer, maybe because he knew, lying is easier than truth and because nobody really wants the truth. Maybe, because truth wasn't pretty but lies could dress up like whores on the prowl. And maybe because lies flowed like a gentle stream whereas truth was rapids, dashing your life and hope on every rock throughout life. Let's admit it, truth is fucking terrifying.

He mumbled these truths to the void or maybe he thought them; didn't much matter. The bartender lifted his grizzled head, scratched at a three-day old growth and looked to see if his only customer needed one more. He'd like to get out of this shithole early one night.

Yeah, maybe one more shot and he could go home to sleep, to dreams, maybe there he could talk to her. Gods knew he'd never actually talked to her while they were intimate. After all, there is intimate and there is intimate. It's one thing to share bodies, but emotion, deepest thought, secrets of the heart, mind and life lived, well, that was just too much. He thought the physical was love, she thought it was just passing time.

He knew what passing time was. Every immortal did. Life passed with ease before time. The sun, the moon, the clouds flew by, you hardly noticed, until mankind came along and found they had a schedule to keep and every other creature had to get on the train. It had been a long ride, thousands of human lifetimes, and a portion of one tired immortal's. He missed her. She was Pyrenean Ibex, smooth, strong spirit, and a helluva species. They had shared a few eons bouncing around this lovely Mother but then extinction took its toll. Immortals were not supposed to spend their lives together, eternity would grind on you. Humans, ha! Humans could mate for life easily; they only lasted a thought or two and then they were dust once again. But it took some real grit for an immortal to hang out with another, there was no end in sight, or so they both thought. And then she wasn't.

It had hit him hard, like a sledgehammer blow to the solar plexus. Except the solar plexus was in his heart, his mind, his soul. Her death had crushed him, his spirit, he didn't care about life or feeling, just stopping the pain. Blocking out every second of torture from this existence. He'd heard about another immortal that had survived much the same excruciating suffering but his had come at the hands of a mortal, not one like himself.

And, really, was he even an immortal or just a guy who felt like every day lasted a century. Maybe he was just a guy who hadn't died yet. He needed a strong drink or a punch in the temple. He gazed at his reflection in the filthy mirror, looked like a goddamn gorilla, though he was Puma, though big for his kind. Yeah, he needed to start taking better care of himself. Well, one more and he needed to find a tree.

He raised his paw to garner the barkeeps attention, one more and he was out of here. If only he could just order by the bottle. He liked the taste of bourbon, though it didn't have the effect on him it would on a human. Shit! If it did, he would've died centuries ago. His liver would've pickled and the pickles would've shriveled and died. Maybe he would grab some of that LSD he'd heard so much about, he could use a trip. A few weeks just wandering around the abandoned mines of the mind and soul. Yeah, a little time off or maybe he needed a nap.

It was sometimes hard to tell what was fact and what was friction. He knew something was rubbing him wrong but he couldn't grab hold of it, to get a grip on the irritant and make it cease. She had said it was the drink, so he'd switched to vodka for a while. Same result. Wine? Removed his spine. Beer? Made him uneasy, queer, though not gay. Language had a tendency to throw him off the beat. Just when he thought he had a handle on what the fuck people were saying some young punk would walk in with a new vernacular and the learning curve would send him into a tree.

He stared down the barkeep who seemed intent on ignoring his one paying customer, well, the one person sitting and drinking with the assumption he was paying. He wanted to feel in his pockets to see if that was the case but didn't want it to appear obvious until the glass had been filled and emptied one more time. If you were going to be banished from a dive, and he had from many, chased down alleys and streets, beaten and arrested, it was best to have a belly filled before the pain came.

Bottle in hand the bored, worn, wrinkled, heavily mustachioed proprietor shambled his way down to where the flop house refugee sat. Hunched shoulders, in need of a bath, four days of stubbled salt and pepper on his cheeks and chin only emphasizing the appearance of box living. That and his refusal to gaze into the eyes of the man with the relief.

"I hope you got cash for this," it wasn't threat or attempted intimidation, more a simple prayer that he would have no need to scamper after the trash today.

Dirty hand in filthy pocket wins the lottery. And it was folding money at that. Now, if only it has a positive numeral followed by a zero. He held it below the bar where the dreamer couldn't see and unfolded the bill. Hmm, a one, followed by...a zero! Jackpot. Couple drinks couldn't be worth more'n a ten spot in a shithole like this. He tossed it on the wood.

The innkeeper picked it up to hold it up to the light. Shit, even in a piss pot like this the guy thought he was being passed a paper sawbuck. It was then they both saw at the same time the second zero. He didn't know who was more surprised, the barkeep or himself. Where in all hell had he come up with a C-note? He wanted to grab it back but knew even a hundred wasn't worth having his head stove in. He closed his eyes and took a deep breath, daydreaming of drinks for everyone at the bar. Oh, he was alone.

His eyes almost audibly snapped open. He'd dozed off sitting at the bar. It couldn't have been for long or the anxious-to-close-and-go-home bartender would've tossed his drunk ass out. Though drunk he was still working on.

The dreams came mostly when he was sober which was why he avoided sobriety as often as his pocket would allow. And he should still have a lot of change coming from that C-note. Unless that was part of the dream.

He felt the hand on his arm. He didn't like to be touched, especially when he thought he was alone. He was about to round house on whoever was bold enough to bother a very large man in a bowery dive when the little brown woman smiled at him. He knew her, but from where?

"Suzette," she says helpfully, "we met while we was trying to help Evan and some good folks save the world few years back."

"Yeah, fat lotta good that did." He remembered. He'd almost ate Bear's kid or grandkid or whatever she was. But hadn't known at the time the girl was the git of Bear! Though now he come to think of it, that might have been the time before when Bear had saved the world. Getting so a soul couldn't keep track of Bear's accomplishments.

The time this pretty woman was talking about was when Bear had got all the family together trying to force humans to give a damn about their own world. That had lasted about a half second until one group took offense at some stupid thing some other group supposedly said on some idiotic unsocial media type goddamn thing and the whole deal blew up. Mankind went back to killing and hating each other, trying to kill the Mother and all her children in the bargain. This woman was one of the People

"I was just sayin' to, uh, eh, well, I guess me, that humans can't be trusted. Can't be honest with anybody, not even theyselves." He made to spit on the floor then thought better. "Can't even get their shit together enough to save theyselves let alone any other on the damn Mother."

"Ya-hay to that. The problem remains. We still can't let them destroy the Mother 'cause we'd go with it and all our children. So, we're thinking of trying, again, to keep them from blowin' up the whole damn thing."

"And how're you planning on doing that?" He scoffed.

"Finding a better class of humans to work with."

"You know some?" He almost laughed but instead held up two fingers to the barkeep who still had the hundred in his hand and pointed at the woman and hisself.

"Might," she said nodding thanks as the barman set down a small glass of brown liquid in front of her.

"Who?" She had piqued his interest. He was tired and no longer believed the Mother could be saved, but if this woman had a glimmer of hope he wanted to see why.

"There's some folks, old hippie types with a bit more miles and experience on 'em, making noise about peacefully helping other humans throughout the world. They been making other humans believe. Old ones like them and young'un's as well. People have been showing up by the thousands and buying into the dream," she sipped at the liquid and smiled. "They seem to give a shit about us as well. Kind of preaching and teaching about an interconnectivity of man, the People, and the Mother. You know, like I said, hippies."

He liked this woman. Might have been a time he'd a tried to eat her but now he wanted to hear what she had to say. "Tell me more." He had watched his kind almost become extinct, if there was someone, anyone, man or beast, who could help increase the numbers, the range, the food supply, he had to be in. It was his duty to his people even if it meant working with man. Even if it was drugged up man.

"Are they planning on saving the world with that noise again?" He remembered the time when young humans had decided to save the world through loud, screeching, ear popping 'music'. He wasn't certain he wanted to try and survive that again. Maybe it would be better for the world to end than have to listen to Iggy Pop and the Sex Pistols.

"Well, it's not Mozart, Beethoven or Brahms," she conceded.

He had liked Brahms, he was quiet, and some of that Beethoven's music was quite pleasant but nothing took the place of the sound of the Mother. He didn't suppose mankind could accomplish anything without all the noise. Though there was plenty of beautiful music going on, if the damn human species would shut their gobs and listen. Man was not good at being silent.

"But from all reports the music of this movement is not unpleasant. And the people making it are cleaner, less smelly than last time. They still smoke that musty, malodorous weed that Bear and some of the others have taken a shine to, though once you get used to the reek it's not so bad and it seems to calm them humans down some, less fighting, less violence," she shrugged.

"Anytime you can make man less violent it is a step in the right evolutionary direction. Killing to eat, to survive is one thing, but killing just to kill," he shivered and made to spit on the floor, the sight of the large human behind the bar with the change for his C-note stopped the action once more. "Especially not in any kind of fair fight. Shit, the cowards are half a mile away when they shoot their godforsaken guns. Pussies!"

"Be that as it may," she forced the engine back on the proper track, "these are not those people. These are the peaceful ones, the ones we should try to advocate and embolden. The ones who kind of believe we are all one or, at least, are trying to be. Or so Bear's thinking goes. Though he wishes to assure hisself and all the other People that is, in fact, who they are."

"So, you are here to do Bear's bidding once again," he snarled. When they had followed Bear before it seemed a good idea but mankind has a way of turning on friends just as often as enemies and cats won't get fooled again. "Hasn't worked out so well in the past, has it?" He nudged and raised two fingers pointing with emphasis at the two empty glasses.

"At least he's trying to slow down the destruction if he can't stop it all together." She made to get up. She'd had enough of those who quit, just rolled over on extinction and the possible death of the Mother. She didn't need to listen to another pissy Spirit belittle those who would try. She was a fighter and expected nothing less of those around her. She guessed that was why she was so attracted to Bear. There was one species that wouldn't go down without one helluva fight.

"Hang, on, hang on, hang on," he put just a minute pressure on her shoulder, not threatening just pausing the motion. "Where is this circus and when can we meet the clowns?" This time he grinned a toothy, challenging gesture, more invite than threat. "I got nothing on my calendar for a few decades, guess I can tag along and listen to what these doped up hippie types got to say."

"They finished their stint here in town last night and head out in the morning. Going south then west. I wanted to catch them out in the boonies, not here, to see what it's like with the rubes in the middle of the wasteland." In other words where they themselves would be more comfortable. There were very few of the People who were comfy in the confines of concrete and glass, preferring the natural environment. He nodded in agreement.

"So, we got time," he downed his shot and motioned for the barkeep to bring him his change.

"We have time to talk and to figure the best way to approach this group, that is what we have time for," she emphasized the word 'time' knowing he had some other use in mind. Shit, even the People suffered from being over sexed and she was nowhere near to being in heat.

The crews were loading gear into the three semis while just a few blocks away small carryon's, backpacks, and valises filled with contracts, ledger sheets, and financials were being loaded into the bellies of the road dog buses. Peadar, Ritchie and Steven had all caught their flights back across the pond, they had kicked around the idea of doing some kind of project together. They would write, produce, and have the best time working with each other, if they could find the time.

The lobby of the hotel was filled with singers, musicians, roadies, and stage crews readying for the first day back on the road. The blacktop called and these were the gypsies that would answer. Empty midsized ballparks soon to be concert venues awaited their transformation. NY had been the Big Apple and more, but it was time to feel the sway of the concrete, hear the hum of tires and make music for the masses across the southern tier of America.

Ian Sperling sat on a small road case watching the busy ants loading, chatting, converging in a symphony of activity. They were happy, happy to have had all that the Big Apple could provide. Happy they had given as much as they had got, happy that each show seemed to top the last, and happy to be heading out onto the wide-open blacktop.

He was lost in his thoughts, they were not happy thoughts, they were old man thoughts. Yes, he watched his crew but he did not see them.

He had never seen himself as old, had never felt the tired weight of decades on the road. He did today. He just wanted to go home, sit on the front porch, drink iced tea, and watch as the rest of life flew by. Which was odd as he hated iced tea, didn't have a front porch, and could never remain stationary for more than a week. Still his mind wandered back down the many miles he had traveled. He thought of, and remembered, with great fondness, shows he had helped produce and artists he had helped elevate, but only for a moment.

As quickly as those memories filled him, the thoughts of all that he hadn't accomplished pushed the memories out of his head, where they fell and broke into pieces on the hard ash floor of life. No one seemed to know why old men laser focus on what could have been rather than being content with what was, but they will and they do. A man could accomplish great deeds in life, cure cancer, save thousands, bring peace to the middle east. Instead, as he neared the final few miles of this mortal coil all he would focus on were the cross words, the missed opportunities, the chance to buy a half dozen acres of prime real estate in Kuala Lumpur, or the dog at the pound he could've saved instead of going to that puppy mill in Amish country. OK, that last one he ought to carry to his grave, but come on, this imaginary man did well. And so had Ian, but he felt he could've done more.

His thoughts wandered as his empty eyes kept time with the march of the tour. Bags and instruments loaded, rearranged, people treated the same, he watched without seeing, heard without sound, as his imagination and mental meanderings wandered along. He should've done more, helped more, lifted more artists with what little leverage he had. Hadn't Peadar McCarthy not long back asked him for his help? If he had the wherewithal to help a superstar, he could've helped those further down the ladder more. Now time was barking at the soles of his shoes and chewing on the leather. Fuck!

The rumbling, stomping sharp retort of thunder snapped him from his self-indulgent reverie. Looking up he saw nothing but clear blue, sun-filled sky. Not even the wisp of a cloud, certainly no thunder heads. Where had that report come from?

Fame stomped around her mountain top creating heat thunder not only around the humans, but her kind as well. Fate stuck her pretty face around the peak, a self-satisfied smirk firmly in place. If Fame was pissed, Fate's day was made.

"What is it. Sister?" she feigned concern. "Don't tell me you are still frittering away over Sperling?" She said the name knowing it would ignite the goddess's passions. She wanted to laugh, Gods knew she wanted nothing more than to cackle, to dissolve into a blather, but decorum won out.

"I know he wants me; he is down there right now wishing for more than he has and thinking maybe he should have tasted my sweet nectar when he had the chance." She turned to face her sister goddess and shrieked, "Why didn't he love me when he had the chance? And why, oh, why can't he admit he wants me now?"

"Maybe you were too needy, too focused on what you wanted. It's possible you should have tried a more subtle approach." Fate suggested innocently though not innocently enough to cool Fame's irritation.

"There's still time," Fame said to herself, forgetting for a moment that Fate was also a goddess and could hear her thoughts and whispers.

" Well, you had best move fast, the circus is leaving town!" And with that Fate returned to the millions of futures she was plotting.

Ian's thoughts coalesced into the information he had been holding back from the rest of the troop. Oh, he was going to tell them sooner or later, but he had wanted to wait until they were well on the road. It would be too easy for someone to jump ship here in NY where jobs were plentiful for great musicians and road crews. And that was the fear, wasn't it? That if he told them what he knew they would most likely quit right here, right now, and tell him to find other targets.

But, if he waited, if he held out, would he not be shattering the bond of trust. Who was he to deny them what he knew? The facts and danger surrounding what lay ahead? Who the fuck did he think he was?

He knew now. He was the guy who would hold the meeting before the buses turned their engines over and one wheel moved. Truth had gotten him this far; truth would either get him the rest of the way or it would all come to an end.

The Sound Of Waves Deciding

She stood silent and still, a statue watching the brightening sky to the east. Clouds skitted across the horizon, the rising sun painting their underbellies yellow and purple, easing into red, though washed out as if from watercolors. The waves lapped at her feet as she slipped into the coming day, gentle, like donning an old t-shirt. Warmth began to fill the morning and, once the sun had risen, it would heat the sands, cooled by the night, but she would be miles down the road before that would happen.

The yip of the large dog in the front seat of the ancient pickup truck roused her from her stupor, it was time to get moving. She had a new life to begin and standing in this ocean would not get it begun. She walked in the soft sand to where the truck patiently waited. Far more patient than the dog and the young man standing next to the open passenger side door.

He wasn't certain where this leg of the trip was going to take him, he was just flotsam caught up in her wake. He was following along because he couldn't lead. Hard to take point when you had no clue where the path lay. Though he'd come this far across the country with her, now they would head back, a lot of motion going nowhere it seemed. Then again, trust is a funny thing.

"Do we have any kind of plan?" Aron stood with his left hand on the bed of the pickup and his right holding the door open as if refusing to get in until she told him where they were going.

"Does it matter?" She teased. He had every right to know but over the past few months they had developed a brother/big sister relationship which she found endearing. She'd never had a sibling and found she loved the intimacy of it without any sexual or romantic pressures. It was playful and he was quick to take the bait.

"Not like I have any choice," he mumbled realizing his precarious position of being left behind and lost in poverty a thousand miles from anything he remotely knew.

"Aron, you will always have a choice. I've told you if you get tired of being with me and my wandering ways, I will give you enough financial support to start whatever life you want." She tossed it like an underhand softball to a small child.

"Nah, I'm finally getting used to you. Don't want to start finding new people to annoy me. Just wanted to feel like we're partners in this thing," he grinned knowing she was pulling his chain.

"Well, I thought we would head back to Oregon where my home is. I have some loose plans of what to do with the rest of my life. You can learn along the way and decide if you want to be part of it. But I wanted to follow some of Kim's journey while we're out this way. So, I am aiming for New Orleans to talk to Henry about maybe having him assist with different aspects of the plan." She sketched as much of a plan as she had formulated.

"You liked this Kim, didn't you? What, were you friends since high school or something?" They had never really dug very deep into Kim and Carrie's relationship. He guessed they had ample time now. He'd known they were close, like twins or besties, kind of thing.

"I loved Kim like no other person I've ever known in my life." The words were soft like the feel of Kim's body when they cuddled.

"What? You mean like," and here he took a steadying breath, "lovers or something?" He shuddered.

Carrie stared at him. She had just assumed since she talked about Kim all the time, he would've picked up that they were a couple, a very close couple. "Yes, we were deeply and passionately in love!" She unequivocally stated.

"Wow!"

"What now? Please don't tell me after all we've been through that you are homophobic!" she would be so disappointed if he turned out to be some kind of bigot, but who knew what kind of an upbringing he'd had. Shit, Kansas, probably some kind of snake wrangling, christofascist cult or something.

"No! I just never knew anybody who was, you know…" he struggled for the word or the concept or something to hang his hat on.

"The word you're searching for is lesbians. And yes, I guess we were and, then again, no, we were just two people who were completely, totally, soulfully in love with each other who didn't get near enough time before she died. And if you say one wrong word here, I am going to leave you here penniless and alone." She'd had enough of bigots and fear mongers and hate. If Aron was coming, he was coming with eyes and mind wide open.

"Sorry, no really," he said to the expression on her face, "it just kind of took me by surprise, I guess. I'm from a small town in the middle of nowhere, I got no reference point. I do now." His grin was sheepish and apologetic. "Look I really like you and respect you, you been through a lot. Been shit on more than most and you're still a decent person. I'm sorry but I just got to recalibrate for a sec. I promise, I got nothing against anybody, least of all you. Just let my brain quit spinning." He tried to find what he wanted to say but jumbled his thoughts.

Carrie understood. It had taken her more than a sec to figure out how she and Kim had come together and the deep feelings they had for each other. "Get in the fucking truck, we got miles to make and we're wasting cloud cover!"

And The Truth Shall
Set You On The Road

Ian called for the meeting in the hotel lobby, the lobby where so much had happened over the past two weeks. It seemed appropriate. Everyone thought it would be a congratulatory meeting for the amazing shows, the dexterity they had shown with different special guests each night of varying degrees of superstardom. They had acquitted themselves brilliantly and they certainly deserved a pat on the back; not to be treated as simple employees with the truth conveniently tucked away in his back pocket. He would give them their props first and then it would be decision time.

The buses and trucks waited patiently on the busy NY side street, every street at every time of the day in NY was a busy street. They really needed to get vehicles in gear and on the move before the crush of 'rush' hour began which would take a half day out of their travel.

Packed into the spacious lobby, Ian depended on acoustics and intense interest in what he had to say to allow his voice to carry.

"I'll make this as quick as possible, as we need to get the fuck outta Dodge before it comes to a standstill." There were a few catcalls, sniggers, and barks of laughter. Someone shouted, "Well, then why are we wasting time talking." To more laughter. The mood was ebullient, they had loved their time in the big city but, as Maggie had predicted, they were more than ready for truck stops, highways, two-lanes, and bad food. "Well, I wanted to personally thank each and every one of you for the professional and superb, first-rate job you pulled off here. And I know what we said when we all voted on the finances for this tour but you will find yourselves aptly rewarded, in cash, in your pay envelopes." A cheer filled the lobby, the side-street, and beyond. This was welcome news.

Jaxson sat over to the side listening. They had discussed the bonus and he had agreed they deserved every penny. But Ian hadn't let him in on the real reason for this meet. Jax had an unsettled, uneasy feeling in the pit of his stomach, something about the way Ian had been acting for the past two days and the suit that had shadowed Ian. It could only be some label or booker come to piss on their parade. Jax didn't like the look of the guy, like a narc, really. He supposed he was about to find out the answer to the mystery.

Ian took a deep breath; this was the rubber skidding across the highway. His discomfort showed in every movement of his body and each line on his face. He knew the chance he was taking but he also knew if he didn't, all would absolutely be lost.

He wished something would happen, so he could quickly and miraculously save a life; he needed the mojo. Everyone appeared too healthy for his liking. Time to jump.

"The man standing just to my left, the one who looks like an FBI agent," they laughed, "is just that." The laughter ceased. "He has come to me with some news from the agency about certain threats on the lives of anyone connected to this tour and its cause. It would appear there are some in this country who do not share our concern for the untouchables, the unseen, and wish to stop our crusade, as it were. They have threatened our lives if we continue through the southern states."

Every sound was siphoned from the room. Every man and woman looked to each other to gauge reaction.

"So, we don't go to the south, fuck 'em!" came the voice of Lee Starling.

"That is an option and one our friend here would prefer." Ian said indicating the stone-faced man to his right.

"You don't sound like you agree," Joya's voice was quiet, questioning.

"It isn't up to me, but I will admit I don't like someone telling me where I can go and what I can do. I especially don't like running from bigots and hate mongerers. But I am not alone and it isn't just my life. Now, I will tell you, the FBI, through our friend Dennis Moore, here, has offered us a certain amount of protection. Just keep in mind there are a lot of us and few of them, so we would have to keep an eye out for each other and those who come to participate."

The murmurs grew with the fear of what this could mean. No one thought playing music, trying to improve the lives of those less fortunate, giving worth and hope to those in short supply of both, bringing a little joy into the lives of fans would lead to their demise, but this was the new world. A world filled with people who hated for no other reason than to hate. Did you want to tempt them? Was it worth your life to stand in the breach for people you had never met, would never meet?

Lee spoke up, "You know, back in '69 we was marching for peace, to stop an unjust war. For peace. Understand, this was before things got real ugly. There weren't no rocks being tossed, no windows busted, no violence, we wanted peace. We marched with flowers in our hands. And then the cops and guard started beating the shit out of some of us. I can still feel the whack of the batons as they hit my head, shoulders, back. I was bleeding like a stuck pig. People were trying to drag me to safety before the fucking cops killed me." He was lost in the very unpleasant memory. A tear, though of sadness or rage no one could tell, raced down his white beard, "I stopped them dragging me. Told them to let me be. So, they laid me on the concrete, on the sidewalk rather than the gutter, and it took everything I had but I got up and I stood and stared down them fucking cops. One made to pound my head, but another grabbed his arm and pulled him back. All I could say at the time to that cop was, 'thank you, brother', and I slow walked to him and hugged him with the last of my strength. Yeah, it was a good day. I despise hate. I ain't running from nobody, so fuck 'em, you need a bass player I'm getting on that bus just like they did in the early 60's. Anyone wants to join me, I got music to play." He walked out the door to the open door of the bus.

Slowly, in twos and threes, the rest of the troop began to move towards the waiting gypsy caravan, resolute in their beliefs though still filled with a dollop of dread. As Joya stood up and turned to make her way in the same direction Jaxson caught her arm. "Are you sure you want to take this on? You told me when we met you were already a target, you're going to have a huge bullseye on your back you come along with this."

"Like Lee so eloquently put it, fuck 'em. I despise hate as well. If I don't stand up now, when will I ever have a chance for peace? When will I ever get the opportunity to live my life? Be me? I got to stand for myself, no one else will. So, I gotta, for me and every other black, queer, beat down human being just like me." She smiled her fear and resolve before wrapping Jaxson in a bear hug. "I'll be alright," she whispered.

As Jaxson's foot found the first step towards his own bus his phone woke up and screamed a Springsteen tune. Several of the band members stuck their heads out of buses laughing at his choice of ring-tone. Jax checked the number to see if was someone he wanted to speak to, which was a rarity, friends being few and far between. It was always assumed he didn't want to speak to anybody on the phone, but this was an international call. Best take the call.

The heavily accented voice on the other end of the electromagnetic wave spectrum called his name as if not certain whom he had called. "Jaxson?"

"Flaco?" Jax was a little taken aback by the sound of his old friend, who he hadn't spoken to for several years. They hadn't had a falling out; it was just the way things go in the music business. You'd work with a musician you loved for an album or two, or a tour, become as close as brothers and then not see each other for a decade. It was Flaco Rodrigez, one of the best Flamenco guitarists in the world. Jaxson picked up right where they'd left off. "Como esta? Que necesitas?" Jaxson was, of course, somewhat fluent in Spanish.

"We're at the airport and they won't let us into the country," Flaco sounded flustered.

"Que aeropuerto? Y que pais?" Jaxson was grasping at straws he hadn't known existed until one minute ago.

"Senor Kennedy's airport in your own beautiful country. Though it would be far more beautiful if they would allow us entry. We have come to play!" Joy filled every syllable as if this were the most natural thing in the world. After another ten minutes of back-and-forth Jaxson finally understood Flaco and another old chum, Kiko Veneno, had decided, after a night of drinking and reminiscing about their time with Jax, while also speaking with great respect about his pursuit of justice for people and the planet, they wanted in. The problem was they didn't have the necessary work permits, paperwork, and licensing to come play in the USA. They assumed since Jaxson was such a well-known man in this country, he could just make a phone call. He couldn't.

As he was talking and explaining these roadblocks to Flaco his phone beeped, another call coming in from another international number. What the absolute...? "Hola" said Jaxson still in Flaco mode.

"Hola, mi amigo," was the response from a voice as familiar as a reflection in the mirror. It was percussionist Tino di Sanchez, who had played on a half dozen of Jax's albums and toured extensively with him over the past two decades, they knew each other.

"Como esta? No me digas que estas en America," Jaxson was feeling a theme here.

"Si, I am at your Kennedy's aeropuerto," the smile could be felt through the phone, knowing how happy his old friend would be to see him.

"And they won't let you in because you don't have documentos," Jaxson tried to keep the languor out of his tone but was only partially successful.

"Si, again. It is like you are reading my thoughts before I can think them to you," the joyous bark of laughter confirmed how close the two were, so close they could read each other's minds.

"Where in the airport are you? Donde esta en el aeropuerto...?" he never got to finish the question.

"Customs, border security, a very depressing office," murmured the percussionist.

"Are there two others with a phone in hand who appear almost as depressed as you feel," Jaxson knew before he asked.

"Si! Are you looking at all of us somehow?"

"No, they are on my other line. The shorter man with the phone is Flaco Rodrigez," Jaxson tried to do intros over the phone.

"The Guitarist?" Now Tino was impressed. "I will meet them and wait for you to come save us," excitement reigned supremo now that he knew he would be sprung and get to hang with his old friend.

"No, I am on a bus heading out on tour, I am going to send a lawyer to help you and he will bring you to me," he emphasized, praying all had packed their patience. Then thought, 'I hope he can.'

"Raj," he called down the line of buses. This was going to be quite the dance.

Jaxson explained to his 'lawyer' exactly what was needed and where they would catch up once he had the three European musicians in tow. Raj asked him where he should take the cash to pay for these expenses. He knew how all felt about the money raised specifically for the 'cause', especially after the episode with Jake. He wasn't surprised to hear Jaxson say he would cover all the expenses himself. Raj decided silently he would help cover most without Jax's knowledge.

Jaxson had finally completed his instructions to Raj, it was time to go. The last of the stragglers found their way onto whichever bus they had decided to ride out of town. The last two to board were the thin, waifish white Appalachian looking woman followed by the dark-skinned slightly heavy-set black woman, twins in song and eavesdroppers for hobby.

As they settled on the two remaining seats of the couch Gillian remarked to Joya, "Jaxson really Is a decent guy, isn't he?"

"Won't get an argument from me," Joya seemed slightly taken aback at the casual observation of a given.

"I mean, with what he is doing for the guys that came over from Europe, paying all their expenses himself. He could've just as easily had the tour pay and none would fault him," a cockeyed grin played about Gillian's lips. She admired the co-captain of the Untouchables.

"He doesn't surprise me, not from what I've come to know," Joya nodded her own approval of Mr. Grahm.

"And I must add I am quite impressed with you, young lady. Continuing on this tour takes great courage. I heard what you told Jaxson before we left. You are quite brave. I admire that. Standing up for yourself, I understand, but for 'your people', that says more about you than anything," she wrapped her arm around Joya's shoulders and hugged her close.

"I don't know about brave," Joya shrunk inside herself, "or having any courage, to be honest I am terrified. It's one thing to have words, quite another to stand eye to eye with hate," a quiver shook the truth from her words.

"You know courage isn't the scarcity of fear, it is being terrified and still standing in the face of it. You are far braver than you give yourself credit for," this time Gillian wrapped Joya in a huge bear hug and squeezed her love into the woman.

"How did you know what I told Jax, I thought we were alone?" She locked eyes with Gillian.

"Oh, I wasn't eavesdropping. It isn't eavesdropping if you just conveniently happen to be out of sight but not earshot of a private conversation," she giggled at Joya's shocked expression before both broke into girlish giggles.

The Road Might Be Silent
But The Mind Has Questions

They had driven along in silence for the first twenty minutes until Aron couldn't take the not knowing, the not being let in, the lack of respect she was showing by keeping him out. Hadn't they traveled across the breadth of the USA together, or damn near? Hadn't they shared adventures and seen a lake as big as an ocean? Been to the biggest damn city he had ever, or would ever, see? Now she's gonna clam up and treat him like he's just some kid? Well, not today.

"So, you gonna tell me or what?" He'd meant for it to sound more demanding but it came out more plea.

"Tell you what?" Oh, so she was going to make him beg, was she? Well, he could be just as patient as she was stubborn.

Another twenty minutes of silence. Oscar didn't care one whit. He had his head in her lap and was stretched out on the bench seat, the bottom half of him laying across Aron's lap. There'd be no help there. He was about to come out of his skin and scream when she smiled.

"I thought we'd just head south along the coast on the Garden State Parkway until we hit Ocean City, Maryland and then stop. We'll grab a bite and see which way the wind blows. If it appeals, we'll hang for a day, if not we'll head down 13 into Virginia and see what we find."

Aron dug the atlas out from under his seat, not trusting his voice just yet, he didn't want her to hear the frustration, though she knew. He studied the map of New Jersey. It was funny, he thought, he'd never have been able to tell heads nor ass when looking at a map before he'd met Carrie, now he was like a professional navigator. Hell, he'd never know'd nothing before she'd run across him in Park City and took him on the adventure of a life. Just some orphaned piece of human by-product, good for nothing, sludge of society, living in an alley and waiting to die. She wouldn't let him.

She picked him up, cleaned him, polished what she found, and took care of him, almost like she cared. He guessed she really did or she'd a chucked him by the side of the road months ago. He should, what? Be more thankful? Show more respect? Maybe just be a better friend.

"We're kind of takin' the long way round if we're headed back to Oregon. I thought you was kind of in a hurry." He wasn't completely up to snuff on her plan but thought she was anxious to get started on whatever it was.

"Well, I thought we'd see some of the south, let my 'plan' percolate a little while longer. I thought we could talk about it while we drove and you could throw in your two cents. I could use a different perspective. I thought we should stop off in New Orleans so I can confer with Henry as well." She spoke as though she was reciting the ideas to herself, to reassure in her own mind.

"He was that doctor you mentioned the one who tried to save your girlfriend at the end." She could tell by tone and verbiage he was still coming to terms with her relationship with Kim. She decided to let him find his own way.

"He was her close friend, before she and I met, besides being her doctor. He is a very smart man and I could use a little medical and ethical advice about my concept. I tried something like this years ago and flopped, because I didn't ask the right people the right questions to do it right," she grinned at her little funny. "This time I am going to ask the experts before I screw it up."

"So, we're going to wander and find the people to talk to? Do you know where we are going to find these brilliant folks?" He wasn't sold on her plan, as it felt more sketchy than planned.

"Yup, just going to ride the rails until we find as much information as is available," end of discussion.

"Might as well be like Deadheads and become music Gypsies," he said to himself or so he thought.

"What?" she turned her head to see if she heard him right.

"You know, folks who follow a band, like the Grateful Dead. There are folks who follow bands and their tours, go to all the shows. Don't know where they get the jack, but they love the music, I guess. We seem to be heading in the same general direction as one of them tours, I think," he Goggled tours, bands, venues along the general direction they were headed. "I mean, if we're just going to flow with life until we finally hit Orleans why not catch some live music along the way. Shit, they got tons of live down south, maybe we could find us an honest to God rock fest or something." He loved live music, from what he remembered.

" We're not hippies traipsing along with the wind and smoking pot, listening to music." The finality of her words were not lost on the citizen at hand.

"No, we're just wandering, saving the world one lost soul at a time," he murmured.

"You talking about anybody you know in particular?" the laugh was cut short.

Carrie was about to query him deeper on the subject until she almost hit the car parked half on the berm and half on the Parkway. She swerved around the vehicle before pulling onto the berm just ahead of it.

"You sure this is a good idea? You know, sometimes people pull over like this in the middle of nowhere," and here he waved his hand in all directions to emphasize how out in the middle they were, "so they can rob and kill whoever is stupid enough to be good Samaritan." His strong survival instinct, which had been honed by years living on the street, was screaming in alarm.

"Then, I'll take Oscar with me while you wait here in case you have to drag my bullet riddled body to the nearest hospital," she smirked and got out of the truck. As she made her way back towards the apparent deserted mode of transport. Aron's paranoia crept up her spine. What was she doing? This could be the dumbest of the many dumb things she had done in her life.

Until she saw the woman slumped over in the front seat and the two children sleeping on top of each other in the back. Rescue and compassion thy name is Carrie. She knocked cautiously on the driver's side window. Nothing. She knocked a little harder. Still nothing. She banged on the window with the side of her fist and one of the girls in the back seat finally stirred. Carrie moved to the back window and pointed at it miming for the young girl to open the window, if only slightly.

The girl shook her head and looked terrified. Carrie became a bit more insistent trying to get the girl just to crack the window so she could talk to her. Finally, she mimed for the child to climb over the seat and wake her mother. Well, she assumed it was the girl's mother, Carrie would soon find out.

Carrie couldn't hear what the girl was pleading, she could only partially read her lips. The silent, 'Mommy, Mommy, wake up, there's a police person here, wake up! Mommy!' until the comatose figure regained life.

She turned her face towards the window where Carrie stood patiently waiting, hoping the woman would respond. As she turned completely towards Carrie, Carrie saw the swollen, deep purple, blue, almost black, and red veined blistered right eye try to focus on her. Recognizing she wasn't a police person or any official of the government she slowly twisted her body to try and open the door. Her left arm wouldn't cooperate with the demands her brain was making, so she reached across her body with her right arm to grab the inner handle. The door swung open and the woman almost fell out.

"The car doesn't seem to want to work," she said as she slipped out of the driver's seat and onto the pavement. The young girl who had roused her whimpered as she watched her mother dissolve.

Aron, who had been watching every breath being taken, every muscle that moved, jumped out of the truck and ran back to the broken-down car. He opened the back door to extricate the children and move them to the cab of the pickup as Carrie tried desperately to revive the woman. They had to get her out of the lane and the car off the road.

"Oscar can watch them for a minute, help me carry her to the bed of the truck and let's get this car out of traffic," Carrie made a gallant attempt to sound calm and in control. Sometimes success has to be graded by millimeters rather than miles.

Neither she nor Aron were gifted with great strength but surfing, swimming, and surviving can build enough strength that adrenaline will take over to do the rest. They conveyed the unconscious woman to the bed of the truck and made her as comfortable as they could.

"See if you can get the car started and move it onto the shoulder," Carrie instructed Aron as she grabbed her water bottle from the front seat.

"You know I don't have a license," Aron reminded.

"I didn't ask you to drive it to Utah, just move the damn thing off the road before there is a much greater disaster we have to deal with." She had had enough and just wanted him to do what needed to be done. Fer Christ's sake, he just had to start the thing and move it ten feet!

Aron Turned the key and the engine made a valiant attempt but the loud knocking and screech of metal on metal told him they would do better to find a couple shovels and bury it. The engine was shot. Great!

"We've got to get her back to the land of the living and see what happened and what we can do," Carrie maintained control by sheer will. The two girls, now very much awake, were beginning to fray at the edges and cry for their unconscious mother.

"Girls do you know how long you were parked here?" Carrie's tone gentle. They stared. "Can you tell time?" She tried another tact. Both shook their heads no. Great! Too young to know anything that would help.

Carrie took her water bottle and poured an ample amount onto a clean rag applying the cool, wet bandage to the woman's forehead. She didn't know if that would accomplish anything but she'd seen it in a movie or TV show. The woman murmured. Maybe this was helping. Carrie poured a little bit of water into the woman's slightly parted lips, some found its way down her throat and she began to sputter, cough, and spit up the liquid.

"Where are my girls?" Her first thought as she slammed back into reality.

"They are in the truck, right up front there," Carrie tried to calm the woman as she offered the now conscious woman a sip of water to complete the revival.

"Why aren't they in the car? Who are you? Where are my girls?" the questions flew like a flock of startled sparrows.

"Relax, everything is alright. What happened to you? Who blackened your eye and hurt your arm? Were you in an accident?" Though Carrie could tell by the condition of the car and the girls, that hadn't taken place. Someone had done this on purpose. And Carrie was now pissed.

They got the woman, Barbara, comfortably situated in the pickup's cab and then settle the girls in the bed as securely and cozy as they could. The girls thought this a grand adventure, riding in the back of a pickup with the great German Shepard as a pillow and Aron as lifeguard. They promised they would be alright with just Oscar. They would behave and keep all hands and feet inside the ride but Carrie insisted and, she was delighted to hear, so had Aron. Carrie couldn't tell if it was just his inherent decency making itself known or if the two girls reminded him of his own lost family.

As the road slipped beneath them, she told Barbara that her car was dead on the shoulder. She and Aron had pushed it out of the roadway and completely onto the shoulder. Carrie didn't know why but she'd had Aron remove the license plates and brought them with. She knew the police would trace the vehicle sooner or later, but she wanted Barbara and her girls miles away before they did.

Barbara gave a brief synopsis of the why and wherefores of how they found themselves broke down by the side of the highway. She actually laughed, bitter and remorseful though it may have been, of how she had grabbed the girls, some hidden cash, and the car to bust out of an abusive, horrid excuse of a marriage. She laughed harder when she explained that she was a counselor and psychologist at a woman's shelter yet couldn't seem to save herself.

"Come on," she chided Carrie's horrified expression, "you've got to see the irony, the absurdity, of someone who has dedicated her life to helping save the lives of others but had to run like hell to save her own!"

"Sometimes that's all that is left to us." Carrie drove on in silence remembering her own run from abuse, until the signpost noted it was but a few miles to the next decent sized town.

"Here's my idea," she roused herself from the deep thoughts occupying the cab stirring Barbara from her own stupor. "This looks like a sizeable town in the shadow of Atlantic City coming up. We are going to find you another vehicle, something you and the girls will be comfortable in. I am going to buy it and put it in my name, don't argue," she insisted putting a hand to stop any discussion, "If your husband is looking for you, we are going to make it as difficult to find you as we can. We'll put the car in my name, I'll pay, believe me, I can afford it. And then I am going to get you some cash so you can buy yourself and those girls some clothes, food, and whatever you need. A phone and I'll call my bank and see if we can get you a credit card in your name, maybe your maiden name, so you can get hotel rooms where you need until you can set up a new life far away from the pain."

Again, Barbara began to protest, "Why?" They had only met a very short while ago, why would this woman care about someone she didn't know? This was going to cost thousands and she had no way of paying Carrie back.

Carrie assured Barbara not only could she afford all this but she felt it was an obligation to a dear friend, though she choked back a sob on the memory, to do so. If Barbara felt like beginning a new life far, far away from the threat to her children and herself, how could Carrie not help in any way she had the wherewithal to do so. Barbara could take her time, enjoy the travel, figure out what her life should be, and meet Carrie in Newport in a month or so. They would exchange phone numbers once they obtained a throw away cell for Barbara. If Barbara wanted to just make tracks across the country Carrie would have an apartment set up for her once she arrived. It was all she could do but thought it would be enough; and Kim would approve. First, they would find a doctor to look at that eye and to check out the rest of Barbara's possible injuries.

This was where the woman put her foot firmly down, there would be no doctor, she was fine, it was just a black eye and would be gone in a day or two, but she was fine otherwise.

She was so vehement in her stance Carrie could not, would not, argue. Let Barbara decide her own health needs, Carrie would not push.

She guessed she would always be ruled by the simple canon, what would Kim want her to do and would that make her a better person and the world a better place. What was the sense of having the massive, to her, fortune if not to lessen the pain and suffering of others? She hugged Barbara, then Izzy and Phoebe, seven and nine sequentially. It would all be accomplished; it might take a full day and a half or more but the work of setting Barbara up would be completed. Then, and only then, could she and her small band of bleeding hearts move on.

Breakfast came early, before the sun, but beach towns made their living off the sun and it only blessed them for a couple months a year. You had to get up early and work late if you wanted to make a years living in a resort atmosphere.

All through the eggs, sausage, sausage gravy, toast and biscuits—homemade if Carrie was any judge—Barbara worried under her breath and aloud about how she could possibly pay Carrie back for all her kindness. Carrie was about to lose control when the idea came to her.

"What did you tell me you used to be?" Their meeting, ride into town, seeking a decent used car lot, motel/hotel that was clean and comfortable for all and would accept Oscar, well, it had been a whirlwind. But she seemed to remember Barbara saying she'd been a professional of some sort.

Barbara blushed as if embarrassed to admit once again, "I was a psychologist and counselor at a woman's shelter. I worked with women and children attempting to flee dangerous situations and hostile, aggressive partners." She sighed thinking of the mess she had allowed herself to be swallowed up in.

"I'll tell you what. We're heading into summer, I'm guessing the kids are out of school, or almost, and you have nowhere to go to get away from what might be hot on your tail. The credit card I'm giving you with the false I.D. will allow you to travel to Newport and get set up in that apartment I told you about." She shushed Barbara before she could begin her protests again, "I have friends out there who will introduce you around and you can get settled. If you want to pay me back," and here Barbara's attention became riveted to Carrie's words, "You can come to work for me when I get my new project set up."

"What kind of work would I have to do?" Now Barbara's warning sense kicked in.

"The same thing you were doing, counseling and psychology."

"Yeah, because I'm so good at it. Look at the perfect life I've forged for me and my girls," despondency washed over her.

"Actually, what I have found is those who excel at any profession are usually the ones who struggled to do so. I have musician friends and the ones who really understand the music and can bring the most beauty to the playing are those who had to work hard to master it, not the ones to whom it came easy. Same with surfing. Some just jump on a board riding like they were born to it, but they don't have a feel for the ocean or respect what she can do. It was those who fought the sea and finally surrendered to her power that became true masters." Her grin was of a memory of Dennis drilling that lesson into her rock of a head.

"I think this experience will make you an excellent counselor. You certainly understand on a visceral level what others are experiencing. Yes, I would love to have you work with my project!" She emphatically nodded her head once in finality.

"I will need to know much more about this project before I can agree to anything." Barbara hugged her girls close with the hope of a new life.

"Well," and Carrie brightened at the thought that just arrived special delivery, "If you've nothing better to do, we're heading in the direction of New Orleans you're welcome to tag along."

They had no specific target date to be in New Orleans. She hadn't called Henry yet to advise him they were on their way and now, had a small retinue in tow. She'd wait until they could give him a more succinct concept of when they'd be arriving. They'd continue meandering their way in the general direction, taking in the sights and culture.

Dip A Toe In River To See What Bites

Ian and Jaxson had met with Ben, Dugie, and several of the elder statesmen/women musicians during their ephemeral time in NY. They knew they wanted to do a southern tour, to bring the message and the music to those who wanted to hear both, but they also wanted to ease into the atmosphere of the old south. They all knew from a lifetime of touring, the 'new' south was not the old south but only just. And with the political climate freezing into polar opposites over the past few years, they wanted to play this safe.

Ian was very happy they had chosen caution once the Feds told him of the threats. People were fucking nuts and becoming more insane. The far edges of the political spectrum had taken to threatening life and limb of those they disagreed with. And they didn't threaten just the of-fender, but everyone in their family. Parents, wives, husbands, children, aunts, uncles, third cousins thrice removed and folks who didn't have an inkling they were related. It was like a bizarro aspect of *Henry Louis Gates, Jr. Finding Your Roots,* then ripping the entire family out by them.

So, they had chosen to begin the southern swing in Maryland. A state that had been torn in half by the Civil War with slave holders in the south and abolitionists to the north. Slightly schizoid but with enough sense to overcome their worst devils.

They'd start the tour in Salisbury a town of about thirty-two thousand people that could pull from the entire Delmarva Peninsula. Ian felt confident they could fill Arthur W. Perdue stadium's fifty-two hundred seats and most of the infield. He was happy Ben and Dugie had recalculated the tour to find minor league parks in or near every town they wanted to hit. That should help the niggling at the back of his neck, ballparks were, and always would be, his comfort zone.

With this being the first show back they had decided, for comfort, to go with the original line-up of singers and players, with the inclusion of Joya and some friends they had picked up along the way. No superstars, no star-stars, just friends again. They had the 'All Girls' Choir', Bonnie, Gillian, Joya, Cinda and Michelle, they would feature each singer for a song or three, round-robin style, with the others acting as backups. They had the guys, James Nash, Graham Young, Jesse Collins, and Jaxson, of course. The only addition had been Emmylou, who had asked to come along for the ride for a fortnight or two.

Yeah, it all felt good, well, except for the threat of death. Ian wondered just how serious he should take that. Very, if he were to trust the FBI and Dennis. Shit, couldn't he have a week or two respite from worry? Maggie sat behind him on the bus and rubbed the knots out of his back. What would he do without her?

"It just hit me," she whispered in his good ear, "you haven't saved anybody in quite some time. Do you think the curse has worn off?"

"Had to bring it up, didn't you?" he chided playfully, though with a scintilla of apprehension. "No, and I hope it never strikes again. People look at you funny when they think you have transcendent powers." He gave her hand resting on his shoulder a reassuring squeeze. "Let's hope you didn't jinx it."

"You're not getting superstitious, are you?" She admonished.

Somewhere, in the far off, distant eastern heavens, thunder crashed and rolled across the pure blue sky. Not a lightning strike could be seen, not a raindrop fell, just the hard crash of thunder, like anger come to life as sound. The surface on the reflecting pool of the world rippled with the sound, blurring the scene below.

"Now what?" Fate thought they had finished with the humans on their gypsy tour, but once the waters settled, she could see that was exactly what Fame was staring at. "You can't throw your anger at all of them. Hell, many of them used to be your acolytes and remain so. Though to a far lesser degree." She threw in just to poke the narcissistic goddess. "What are you pissed about now?" It certainly couldn't be that one human. Fate had followed his lifeline and could have informed Fame he would never succumb to her wiles, but what fun would that be?

"So, he thinks he is done with me, does he?" Fate did not have to ask who the 'he' was Fame was pointedly cursing.

"What did he do to raise the ire of the great Fame?" Best to let the wound bleed so they could have peace in the valley once again.

"He just told his hag that he believes he gets to decide when the curse of saving lives is lifted! He! The human will decide! He will tell a goddess when to back off." She stomped her foot so hard Fate feared she might bring down the whole mountain. "Well, let me tell you no human tells this goddess when to back off, when to mind her own. He thinks he's seen the last of me but he hasn't seen the beginning of my ire!"

"Ah, Fame, you are fickle and pigheaded. Why can't you let this go? He doesn't want you!" That came out as a much stronger statement than she intended but then upon reconsideration it might be just what the screaming bitch needed!

"I'll tell him what he wants! I'll show him what he needs! I am the goddess of Fame! Millions throughout the history of his petty little species have worshipped me, craved me, would kill, cheat, and die for me! Who does this puny mortal think he is to deny me?" Fame was on a roll and not a good roll.

Fate walked away to lay on a beach on Bora Bora where, hopefully, distance and the crashing of waves would drown out the tirade. Nothing worse than a goddess rebuffed while in the buff!

"That's the second time in as many days that I have heard thunder where there isn't a cloud in the sky," Ian's concern disturbed Maggie's mood.

"It's just some kind of anomaly. I'm sure it's nothing to do with you. Believe it or not you are not the center of the universe. Weather, events, the workings of mankind and the gods do not orbit around planet Ian." She hoped her jibe would snap him out of the funk he was working himself into.

As the buses settled into the back lot of the Residence Inn Ian hollered to the back for Jaxson to get up, they had arrived. The sleep filled response was not what he expected. He strode to the back of the bus with intent.

"Come on, sleepy Pete, we're going to go check out the Field and preparations while the rest of the tribe checks in and cleans up. I want to do a sound check this eve so maybe everyone can relax into tomorrow's show." He shook the ostensibly snoozing form to roust him into action. "Let's go! You can't be tired from a few hours of road! Shit, man, you've been sleeping in a comfortable bed for two weeks! Time to get your road legs back in order." He shook the prone form again to murmurs of protestation. "Lazy bastard!" He pulled the form out of the sack and onto the floor.

"What the fuck?!" The exclamation was half jovial half irate, "Can't a body get any rest around here? I've been jostled and bounced all down the Jersey Pike, and now my own friend dumps me on the floor like trash!" He feigned fatigue, though truth be told he was, as Ian had pointed out, well-rested. He also had no desire to go to the park and check things out, that was Ian, Ben and Dugie's job. He was the star of the show. Yeah, that and two dollars would buy a pencil so he could write about it. "I really would prefer to lay about for one day. One freaking day, is that too much to ask?"

"Yup. Now rise, oh, great superstar and idol of millions, we have work to do." Ian left him in the pile of covers and pillows on the floor.

"What about my gear? I don't want it sitting in the bus all day while we gad about playing road warrior," he thought he may have found an escape route.

"Dugie has already assigned Gabby to load your load into your room. Get dressed, I have a rental supposedly waiting at the front." Ian shouted from the open bus door.

"Why don't we take the bus?" It was a little whiney but he really just wanted to lay back for a day.

"Then how would anyone empty your trash out of this hovel into that hovel?" Ian Barked a laugh, "Let's go!"

After assuring himself that the hotel had the entire retinue under control, he called the purveyors of Park Perdue to let them know he, Ben, and Jax were on their way over. All would meet at the ballyard and check things out.

Ian drove, Ben rode shotgun, so Jaxson stretched out in the back of the minivan. Ian had ordered a sedan, to which he was more accustomed, but the rental company had sent what they had. Smaller towns, smaller selections. They rode along, each lost in their own thoughts, which meant they were thinking of getting back to the hotel, having a 'smoke' and relaxing for the eve.

"Explain to me, again, why my presence is necessary on this little jaunt. We have been traveling the highways, byways, your ways and my ways for the past three months and my companionship has never been required. Now, at the break of the new day, I am essential." Jax's tone wasn't exactly petulant but curious.

"I thought you might like to stretch your legs and experience the great outdoors, or at least, outside the confines of the stage at dark and the hotel while in slumber," Ian's response betrayed not the jovial intonation he'd heard in his head but one of uncertainty. Why did he almost demand Jaxson come along on this errand. It was true he hadn't come to inspect any other venue, so why here? If Ian was honest with himself, and shouldn't one always be, there had been an insistent and nagging pressure at the back of his neck that he bring Jaxson with him, almost a warning. But a warning about what? They were safely ensconced in reputable digs. There had been no immediate threats, Dennis, their personal G-man, had assured him. There almost always was a taunt before someone attempted a physical assault. As if tempting the authorities to try and stop them.

Yet, here was Jax bemoaning the fact he was stretched out, unpleasantly, in the back of some kind of minivan going to waste time on something he had nothing to do with. And Ian couldn't give him a logical reason why.

"Maybe I just wanted the pleasure of your witty repartee and sunny personage," it was the best he could come up with on the spur.

"You've had my company for the past three months and you required one more afternoon?" Jaxson slapped the back of Ian's head. "Nimrod!"

"Wait! There's more, isn't there? You thought something, saw something, dreamed something, you are something. What?" Now Jaxson sat up straight on the bench seat.

"We're here," announced Ian as they pulled into the lot and headed toward where the welcoming committee awaited.

Introductions were made as they made their way inside the small but cozy ballpark. Just what Ian hope for.

"How's ticket sales?" He asked the tall, mid-forties, brunette, Allyson, who was the person obviously in charge.

"If we had a shoehorn the size of a frontend loader," and it was evident she knew of which she spoke, "we couldn't get more folks in here. I could've upped the price by double and we'd still not have enough room, but you specifically said the price was the price. I get it, but man we could've made a killing on this show." The businesswoman in her saw a golden opportunity slipping away because these old hippies had those, oh, what the hell were they called, scruples. You were supposed to make the buck when it was seductively beckoning.

"Excellent!" Ian smiled his happy, this-is-the-way-the-universe-should-work, smile. They would make their nut and more, the venue would do well, though not as well as this woman would like, and all the people could afford to come to the show. He was a happy, little, ancient hippie boy.

Ben checked stage set-up and backstage area to assure himself they had the power and space for all their needs and was satisfied. It was a quick once over and they were on their way back to pleasures of the mind and body. Ian was quite certain he had spied a few local dining establishments close by the hotel.

The scent of smoke greeted them as they turned into the hotel parking lot. Several firetrucks were parked near the buses, particularly the bus that Ian, Maggie, James, and especially, Jaxson had ridden in on. Most of the crew and band members were standing, watching as the firefighters finished cleaning up and putting out what they'd pulled out of the back of the bus, the apparent site of the fire.

"What the hell is going on?" Ian, as the titular leader of this rover band, asked the firefighter in charge.

"Something caught fire in the back of the bus," said the smudged firefighter who'd come to talk to Ian.

"But what? How?" Ian saw the 'Chief' in the front of his turnout coat. "Chief."

"We'll have to get the arson boys out here, probably today, to figure it out." He saw the expression on Ian's face and cleared his throat, "To be perfectly frank I would guess electrical or some such, I don't think it was intentional but it was a good thing nobody was in that back bed or they would have suffocated on the fumes. Closed in area like that, lots of smoke and carbon monoxide, well..." he gave Ian's shoulder a reassuring shake. "It's good, nobody got hurt, just a mattress and some interior stuff. Your crew told me they'd gotten all the important stuff out earlier. You are a lucky man." He shook Ian's hand though Ian never noticed as he stood traumatized staring at the burned out back of their bus.

He did, however, notice the expression on Jaxson's face as he turned to reassure the rest of the crew. "Don't even," he pointed a finger at his lifetime friend, "I had nothing to do with nothing even if something happened to something. We were well away from here. Don't even begin to think," but it was too late the wheels had been engaged, gotten traction and were in full forward motion.

Jaxson knew, Ian had saved his life.

And The Music Goes Round And Round

For the first time on the tour not everyone wanted to dine in the same establishment. Ian should not have been surprised, they had all been traveling, living, eating, sleeping as one for the past almost four months. They all needed a break. Some wanted Italian, of which Fratelli's would fit the bill, others wished Americana, so off to the Market Street Inn, the boys and girls of the road crew thought the brew pub up the way sounded just right, so they sailed on Brew River. Ian and some of the more health-conscious group chose the Cactus Taverna as they offered vegetarian fare. Ian dutifully hopped into the trusty mini family van and presented his credit card with instructions to feed the hungry horde whatever their hearts desired, knowing they would not break the bank. They would consider the financial repercussions of the great cause of the Untouchables. The sanctity of the purpose had not lessened with miles and time, if anything, it had become even more sacrosanct.

Ian, Maggie, Ben, and Gillian looked forward to a quiet, relaxed meal, convivial companionship, away from the hubbub of band, crew, and hangers on. Jaxson was quiet, remote, keeping mostly to his own thoughts, sneaking a sideward glance at Ian from time to time yet saying nothing. Ian knew what he was thinking and was quite content to let Jax keep his thoughts to himself. The last thing he wanted right now was for the crew to allow their distant revere for Ian to reawaken. As far as he could ascertain no one had put Ian and the incident together.

The dinner had been pleasant enough with small talk about the upcoming tour and especially a nice sound check tonight under the lights and laid-back show tomorrow. Jaxson remained reserved and mostly to himself just adding a few remarks when pushed. Ian assumed he was thinking of what might have been had not he been pushed to join them at the venue; it was only normal when one had perceived having a close brush with taking their final breath of the sweetness of life. He'd get over it.

Jaxson asked if Ian could drop him by the hotel so he could change strings and shower so as to be ready when it was time to head over for sound. He dropped off Ben and Gillian for the same concerns while he and Maggie could spend a little time alone paying the various bills and collecting receipts.

They popped in at the Brew River to get the road crew paid up and, on their way, to finish the unloading and setup. As they entered the establishment they were assaulted by the raucous laughter and boister-ous voices of the crew enjoying an eve among their own. The moment Ian and Maggie's presence was noted silence wrapped the formerly gay exchange. Not unusual when the boss shows up unless it was this crew and this boss. Ian didn't like what this might be signaling.

"Everybody get enough to eat without getting enough to drink?" He chided in a playful manner hoping to kick start the jovial mood.

"Absolutely. Good grub," they chimed back. "see you at the ball-park." They attempted geniality but it felt forced.

The same greeting met Ian and Maggie at the Italian joint and Market Street. Something was up and Ian intended to find the bottom of that up. And since Dugie seemed to bear the most guilt upon his features, that would be the place he would begin the search.

Load-in accomplished, set-up complete, cords run, mics set, am-plifiers plugged in, keys to stage left and drums to the right of him, Ian rode into the valley and found Mr. Dugan.

"So, dinner was satisfactory?" He began the dance.

"Quite." responded the quarry.

"Any particular subjects come up during the feast?" Ian pushed ever so slightly.

"The usual ball busting. Nothing out of the ordinary." Why did his eyes seem to be seeking an avenue of escape?

"Nobody mentioned the fire?"

"Not that I recall." Was there a tremor of contrition riding the answer?

"Interesting, I would've thought that would be the main topic of conversation." Now Ian had the hook in and was playing with the catch on the other end of the line.

"Look, of course everyone was talking about it," Dugie broke. Kevin was great at many things, lying was not his forte.

"And what was said?" Now for the kill and the answer he knew was forthcoming.

"Everyone was jittery, especially after what you told us before we left the City. They know it was probably just an accidental occurrence, a frayed wire, something natural but they still were freaking a bit. And what Ben told me might have slipped out as a way of calming some ragged nerves." He wanted to stop there but the look Ian gave him would not allow the wound to be staunched.

"And what can of beans did you open and spill all over my life?" Ian could feel his temper taking hold and took several deep breaths. A lifetime of containing the fury came as natural as deep breathing. He would not lose himself with a friend.

"Ian there were some who wanted to bail on this leg of the tour!" Dugie pleaded the need.

"And who might those folks be?" He really didn't want to know but he was in the mood to push.

"I ain't telling. I might confess to my part but that's it. These are my friends, my people, folks I've worked with on and off for years. Musicians I respect, I ain't narcing so go ahead and fire me!" If this was a C or D movie Ian would've shot him in the leg, but since this was a B or better with a family theme he didn't.

"Nobody's firing nobody 'cause nobody did nobody wrong except maybe to me. And I need to know what's been done to me," Ian was a patient man with an impatient soul, something was about to give and he hoped it was Dugie's conscience.

"Well, they was talking about this tour not being worth their lives and all. I told them we were doing something that would be talked about by musicians and crew for a hundred years, that we were putting all on the line for others, not our own egos and such. They didn't care, they were scared. So, I told them how you saved Jaxson by insisting he come along with you. That you'd had a premonition. That you'd protect us. You'd take care of us and wouldn't let nothing happen to anybody on this crew." Dugie whispered the last of his confession knowing he had gone well over the bounds of what he could promise and Ian could perform, but he'd done it the heat of the moment.

"Shit, Duge, I'm not the fucking Messiah or even a good magician. The only thing I can make disappear with any regularity is money. I certainly do not have any power to protect people," Ian's thread was frayed and quickly unraveling.

"But you have saved people, everybody here knows that and consider you to be a lucky charm." Duge pleaded.

"By accident!" Ian almost shouted but held the frustration in check.

"Doesn't make any difference, they believe," said the road manager, "and to be honest so do I." He shrugged and went out to where the sound man was completing his check list to see if he could help in any way.

Ian made to follow until he felt Maggie's hand lightly settle on his arm just above the elbow, staying him. "Leave him be. Musicians are superstitious, people want to believe, if it settles their nerves..." she gave her own shrug.

"And then what do they believe in when someone does get hurt and I couldn't stop it!" He glared.

"We'll cross that corpse when we come to it," she smiled.

He laughed out loud, a hearty release of pent-up emotion, "That's the dumbest thing I've ever heard!"

He would've said more but the roadie standing patiently waiting for his attention was slowly dribbling that patience on the ground.

"Whatcha need?" Ian didn't mean to be short but at five foot nine he was hardly a giant.

"Excuse me, Mr. Sperling," the roadie, shit, what was his name? Ian knew every roadie's name but this one.

"Ian."

"Pardon?"

"Ian, my name is Ian. My grandfather was Mr. Sperling because he owned a car."

"Yeah, uh, Mr. Sperling, Mr. Grahm and another guy want to talk to you over by the bus." Message finally delivered he headed back to work.

"And his name is Jaxson!"

"I grew up listening to his music. I learned to play guitar learning his songs, he's Mr. Grahm," Shot the road man over his shoulder.

"Now what?" Ian said to the clear blue sky as he, with Maggie in tow, went off in search of Mr. Grahm.

They found their star with his back to them talking to someone Ian couldn't quite make out, standing between two of the buses. As he closed the distance Maggie heard Ian utter an expletive and pick up his pace. She glanced at the object of the expletive and picked up her own.

"Bob," Ian reached out a hand to shake the hand of one of the most recognizable people on the planet. "Some guy, says the roadie." He muttered to Maggie. "What brings you to the bottom forty?" Not that Ian wasn't beside himself that Dylan Roberts would show up but why? Though his name was Dylan everybody referred to him as 'Bob' because of the 'Roberts' thing, somebody thought it was funny.

"Heard that you cats were putting on a show to save the world and thought I'd drop by and see if you could use an old singer," His grin widened as he wrapped Maggie in his arms.

"You do know we were camped in New York for the past two weeks, don't you? I would've thought you'd have come out to play while we were in the Apple," Jaxson was bemused that one of the greatest and most famous people in the history of music would show up here.

"Yeah, I heard. I also heard everybody and their brother was showing up just to share the stage with you cats. Thought I'd wait until you got a little closer to where we were camped to join forces." He slapped Ian companionly on the back.

"You got a place down here?" Ian thought of Dylan as a city guy not one to take the pleasures of the rural life.

"Yeah, it's quiet. Nobody bothers us while we're hanging. Got a nice house away from the action where we can run to the beach if we so desire or we can just cookout in the backyard and sit around the fire playing old tunes. We play some tunes, every once in a while, at a roadhouse between here and OC. People keep it on the QT as they like the tunes but don't want the bother of crowds. They're nice that way down here," he laughed at their shocked expressions. "Come on guys don't you miss just setting up and playing whatever comes to mind?"

"Guess it's kind of what we're doing, for the most part, by avoiding the large venues and big cities," Jaxson had to admit to himself he did kind of miss just playing to play.

"Besides why is it only the big towns get the best?" Dylan took in all three standing in a semicircle around him. "Don't the folks out here deserve a wild night out once in a while? So, what say you? Want to have a little fun tomorrow night? Just a couple few tunes and a lot of love."

Who could argue with that? It was decided they would keep his appearance quiet. They had tried to keep expectations down as far as 'special guest' appearances. They didn't want the fans to always expect there to be superstars at every stop. The tour had begun as a fun, family of musicians out on the road to share time and tunes, they really wanted to get back to that concept. Of course, also while raising money and awareness of the plight of so many around the world. Yeah, lots of love and fun, this would be good and it might take the crew's minds off of Ian as their savior.

The Show Must Go On And On And On

The show was exactly the diversion all required. Everyone drew energy and love from the crowd, the surroundings, and the ocean, only thirty miles away. Ian had promised they could get up a little early and run down to the sand and sea for a few hours before heading south and west to Salem, VA.

'Bob' had been brilliant, blending some of his most famous songs—"Give the people what they paid to hear"—exclaimed the almost eighty-year-old minstrel laughing. "If you piss them off too much, especially without a backup plan, you'll soon find yourself out of the business and looking for day labor." And he would know.

He had come up a folk singer and songwriter of no small repute and then, for a reason not even he could discern, electrified. No, that wasn't exactly right, he had a reason, he wanted change. He thrived off of change, boredom was the death of the creative spirit. So, he'd pissed off his share of old fans and found new acolytes who believed in and loved the new version. And there he was, on stage showing the brilliance of the change. He even threw in a couple old rock and roll standards because he thought it would be fun. Everyone, band, backup singers, frontmen and women sang along, both backstage and then joining him onstage.

The road crew danced; the lighting folks stepped up their game flying by the seats of their pants, putting on a light show for the ages.

Emmylou jumped up with the All-Girls' Choir and if it hadn't been perfection before it was certainly heavenly perfection last night. It was hard to tell who was having a better time, the folks on stage or the folks on the grass, literally and figuratively.

Even if they took all back roads, they could still easily make Salem by early evening next day, a stop at the beach and all. The tour was off to as good of a start as Ian and Jax could have dreamed. New York was behind them, the whole country in front of them and everyone had forgotten his premonition and Jaxson's close call with the Reaper.

They could ease into Salem—just north of Roanoke—and slip-slide into another evening of joy. Salem Memorial was another old ballpark, as far as the minor leagues went. The small parks didn't last long, hell, the new modern billion-dollar ballparks didn't last long in the scheme of things. Ian thought of the places he had visited while touring Europe. Well, the places they had driven by and seen through van windows, you didn't do much touristing while on tour! There were buildings a thousand or more years old still in use. They didn't tear everything down after a few decades in Europe, they built them to last the test of time.

There was an atmosphere in a place that millions had walked through to watch great entertainment—lions eating people, people killing other people, blood, gore, guts, wholesome family fare—for centuries, that made you feel the weight of time. Ian would settle for an almost seventy-year-old ballpark. In American terms; ancient.

The stop by the beach had been as advertised. There is something about dipping the toe in waves that had traveled a few thousand miles just to kiss those toes, that refreshed the whole body. Ian was not a swimmer, though he'd been in the water, so a toe or two was about the limit of what he would experience, but he was happy watching the others frolicking in the waves. Some just stood, some, like the athletic, well-maintained Mr. Grahm, did some body surfing. It was early in the season so the beaches weren't packed, though the temperatures should have tantalized more than were present. Mid-week wasn't a draw for the working classes.

As they prepared to board buses and make the journey west Ian saw one of the road crew caught up in a small riptide. Try as he might the guy couldn't break loose of the pull of the current, it was pulling him out to sea. Well, Ian could do nothing but shout for help. He, as mentioned, was not a swimmer, as in 'could not swim'.

As he stood trying to get someone, anyone's attention, the new roadie, who had hipped him to Dylan waiting to talk to him, ran by Ian almost knocking him over. He dove, like a cast member of Baywatch, into the center of the riptide. He didn't struggle, instead swam with the tide allowing the strong current to take him directly to the struggling other man. Once the two collided he grabbed his fellow road crew member under the chin, somehow coaxing him to relax as he swam perpendicular to the tide. After much struggle and, once again, using the force of the water he dragged the waterlogged victim up onto the beach. Where he applied CPR until said victim spit our half the ocean and smiled his thanks.

The tour had their new hero. One who had braved certain death to save another. Ian was officially off the hook. The savior retired.

The rest of the crew and performers were congratulating the lifeguard roadie, with cheers, slaps on the back, hugs, the usual, while helping the nearly drowned back to his feet. Ian suddenly realized the guy who had come to him with the message from Jax, the one being congratulated, wasn't. His brain spun with dizzying speed, the guy wasn't a guy, but a girl. Sure, she had short hair and her strength showed in the definition of her arms and legs but she was a 'she' not a 'he'. Maybe Ian was getting too old to recognize the difference between the sexes or maybe they were morphing but, shIt, he should've noticed. For now, he was caught between relief that the load of hero had been passed on to another and the horror he couldn't tell male from female.

As he approached to make his own gratitude clear he saw Gabby hugging the woman in thanks for saving one of their own.

"That was amazing," he gushed, "the way you dove right in, knew just what to do, how to save, well, it was just the most amazing thing I ever seen," Gabby couldn't seem to stop his tongue from flying. It looked as though Gabby, like the rest of the clan, had found his new idol. He stepped back as if realizing he had overstepped and intruded on her 'space' before extending a hand, "Gabor," he offered. "and it looks as though we might have two good luck charms on this tour. Guess we might be needing both from what Ian said." He spoke to himself though she heard him quite clearly.

"Soteria," she shook his proffered thanks.

"Soteria?" he asked, amazed he got the pronunciation right.

"It's Greek," she hesitantly explained, presumably, not for the first time in her life. "My friends call me Teri."

"Mine call me Gabby. Which since I can't seem to control my mouth and tongue would be appropriate at this moment," he said through his own timidity.

Ian and Maggie inched their way closer not wishing to disturb the two dancers.

"Care to do the intros, Gabby?" Ian asked with a quirky smile. Did that huge man just turn beet red? Ian wanted to jump for joy. Gabby had been this enigma of a large, good looking, hardworking, decent man who was destined to be alone for life as he couldn't get past his own bashfulness around members of the opposite sex. Ian could feel the attraction from where he stood.

"Shit, yeah, boss, sorry. This is Soteria, she's from Greece!" he gushed.

"Just the name is from Greece I'm from Queens. You must be Ian, the lord and master of the great and honorable circus maximus!" She grinned as she offered her hand.

"I don't know if I'd put it quite like that, but yeah, kinda. This is my wife, owner, and boss Maggie."

"She seems nice, for a boss," Soteria affected the gravity of meeting the true superior.

"She has her moments," Ian laughed and was slapped on the arm for the transgression. "Am I to assume we picked you up while in the City?" Ian couldn't get by the fact he hadn't met her before. He always wanted to know everyone on the crew. It was family, so even distant cousins were acknowledged.

"I got hired the day before you loaded out and headed to the open road," here she laughed. There was no such thing as an 'open' road in New Jersey.

"I shall have a harsh word with Dugie or Ben, whoever brought you on board, for neglecting to introduce us. I like to know my crew, especially ones who are as adept at lifesaving as you," He gave a quick bow of thanks. She didn't have to know the why and he wasn't about to divulge his secret.

"Glad I could be of assistance. You do know there are rumors aplenty about this group." She swept the retreating group making their way towards the waiting buses.

"Well, don't believe everything you hear about tours from other roadies and musicians," cautioned Maggie as she took Ian by the arm and steered him in the general direction of Virginia.

"They're good people. You'll like working with this group. They're all like family. They watch over and protect each other, so you'll fit in here perfectly." Gabby gently took her arm and was pleasantly surprised by the strength he found there as they walked up the beach to the traveling Untouchables Bandwagons. He knew he was feeling something, deep down where he never had before, a pleasant something. He would have to ask Ian about that.

"Crew or singers?" He asked. Her confused expression was his answer.

"You can ride on whichever bus you like, with who you're most comfortable," he clarified. "Some folks jump from bus to bus depending on mood or who they need to talk to about whatever is happening in the show. Some of the women are more comfortable around the other women, the crew around the crew, you get it," he shrugged as if it made him no nevermind.

"And where do you ride, Gabor?" he liked the sound of his given name on her tongue, it tingled.

"Well, I'm kind of a loner. So, I ride where I can find some peace, unless someone wishes a word or two about the castes or what they require of me on the stage," again a noncommittal shrug.

"You have been with these people for months and yet you still ride alone? It must be very lonely," she stared deep into his eyes as if she could read what was carved in his soul.

"There is a chasm of difference between lonely and alone. I come from a people who keep to themselves out of self-preservation. We learn very early on to be comfortable and content within ourselves." He stared to the south to a place she couldn't see, though she turned her head as if she could.

"I think I'll ride with the crew as I am one of them, to ride with others would be to rise above myself, which would be considered arrogant where I come from." Gabby felt she wanted to be embarrassed by the admission but couldn't, life was what life was. She knew her station in that life.

"But don't you see, that is exactly what this tour has become about, stopping that way of thinking. Allowing people like you and me and all the others like us in India, Africa, South America, shit, America, to stop thinking we are destined to be only one thing. That we can't rise above what others tell us we must be." He stopped in his mental tracks, lost in the thought for a moment but not wishing to cut the thread. "These people," and his waving hand took in all the people on the buses and trucks, "they have given up a lot of money and time to raise awareness and funds to lift us out of that way of thinking. The very least we can do to show our gratitude is to try. To dream. To see ourselves as more than detritus to be used and thrown away."

"Do you believe that?" she wasn't mocking, she was curious.

Gabby had to stop and think, did he? Were these just words? No! He had seen the difference in the Lakota people when they believed someone cared and would give of themselves to improve the lives of these native people they had never met. He saw the way the crew and musicians, even the superstars reacted when this burden was put on their shoulders, they stood taller, straighter, prouder. That was it. There was great pride in lifting others. There was honor in standing up, giving of yourself for the benefit of people you had never met and, probably, never would. To give selflessly of oneself with no expectation of any reward, not even thanks, only knowing it was right.

"Yes, with all my heart and with the soul of my people, I do."

"I still think I'll ride with the crew as now I have many questions. Which transport do you take?" She gave the impression she might like it if he joined her.

Gabby was about to say, 'wherever she rode', when he heard Ian clear his throat behind the big man. "Gabby, I am very sorry to interrupt but would you mind riding with us for a while, I need your expertise." Gabby knew what he wanted to say, and maybe should have said, so she would see what he was talking about, but Ian's tone had been one of request, not demand, with respect. He couldn't say no. He would talk to Teri later. He bowed to her as he turned and joined Ian walking towards his bus.

Every Road Leads To A Show

Each driver radioed they had all on board who were supposed to be. Ian held up a hand while he gathered in all who were in his charge and hustled them into their bus, then stared out the window at the empty beach. Satisfied he gave the thumbs up and pointed west, the drivers engaged. Actually, they would head north for a few blocks up from the end of the boardwalk where they had parked the buses, then they would swing around onto Philadelphia Ave. come back south a couple blocks to where they could pick up route 50 again. They'd head back the half hour to Salisbury where they could pick up route 13 south across the mouth of the Chesapeake Bay, swing around Portsmouth and Norfolk where they could pick up route 460 and take the back roads to Salem. It certainly wasn't the shortest or quickest way but they had time and Ian wasn't in any hurry.

There were pieces of puzzles he hadn't known existed and he wanted to get a handle on what had happened in Ocean City, Soteria, the popping in of Dylan Roberts, though that was easily explained, yet all seemed tied together somehow. He just had to figure out the somehow.

As they crossed the bridge into West Ocean City and the highway opened up a little towards Berlin Gabby sat down next to Ian. "You said you wanted to talk to me, Bo...Ian?" He stumbled but corrected before the fall.

"Yeah. You seemed kinda tight with that young woman, Soteria? How long have you known her? I don't remember her from the rest of the tour," Ian was fishing with scant bait.

"Actually, I just met her. Said she jumped aboard just before we split the City." Gabby indicated his indifference with his customary shrug.

"I guess I didn't know we were short a man," Ian prodded.

"Ain't my purview," Gabby thought this was a good time to practice his word for the day.

Ian turned his head and grinned proudly, "You been learning on my tour?" He kidded.

"Well, the thinking went, if we're going to put all this effort into helping others raise themselves up, maybe I ought to do the same. So, I'm learning a word a day. Glad I got it right!" his pride touched his eyes and his smile was broad as the horizon. He liked being thought of as more than just a guy holding down a spot any other guy could hold down just as well. He worked hard and he was proud when it was noticed.

"Please, keep it up. You continue to impress me every day," Ian meant it and Gabby blushed with the praise. "Guess I need to pick the brains of the wonder boys. When we stop for vegetable oil, please tell Ben and Dugie I would like to see them. If you'd like, you may spend the rest of the travel time with the young lady," Ian gave him a paternal shake of the shoulder.

There was a Love's truck stop up on route 460 before Petersburg where they would stop, fuel up and feed the masses. Ian would pick the brains of the brilliant lights at the top of the road crew. Normally Ian wouldn't concern himself with who the fellas hired or fired but with what Dennis had imparted he couldn't take anyone's presence for granted. People always assumed the assassin was male. Women, Ian knew, could be more deadly and more subtle. He wanted to know what cloud this woman floated down from.

Dugie and Ben each thought the other had hired Soteria as neither remembered ever meeting her before she saved Howie the bass tech. Dumb bastard shouldn't have been swimming what with him only having one leg and all. They both stared at Ian for a moment. "Why didn't you save him?"

"Number one, I can't swim a stroke," and they both gave each other a 'yeah, there's that' roll of the eye. "Numero dos, I don't save people on purpose, apparently, only accidently. She jumped in the riptide and knew exactly what to do. Who have you ever met who would know exactly what to do in that circumstance?"

"A lifeguard I dated thirty years ago used to tell me horror stories about saving people. Maybe she was a lifeguard before she joined up," deduced the Duge.

"Probably," scoffed Ian, "Then got tired of the glamorous life of saving people, sitting in the sun, looking out over that beautiful ocean, and thought, what I need to do is haul amplifiers, trap cases, and spend my life moving from shithole to shithole in the company of reprobates, drunks, and perverts," Ian laughed and the other two couldn't help but sheepishly join in.

"We ain't all like that," Ben defended his crew.

"Yeah? You ever sit around and listen to these saintly, pure fellows talk about women in the crowd?" Asked Ian, knowing he had. "Here's the deal, keep an eye on her. She does anything, and I mean anything, weird, threatening, oddly indicating a violent temper I want to know. Please keep in mind we have been threatened and I don't intend to let anything happen to anyone in this circus," End of discussion.

She climbed aboard the bus wishing Gabby were still with her. He would mitigate the discomfort of her not belonging. She dug into a glamor of inclusion and belonging hoping she had enough sway left in her to convince enough of the crew that she did, indeed, belong with them.

She inserted herself gently into a conversation about the upcoming tour and shows and what a blast last night had been. Imagine, Dylan Roberts popping in out of nowhere in the middle of nowhere and making it somewhere. Teri didn't add anything, not yet, it was best to blend into the background, become part of the road atmosphere so she would espouse the aura of someone who had been part of this tour for a few days. She would look familiar, feel to the others as if she fit, even if the others could not quite place where, who, or how she came to be among the Gypsies. They would assume that she should. It was a trick but only for a short while, soon she would fit like a hand in glove.

It wasn't long before the comments included Gabby, her ears perked up as that was the object of her interest.

"He's with the bigwigs, again," harrumphed one of the older road crew.

"It's not like he asked to go with the mucka mucks," defended a long-haired, bearded guy who obviously couldn't have cared less who rode with who. "You guys make way too much of minutia. It was Gabby who got us pointed in the direction of where this tour ought to go. He is the one who taught us about the treatment of millions, if not billions of others on this marble. He has never asked for, nor received to my recollection or observance, any kind of special treatment or favor," he glanced around the gathered who all shook their heads in agreement. Some grudgingly.

"Look I been on tours since most of you was babes without a hair on your asses. This is the best one of all time, don't fuck it up with imagined slights or jealousy. We're all in this thing together, for the benefit of the Untouchables," at this they all agreed wholeheartedly.

She was amazed by the turn of attitude from one of resentment to one of esprit de corps. She bathed in the emotion for several seconds until a man hobbled in her direction with an almost a drunken gate, swaying with the motion of the bus, attempting not to fall on any of his fellow roadies as he made his way to stand in front of her. He looked familiar but she couldn't place him. She thought the fact that he only had one real leg and one prosthesis would stick in a person's mind.

"Guess I owe you a debt of gratitude," he began, the others regarded the scene as if watching a play, "maybe a lot more than gratitude. I owe you my life. Thank you, will have to do." He reached out a hand as the bus caught a chuckhole and he almost fell until several of the others caught him, as if a natural, common occurrence, and set him up right again. It was then she knew. Howie, the guy from the ocean.

"It was nothing, really," she blushed, humans did that in these situations, "I used to guard lives on the beach. Guess I just slipped into automatic mode. I'm glad I could help and very glad you are alive and well." It was a stinted turn of phrase; she would have to work on her English if she wished to belong to this group, not constantly try to explain her colloquialisms by claiming to be from Queens.

The road crew turned their attention to the new crew member at the sound of her voice. It was as if she had materialized out of thin air right before their eyes where no one had been previously, "Ah, our new charm," said the ancient, bearded hippie. His smile was warm as midafternoon and welcoming as a grandfather to a beloved child. "So very glad to have you with us, I'm Lee," she stuck out her hand to shake his, though not proffered, and he shook his head 'no' as he enveloped her in an all-encompassing bear hug. "Welcome. If you need anything we are all here for you, sister."

The two women, trailed by two small girls and the young man who appeared to be their elder brother, walked up the boardwalk with a small bucket of French fries enjoying the mid-seventies temperatures and sunshine. The waves of the ocean had kicked up enough the women didn't think it prudent to allow the girls to do more than stick their toes in but it did the trick. Sometimes it was the smallest of pleasures that brought great rewards.

"I know you two can't be hungry," grinned the elder of the two women to her daughters, "but we need to get a sandwich or a salad, if we can find one on this desert of deep-fried cholesterol." She grinned to take any accusation out of her words.

They found a small Italian place on the lower floor of a seven-story condominium complex—what would be the basement in a city—that offered pasta, sandwiches, and the Lord be praised, salads. Seated at the five top, converted from a six, they gazed across the beautiful, tan sand to the rolling waves crashing a hundred yards away. There was something comforting in the sound, the rhythmic pounding that wrapped all in a cocoon of familiarity. It made them a family, of sorts. A family formed in days that felt lifetimes.

"We haven't had much time to talk," began Barbara tentatively, "since we're driving in separate vehicles but I have some questions and thought we could use the time to get to know each other and the future a little bit better."

Carrie sipped her water, keeping a careful eye on Aron who looked to be completely smitten by his two new 'sisters'. She smiled at the fullness of her heart and then thought, 'it must remind him', before closing that door. If it did, it did, and if it brought him a small dollop of joy at the reminiscence then so much the better.

"What is it you would like to know?" Her attention returned to the other woman.

"Well, everything. What is your plan? What do you hope to accomplish? Where do you hope to accomplish it? Where does the financing come from? How? Why? When? Everything," she laughed at the enormity of what she asked.

"Hmmm, where to begin. Life shit on me pretty hard when I was a kid, a teen. Lost both my folks, got Harry Pottered in with an abusive uncle and a drunk aunt. Tried to kill myself, if I'm to be honest. I got saved by chance by an old broke down surfer who taught me everything I needed to know in life. I was handed a wad of cash from my long dead folks, money I would have gladly traded for more time. Then fell truly in love, once. She died, left me a wad of cash, and now I want to do something worthwhile. Kim," and here was the ever-present catch in her throat anytime she said the name, "would've wanted me to do something to help others. It was her way. She would've allowed me to wallow, though probably not as long as I did, and then she would want me to alleviate the suffering of others. So, that's what I plan on doing," she was attempting to be succinct but honest.

"As to where, I would like to start on the west coast, somewhere in Oregon, probably around Newport, since that's where I know the territory and have friends. There are people who are dedicated to their particular specialty but don't fit in with the status quo. So, they wander aimless out there, jumping from job to job, not fitting in, who will jump on board if I can mold this into a cohesive concept." Her smile was sad at how nebulous her plan was but there was determination as well. "That's why I hope to find people like you. People who need to help others and in so doing help themselves. I think you would be a stellar counselor because you know, you've lived it. You would come at it without any judgements, just a clean slate of knowing." Kim shrugged her impotence wishing she had a more concrete concept. But that had been the plan, to take her time crossing the country, talking to Henry and any of the others Kim had told her about. She hoped by the time she got back home enough would be formed in her own mind she could explain it to others. They would add their two cents or ten dollars of experience and between all involved maybe they could accomplish something good.

Barbara sat back in her chair, staring out the window at the blank slate of the ocean. Did she want to get involved in this dreamer's blurred project? She had the girls to think of; their future. Could she afford to make such a massive mistake? Or was she being offered a new beginning? A fresh start on a good life? Without fear, violence, constant drunken battles with the shards of love?

"Hey, ladies, ready to order"? the young teen of a waitress broke the concentration of life.

"I'm sorry, we were wrapped up in conversation and hadn't looked at the menus yet," Carrie's embarrassment evident in the red sprouting from shoulder to cheek.

"It's OK, everybody seems to still be in a tizz after the event. We all seem lost in how cool. We don't get folks like that often, nor excitement!" She could hardly contain herself and was slightly taken aback by their blank stares. "Did you just get into town? Not from here?"

They shook their heads emphatically, no. "Well, let me tell you. You know that tour that's raising money to help people who have been shit on for thousands of years?" she stopped herself and covered her mouth with one hand and silently apologized pointing at the girls. Barbara shook it off like a pitcher not liking the called pitch, before, again, shaking her head no. She'd been too busy trying to survive to know anything about touring bands or festivals.

"Well, these musicians, some of them pretty famous, got together to help people all over the world. The 'least fortunate', they call them, 'The Untouchables' cause their so poor and below the normal people they're not even considered people. Can you imagine? So, these musicians, like Jaxson Grahm, Bonnie Welch, Steven Gatos, James Nash, bunches I ain't never heard of, course they were before my time by a lot, but they decided to bring awareness to the fact these folks were being treated like, well, horribly. Just like black folks used to be treated here.

"I guess a long time ago black folks were treated real bad, they were beat and lynched just for looking at some white person wrong. Can you imagine? Couldn't own land, weren't even allowed to learn to read or nothing. I'm just starting learning about this stuff because these folks cared enough to give up a lot to teach us that this stuff is still going on. We never learned about it in school, ain't that just wrong?" As if she realized her train had taken a side rail a long ways back, she pulled out her pen and pad ready to take their order.

"Not yet," Carrie said gently pushing the pad down, "so, what happened here?"

"Well, they did a show over in Salisbury, about a half hour that way," she waved in the general direction of inland, "and decided to come over here to dip their toes in the Atlantic. Most of them are from the west coast, so they'd never. And while they were here one of 'em got caught up in a riptide and almost drowned. People don't realize a storm out to sea, big storms hundreds of miles away, can really affect the tides here. Well, this riptide pulled him out and one of the others just jumped in and rode it out to him and knew exactly what to do to bring the drowning guy back in. Musicians! Who'd a thunk they'd be smart enough to know life-saving? It was all the talk along the boardwalk. They wanted to give the guy a medal and stuff but the buses were well away by then. Ain't that something? Saving someone's life and not waiting around for any rewards, no plaque, no certificate of thanks from the governor, no nothing. Just like it was something they were supposed to do, nothing out of the ordinary." This time the pen and pad meant business.

"Lotta excitement along the coast last couple of days," mused Carrie.

Check paid, children and Aron herded, they decided to walk off a few calories before heading inland themselves. Carrie had checked the maps with Aron and they decided the best course of action was to head towards Berlin and take route 113 south to Virginia swing around

Chesapeake and pick up route 17 south into North Carolina then find lodging somewhere before they hit Raleigh.

"We have plenty of time to talk, discuss, and butt heads before we have to make concrete plans. There are so many details to go over, and that is one of the main reasons I want to get to New Orleans to talk to Henry," Carrie was adamant. Though whether trying to convince herself or Barbara she couldn't be certain. She knew she only had the outline. Maybe finding Barbara had been the best thing that could've happened, now she had a hard brick wall to bounce ideas off of, someone with the smarts, the experience, the balance to offset Carrie's dreamer ways.

If You Want To Dance To The Music, You Gotta Leave The Trees

Suzette and Nash—she'd about had to pry his name out of him with a long knife as they stood in line to buy their tickets. Spirit Guides could be such superstitious creatures believing their name, once known, could be used to control them. He needn't have been so concerned. First off, she knew his real name, Nashdoitsoh. After all she was of the same immortal fabric. Secondly, the name thing wasn't true but he'd read it on the interweb and nobody and nothing could convince him otherwise.

Nash had lobbied to wait until the tour was leaving man's civilization behind. She had agreed. They had considered Salem, VA, as it appeared well into the mountains according to the map, but the reality of Roanoke loomed large. So, the decision was made to wait for deeper mountains.

He and Suzette wandered the hills and valleys of the Great Smoky Mountains. They could avoid the great towns of humanity while traveling through forest, their natural habitat. They were in no hurry to return to man's domicile. As they meandered their way west and south through the deep forested hills and craggy mountains of East Tennessee and West North Carolina they enjoyed the sounds, scents, and sights of the Mother.

If need be, they could just move through space and time and be where they wanted in an instant.

Suzette chittered and chatted about Bear, the miracle return of Rebecca and the surprise of Alexandra's well-kept secret. She made small talk informing him of her many cousins and children that lived in the general vicinity, though small in number they were doing what they could to increase. The main component they required to expand their food source was habitat, she said. Though he knew.

She gloried in the venture, the walkabout intensifying her mood and the beauty filling her heart and verbiage. Nash had remained for the most part pensive and silent over the two days they skitted hither and yon, seemingly without direction or any pressure of schedule. He would hit the small pocket flask regularly to lessen whatever internal weight he carried.

As silent as he had been on the journey, he was stone faced as they stood in line to purchase something they could have avoided, along with the happy hippy late comers, by shifting position metaphysically. His spirit lifted as he realized they would not be using the cash left from his C-note, she was paying. They sulked their way through the darkness of the small ballpark toward the beckoning sunlight and the luxurious green grass of the ballfield.

"Are you alright?" Suzette was concerned, her natural state. Nash had never been loquacious, more surly and bitter than convivial, but he had morphed into a depressed, sullen state.

"It is the loneliness of an animal spirit whose children's numbers no longer are limitless, instead they are extremely limited. You see, whereas your people increase, humans find them cute and their fur no longer of value, mine are hunted out of fear every day. There was a time when my children, as well as myself, were considered Gods to man, then the white man came along with his fear and loathing of anything natural. Any scent of the Mother burned his nostrils. The very essence of what he had evolved from now offended his sight. Nature should be dynamited, clear cut, burned, and killed." He spit on the hard surface of the warning path, "The sight of these breeding horrid masses only acts as reminder of the number of my glorious scions now long gone and still dwindling. Yes, it breaks my heart knowing extinction, the loss of magnificent creatures, hardly passes their notice. They disgust me." She saw him shimmer and knew he fought the transition from man to beast.

"We are here to find those who are not what you describe. We are here to listen and observe, to find humans who are decent and understand what you say and want to change their course. We are not here to judge by the past but to hope they represent the future," her words were whispered steel. She was a believer in Bear's vision, she had to be, it was their only hope.

The mood inside the park was one of joy and celebration. These people were here for a purpose and the purpose was greater than the sum of the total parts. If belief, heart, mental determination, and optimism could change the world, these thousands gathered here would wake up to a new day of peace, glory, and renewal throughout the land.

The air was filled with laughter, earnest conversation, beach balls, and pot smoke, though not all partook of the mighty weed. Each person brought a piece to the puzzle of how to change the world for the better, some would fit, some would be thrown away. But all would listen, given honest and careful consideration, then respect would guide what could be accomplished. Suzette allowed herself to bathe in the esprit des corps. She might be mistaken but Nash's despondency appeared to be lifting.

A joint was casually passed their way, the passer not looking to whom he passed it, nor caring, as he was deeply involved in conversation. People—Nash assumed with the show—wandered throughout the crowd checking cables, adjusting lights and sound, making minor adjustments to where speakers were placed throughout the ballfield. Nash could only guess what horrors were about to emanate from those same speakers, he wanted to move away from direct exposure.

He took the joint without thinking and puffed it twice before continuing the procession of the pot parade. He couldn't tell if it was the drug or the good vibrations blasting from the assembled but he felt his mood lighten and when the music escaped the black boxes set up by the crew it was pleasant to the ear. He detected no overwhelming desire to run and hide, covering his ears and howling. It was Brahms.

The quartet on stage eased into Mendelsohn's String Quartet No. 2 in A minor, Opus 13. Nash found his full attention riveted to the sound, the beauty of it moved him as none other ever had. He stood, stock still, in the midst of all this unwashed humanity and closed his eyes, the better to allow the sound, the notes, to wash over him, cleansing the displeasure he had experienced when he first walked through the gate. Tears flowed gently down his cheeks, disappearing into his scruffy beard.

""Well, I don't know if the Quartet was a grand concept for everyone," grinned Jaxson, "but for at least one it was the greatest we've had." He pointed at the tall man standing where most sat, light brown, almost blond, hair—no, it was tan—and a beard of the same, eyes closed and weeping. Ian, Maggie, Gabby, and Ben had no problem picking out who he meant.

He was tall, standing next to a smallish, well, compared to him, brown woman. Those seated around him quieted as they took notice of this large, powerfully bult man weeping as the music obviously resonated with his soul. Silence rippled out as if the service had begun and attention was demanded by the assembled. Then as if to proclaim each was Spartacus, they began to stand, to allow the magnificence to wash over them, to experience what this man clearly was witnessing. As the music faded the roar of approval washed over the players as they stood as one to thank the assembled for hearing their musical words. And the crowd demanded more. The four glanced to the side of the stage where Ian and company stood applauding and motioning them to please continue. Beauty wins again.

Ian was as content as he had ever been in life. Allowing people to ease into the concert space, find their piece of turf, and settle while the strains of Mozart, Beethoven, Hayden, and Mendelsohn wafted on the air was perfect, even if their A&R guy was the sleaziest human on the planet. Vilhelm was not going to change his style, it was his and his alone. It made him stand out. Boy, did it ever, thought Ian. But the guy was growing on him.

The show in Salem had had a few bumps but nothing drastic. It was their first show in almost a month without some superstar showing up and transforming the rhythm of the show. It's not that that had been horrible, but you can't have a Dylan Roberts show up, or a Bruce drop in and not disrupt the cadence of the show. It had been fun flying by the seat of their pants. But now they were back to the roots of the show. This was the essence of the show, the soul, the raison d'etre for the tour. These people, stars in their own right, who had agreed to give of themselves for a cause, a worthy, just cause. All the bumps and rough spots would be buffed out tonight while they remembered who they were and why they were on the road together. They had the capability, the talent, the love to carry the weight of the show and the cause. A burden shared, especially by ones with so much talent, was a burden caressed and loved. If it took a village this was the capstone.

He decided to let the quartet play another twenty minutes while the crowd settled. If they all picked up on the vibe of the tall fella weeping, they should be primed and ready for the 'All-Girls Choir plus One'. The five, now six with Emmylou, women singers each brought their own sensibilities to the choir. They came from as disparate backgrounds as you could find. Gilliam from the hills of North Carolina, Bonnie from musical parents on the outskirts of L.A., Cinda from the hills of West Texas, Michele a Nashville girl, and Joya, dear Joya, from Nigerian parents who settled in southern New Mexico, along with Jesse, old pro of fifty years, guitarist extraordinaire, the plus one, the seasoning. Ian dared anyone to find a more impressive, outstanding melding of voice and talent, harmony and love anywhere on the planet.

Yeah, and the rest of the crew was just as good. They would recall the purity of purpose and the joy of each other's talents tonight. If his grin got any bigger It would cut his head in half. Time to go out front and check balance, comfort of volume, and soak in the vibe of the masses.

The skies were clear, the sun warm without beating them to death. It would be a perfect evening of music, kinship, and optimism in Asheville, NC. Ian took in this beautiful old ballpark, McCormick Field the third oldest minor league park in the nation and the oldest outside of Florida. Shit, Babe Ruth played an exhibition game here. He wanted to cry with the history of the place. This was baseball personified. It was why he wanted to do a show here.

Dave Rogers, the manager of McCormick Field had taken him on a tour of the place. It was solid, the way they built things in 1923, built to last. Even if some money-grubbing millionaires would tear most of these places down in the future this one had survived. He wanted to howl. Like a wild animal calling to a mate, he was complete. Rain might be predicted for tomorrow but love would hold the evening in its soft hands.

Still his attention could not be ripped from the tall, bearded cat in the middle of this small mass of humanity. There was something about the guy that just didn't 'fit'. The way he soaked in the music, the energy all around him. Almost as if he wasn't really human but feasting on humanity's vitality. Or it could be that tan hair. Who had tan hair?

He moved in a languid, stealthy, fluid, almost stalking way, smooth as if he were above those around him. There was no need to hurry, no need to worry, these creatures were below him, non-threatening, he stood above them all. And the small black woman at his side scurrying to keep up as he casually weaved his way through the crowd. A strange pair. Ian should mention them to Dennis, wasn't this what he had explicitly told them to watch for? Though if Ian saw, Dennis had seen a half hour before. They guy was scrutiny personified.

Relax, son, Ian told himself, all is under control. That didn't stop him from jumping at the touch of his arm. Dugie stood there with computer open and operating in the crook of his left arm as he got Ian's attention.

"Might have a problem," he told Ian as he turned the computer around so Ian could see the screen. There was a large red, orange, and yellow blob across the screen with a small blue dot at the far-right hand corner.

"That's a storm, a big one," he said pointing at the blob, "and this is us." He pointed at the blue dot.

"How long?" Was all Ian asked.

"Forty-five to an hour," Dugie closed the computer.

"Shit! Alright get the girls on, one song and I'll get everyone as secure and inside as we can get them," Ian's gaze took in the woefully inadequate shelter facing him.

"Maybe we should try and send them home?" Ben had stepped up and caught the tail of this beast.

"No time," Ian took in the crowd and the exits, "They'd still be trying to get to their cars when this hits. Get me one of the officials for this joint so we can make a very quick plan. And I want everyone on board either taking down and storing equipment wherever possible or directing people where we can. Tarp what we can't hide." Ian mode engaged.

As the 'choir' let the last note of their only song ring out, Ian took the stage and the microphone. "Ladies and Gentlemen, we have a bit of a weather condition moving in. We do not believe it would be wise for you to try and make it to your cars and home. We are asking that you move under the stands as much as possible or under the protection of the overhangs. Some of you can fill the outbuildings and hold each other close. They are not predicting tornadoes or damaging winds but if you live in this part of the country, you know that can change in seconds. Please look out for each other, we have time, we just need to remain calm, orderly and think of your brothers and sisters. Remember why we are here and we'll all be alright."

To his surprise everyone seemed to be doing as he asked. They moved in an orderly fashion sharing bottles of wine, laughter, joints, pipes, stories of storms and festivals they had survived. It was a merry old time. The roadies were tearing down and storing the equipment in the trucks and under the stage, covered by tarps and weighted down with anything they could find. It was going to be alright. Where did he hear that laughter coming from? Oh yes, inside his head, ah well.

People scampered up the stairs to the relative safety and protection of the iron supported overhang in the upper decks as others headed to the interior. There was no vibe of fear or worry just folks out for a great time with a minor interruption. Ian told most of the sound, roadies, and light guys to head to the buses. Save the interior of the park for the paying customers. It would be tight squeeze in the small structure of the ballpark, but everyone should remain dry and free from harm inside. The singers, musicians, and 'stars' were to shelter in the buses as well. He wanted to know where everyone was and that they were safe and together. Ian would go with the fans to act as head cheerleader. He would reassure, talk, make jokes, tell stories of the road and famous people. He would be lead distractor, with Maggie, Ben and Gabby acting as aides.

The sky darkened and with it, night fell in the early evening of the day. It pressed down on the small ballpark and those hidden within. Loud talking and laughter became muted whispers, a guarded wariness enveloped the gaggle huddled within. Flashes of lightning illuminated the way for the clusters of booming thunder as the storm drew close. Wind howled and loose debris slammed up against the concrete structure breaking several windows. A shiver of trepidation wobbled through the assembled. If this ignited, people would stampede and fans would be hurt, he had to quell this before it got out of hand.

And then the rains came. They were mostly protected from the worst of it but with the swirling winds a river of water was developing down the concrete runways. Most of the assembled were either in bare feet or flip-flops and didn't much care about wet feet, but Ian had always been a bit fastidious about his footwear. He stepped up on the two-by-fours holding a section of scaffolding where the owners were making minor repairs. In ancient real estate there were always repairs that needed repairing. Anxiety flowed with the rippling stream of water, ponding at Ian's dry safe harbor.

It was then he heard the most idyllic, breathtaking consonance ever birthed by humans. It was the All-Girls' Choir plus One, they had disobeyed his orders to go to the buses. They had come to soothe the fears of the followers. A Capella, with a richness born of the Mother and carried on the wind for thousands of millennium, the harmonics soothed fraying nerves. Tears of joy replaced whimpers of unease.

As Ian stepped from the two-by-four up onto the scaffolding to gain a more advantageous view the deafening crack of thunder caused everyone to reflexively duck their heads and cover their ears. Ian's grip, slipped, and as he slid from the scaffold to the precarious wooden framework his foot lost purchase causing the break on the front right wheel to let go, a two-by-four shot from under his left foot bouncing off the metal guard running alongside the base of the runway where it ricocheted back to release the brake on the other front wheel just as he looked up and saw where the 'thunderclap' originated.

Apparently with all of the weight of the people crowded into the restricted space of the covering on the upper decks, along with the minor repairs not yet completed, the strut from 1923 was losing the battle with physics. Just as he saw the disaster about to happen, he slipped the rest of way onto the hard concrete surface pushing the scaffolding down the runway where it came to rest just as the strut gave way. It bent, groaned, cried out but held. All the dozens camped under what would have been certain death were able to scamper to safety.

Ian's head whipped around to watch in slow motion as he, sure as life is given the newborn babe, saved those dozens. He lay in the raging waters of the river McCormick. He raised his head enough to stare directly into the astonished eyes of Soteria, who grinned.

Thinking Is A Relaxed Way To Travel

As they neared Greenville, North Carolina all agreed they had seen enough of the backroads of America for now. Aron did his usual workman like search for the best hotel for all of them, that included kids, dogs, crazy women and one lone teenaged boy. Holiday Inn. They had recently renovated, they accepted pets and children and there were plenty of food choices nearby. Perfect. They even had a pool.

That would be nice for all involved. There was nothing much better after a day on the road than a little clean-up and relaxation by a pool. It was warm outside, not hot, low 80's, but warm enough to swim.

Aron and the girls were ready as soon as they saw the pool and had a room to change into suits. Carrie and Barbara would unload, unpack, settle in, maybe have a quick libation then meet the kids at the pool. Carrie was a seasoned traveler by this time so had settled within a short time and was ready for that drink and the pool. She knocked on Barbara's door to no answer. She knocked again. No answer. She knocked a little harder and the door swung open a little, apparently not latched in case the girl's needed something.

Carrie kept knocking as she slowly eased the door open, calling Barbara's name so as not to startle the woman. Water was running in the bathroom so Carrie decided the better part of privacy was for her to back out of the room and return in ten.

Just as she turned to leave the water shut off and Barbara exited the bathroom in bra, panties, and a scream on finding Carrie there.

"The door was open, I'm sorry, I knocked and called out your name, I'm so sorry," Carrie repeated and would have again had not the sight of Barbara's bruised body shocked her into silence.

"Yeah, now you know why I couldn't go to the doctor," Barbara said as she covered herself with a loose-fitting kaftan. Though the damage had been done.

"No, that is why you need to go see a doctor!" Carrie retorted, "Those bruises are bad, there might be broken ribs, internal damage, we need to get you examined!"

"And tell them what? That I fell down the stairs? Walked into a wall? Got run over by a rogue wave? No, there would be too many questions and this will heal. They find out my husband did this then there are cops and lawyers involved, then he knows exactly where I am. I am not going. This will heal," Carrie thought Barbara wanted to break down and cry, but she wouldn't, not here, not in front of Carrie. Certainly not in front of her children. Barbara might not have much she could call her own, but this was hers. She would bear it. She had borne the burden for years; those years were coming to an end. She would heal and leave the pain and suffering in the past.

'I want to take pictures." Carrie said to Barbara's violently shaking head. "Yes, we have to document this."

"I won't. I want no souvenirs of nightmares," Now the tears began to find their escape. "I don't want to relive this. He can't hurt me anymore." On this point she was as firm as any human could be.

"What about others," Carrie thought of the battle she'd fought to free herself of her despicable uncle. She'd had to stand up to insure no other child, no other woman, no other human would ever be harmed by him again. She knew the pain Barbara faced. She also knew the weight of the pain and guilt Barbara would feel if she heard he had done this or worse to another. "I promise we will never use the photos unless it is absolutely necessary."

"You promise on the life of those you love?" Barbara's words were steel, she would have an answer, and it had best be the answer she demanded.

Carrie thought hard, 'who did she love?' There were not many. Dennis, for sure, Aron, she guessed she did, Henry, Oscar, her beloved guardian, Kim. Oh, yes, Kim. If she swore this, she swore it on the memory, the love that filled her heart, Kim. "Yes, on those whom I ever loved and still love, I swear." She heard the door clank shut. Truth.

It was not a fun session and was over almost before it began. Less than a dozen, more than a lifetime. They silently hugged and walked hand in hand to the bar for one shot to seal the deal, then out to the pool and joy.

The pool area was filled with shouts of laughter, splashing and 'quit its''. The young ones were enjoying this 'vacation' away from the stress and fear of their home. Izzy and Aron jumped into the shallow end of the pool chasing each other, dunking the other's head under the clear water. Aron would dunk her then, turn about being what it was, allowed her to dunk him. Phoebe sat at a table under a sun umbrella quietly watching, lost, for all intents and purposes, in herself.

"Was she always this quiet?" Carrie softly spoke the question.

"No. when she was younger and Rod was still play acting, she was a happy, normal child. She was so full of life and bliss you didn't think anything on this world could stop her," the sigh held such agony Carrie thought she might break down right here. "and then Rod lost it. Whatever thread he'd clung to so he could appear as he wanted, or maybe as we wanted, needed, hoped, I don't know." Her eyes never left the silent curled up figure of Phoebe, "He hit her. She hadn't done anything to warrant it. Damnit what could any child do to warrant being struck by an adult?" She took a deep breath, "And then he couldn't seem to stop. I jumped him from behind to make him quit, to hold his arm, to weigh him down. But it was like I was a doll, small, insignificant, an irritant, he threw me down and started hitting me, punching me. Phoebe grabbed Izzy and ran to the neighbor's house." Her fixed glare emptied and she forced her eyes from the silent child and gazed off into infinity.

"Rod finally got hold of himself. He begged me to forgive him. He wept, swore it would never happen again. He vowed on all he held holy he had no idea why or what caused this but it would never, ever happen again." Her glare embraced a past of lying, deceit, and pain. "It didn't, not for a while but his hold on all the pent-up anger, hate, whatever grew tenuous until he stopped trying to hold it in check. I guess it was the booze, but that was just the grease on the rails. They had already been laid long before I knew him. His old man and his old man before him had the same disease. Blind rage and no control. I tried to leave a hundred times, but he kept finding me, begging me, and promising me," now her own pent-up anger showed its pretty little head though whether that anger was for him or her, Carrie couldn't tell. It didn't matter; she let Barbara have space. If she wanted to say more, she would, if not Carrie could fill in the spaces herself.

"See, I never had nothing, no one, really. No knowledge of the rest of the world. I was cocooned in my own little creation, kids, house, job, husband, I never traveled or went anywhere. I didn't know anybody outside my tight circle. I had nowhere to go. I wasn't well traveled and wise beyond my domain, not like you," again her eyes found her elder daughter and she sighed what might have been.

"Hell, before Kim came along and shook up my world, I'd never really been anywhere either. I'd just been in my town, my house, on the ocean and in love. She's dead." Carrie always tried to come up with a nicer way of stating reality but she never could. She hadn't gone to the great beyond. She was dead. Except in Carrie's heart, memories, and soul, that was where Kim would always be alive.

"Shit!" Carrie exclaimed, "Well, aren't we a pair!" she barked a mirthless laugh, "our path is not back there, it is forward. I'm not saying we forget the past but learn. You can't live there; we live in the future and that's where we are headed. I've wallowed as long and as deeply as I will ever need. I carry the past as do you, but it doesn't have to be a burden, just a starting point. So, let's start having some fun, we are on an adventure." Carrie had found herself as she would try to help other women find what was locked in them. Kim would suffer no less.

"We hang, we swim, we eat, drink, live and tomorrow we find the highway and head southwest to New Orleans!" She hugged Barbara and they in turn walked over to hug Phoebe out of her funk, if only superficially before being joined by the sopping wet Aron and Izzy. "Ever been to New Orleans?" she asked the sky, and the four responded. "No!"

"Well, neither have I, but we got friends there and they have food and music," They may not have felt lightness all the way to their souls, but they felt something positive and that was a beginning.

The Show Must...Oh, You Know

The storm had passed, all survived, attention could be paid to other oddities in life. Now they would see how much of the show they could salvage. Gabby used the long-handled squeegee to swab the stage so they could try to reset as quickly as possible. The equipment had stayed dry under the stage and stored in the trucks, it should only be a matter of a half hour to reset and then they would try a quick sound check while the Choir sang. It would be far from perfect but it would have to do. The fans would be happy to end this day on a musical note. This was one of the primary reasons Ian and Jaxson had specified they wanted an-alog sound boards. If you had a set-in stone set with one or two bands digital was wonderful, it would run itself. But give a good sound man free reign and an analog board and he could mix by the seat of his pants and the sound in his ears. That was going to become extremely necessary in about forty minutes.

As Gabby wiped down the last of the ponding, he set towels and squeegees aside to grab a base bin and wrestle it into place. He struggled for a moment until for some reason the burden lessened by half. He looked up from where he had been concentrating and saw the cause of the lightened load. Teri grinned at him as she helped ease the big cabinet into its spot.

He nodded his thanks when she joined him to lift the next one.

"So, tell me about your leader?" As off the cuff as one can be when lifting a hundred- and eighty-pound speaker.

"Oh, Jaxson? He's great. I grew up listening to his music, he's really one of the best songwriters and musicians there is, in my book. A real swell guy as well," he knew he was talking too fast but he wanted to stay away from who and what he feared she was getting at.

He didn't know if Ian had performed another accidental miracle. He hadn't heard any talk but she had the look that only people who had witnessed such an occurrence get. A look that said deny it if you can, I don't care. I want and will get verification of what I saw with my own two eyes. He had seen it in Jeanette's when he'd saved a half dozen folks at that show in Pittsburgh. Shit!

"No," she looked him right in the eyes daring him to lie, she knew he couldn't, it wasn't in his Mayan nature. "Ian." The name came out as an accusation, a goad.

"Oh, he's great, too. He's the one who took up the whole stand against the caste thing. The reason for the whole Untouchables tour. He's that kind of guy," he grunted with the weight of the bin. She grinned lifting her end.

"And he has a hobby of saving people?" she had him by the short hairs now. She knew something, something Gabby did not.

"What are you talking about?" Play dumb, son, play real dumb. He didn't know this woman. He liked her, she saved Howie, didn't she?

"Look, when the storm hit and everyone was concentrated in limited areas one of struts down below cracked and would have crashed down killing and injuring dozens of people, no way they could've gotten out of the way. Yet, completely by accident, I know I watched the whole thing take place, Ian saved all those people. In the way he fell, cut loose the breaks on a scaffold, again, quite by accident, and pushed it into the exact spot to stop the whole collapse. Now, I know what I saw. And the thing is, no one, not one person he saved seemed to realize it. No one said thanks, no one acknowledged it, no one took notice. It was as if it was expected!" She wanted to scream yet kept her voice in control. "What's his superpower, or what the fuck is going on?" Now the volume peaked and a few of the roadies peeked over but did not intercede.

"I don't know. Nobody knows. I don't think Ian knows, it's just something that happens, has for a year or so. Some kind of weird mojo or curse, or maybe he's a minor deity." Gabby uttered a strained laugh, though it sounded more like a cry as he set the speaker down. He was getting flustered and his words tumbled like an avalanche. He wished someone would come and rescue him but he stood alone, atop Mt. Ian and no other worshippers took a knee.

He gazed at the sky as if in prayer, closed his eyes to breathe and opened them to the prayer answered. Ian smiled, patted him on the back and turned to face Soteria. "I'm guessing you have some questions you would like to have answered." He took her by the arm and led her off the back of the stage.

Just as they were about to take a seat at the picnic table, now occupied by Maggie, to help explain Ian's affliction, Dennis motioned he would like a word in private with the lord of the drifters and vagabonds. Ian excused himself.

The women watched Ian and Dennis head-to-head in a very quiet, private meeting. After several seconds and a raised word or three Ian excused himself for just a moment.

"It would appear my presence is required elsewhere for a bit. As I would also like to be a part of this discussion, I'm afraid it will have to wait until we mop up this show and have time to talk." He shrugged his impotence to the women with a silent promise to Teri they would have their time and she would have her explanation; it would have to wait.

As Ian walked off with Dennis, Teri had conflicting feelings, as if she had just dodged an avalanche by ducking behind a small boulder yet missing a grand opportunity to discover one of the world's great secrets. She'd wanted to talk to him. She had experienced some kind of bizarre phrenic connection between the two when the incident happened. She had no idea why, something out of the past, some psychic/supernatural linking she couldn't describe and had no idea of the why. Some other incidents in her past had triggered a mist shrouded memory, but what? She had no recollection, not past the last few years and they were sketchy at best. Maybe a trauma of some sort blocked her earlier life. She had no recall of family, friends, school, nothing, not until NY, and she knew she didn't fit in there, but who did? It was like she had been dropped here from another planet, another life and she was constantly adjusting her words, her actions, to fit in with humans. Like why did she think of them as 'humans'? She was afraid to bring it up to others, she was quite certain they would think her insane. Ah, the life of the musical gypsy and their superstitions.

Dennis pulled a sheet of paper out his back jeans pocket. He, of course, was outfitted in jeans and tee with work boots for accessory, so he would 'fit' with the roadies and crew. It would have been perfect if it hadn't been perfect. None of the other vagabonds bothered to iron their stain free and fresh-as-the-outdoors scented, T-shirts and jeans nor polished their work boots to a brilliant shine. He stood out like a shiny nickel in an outhouse, but he tried.

"This came across from the boys in D.C.," he passed the paper to Ian.

It was, as Ian had feared, another threat on the lives of the crew and performers. The strange thing was it had Ian's email address with a cc to Jaxson, who happened to walk up just as Ian perused the note. Ian passed the threat to Jaxson. Ian thought Jax might cancel everything right then and there out of concern for the safety of his people. Instead, it had the opposite effect. Jaxson's expression transformed into one of anger. Ian had known Jaxson Grahm for half a century; he had never seen the man truly pissed. He did now.

"Who the fuck do these reprehensible sonsabitches think they are? They think they can intimidate me? Us?" He kindly included Ian and the rest of the Untouchables. "Do they know who they're fucking with? We are road bards! We have worked some of the shittiest dive bars and hellholes in this country. Threaten us? I had a club owner put a gun to my head when I demanded he pay the band when he wasn't going to! Asshole pulled the trigger back and was going to blow my head off. Or so I thought. But I stood my ground and he fucking paid me! Fives, tens, nickels and quarters but I got my money. This jagoff thinks he can intimidate us? Well, bring it on!" Jaxson was not known for macho bravado and Ian found it amusing he would act out some bizarro inner id attempting freedom. Jaxson noticed.

"You think this is funny?" Though on further review, observing from outside the safety of that id, he had to laugh as well. "Ok, I'm not some macho hairy ape, but I can stand up for myself and my crew, can't I?"

"Yes, and you did it magnificently," Ian ceded. "but the question is what do we do about the threat?" He turned, directing the question at Dennis.

"Well, you know what I think you should do," he began.

"We're not giving in to fear and intimidation," both the showmen almost said simultaneously.

"Yeah, I know, the show must, whatever," Dennis gave up that line of thought.

"Dennis, I'm sorry. No, no, I'm not," Jaxson was steadfast, "It's not just some saying. It's not a challenge, it's a promise. A promise to the paying public, to the fans, to those who might only ever get one opportunity to see a show in their lives. That if they show up, so do we; threats, floods, thunderstorms be damned. Whether we have hundred and three temperatures, dying mothers, sick children, whatever, come and we owe it to you to give you our best, always." Jaxson had proven that over and over throughout his decades on stage. Even if he had to cancel the show halfway through because he couldn't sing, he would give the audience their money back and make good on the date. The promise was sacred to old school troubadours. "So, what are the other options?"

"I think we should get some backup," a simple statement with obvious severe repercussions.

Ian didn't want to bring in the National Guard or a bunch of uniformed cops, or more FBI agents who would stick out even more than Dennis. This was supposed to be a tour of goodwill and hope, not an armed camp of terror. Old Hippies tended to be a bit skittish around the feds and bulls who used to beat the shit of them with clubs for wanting peace.

"I don't suppose you have any undercover types like they do on the TV shows that would fit in with..." Jaxson gestured to the oddities working their asses off around them.

"Let me see what I can do, but I want at least a dozen trained professionals on this," Ian was about to chime in when Dennis chimed him out, "no negotiations on this. My job is to protect you whack jobs. And I am going to do everything in my power to keep you dreamers safe. Believe it or not, I've kind of come to see what it is you are attempting to do, and I'm beginning to buy into this whole fantasy."

"Ok, but no narcs, no DEA, these folks are here for a good time, to help others and all they're doing is smoking a little dope and eating some gummies. Nobody is shooting up or selling fentanyl or crack or smack," Ian didn't want people getting paranoid and avoiding the cause. Shit, did people still do all that stuff and did they still call it that? He didn't know and didn't care; he also didn't want that shit anywhere near but they couldn't be an armed camp, that was final.

"Well, I'd keep an eye on that big guy who was standing up earlier and his little black friend. I ain't a bigot but those two are up to something and that's usually not a good thing." Dennis began dialing on his cell to set up backup and direct them where they could catch up with this circus. Of course, he had noticed Nash.

Hiding In The Open Spaces
Between People

"I am still a bit confused on the necessity of hiding with the weak and fearful. We do not fear the Mother. Why would we hide from her when she is at her most glorious?" Nash was not of a species that hid from danger but one who faced it dead on. There was no fight or flight, only fight. Oh, if things got tempestuous, if Mother was on the warpath sometimes the better part of glory was to lay low for the nonce. This had been a storm, and a brief one by Mother's standards, so he had been inclined to stay out where he could experience it full on.

"We wish to fit in. If we are to gage the depth of commitment, if we are to know their hearts, we must be one with them. To understand them on a visceral level." Suzette attempted to appeal to his higher cognitive abilities, to move him from instinct to a more deliberate reaction to humans.

"One would think that after suffering the existence of these vermin for millennium after millennium, observing their fears and hatred of anything not of them—and of themselves more often than not—we would know them intimately for who and what they are. I know their terror of my people. I have had ample opportunity to experience it full on for the past few thousand years or so." Nash explained, though he knew he spoke to a stone mountainside. "Usually, we were forced to protect our own rather than attack these. Why would we attack them? They don't taste good and they smell worse. Or certs used to!" Here he allowed himself a chortle at his own clever retort.

"We seek allies to protect not just our people but our habitat. For what is survival without a place to live and hunt," she appealed to his baser instincts. Yes, they could survive on the meager portions that humans would allow, but they lived on the hunt. One didn't want scraps when one could draw on stealth, intelligence, patience, and power. "If their hearts be pure and their cause be just, then, and only then will we come together."

He sighed. His children knew patience, he knew patience, but sometimes you were ready for the kill. "Let us hope the disruption in the weather has not disrupted the beauty of the song." He watched as the roadies scurried like ants over the stage rebuilding what they had only just a short time ago torn asunder. He watched the big man struggle with the large boxes on the front of the stage, the woman of magic had been called away. Making a quick decision he made a fluid turn and with a deceptive speed and supple grace made his way to the stage and easily helped lift the cumbersome object.

No words were exchanged between the two large, powerfully built men just a nod of thanks from Gabby to Nash and an accepting nod and smile in return. If Gabby thought that would end the assist, he was pleasantly surprised when the fella went over to the next bass bin and again silently nodded, he would help.

They made quick work setting all bins where they should be, Nash shook hands with Gabby in the way of humans and left him to complete his work. Now Nash could only hope that he had not occasioned the torture of his own ears.

There had been no conversation between the two men for several reasons. First off, when you are executing heavy lifting, you save your strength for the lifting not the chatting. As for Nash, he was not one for gab, it was not in the nature of his species nor him in particular. They were solitary creatures not social ones. And Gabby was still digesting what he had witnessed. He, obviously, was over tired and stressed from the tear down/set up in such a short time.

As he had struggled, slightly, after Teri had gone off with Ian, to set the front bin in place, he'd seen the large man make his way to the stage. He didn't think he'd ever witnessed a human being move in such a smooth, supple way. It was as if he slid through the massed horde gathering in front of the stage.

They could see that, at the very least, some of the concert was going to proceed and they wanted prime viewing and listening accommodations. No one noticed that an extremely prodigious and lithe human was slinking through them, not even security. It was as if he didn't exist for anyone except Gabby.

He wanted to yell at the security guy, who appeared as vigilant as any person could be, that he were staring right at a threat and allowing it safe passage. Did everyone forget the FBI warning? Gabby set the bin back on the stage so he could be ready if this guy went after any of the performers. He might not succeed in stopping a man of such discernible strength and ability, but he could slow him down.

That's when the man walked to the other end of the bin and nodded for Gabby to grab his end. They easily moved the large, heavy box into place before continuing on with the other five. That was not the weird part, the part Gabby was having the most difficulty grokking.

He couldn't quite focus on the guy's face or features other than he was big and sleek at the same time. But his features kept coming in and out of clarity and definition. Gabby knew intellectually that what his eyes saw was impossible, but he couldn't make his brain accept the reality of it.

If he was to believe the irresolvable, that was not a human person. His features morphed between human and some kind of animal. Gabby's Mayan history told of gods or spirit animals that could jump between human and animal, but they were myths, folklore, legends born of ignorant, naïve, superstitious minds. He was not that, he was an evolved, modern, civilized man, and yet...

He shook his head as if he could shake the vision from it, though all he accomplished was rattling it about in his cranium. This was stranger than the incident when Ian had saved Gabby's life and limbs.

"What's wrong," Teri asked his troubled expression.

"Nothing, just losing what's left of my mind." What could he say? That an ancient myth had come alive before his eyes to help him set the stage? Yeah, that would ease her mind about him.

"There is some weird mojo surrounding this circus," she said not accusing, just feeling about for some place solid to plant her flag.

"I'm not sure I understand what you're getting at," Gabby would never win an academy award. He was too honest.

"You know exactly what I'm getting at. There is nothing but weirdness and strange occurrences that surround this tour, and everyone just seems to accept them as the normal day to day." She looked him dead in the eye knowing he couldn't lie, couldn't dance around the truth, couldn't even two step it. There was something transcendental, like a little bit of magic, and everyone was superstitious enough they didn't want to say anything for fear that voicing the truth would make it dissipate like some ghostly spirit. She didn't know how she knew, but she knew. "I haven't been roadieing my whole life like a lot of these guys, but I know this ain't no typical rodeo."

"What did you do before you joined us?" Gabby took the offered offramp.

"Nothing, really," she responded instinctively, "Guess I was a bit of a roustabout. Just picked up gigs here and there." Gabby sensed she wasn't attempting to hide her past so much as try to grasp it.

"You don't know, do you?" not an accusation more a lifeline.

"I don't want to... I can't...look, this is not about me. This is about this tour, these people, whatever, is...I don't know," she turned and walked away. She knew there was some way to say what she wanted to but she couldn't hunt down the words. And she couldn't remember her past. And she couldn't admit that to anybody, especially this big Mayan. The only thing she did know was she belonged here. She couldn't say why, but she knew in her gut. And she didn't need anyone digging into things she couldn't recall and possibly coming with some reason she would lose the first place she knew she belonged.

Before Gabby could protest innocent intent or attempt any kind of apology she was gone. What the hell had he said? He thought he sounded concerned, after all, he was. How could someone not know their past. Unless some kind of physical or, worse yet, psychological trauma caused this. Shit, maybe she was abused by some guy or guys. What kind of quicksand had he stepped into? Didn't matter, he'd scratched the surface of this wound and opened it, now he had to do all he could to heal it. And he hadn't a clue how.

She didn't know why she was so pissed at Gabby; he hadn't meant to pry. He'd unknowingly pulled a scab off something she couldn't remember. Frustration boiled and anger escaped. She wanted to be alone in her own thoughts. To try and find the key to her lost past. Shit! She hadn't thought about amnesia but did anybody. She didn't think anyone knew they had it until someone asked a question and there were only short glimpses of recent history and then life faded to black. Lost in her thoughts she almost ran into the pretty, black woman making her way into the backstage area.

"Have you seen Ian or Maggie?" The woman searched the hustling men and women completing the return to concert mode.

"I'm sorry, what?" She'd caught Teri adrift in the darkness of space.

"You work here, yes?" Again, seeking information. It was then Jeanette noticed the confused, disoriented expression on the other woman's face. An expression that screamed she had at some point recently witnessed a Rube Goldberg chain reaction that, more than likely, ended with a certain man saving lives quite unwittingly.

"Are you alright?" Jeanette gently took hold of the roadie's arm and peered deep into her eyes. Time to gauge this situation.

"I'm sorry," Teri didn't mean to continue apologizing but the words were there why not use them? "Can I help you? Should I know you?" Still the desert bore no fruit.

"My name is Jeanette, I am a friend of Maggie, Ian, and Jaxson's, do you know where I might find them?"

"Somewhere, storm came, everybody took shelter, weirdness, They're back there somewhere still, I think," her eyes trying to focus on something only she could see, and Jeanette knew.

"I don't know what happened, but understand this, if you saw it, it happened. It was not a hallucination and all will be explained, just go with the flow, hang on to something solid, like work, until Ian or Maggie come to rescue you, ok?" She gave the roadie a reassuring shake before leaving her to muddle through whatever miracle Ian had performed.

Teri heard the word work and came out of her stupor. Yes, work. She should find something to do, help lay cables and mics, see if anyone required an assist setting up the backline or monitors, the just-in-case monitors. It was funny how everyone loved modern technology, Bluetooth, wireless everything, but still needed the security of having old school backup. She set her shoulders straight, took a deep breath and concentrated on the work at hand.

Jeanette found Maggie sitting at the picnic table in the temporary commissary behind the stage, reading and staying out of the way of the frenzy of activity out front. She took her attention from the page just as Jeanette approached. Smiles filled eyes and features as the two women hugged and shared a joyful reunion.

"I wasn't sure I'd find you all still here. That was one hell of a storm!" Jeanette said embracing Maggie.

"It passed through pretty quickly, nothing got damaged, everything is in working order, last I heard. They want to give those who stayed a reward, and those in need, who live in the area, will get much of the gate receipts," Maggie smiled.

Jeanette thought, 'How typical of this group. This massive storm blows through, probably did some damage here and the surrounding area. There would be cleanup and money needed. Of course, these people would give of themselves and try to help out the locals.' Her better angels did a jig and celebrated. She could not have been happier to be anywhere than in the warm embrace of the Untouchables.

"Well, you might have some damage backstage that you will need to dance lightly around so as not to spook," Jeanette's gaze took in the subsiding activity and she thought of the young woman she had encountered.

"Ah, you're talking about the new roadie, our Teri," nodded Maggie, "Ian tried to have a word with her but was pulled away by our FBI escort." She said the words as if it were the most natural sentence ever uttered.

"Your what?!" Jeanette said much too loudly, but what the absolute...

"Oh, we now have an FBI agent, Dennis, who travels with us and might be adding more. Turns out we are not popular with the far-right crowd. They don't want us messing with the whole caste system. Seems they would like to return to the 'good old days' when the wealthy white, male, minority was permitted to lord over the rest of us peons." She grinned but it was not pleasant.

"Are you saying you've had threats on your lives?" Jeanette was shocked beyond further expression.

"Apparently, though not just Ian or Jaxson or the usual suspects, but the entire crew. Dennis has to inspect every bus and truck before we leave, he has to vet every place we stop for food. It's a real pain in the ass. But better safe..." Maggie would have said more but the loud crack stopped her.

For several heartbeats the world stopped spinning. No one ran or dropped to the ground, they all stood or sat stock still. Where had the sound come from? Was it what it sounded like? Everyone looked around them, front to back, side to side to see if anyone appeared injured or harmed in any way.

Dennis and Ian ran out onto the stage to survey what might or mightn't've happened. Probably not the wisest choice, they both thought at the same time and were about to seek shelter when Jaxson strolled out on the stage. Thunder rolled across his features; lightning flashed from each eye. If there was ever anyone in history that had been more pissed, no one had lived to identify them.

You Can Stand Ten Feet Tall, You Just Make A Better Target

Jaxson stood for several breaths, composing himself and surveying the crowd, the facility, the stage, and crew. He took a hesitant step towards the microphone before pausing and gazing down at the floor of the stage, as if gathering his thoughts once more. He took one more long glare at his surroundings, scrutinizing everything and everyone within his purview. Satisfied, he completed the trek to the mic, stage center.

Taking another cleansing breath, he began to speak, "We..."

A second loud, sharp percussive crack rang out. He flinched before regaining his composure. Ian had no idea what his friend was up to but he was both proud and terrified simultaneously. Jaxson was taking a huge gamble, or he knew something no one else did.

"We will begin the show as soon as I explain something. There are rumors flying everywhere about this tour. That is the state of our society. Conspiracies rule our lives. I believe in music. I believe in people. I believe that sometimes trap cases falling onto a wooden stage can make a frightening sound in a country awash with guns and death. I will not be ruled by bullies, threats, intimidation, or ignorance."

And he sang A Capella;

"Some people are dreamers
Some plot empty revenge

Some try to crush the love and hope
Instead, dreams crush the attempt."
"We are the dreamers,
We are here to fight the hate,
To lift the abused, the exploited
To open Heaven's gate."

"Let there be music and let the music heal." He bowed to the crowd as the All-Girls' Choir plus One took his place with Joya in the center, protected by her sisters and Jesse. She began to sing *"Look Up"* as she had in NY.

Each group and soloist performed an abbreviated set though those in attendance would later claim the show had lasted all night. Everyone came on stage for the encore, Jesse's *'Love Now'*. The audience joined hands, wrapped each other in a bond of love, of hope, and sang along. It was a very hippie ending to a weird, bizarre storm filled day. Perfect.

Nash and Suzette stayed until the end. Nash was astounded by the courage of the troop, the beauty of the music, and the solidarity and fellowship of the gathered humans. He would not have thought that possible. He had always thought of humans as narcissistic, self-serving, greedy bastards who would kill their own mothers if it brought them more. That seemed to be the dictum of humanity, 'It's never enough, We need more'. And more of what didn't matter. More money, more land, more than the other guy, more, more, more. He who dies with the most toys wins. He could never understand that way of thinking.

His kind took their fill, that was all. What was left was for others to scavenge. One didn't kill to kill, for sport, for the joy of the killing. And you never tried to hold more territory than required to live. If another came and tried to take your territory you chased them away, no need to kill. Make your point and be done with it. Respect. Something humans just could not grasp.

But these, these humans, did not crave or envy what others had, they shared the wealth. Food, wine, drugs, cover, and warmth. These humans were almost animal they were so giving.

"What do you think?" Suzette considered his ever changing, watchful expression. He hadn't misjudged humans; he had merely lumped them into the same steaming pile of excrement.

"I think this might be an aberration." He would not let go of long held beliefs and observable behavior because of one day. He was immortal and had witnessed cruelty for centuries, it would not be dismissed so easily. "When does Bear plan on making his move?"

"Who knows the mind of Bear? When he remembers he sent me and wants to know what I have discovered, he will request I pop back to the homestead and we will discuss." She smiled her indifference. They did not think in terms of days or months or years. Time had no meaning; it was an invention of man. When one existed for eons, you realized things would come to pass when they were supposed to.

"Did he ask you specifically to come find me? Or was that your idea?" Nash wondered why he hadn't asked the question previously. Because it didn't occur to you, he answered his own unasked query. He gazed at the stars through the bright lights of the emptying ballpark and saw Bear and his child passing by. And a stab of envy passed through his pure heart. Why was Bear one of the few who was given space in the heavens? The second passed and he once again didn't care because he didn't consider it important. It was time to leave.

They sat in the almost empty bar just this side of the forest where they would rest and check on their children. A small glass of brown liquid sat in front of each with a water back. Silence wrapped them in a convivial embrace once the last song blaring from the jukebox rang out. Nash knew it would be the last song as he has jimmied the machine to not accept any further requests.

"Why would Bear or you, for that matter, still want to work with these," he asked quietly, though not as quietly as he meant to. "They will turn on you the first chance they get. Have you all forgotten what they have done to our children? Because I certainly have not!" His voice grew more intense, louder with each word. What did he care if these few heard him, heard his anger, his betrayal, what could they do to him? He would call down his vengeance before they could raise a fist. He slowly sipped the brown liquid.

"No one has forgotten anything," she hissed, "what we have done is learn to differentiate between good and evil, between those who truly care about the Mother and all of her children and those who would do harm so they can display that lack of compassion on a wall." She glared at the head of a magnificent stag hanging, dusty and uncared for, above the bar. Shit, If these people wanted to display their great courage of killing something from a quarter of a mile away, the least they could do would be to care for the trophy.

"I still feel every cut, every child drowning in a trap under what should have been home to them, gasping for breath. Being shot for sport and pleasure without thought they might have a family." She regained control of her runaway temper. Nash had hit close to the bone. Yes, she was pissed, and would be until the end of time, literally, about the cruelty shown her kind, but she also knew her anger, her revulsion at the mindless destruction of life would not bring them back. If she was to preserve the remaining children, she had to find allies, and those at this concert seemed the best place to start. She had to make Nash see that; if she could win him over, there was hope for all.

He watched her eyes dance from concern to worry to thoughtful to hope. Yeah, he knew what she'd been through since mankind showed up on the Mother, he knew because he had experienced the same. Some species had not done as well; they had been exterminated by man's bloodlust. She'd been to the very edge and back several times, how much had that cost her?

"Alright, here's the deal," he shifted on his barstool so he could face her, so he could see into her essence, "I'll give you two, maybe three, more of these displays. We will weigh the intent of the humans who attend. No guarantees! And keep this in mind, my Mustelidae friend, we are headed where humans tend to be the most bloodthirsty especially for our kind but also for their own. They kill for the love of it and hate because it is tradition. You are behind the eight-ball here but I will give you the benefit of our kind." He downed the brown liquid and held up two fingers for the bartender to see.

It was all she could ask; all Bear could ask of her. If she could show the skeptic the worth of joining forces with those he abhorred, then she and her allies back in Fort could have promise for the future. It was scant to hang her hat on, but then she didn't have a hat, what did she have to lose?

The buses pulled out of the shadow of baseball history and headed south towards Columbia, South Carolina and Segra Park, home of the Columbia Fireflies of the Kansas City Royals baseball team. It was only a few hours and they had hotel rooms reserved. They would spend the night, set up, play and move out the next night.

Ian, Ben, Dugie, and Jaxson thought it a good spot to enter the deep south as it had several colleges and universities. So, their hope was for a hospitable reception. They were well aware that at least some of the threats had originated in the southern states, still, the tour had begun well. They wished to keep the string alive. Shit! They wished to keep everyone alive.

Gabby and Teri sat in silence as the bus bounced down the highway. Each deep in their experiences of the day, each not wishing to discuss with the other for fear of the reaction. Yet, neither could make sense of something they had witnessed and desired a confidant, not realizing they were sitting next to their best possible candidate. Gabby was certain beyond any reasonable doubt that what he thought he'd seen was a figment of his imagination, a mirage. Teri was certain what she had witnessed was an impossible series of events that only she would believe had saved dozens of others. Yeah, and the fairies and woodnymphs of old were coming to tuck her into bed tonight.

Their silence began to pervade the bus. They sat, staring in opposite directions afraid to make eye contact. Several roadies and two musicians hopped on board to share war stories on the three-hour ride to Columbia. This was a wonderful way to share time and catch up on the news of the decade. And, with just a short ride, a pipe, and a bottle or two.

Many on this crew had worked together on shows, festivals, benefit concerts and recording sessions, they shared history. There were no 'castes' in the music business, at least not among those who have survived for decades. They shared a love of music, of the road, of creating.

Hell, some of the road crew had served as sidemen and women to top artists, they were as good if not better musicians than the band, but they kept that to themselves. They had chosen the steadier gig of roadie and techs. A regular paycheck exceeding the glory of the spotlight.

So, it was no surprise that all noticed the dead air between the two on the couch. There could only be three possible reasons these 'kids' were radiating such an uncomfortable vibe. One, they'd had an accidental tryst and either didn't want it to continue or one wanted it to but the other didn't. Two, they'd had a falling out about something entirely unrelated to work. Or three, something bizarre had happened, which both of them had witnessed, and they wanted to pretend neither of them had. No matter what, this required a bit of nippage.

Yogi Mahesh, guitarist extraordinaire, didn't have quite the years of Lee or Russel, though he was not that far behind, but what he did have was over forty years of marriage. Relationships, and keeping them together, was his forte! He sidled over and wedged himself between the two, neither glanced his way.

"I may not be the smartest or most observant man in the world," he began in a dry, droll manner, "but there seems to be a teeny bit of friction between two of our crew, and we can't have that, can we? I know you have worked on other crews, and I don't know how other crews function, but here we work as a well-oiled machine. We have to, as we are about two bones beyond a skeleton staff. We can't have friction, it kills the machine." His words gentle, supportive, though the point would be made. "So, if someone is pissed off at another, we resolve it. If feelings have been hurt, someone feels as though they've been taken advantage of, we beat the shit out of the reprehensible sonofabitch that caused it!" There was an intake of breath from those pretending not to be listening before a huge gale of laughter swept through the bus. Gabby and Teri made eye contact and grinned, yeah, they could use a bud right now. Tension deflated, spirits lifted, it was time for bloodletting and relief.

"What the absolute...?" Began the latest tirade from the lovely, well-shaped, Fame. "There were dozens of humans standing right there, watching him fumble his way through saving their insignificant lives, they saw him! And yet they say nothing. They do not worship the man who gave them a second chance. They do not raise him on their shoulders and parade him up and down the avenues of town! They do not demand their television and radio stations blare his name and likeness so all can see what a miracle he has performed. They ignore the man's due. He should be tasting my essence and demanding more, more, more!"

"Maybe there are other forces at work," shrugged her associate, Fate. "There might be more mighty gods who wish him to be just what he is." She wanted nothing more than to laugh in Fame's face, to glory in her frustration. Not yet.

"Who is more powerful than I?" Pouted and sulked the minor goddess being forced into her place in the pantheon of immortals. "Without me even the most powerful god himself, Zeus, would be nothing. No one would know of his mighty exploits or his greatness without my skills!" She had rediscovered her ego and it fit like the skin she wore so well.

"I think I might mind my tongue if I were you," warned Fate, "Zeus has sensitive ears and all the other gods enjoy gossip. I don't think it would be wise to anger the Father of All Gods!"

"Ha! What is He going to do? Spank me?" A tinkling of laughter escaped her perfect lips. "I have been spanked by the best and it only excited my amour!"

"Yeah, well if Zeus takes it into his head to punish you, you might consider armor to amour," Fate fell out laughing at her turn of a phrase.

Fame, famous for her own temper, stomped away to gaze at herself in the reflecting pools of life.

Is That The Big Easy In The Distance? Yes, I Think It Is

As Carrie and Barbara ordered one more refill of their coffee mugs and the girls squirmed in the chairs ready for motion, Aron flipped open the atlas to the two pages containing the map of the United States. The atlas was getting worn and bent opening to the same spot so many times, but this was where every adventure began.

"We have three really good choices here," he began as he turned the map so both women could see where he pointed. He had no problem reading the map upside down, he had studied it and knew each dark blue line. He almost laughed when he realized what he was doing. Jeez, a few months ago he could've looked at this same map and not been able to read it upside down, inside out, or right side facing, it would have all been indecipherable. Now, he was an expert. "Here we are," his finger jabbed a spot to the east of Raleigh, "We can take route 254 to 64 down into Raleigh and pick up interstate 40 all the way over to Memphis before heading down to New Orleans. Or we can take 254 to Interstate 95, and here's where it gets interesting, we can hop off on Interstate 20 through South Carolina, Georgia, Alabama to Interstate 59 into the Big Easy or stay on 95 all the way to Interstate 10 and it's a straight shot from there," he grinned at their astonished faces. He had studied the roads and mapped out three excellent routes.

"Which way would you prefer?" Aron had done all the work, it was only proper for him to pick the route, thought Carrie.

He took a quick glance from under his bowed head at both of the women. Were they serious? They were letting him pick the routing this time. Well, he took a few breaths to think, 'where would he most like to go?'

"You know," he focused on Carrie, "when I was squatting in Park City, I used to dig old magazines and books out of the trash. Why not, that was next door to my place," his expression wry with memories of hard times and a little pride for survival, "there was this travel magazine with a feature about Savannah. It was beautiful. With this moss hanging like curtains from every tree. Tree lined streets and parks every block. Old, ancient buildings and cobblestone streets right on the ocean. It was, it was, breathtaking. If it looks half as beautiful as those pictures it would be a sight to see." He was focused on a place a thousand million miles from what he thought he would ever get to witness. Carrie nodded.

"95 south it is," she saw Barbara nod her assent.

"Though," Aron added quickly for fear this would make them squelch the plan, "If we're going, we can't just drive through. We would need to spend a night or two to see it all, or enough of it to satisfy." He avoided watching their possible nixing of his dream.

"Then you'd best find us a nice hotel that has no problem with Oscar!" Carrie laughed as she gestured for the waitress to bring them a check so they could be making tracks.

The Staybridge Suites had three rooms available with dog and children included. Since all the rooms were suites, it was easy to set up one for Barbara and the girls, one for Carrie and one for Aron. He had wanted Oscar to stay with him but was outvoted by Carrie who was pay-ing the toll.

Aron found a place called the Cha Bella that was farm and water to table. It would not be cheap but it would be an experience and they had a patio that was dog friendly. They'd been eating quite a bit of deep fried everything for the past few, so this sounded like it might be the perfect change of pace. Best of all, they could seat them early this evening on the patio. They would arrive in Savannah just after noon, settle in, see some sights, walk off the drive and fill up their bellies. In other words, a damn fine day!

The few hours they'd had to explore before dinner were perfect. The weather was warm without being overbearing and the kids were fascinated by just about everything they saw. It was pretty much waterfront, stores, history, shopping, more history, and splendor. Dinner would be welcomed like an old friend too long in absence.

Aron had attempted to look up the menu online, to prepare the girls and himself, he admitted, to what lay in store for the evening's repast. Though, as the restaurant was farm to table or ocean catch to table, they could not be specific about what was coming out of the ocean or the ground. It would be good; he was assured by the voice on the phone.

The dinner had been as advertised. Fish fresh from the ocean and river, greens and vegetables from a garden. Carrie and Barbara had ocean, Carrie Grouper and Barbara White Shrimp Risotto, and a bottle of Mer Soliel Chardonnay, the girls surprised everyone by ordering the Confit Duck, Aron decided on the chicken as it was the closest thing he could find that he knew what it was. Oscar could sample some of each. They thought about desert but the distended bellies told them the better part of pluck was to know when to call it a night, though a cup of coffee would go down well.

Sitting, enjoying the quiet murmur of satisfied diners on the patio, the night wrapped them in a warm embrace, yet it could not hide the melancholy of Barbara's expression. At first Carrie thought it was the look of too full but she soon realized Barbara was locked in remorse once again. She knew she shouldn't have been surprised. No matter the horror of the home, no one got married to get divorced. The fights, the pain, the yelling, the slammed doors and punched walls would take years to knock down what should never have been survived. And it would take that much longer to heal the regret, the what ifs, the why didn't I's. But you cannot rewrite the past. That is the one thing carved in stone. Though like any carving, it should be studied and learned from, not disregarded, or ignored. She let Barbara have her thoughts without intrusion.

The walk back to the hotel was quiet whispers between the two women walking hand in hand, reassurances, support, promises, and hope for the future while Aron did all he could to distract Phoebe and Izzy with oddities he could find in store windows and along the road. They taking turns with Oscar's leash. He was a good kid. Though Carrie had to wonder if he was just trying to make up for time and family lost. Either way, did it make any difference?

As they continued their voyage further south Carrie realized the one thing Aron had not taken into consideration was the coming on-slaught of summer. Both she and Aron were of the northern climes where in normal times winter eased into spring allowing one to become accustomed to warmer temperatures and sunny days. This would prepare the person by thinning the blood gradually in anticipation of the heat to come. When one drove south this happened within hours. The sixty- and seventy-degree temperatures enjoyed would feel chilly compared to the upper eighties now assaulting them with the nineties in reserve.

They had enjoyed their romp through Savannah, it had delivered to Aron all promised from an old, sodden, and stained magazine rescued from his neighbor, the trash bin. He took picture after picture of moss hanging and wafting in the cool ocean breeze from the Southern Live Oaks. He knew that now because he couldn't contain his curiosity and had asked person after person until they found an old Savannahian. He was kind enough to take them on a walking tour of the beauty of his city. He took them block by block and showed them the small parks with their fountains that pocked each of those blocks. The towering trees covered with Spanish moss and the lovely residents who stopped to talk and were ever so pleased that these folks from far away had come to their town. The locals chatted with the children, some finding gumdrops and hard candies in their pockets to share and told them the best places to eat or see the sights. Each, of course, different from the last recommendation. Savannah had been Aron's dream come to life.

So, it was with light heart and joy they hopped back into vehicles the next morning and headed south. The truth in old sayings come to life by living them, it wasn't necessarily the heat, it was the oppressive humidity.

Carrie loved her 1948 Ford Pickup. She loved the style; the way folks would turn their head to gape at it until it faded from sight. She loved the way it handled—she'd had the suspension updated and all new steering components fitted—what she was coming to terms with was the lack of air conditioning.

When living and spending all her time on the coast of Oregon that had never been much of a consideration. Oh, a day or two here and there but they would soon pass, but here, in the hot humidity of Florida, the interior was oppressive even with the wing vents turned all the way inward and all windows open. Oscar had intelligently hopped into the bed of the truck in anticipation of this discomfort to avail himself of any and all amelioration. The dog's instinct was superior to the humans supposed greater intellect.

She could only hope their bodies would adjust as completely as the many folks she watched passing them with windows down, wind blowing through their short, cropped hair and smiling. It was a fascinating observation that even folks with newer, more expensive automobiles had their windows down, wouldn't you think those people would have AC? Though it was mostly Black folks, she noted, who refused the benefit of cool air. Almost as if they wanted to say to the privileged white folks passing by, 'look we don't need to be comforted by modern technology, we are comfortable in ourselves.' Superiority is where you find it.

Carrie supposed she should be grateful that the used vehicle they had found and bought for Barbara and the children had AC and they were comfy. She had suggested Aron ride with the family so he would be excepted from the severity of the heat and humidity. He, of course, refused. If she had to ride in this heat, so, would he.

It was mid-afternoon when Carrie's brain screamed, 'Enough!' she was tired from the heat, beat down from the oppressive damp, stickiness of the air. Even a stop for lunch in a nice family—air conditioned—café had only revived her enough to get this far. And where the hell was this far? Was she close enough to any sized town that would have rooms to let with AC and allow Oscar? She could only pray.

"Where in hell are we?" Said asked, literally.

"Just east of Mobile according to the last sign back there," Aron didn't seem bothered by the conditions.

"Find me a hotel with AC!"

"How much do you want to spend here?" Aron was becoming financially conscious and responsible.

"I have been sitting in an oven all day with the weight of a massive cloud pushing down on my spirit, my life, my desire to continue to breathe. I want the nicest joint that will accept Oscar!" If someone had decided to draw a picture of the epitome of frayed human's nerves, they could have just as well taken of picture of Carrie at this exact moment in time. Her hair was akimbo, and that was a considerate description, sweat stained tank top and shorts that were riding up her butt like an invading army.

"Well, if you don't care and we want to experience historical Mobile," he scrolled through his phone screen one more time, apparently taking longer than the short fuse next to him thought appropriate.

"WHAT?" The fuse had burnt down to the powder.

"The Battle House Renaissance. Right in the heart of the Church Street Historic District, close to air-conditioned restaurants and they love big dogs," he smiled.

Her discordant mood instantly began to deflate, replaced by the promise of relaxation, a tall cool drink, and a nice cool room.

"Book it, Dano." He stared. "It's from an old television show," she encouraged. Nothing. "Nevermind. We need three rooms."

He knew that but kept the knowledge where it couldn't cause him harm.

They unloaded bags and dog so they could check in and go straight to their rooms. Carrie was buoyant when she discovered her best friend Aron had found not just a hotel, but a hotel and Spa. The bags could unpack themselves; she was going to get a massage and then swim. She prayed to all the gods and goddesses that the pool would not be bathtub temperature, but a nice cool dip in refreshing waters, or she'd go jump in the river, either or made no difference.

Just a Hop, Skip, And A Couple Hours

The sun peeked over the top of Mount Pisgah deciding whether to burn off the light fog that had settled into the valleys overnight or allow it to sleep in and leave of its own accord. Two figures materialized in the shadow of the mount, stretching out the limbs of corporeal forms discarded the night before. They had used the night to do their due diligence among each family. Native Spirit guides found it humorous that white folks couldn't believe any entity could traverse the Mother in one night performing their duties. Shit! How did they think one spirit could watch over so many children without the capability? Suzette had the more difficult task as she had far more offspring that Nash, whose children were dwindling. She did not envy him the ease of his task.

They decided they would walk, run, and romp through the dense forest for a half day before making their way down the backtrails of the other side of Pisgah. Time and distance were concepts that served mankind. If they would only open their minds eye, to move outside the confines of the mortal coil, to expand their narcissistic sentience they would realize there were no boundaries. They could travel and experience a true limitless existence, but such was humanity.

The day warmed as the two traveled in contented companionship. In the 'real' world they would have been predator and prey, that was the way the Mother had set things up. It was her way of controlling populations, keeping the sick from pulling down the healthy and giving new life room to grow. Sometimes you needed a good fire to clear the land so seeds could take hold and begin life anew. The scent of life coming into full bloom filled their nostrils as summer closed in full fury. Yes, there were moments when having a physical form had its advantages.

Suzette had explained to Nash that the traveling musical revue they had witnessed last night would once again come to life in a new location today. It was not far, even for humans, to travel from Asheville to Columbia and the whole magilla would commence with different folks out in the audience while the same folks appeared on the stage. To him it seemed a silly, futile exercise. To each their own.

He wished to arrive early enough to hear the joy that caressed his ears the day before. Suzette was pretty sure the foursome would be part of the show once again, or so she hoped, if for no other reason than music hath charms. She coveted his acquiescence as he was a hard mussel to crack, she needed a bigger rock and that was for the vibe from Asheville to return in Columbia.

The gathering outside Segra Park had the feel of a carnival preparing to open. An electric current ran through the assembled in anticipation of the day's entertainment. Yet, it was more. It was not just the music or the performers or fame, it was a coming together of like-minded people who, through their sense of right and responsibility to their fellow man, were here for a purpose, a cause, much bigger than themselves. Yes, there was pot and wine and who knew whatall, but that only intensified the exhilaration and pleasure of the day. Nash even tempered his customary irritability. It might be a very good day.

A bucket was passed down their way, Nash took a look inside and was confused. It was filled with paper money displaying varying ranges of denominations yet was heavy, as if filled with rocks, and clinked when he shook it. He shook it again to determine what might be in the can when someone shouted, "either put something in it and pass it down, or just pass it down. If you shake it more than three times, you're playing with it!" The sound of laughter showered down on him as everyone with hearing was chortling at this, apparent, humorous retort. He passed the can in the direction of the voice.

"You cats from out of town?" asked a couple, he of long hair, beard and no shoes, she in summer dress, hair in dreadlocks both reeking of pot.

"I am the Cat," responded Nash, confused that this white person could recognize that fact, "she is of the Otter clan."

"Otter, eh? Sprechen sie Deutsch?" Asked the hippie woman to blank expressions. Realizing her mistake she apologized, "Sorry, man, I thought Otter, it sounded German." She nodded her head a couple times as if that cleared everything up. "You from around here?"

"No," replied Suzette quickly before Nash could explain further, "We're from out of town."

"It's just your partner seemed confused by the donation can," emerged from the beard.

"No, he's just a bit high right now and was staring into the depths of the unknown," Suzette continued her fumbling explanation.

"Gates are opening," saved any further discussions.

The herd of humanity moved in the direction of the gates that were now open and manned by ticket takers. Nash and Suzette stared at the pieces of paper in hands or the holding up of phones as folks entered the intended venue. Once again confused by the ritual, as they had bought tickets at the stadium last evening, they didn't know they had to repeat the process. They were cash poor.

"It's alright, man, if you ain't got a ticket you can go stand outside the right and center field fences and catch the vibe," offered the dreadlocks, pointing to where apparently the right and center field fences might be.

"Thanks," said Suzette as she steered Nash away from the officials at the gate.

"We may have need to walk a back road into this facility," Suzette whispered as she moved Nash further away from humanity.

"Hey!" called a voice from the direction of the 'gate'. "Hey!" Came the cry once again.

Nash had no idea why but he thought the cry might have been directed his way, it had a familiar aura to the sound.

They searched the area wondering who would be calling to them when he saw the large Mayan towering over the mass of humankind. He was waving his hands to garner their attention and waved even more furiously when he had achieved same.

Pushing his way against the slow moving, hard current of people he finally made his way to where Suzette and Nash stood motionless observing his progress.

"No ticket?" asked the Mayan smiling. "Don't worry, you won't need one when I'm around, just follow me," he said to their confused yet contented expressions. "I got pull."

"I didn't thank you for the help yesterday," Gabby bowed his head slightly in recognition of a good deed done. "We were trying to get everything back up quickly and there were a shit ton of things going on at once." He spoke quietly and reverently as if speaking to a god. His sidelong glances were meant to go unnoticed, at this he failed.

Nash nodded his acquiescence though kept silent. He noted the Mayan's trepidation at regarding him directly. Could it be? He had to question the possibility. White men, he knew, could not see what they did not believe yet believed much of what they could not see or did not exist. It was as if they enjoyed making up beliefs based on the currency of public opinion of the day. But this man was not white; he was of the people. Could his blood be pure enough, not diluted by white conquerors over the centuries, that he could 'see'? It was an interesting proposition; one he would have to discuss with Otter once they were alone again.

Suzette kept her own counsel as she watched the interplay between the two. She was having the same inner dialogue along the same lines as Nash. There was something about this man, some purity or virtuousness, that emanated from him. One could almost feel the warmth as if basking in the love of the sun.

"Are the same people playing this afternoon as yesterday?" Asked Suzette breaking the silence.

Gabby stopped walking to consider before continuing his progress, "Yes, I haven't heard of any guests showing up, though that can be very last minute." He chortled though neither Nash nor Suzette could see the humor in what he'd said.

"The quartet?" Suzette prodded.

"Oh my, yes. They have become quite integral to the show. People love hearing them and they have a calming effect. It puts the audience in a listening mode, not like they don't come in that mode to begin with but the quartet settles them and quiets them. And it's nice," he added his own opinion on the subject.

"Good." Nash and Suzette agreed simultaneously.

"Would you like to go backstage and hang out?" Gabby offered; again, to blank expressions.

"Behind where people are performing?" chanced Nash.

"Yeah, you could meet some of the performers," he was about to suggest getting autographs though immediately changed his mind. These were not autograph seeking folks. Hell, he wasn't certain they were 'folks'. When he attempted to look directly at them, he couldn't quite focus on their faces as if there was a heat shimmer or waves in the air that pushed his attention away from seeing them clearly. He rubbed his eyes. He has got to get some sleep.

Ian watched as Gabby gave the fifty-cent tour to the couple they had taken note of at Asheville the day before. There was something very odd about the guy, besides his size, he was threatening just by existing. And the woman with him didn't fit any better. Small, chocolate brown, pretty as any woman Ian had ever seen yet wary, constantly in motion as if expecting an attack from everywhere at once at any moment. They made Ian feel uneasy and the only way to relieve the discomfit was to stare the bull in the eyes.

"Hey Gabby, looks like everything is coming along. Have you seen Dugie or Ben?" Ian was making an excuse to join the trio and dig a bit.

"Yeah, they were over by the monitor mixing board last I saw. Ian, I would like you to meet a couple folks that were at the Asheville show yesterday and came down here today," he beamed wanting to tell Ian exactly why these two were backstage. "This is..." he faltered, realizing he had never gotten either of their names.

"Suzette," she extended her hand and shook Ian's, "and Nash." Who just head bobbed a hello. "We loved what we heard yesterday and wanted to catch the whole show," she smiled her anticipation.

"The joy of outdoor shows," laughed Ian. There was something about these two he couldn't put a finger on, but they didn't configure to normal. They were First Nation folks, that was obvious, but he couldn't quite detect from which region, not that he was any kind of expert. One would've thought some nation here on the east coast, as that was where they were, yet they didn't fit. He couldn't bring their faces completely into focus.

"We're visiting family from out west," it wasn't a lie. Nash had danced nicely around the truth and Ian's suspicious eyes.

"Nash helped get the bins back in place after the rain yesterday. Everybody was running around trying to get up and running and I kind of got left alone on the fronts. He saw and just came over to help out." Gabby glowed with the joy of the act of kindness.

"Well, we certainly appreciate your help," Ian reached out to shake the man's hand and Nash hesitantly obliged. "We really wanted to end the day on a positive note. It is always best when the fans leave a show feeling the joy. You want people to have an excellent experience not wishing they had done something else."

"I guess that helps with the collection plate," Suzette prompted to dig into this man's psyche and motivation.

"Oh, it helps, but that's not the reason." Ian defended, "We want people to give because they believe in the root cause of the tour, to help raise those who have been held down by the powers that be. To lift the spirits, the hopes, the realities that life can be better. Those who have been led to believe they are lesser than, can achieve greater things. That someone out here is willing to put their money where their dreams are to improve the lot in life of those shoved in a caste not of their choosing. That they matter. As my friend, Gabby, has made quite clear," Ian patted Gabby on the back in appreciation of all he had brought to the table.

"You know Gabby, if your friends here wish to hang out back here, or have full access, we need to get them laminates," he raised his two-way radio to get Ben or Dugie to bring the passes. He didn't know why, but he wanted to win these two over. He could feel their mistrust radiating like a cold front, it reminded him of Joseph Standing Bear in Rapid City. He also thought their good will could go a long way with other doubters. There was a powerful force, an energy emanating not just from the large man but equally from the small woman. A year ago, Ian would have thought it was his imagination but after all the events of the previous twelve months he could not discount his gut.

Ursa Major With A Minor Dilemma

The fledgling summer sun showed its youth by getting up earlier every day and staying up later in the evening, warming the land before allowing the night to cool it back down. The next morning, Helios would begin the cycle once again. Soon he would conquer the night and the Mother would stay warm through the darkness.

Bear's mood did not reflect the positivity of the changing seasons. He rode the roller coaster of highs when he thought of his family, his dearest Rebecca, soul mate and partner forever, and his Alexandra, the granddaughter who would now take over the family business as well as continue to lead the charge to save the Mother. Both were now immortal. No other Spirit Guide had ever had a family, not even for one human lifetime, let alone for the rest of time. Bear was overwhelmed with a sense of gratitude and humility that he'd been granted such a boon.

Then there was the other side of the coin, when he was despondent that his unrealistic belief in mankind had been shattered once again. He honestly thought that when they had gone and forced the members of the United Nations—representatives of every face of humanity gathered together in one room for the purpose of the betterment and peace of mankind—that they would save the Mother. How could humans not see past their own petty interests? How could they not view the greater picture of saving not only themselves but millions of other species?

They had begun with the esprit de Kumbaya, all working together towards the common good. And then man's innate nature kicked in. Countries grumbled that some were giving more than others and receiving less in return, not self-aware enough to note they already had more than most. And those with less wondered why they should not have what the richest did before cutting back on their fulfillment. Shouldn't they be allowed to reap the rewards of what the more powerful had stolen over centuries before giving up more? There should be retribution before sacrifice. Arguing became grumbling begat skirmishes begat hostility begat bloodshed, begat battles, begat war begat a collapse of any and all agreements. It had been a clusterfuck of biblical human proportion.

Now all his hopes lay with Suzette. They had not heard a squeak or a bark out of her in the last month. She was of the belief that this ragtag group of musicians and hippies could be the solution. Bear had his doubts. Then again, where else could he look?

Rebecca sat at the kitchen table across from Alexandra watching her husband pacing the backyard as if caged against his will. He had been in a foul mood since fighting had come into the open between the factions of mankind. He did his best to tamp it down when she was around yet she could sense his anger and despondency, his futility with man. She wished she could take the burden but she knew her husband too well.

Alexandra watched her grandmother watching her grandfather and had never felt more impotent in her life. They both needed a distraction, but Alex had nothing. What they all required was a report from Suzette. She hadn't checked in, in far too long. If only some of the uncles could pop their lovely heads in with a bottle, pipe, and stories to divert Bear's mood.

The knock on the front door startled them both almost more than the sound of that same door opening and a loud, 'Ya-Hey', in greeting. Impossible though it might be, Alex's thoughts seemed to have sent a silent call to the uncles. One may just have answered.

Sung leaned against the door jam, a grin sparking the sparkle in his eyes, the outline of a bottle on the inside of his leather jacket. "I told the others to sneak around the back and surprise the old codger." He laughed and all the nymphs and fairies' laughter tinkled in crystalline chimes. He pointed out the back door as Tatanka, Elk, Oscar, and Glen, dear, sweet Glen, all took turns hugging and laughing while staring at the back door awaiting the delivery of the bottle from Sung.

"This is the restorative we prayed to the Mother for. He has been in such a funk since, since, well, you know," Rebecca found the pain had settled into her chest as well. Such hope, such progress, such a short time, such a fall from grace. Her heart hurt hard for her husband.

"You think we didn't know?" Sung barked a howl, "Every creature with any empathy has been agitated by the great one's mood. Remember, he is the leader, the protector of the People. His pain, his distress is lived by all. We came because Bear needs us, come, let us adjourn to the back forty." He ushered them out.

Bear's grin became wider, deeper, and love spilled from his expression at the sight of his old friend. He wrapped Sung in a great Bear hug refusing to let him go, until Sung pushed back and pulled the bottle from the inside of his jacket. All gathered around the picnic table on anything that would hold them. For Tatanka and Lawrence the Elk, those were upturned chopping logs, others chose chairs, Glen laid out on the on the grass. Though he was their neighbor he spent more and more time traveling the world, doing all he could to take care of his millions of children. Collecting them, loving them, finding family and homes for them. A vocation he knew would take an infinite amount of love and patience.

Bottle open, hearts open, fires, pipes, and blunts lit and passed, the stories began to roll from tongue to tongue, laughter filled the darkening sky. For just a few minutes, immortal time, Bear shed his worries like an old skin. This would not heal the wounds but would lessen the soul crushing disappointment so he could think, reason, plan.

"I heard through the grapevine that Suzette," Sung spoke, seeking the woman but knowing she was not present, "has decided to become a disciple of some traveling carnival or gypsy group." It wasn't a question, per se, but he threw the statement over to Bear, who would know all.

Bear noted Sung appeared stronger, his features filled out and body well-muscled, though he still wasn't the Wolf of old. He would have to ask his friend how his children fared once they had a moment alone. "She is assisting me with a possibility," said the Bear enigmatically. He was giving no ground, not yet.

"Still the Bear with the plan, eh?" rumbled Tatanka.

"Here's the thing; we only have the one Mother and even if there were infinite Mothers out there, She is ours. We either love Her, protect Her, try to help Her heal or She dies, and all of us with her." Matter of Fact just as Bear always was around his own.

"Every time we put our shoulder to the wheel, humans' step on the brake. I am quickly coming to the conclusion," said someone who had lived a million lifetimes, "they will never change. They cannot see their death standing in front of them, they only can conceive that someone might have one ounce of anything more than they when they die. And when you die who gives a shit who has more of what?" Mika, Coyote, strode up from the darkness. He plopped down next to Glen and let out a forlorn sigh and whimpering howl. Someone passed him both the bottle and a joint. "Sorry I'm late, had a thing." That was explanation enough.

"Well, we don't have any choice but to try. Too many of our children have perished, extinct, gone forever, and I don't want mine to join them," Bear exclaimed to Ya-heys and growls of assent. "So, I have to try, to plan, to never give up hope. Suzette thinks these humans might help and I'm willing to try anything, any human, seek any glimmer of hope that is out there." Bear took a tug off the bottle and passed it on.

Rebecca took in the gathered, "You know you can trust Suzette's judgement. She is fact finding, that's all. At least give her the benefit of time, we all have that! We hope," She added under her breath.

"I heard she's traveling with Puma," Coyote threw out into the circle, " he ain't exactly a joiner. Isn't he the one that almost et your grandchild?" Coyote glanced to where Alexandra noticeably shivered.

"Well, he didn't know who she was and he was only reverting to type. He saw a meal. His children were hungry and he felt that. Nothing more, nothing less. He is a skeptic of the nth degree as you all know, I approve the linking up. Two good minds are always superior to one. Betwixt the two they should get a complete picture of what this traveling entourage is at heart." Bear bobbed his head in agreement with hisself, "I am hoping to hear from her by the new moon."

The talk, laughter, meditative, introspective, reminiscence of infinite history passed like quiet whispers of a mountain stream in midsummer. There had been donnybrooks and conflicts within the People but they had never come to full blows, no wars, no animus. The bad blood had been left on the ground at the end of the misunderstanding. The People kept their children in check to assure hatred had no foothold. Man could learn much from animal.

Bear's thoughts rode the cosmic back roads considering his options once he received information from Suzette and now, Nash. Bears could be very patient creatures, though that quality was being stretched thin in the case of The Bear. He knew he should be thinking and planning in Bear time, not human, but the pressure of the moment canceled that option. The possibility of thousands if not millions of deaths within the families of those gathered weighed heavy on his broad shoulders.

The talk became sparse, the laughter died down, thoughtful replaced gaiety, as all focused their attention on the problem of saving as many species as was animally possible. Quiet wrapped those present, they wondered if more would join them again, then realized the futility of wondering. Almost every species of animal, insect, fish, fowl, avian, and mammal, land, sea, and air, had joined forces the decade or so before and what had it brought them? More disappointment, greater realization of man's innate self, depression, and angst.

"I don't get it. None of it makes any sense to me." Glen said to no one in particular, yet to everyone sitting around the dying fire.

"What?" There were so many possibilities, so many 'things' not to get. So many actions that made no sense. Bear couldn't picture them all, let alone to pick just one.

"Why is it man is so self-destructive?" Glen pleaded with every emotion for answers. He had witnessed the depravity, the wickedness of humans. There had to be a reason why they seemed to hate everything.

"Demons," said Bear.

"What?" came the chorus.

"Every man has demons," Bear stated flatly.

Oscar blinked his massive eyes as if to focus on Bear. "Are you implying that man is beset by something that doesn't even exist? We, all assembled here, know there are no such things as demons, they are a construct of a warped mind."

"If you believe, if you are taught to believe, then the belief becomes reality. Man suffers from demons of his own creation, demons inherited, demons born of his culture, demons created and made real by his religion. We know that, if a man appears evil, it is because his spirit is out of balance, twisted. All we need to do is heal the spirit and the human is healed. But they don't believe that, not most of them. They believe demons rule their every evil thought, action, and deed. It alleviates the guilt of responsibility. 'I'm not a bad person, demons rule my life and I am not strong. I cannot fight them; they are too strong.' Saith the human. Therefore, it is not the fault of the individual but of the possessor." Bear shook his head at the insanity of convincing oneself of a lie to assuage the conscience. Culpability blamed on another is culpability dismissed.

"But it isn't true," pushed Glen. "there has to be truth."

"Not where there is belief. The true believer needs not proof, as a matter of fact the true believer despises any fact or data that would prove their belief unfounded." Bear bowed his head in frustration. "We have to find people whose belief is in truth, facts, observable data, reality and find a way to build our movement on them."

"Good luck with that," guffawed Coyote, "man only believes in possessions, demons, money, greed, avarice, lust, and owning something he can only possess for a nano second of the Mother's time. They don't realize that you cannot possess something that doesn't belong to anyone but everyone."

"Ya-hey to that," all agreed.

"Well, we shall wait and see what news Otter brings. Pray to the Great Spirit it is positive and brings promise." Bear took a long toke of the offered pipe and washed it down with the brown liquor.

And Then, The Worm Turned, And It Was Not Good

Ian watch as Gabby led his two new friends on a quick tour of the backstage so they would know the limitations and where the grub was. Ian thought about reenforcing the concept of not bothering the musicians but realized with Gabby that was unnecessary. He had finished his quick meeting with Dennis and had approved the addition of extra Agents. Protecting his people was number one priority, so if Dennis thought he needed more, Ian was on board.

As Ian went off in search of his love it struck him that he might not be able to describe the two people he had just interacted with, as he couldn't get them in focus, but he knew they were native, First Nation folks.

He watched the crowd entering the ballpark and it struck him like a fresh fish to the jaw, a large percentage of the attendees were either black folks, Asian folks, native or Hispanic folks. At most shows that would never have registered but these performers, for most of their careers, had appealed mostly to young white kids. They hadn't meant to or geared themselves to, it was just the kind of music they played. Different genres of music appealed to different folks. Though many artists would crossover to a larger swath of the population. The music Jaxson, James, Jesse, even Bonnie played, resonated with young white kids. That was apparently changing and that fact made Ian very happy.

Music, he had always believed should appeal to as many people as possible. Music should be a bridge without tolls, without restrictions, allowing all who wished to cross it to come. Black folks should give country music a try, and many were. Country folks should sit and listen to the blues, jazz, and R&B. Old folks should just try and remember when they were young and not be so tight assed! Straight people should listen to LGBTQ+ artists without judging and everybody should dance to the Klezmer band.

It was with a happy heart he found Maggie reading off in a corner where she couldn't be disturbed except by a loving, content husband. He say down next to her on the steps of a fifth wheel being used for an ancillary dressing room without saying a word, just wishing to be near her.

"Save anybody today?" her tone light, teasing, he appreciated every syllable.

"Not yet, but the day is young," he responded in kind, "I did OK an increase in FBI protection. Dennis felt it was necessary and if we are going to trust him with our lives we should also listen to his counsel. They'll meet up with us in Birmingham."

"I'm shocked you would take any advice from anyone. Here I thought you knew everything," this time she laughed.

Ian was about to say something he probably shouldn't've when his radio blasted a pinging repetitive tone announcing his presence was required elsewhere. "Sorry hon, I would love to stay and play some more but apparently the world cannot continue its orbit without my help." He gave her a quick peck on the cheek before bringing the radio up to his ear and speaking into the microphone.

Ian turned to head towards the front gate where a ruckus had commenced and the people commencing it had said they wanted to speak with Ian or Jaxson. And only one of them spoke passable English, the others were irate in another dialect. He almost ran Jaxson down as he was heading in the same direction.

"I got the call as well. I think I know who, why and what this is about, though I didn't think it would happen this quickly. Still, it should be quite the hoot," his boyish grin almost split his face.

"Glad you could clear up what this is all about," the sarcasm was lost in the deep end of Jaxson's joy.

The two rushed as quickly as two elderly men could against the current of incoming patrons especially with people stopping Jax to ask for autographs or just to say hello. It was a good ten minutes before they arrived at the scene of the disturbance.

Ian was slightly taken aback to see Raj, standing as tall as he could, trying and get in the face of the six-foot six-inch security. It would have been more comical had not Raj's blood vessels appeared to be on the verge of exploding in his neck and forehead. First thing Ian had to do was calm the man before he had a stroke. The other three were emphatically expressing their thoughts, though from what Ian could hear they were in a language no one at the gate spoke. The Marines had arrived just in the nick of time.

And immediately fell under friendly fire. Flaco and compadres immediately set upon Jaxson speaking Spanish with great passion and speed. Jumping between the joy of seeing him again and their mistreatment by the security at the airport and then again here. At least, that's what Ian thought from their waving arms, hugs, and intonation. He decided he should get between his small lawyer/roadie and the large security dude. Someone was bound to get hurt and Ian wasn't certain it would be Raj.

Ian sauntered over to where Raj was having his discussion with the mountain. So, intense was his temper he had failed to note Ian's approach. The mountain hadn't. He turned his attention from the angry Indian to the approaching elderly man.

"Something I can help you with, sir?" his tone dismissive, his attitude one of superiority.

"No, but there are probably a few things I can assist you with," Ian's attitude one of relaxed camaraderie. No need to antagonize the situation by jumping on anybody's toes.

"I think you can assist me by going about your way," Well, alright. If this mass of humanity wanted attitude Ian had brought his whole supply.

"Here is what I will tell you sonny, if you would prefer to avoid one heaping helping of shit, you might want to turn that attitude down a notch or three." Not threatening, just the boss having had enough of this horseshit for one day. Raj had gone quiet and subdued at the arrival of the King of this particular Gypsy caravan.

"Or you'll do what?" this guy wanted to push every button he could find.

"Let me try to explain something to you and I'll use the smallest words possible so as not to lose you along the trail. This show that is about to transpire within the confines of this beautiful palace of the greatest sport in the world, is my concert. I am the promoter, booker, manager, head honcho and bottle washer, capiche?" A little Italian goes a long way out here in the hinterlands.

"You know, pal, if I had a dollar for every stoner that demanded to be allowed in because they are the boss of this, I wouldn't have to stand out here and listen to idiots like you," his stare was challenging.

Ian was about done with stupid; it was time to do a little edjumacatin'. "Come here. Come here." He declared in soft firm tone, the one that usually got the attention of the intended.

The big guy did as directed, with Raj on his tail. Whatever Ian had in mind; Raj wanted to witness. As they closed the gap with Jax and his three overzealous friends Ian pointed directly at the concentration on Jax's face as he attempted to corral as many of the words these three were winging like darts at an oncoming train.

"Look at his face, memorize every feature, chisel his features into that neanderthal brain of yours and then step over here." Ian pointed at the very large concert poster hanging on the brick façade of the ballpark. Jaxson stood in the center of the assembled cast of the Untouchable's. "Does that man on the poster look even the slightest bit familiar to you?" Ian found he was beginning to enjoy the plowing of uncultivated soil.

The mountain began to move back to his previous post, shaking his confused brain. Ian grabbed him forcefully by the arm and pulled him back to the poster. Just then, in a car circling the parking lot, somebody dropped a lit joint right on top of a very sensitive part of their anatomy, effecting an immediate response where both hands left the wheel beating himself about the groin and the car jumped the curb crashing headlong into the side of the edifice where the mountain had just moments before occupied said turf.

Three pair of eyes locked on Ian. He ignored them, glaring at the auto which was now nestled in the warm embrace of building and gate. The mountain began to crumble, the sky laughed, Jaxson grabbed the three musicians, Raj grabbed Ian and they all made the sprint to the relative freedom inside the ballpark. Ian muttering, "I don't fucking believe it, I just don't fucking believe it. Fuck, fuck, fuck, fuck, fuck." However, the exercise did not seem to elicit the proper lalochezia.

Ian plopped down on a folding chair near catering, it was between meals and stage time, he would be alone. Well, until Maggie and Jeanette saw him. They knew immediately without Jaxson explaining what had happened. They welcomed Raj back in the fold and Jax did a quick introduction of his three guests from over the pond. Jaxson knew that Ian was in good hands with these women watching over him. He needed to run through some songs for tonight with Flaco, Kiko, and Tino!

Raj stood still, not wishing to be noticed and dismissed. He wanted to hear the details of what Ian thought happened and see if it meshed with what he had seen. Suddenly he was three feet off the ground, dangling in midair.

He thought for sure that the mountain had come backstage just to mess with him! He grinned. He was here amongst his friends and people who could vouch for him. He would not have to suffer the idiocy of this troglodyte within the safety of his people.

The cackle that tickled his ear told him he had no worries, not today. He turned his head just enough to take in the buoyant, cheerful face of his Mayan friend.

"We didn't expect you for another few days!" Gabby crowed. "This is the best surprise of the tour." He hugged the little man close. He had never had anyone he would consider a friend, certs not a close friend, now he did and he reveled in the relationship.

"Well, it was very propitious to find I have an uncle who is well stationed at the customs and immigration of these Unite States. My mother's brother, so he was more than pleased to assist his little sister's son," He grinned and made a ta-da as an exclamation of triumph over evil.

"Why didn't you call one of us, we would've picked you up at the airport. Shit, do they even have an airport here?" again that chortle.

"I'm afraid Mr. Grahm's friends had had enough of airports and they had guitars and percussion and a plethora of electronic accoutrements. We rented a van, not my preferred mode of travel, and I drove the whole way," he stood to his full five-foot six height with pride.

"Why didn't they help with the drive," now Gabby was getting miffed in protection of his 'brother'.

"Oh, that would not have a wise concept. They have no idea how big this country is or where anything is located. I fear we would have found ourselves wandering in the wilderness for all eternity. I can read a map, especially when it is the great and wise Goggle. The lovely lady in the box was very patient with me and very succinct in her directions," he patted Gabby on the back so he would not worry nor seek any kind of retribution. "Now I need sleep very badly. Where is the closest bus with a bed?"

"I'll take you."

Ian sat with head down, lost in what this quirky run-in with fate meant. Shit, he had almost been able to justify the Goldberg happenstance in Asheville. The further the distance to an occurrence the more it lacked a solid foundation in reality. The weirdness gave license to become dream to become an incident that befell another.

He shook his head as if that would dislodge the memory, instead it forced him to see Maggie, sitting quietly, tolerantly, waiting for him to come around to the point he could talk about whatever happened.

A few deep breaths, he gazed at the clouds passing by and the solidity of the earth, there was strength there, he had to tap into that energy. Maggie waited, as patient as paint drying, Jeanette next to her like another wall. She knew he would come around and expound on the miracle of the day. She also knew she didn't have long to wait. The show was scheduled to start in about a half hour. If there was one thing Ian would never let happen, if it was in his power, would be a late start. People showed up on time, if you wished for that to continue you had to begin on time. The quartet was due to begin any moment. That would be his signal.

Mozart's String Quartet No. 21 began and Ian turned to his wife.

"It wasn't my fault," began the confession, though he had nothing to confess or apologize for, this was a power that was out of his hands. "You remember the radio began screaming at me?" Of course, she did, it was only about a half-hour previous. "Well, it was Raj and the three Spanish musicians, friends of Jaxson's. Since we didn't know they were coming and they hadn't phoned ahead, dumb on Raj's part really but, apparently, he'd been driving all night and was not working on all cylinders. Be that as it may, they had asked the security, not one of our people, someone hired by the ballpark with an attitude, to call me. The fella being of small mind and refusing to think outside his teeny box refused any such request. Raj tried again and again, then decided he would come find me. That was where the fight began. Though it wasn't really a fight more of a donnybrook of words. The security guy being a mountain and Raj being the molehill. One of our guys was out front, tried to intervene, which only made the huge guy more pissed and that's when the call came through. Jaxson and I headed out front to quell the impending war only to find not only didn't the Troglodyte not recognize either of us but refused to try. I pulled him over to the massive poster on the wall so he could compare Jaxson to the handsome stranger in the middle of the picture but apparently Cro-Magnon's cannot recognize similarities between people, only dinners. He began to walk away, I pulled him back, the car missed him, hitting the wall. We booked it into the crowd, lost ourselves in humanity and, voila, I am back on top of the hero list." He took a long steadying breath, then another, shook himself, stared at the sky, the ground, the stage and then into her eyes. "The worse part, the very worst part was the look in Jaxson's, Raj's and the Neanderthal's eyes, as if I had just pulled a 1971 Oldsmobile Cutlass out of my ass." He was done.

"If it makes you feel any better, we," and here she pointed at the quiet as a turnip and patient as death Jeanette, whom Ian had failed to note as he concentrated only on his wife. Jeanette, who sat off to the side with a look of astonishment on her face. She had seen these happenstance previously but to find Ian had not been cured shocked her. Would he have to live the rest of his life saving, helping people? "We don't think you are anything special. Just a little old man who performs miracles for those closest to him. I hear Mendelsohn, if you are going to introduce the show, you'd best change into your robe and pass out the fish and bread." She kissed him on top of his head and then squeezed him as tightly as love.

Just as Raj had seen. He was happy to have his hallucinations confirmed.

Chapter And Verse, Almost A Hearse

Nash had moved back to the front of the stage. He sat front center forty feet from the stage. Leaning back, he took in Mozart as if it were life giving breath. This filled his Spirit, his soul rejoiced in the beauty of the composition. Tears flowed and he stood, wrapped in bliss. Anticipation. He felt jittery knowing, in his heart, deep in himself, who would be next. Closing his eyes, holding himself back from experiencing before the actual hymn began. Mozart rang out and breaths were taken, a sip of water, the hush of whispers as the crowd settled into stasis. Instruments lifted, a nod, eyes locked, a second nod and Mendelsohn cascaded.

If all of humanity were as gifted as Mendelsohn, thought Nash, he would love them unconditionally. He watched the scene play out behind his closed eyes. Music, he was pleasantly surprised to find, would create its own story, its own visuals, its own movie, without lyric, without narration.

As the rest of the crowd took note of tall Native standing wrapped in majesty. One, then two, then a group, then a section of humans stood to join in the ritual of accepting this gift. They stood, silent, their heads moving with the sound of the instruments like sunflowers following the sun. Even the hundreds of folks parked outside the ball yard, standing along the low fence in center and right field stood. The beauty of this ballpark was those with limited funds could stand or sit around the outfield fence, outside the park, and listen to, if not see, the concert.

As Mendelsohn faded into the afternoon sunlight the crowd settled down for the long show ahead. Ian walked slowly out to the center-stage microphone taking in the assembled like a preacher heading to the pulpit. These were his people, this was his church, let the service begin.

"Thank you all for coming and supporting not only this concert but our mission." Applause. He heard several musicians plugging in, setting tone and volume, one last check of the tuning. There would be three backing musicians, keys, guitar, and upright bass, not drums or screaming guitars, just support for the All-Girl Choir plus One. This would be beautiful. "Please welcome, from all over the country, from the Appalachian Mountains to the swamplands of Louisianna, and the desert of southern New Mexico, the sound of the angels in glory, The All-Girl Choir plus One!" thunderous applause and cheering greeted the four women and Jesse.

As Ian turned to walk to his spot over in the wings, his foot caught on one of the mic cords that hadn't been taped down. He tried to right himself but crashed into the brace of singers. Two tumbled to the ground, two teetered on the edge, Jesse avoided the accident. The musician's natural reaction was to jump back out of the way and save their instrument.

The sound of the rifle shot from somewhere beyond the right field fence behind the stage froze all within ear shot, rippling forward as others inside the ballpark began to realize what was happening. The bullet ricocheted off the swaying mic stand to the back of Ian, taking Ian in the shoulder before It could strike any of the women singers to his right. He went down hard on the stage. Sharp pain in his shoulder paralyzed his right side, he could only guess it was caused by the fall. Until he saw the blood pooling on the stage beneath him. Shit! He raised his head enough to see all the singers either prostrate on the stage or hiding behind the fronts to his right. The crowd had fallen where they stood seeking comfort and protection in the grass. They couldn't tell from which direction the shots rang out so instead of panicking and running blindly they responded sensibly and made themselves into as small of targets as possible.

There was a blur of something moving in the audience at the speed of thought from the front of the stage, onto the stage, rushing behind the stage in the direction of where the rifle shot had come. Ian felt the rush of wind as it passed by him though he couldn't see who or what it might be. Within seconds, though, the scene settled into stasis. The screams behind the stage where Ian was certain the sound of shots had come from were quieted.

The sharp crack of something being snapped and a momentary scuffle was quickly followed by applause and cheers. Ian's vision was blurred from the pain though he was fairly certain he saw Gabby's new Native friend hopping back over the outfield fence clutching a broken rifle in his left hand and an unconscious form slung over his right shoulder like a bag-o-taters. He landed without a sound and marched his spoils to the back stairs of the stage where he ascended and presented the booty to Ian. Who immediately passed out from lack of blood and shock.

He was quite certain he had died when he heard Maggie's voice, calm, reassuring, filled with love hollering for him to stay with her. Followed by the wail of sirens, beeping of machines, and a bumpy ride to heaven, which had been administered into the large vein on the inner side of his right arm. Cool found its way into his arm, up through his shoulder and into oblivion.

It was night when the weight of Maggie lying next to and on top of him woke him from the drug induced coma. She snored quietly, like a purr from a large cat, and he hated to disturb her but his whole left side seemed to have gone to sleep on its own. He couldn't move his hand, his ankle, leg or much of anything. If he was paralyzed it tingled.

Maggie woke with a start as he tried to move what parts of his body he could. "What are you doing," the words slurred by exhaustion and unconsciousness. "You are not supposed to move yet. They want the incision to heal."

He was glad she didn't sound worried, that reassured a confused and muddled mind. "What incision? What happened? Am I going to live?" He thought of the episodes in NY and scolded himself, 'this is becoming repetitive and I'm too fucking old for this!'

"You took the bullet meant for Joya, apparently. At least that is what the sniper is admitting to or so the police say. Thank God for Nash, he stopped what could have been a very ugly situation." She smiled as if that would convey all he needed to know.

"Start from the beginning. I was shot?" Ian had been mugged once in Manhattan in the 70's, beat up as a kid, threatened on many occasions but had not actually ever been shot, until now, apparently. He wanted to know every detail.

"The All-Girls Choir plus One, was walking on stage and you were walking off. Just as your foot got tangled in the microphone cord," she locked eyes with her husband. Both understood exactly what would happen next. "The mic fell, in slow motion according to my recollection, as you began to tumble, the ladies fell back so as not to be taken down with you. You bumped Joya hard knocking her to the ground. I heard a crack, I'm guessing it was the gunshot, just as the stand was falling behind you. The bullet hit the stand, where Joya had been standing, and lodged itself in your shoulder. Hence the incision to remove said projectile from where it came to rest up against your shoulder blade. Nash moved with a speed I would not have believed had I not seen the blur, the jump, heard the crack of him breaking the rifle in half and hopping back over the outfield fence with said weapon and the unconscious sniper. We owe him more than we can ever possibly repay. He and his woman wish to speak to you in private and I would advise you to take the meeting. Joya placed her stage towel on your shoulder to staunch the bleeding, cops and EMTs showed up and here we are," she bobbed her head one time at her succinct accounting of the day's events.

"Holy shit!" Not brilliant but what he had. "How is everyone else? Did I hurt Joya? Tell her I'm sorry. I didn't hurt anyone else, did I?" Maggie thought it was typical of her husband that here he lay in the hospital recovering from a gunshot wound, though non-life threatening, and his thoughts were of his crew. She kissed him hard on the lips. "What was that for?" He glowed.

"For being Ian Patrick Sperling, my love," and kissed him again.

The knock on the door broke up the scene. "Geez, don't you two ever quit?" Jaxson laughed, he could, now that he knew his closest friend was going to be fine. "Get a room!"

"Got one and you're intruding," Ian tried to sit up so he could hug his friend. The pain had other ideas pushing him back down. "Bit of a day, I guess."

"Yeah, well, thanks to Gabby's newfound friend, it was a day saved by people who care and are amazing athletes. I don't know what that guy used to do or play but he makes Gabby seem small and weak by comparison. Wow!" Jax shook his head in amazement. "We should see if he wants to be part of our security or something. And he's very quiet," Jaxson wanted to be the only chatterbox on this party train. "He wants to meet with you."

"Yeah, Maggie told me. Guess that's a must," Ian withdrew back into himself. There was something, but he was too shaken, not stirred, to find whatever was bothering him. Too much had happened, again, for him to focus on what was odd about some native cat that happened to show up on this tour. The whole Doug/Jake thing, his missing years as a child, almost dying, the secret his family kept from him, and now this. It was like he was living two lives and both had wild and not necessarily pleasant occurrences. He wanted to rest on a beach somewhere. That weren't never gonna happen.

"Yeah, I think it's a must, he saved the show. It went on, once all the cops and ambulances moved on, without a hitch. People stayed, righted their chairs, popped open another bottle, lit another pipe like nothing had ever happened. It was pretty wild. These folks that follow us are pretty resilient, turns out," Jaxson laughed hard, "But we gotta get back on the road if we're to keep to our schedule. Think you can travel?"

Ian's focus settled on Maggie, the final arbiter of that query.

Maggie walked Jaxson out of the hospital room. They were old friends met through Ian, as close as any two people could be.

"Do you think he can travel or should we continue without him?" Only Jaxson could ask such a question and not be berated or dressed down for having the audacity.

"I think you know the answer to that. So, it would be best to find him the most comfortable bus, make certain we have all medical supplies and personnel," she glanced his way and he nodded making a list in his head. They would have to find a qualified nurse, willing to travel, so, no family or immediate imperative obligations. No jealous boyfriends or a husband, no parent requiring at home or constant care. In other words, an angel not tied too tight to heaven.

"I'll get on it while the teamsters hook the mules up to the wagons. Shouldn't be too hard of a chore to find a brilliant, untethered nurse with an insatiable wanderlust, looking for a gig." He hugged her. She had enough to worry about with a husband, wounded in battle and unwilling to rest. Yeah, he'd known before he walked through the door there was nothing, he nor Maggie, nor all the gods and godlings throughout history could do to stop the great Ian Sperling from continuing on this tour. It was his dream. Crossing the continent in the service of something far greater than he, making the music possible to do what he believed it was created for. No, this was Ian incarnate. The curmudgeon who could only do for others. Jaxson had to laugh; he had just described himself.

The Impossibility Of All Possible Possibilities

Maggie turned to go back into Ian's room and stopped short at the shock of seeing the Native, Nash, standing at the door as if guarding the room. He had not made any sound slipping in behind her. She completed her stalled step walking towards the door to see if he would attempt to refuse her entrance.

He smiled. Nash liked someone with caution but moxie, yet did not move out of her way. When she was within a breath of where he stood, he half bowed to her as the mate of the man he'd come to see. "I have a favor to ask," his voice a whisper, though a whisper of steel.

"If it is something I can grant I will," she said nonchalantly. She had no idea what this man might want but he gave off no indication of menace and he had run down and captured the gunman from earlier. There was nothing to fear.

"I would ask several minutes, quite alone, with your husband and leader of this tribe," it was a simple request not a demand. He waited patiently.

"You would want..." she began.

"Yes, to be alone with him. I need to talk to him and I believe he would be more comfortable answering my inquiries alone than with someone else in the room." He was not going to explain further.

The discussion taking place in Maggie's head was one based on the concept of trust. Could she trust this man alone with her injured husband? And if she couldn't, why was she still standing here talking to him? He did not emanate intimidation. This was stupid. "If you need time with him, I'll stand guard so you will not be disturbed." A soft chuckle escaped her lips as she imagined herself as security for the man she loved. But, then again, why not.

"I promise not to take more of his time than is absolutely necessary." And with that he slipped into the room.

Maggie knew Ian would be safe, she couldn't say why, but she did. As far as the curiosity clawing at her stomach and inside her head that could be easily assuaged as soon as the large man left the room and she could have her own few moments with her husband. Ian might be many different things to many people but to her he would always be an open book. He could no more lie to her or keep tasty tidbits from her than he could hold his breath or climb a hill. He would succumb to her wiles and spill each and every bean on the floor at her feet. She hoped this didn't take too long or she'd go goofy by the wait.

Twenty minutes passed before the door whooshed open and the large man silently stole from the room. Maggie might have missed him in the pages of the magazine she pretended to read except the door was not quite as silent as the man. He nodded his thanks and slid down the hallway without another word.

She was through the door almost before it closed. Ian stared out the window. "Two breaths. You're slowing down," he turned his head and grinned taking any accusation or bite out of his words.

"Pardon me?" He had caught her off guard, thinking she would find him pumped and ready to tell her everything.

"In the olden times, you would have been through that door and to my bedside within one breath, now it takes you two. I guess we are all slowing down and need to reassess our lives." He was oddly reserved. Whatever the two had discussed he remained deeply in consideration.

"Everything copacetic?" Time to trip the light fantastic. This was Ian in transitional mode. Whatever these two had discussed it was settling deep into his being, the very marrow of his id.

"Yeah. I need some time to come to terms with what I believe or consider possible. He told me there are folks who would like to assist us in our mission but would also like to enlarge it for their own self-interests. Not selfish, but to expand who all we wish to help. He feels we are being too species specific." He laughed, "I think he means we should include all of life on this planet. That we should try not just to lift humans out of depravity, poverty of hope and habitat, but all life." He slipped back further and deeper into thought and possibility. "I don't know, exactly, but I seem to remember a few years back there was a group trying to rescue animals, fish, mammals of the sea, insects, all kinds of life from anthropogenic extinction."

"I'm not quite understanding," Maggie didn't know what she expected to walk in on but this was well outside the realm; it teetered on the fantastic.

"I'm not sure I do either. Going to take a lot more thinking than I've been allowed thus far." He shrugged, "I told him I would give it great thought and I'd appreciate it if he could travel with us for a while so I could ask him some of the thousand questions running roughshod through my teeny brain. Help me get my clothes on, the wagons wait for no man and I want a comfy birth on the looney train." He slipped his legs over the side of the bed, disconnecting one of his IV lines and setting off an alarm.

The nurse was not amused to find Maggie helping him dress and, after a few choice words, went to find a physician. The doctor having no more sense of the absurd than his nurse attempted to force Ian back onto the bed, until he saw the incision. It had not healed but it had walked the first hundred miles towards it.

"Impossible!" He proclaimed.

"I'm a quick healer," grinned the patient with a secret.

Maggie wanted to say something else but prevented everything that would have followed the 'F'. She was as astounded as the physician but would ask her questions once the wheels were turning. For now, it was obvious the wound might be healing but the patient was still in a painful portion of the healing protocol and she wasn't certain Jaxson would wait on the convalescence.

Jaxson came back to camp with more questions and chores than answers and accomplishments. The crew was completing pack up, load up, and giddy-up. They would be ready to start turning wheels within an hour. He had to complete his most important task, finding a nurse for Ian. The last thing he needed right now were any impediments to accomplishing said task. So, he was not pleased to see the diminutive brown woman hanging by the door of his bus. Shit, now what? Though wasn't she with that big Native cat who saved the day?

"Can I be of assistance?" No cause to be rude.

"Or can I be of assistance to you?" she asked to his blank expression. She continued, "My friend has gone to have a meet with your brother." Jaxson's puzzled expression told her more information should be forthcoming. "The leader of this tribal community, Ian. Is he not the leader?" Now, she appeared confused.

"Well, we like to think of ourselves as co-leaders, I guess, but sure," no need to belabor the point.

"We require to know your intent for this," here she waved a hand at the commotion surrounding them.

"To be honest I thought we'd made that abundantly clear. We are attempting to shine some light on the plight of those who are being suffocated by the most powerful. The rich, the ones who own most of the natural resources of the world and refuse to share or preserve those resources for the benefit of all. They destroy not just the environment, but the hopes and dreams, the possibilities of those who are economically beneath them." He really didn't have time for this. They should print up a pamphlet so he could just hand them out.

"And the others?" Not accusatory just wondering.

"Others?" Jax thought he had included the primary colors of this piece of art, this woman wanted more detail. Maybe she should stand back a little and see if all didn't come into focus.

"Those who humans consider below even the lowest of them-selves." Now her eyes were sharp as knives and he didn't care for the way they cut into his psyche.

"There aren't, ahem, uh, any humans consider lower than those we refer to as Untouchables. And in that," he did a twist and nailed the landing, though just. "we mean Native cultures, black and brown people," he emphasized for her benefit, "those born into and expected to remain in poverty. Women, people referred to as the 'others', those who have been treated as less than human or as property." He thought that cov-ered most bases. He had to find a nurse and he was running out of sand.

"Would you mind if my friend and I traveled with you for a while to assess your motivations?" It seemed a simple request yet also an ac-cusation.

"Miss, I like to help you but right now I have an extremely im-portant job to do and I can't do it while you're asking all these questions," he tried to explain but he was running extremely low on patience and time and really didn't want to seem like a dick but...

She stared into his eyes as if reading his thoughts. "I can help you and us, I think." She grinned, "You require someone of healing experience to care for the injured chief, yes?"

Jaxson took a minute to translate, "Yes, I have to find a nurse to take care of Ian while we continue the tour."

"I am that person. I have trained in every aspect of the healing of humans for many, many, many years. This will benefit both of us. I ac-cept." She said it in such a final way he couldn't think of a reason to say no.

He apparently had found his nurse, and the taxi bearing Ian and Maggie announced it was time to be rolling out.

"I will need you to ride with us, as that is where Ian will be," Jaxson reminded the woman whose eyes searched the lot apparently seeking her consort. "If you want, your friend can ride with us, but I need you in this bus."

"He will meet us in the next camp. He has his own way of travel, which is necessary for us." She turned her attention to the good-looking man with the flowing locks of hair in front of her. There was a sincerity that lived in those eyes. There was an honesty that she could read as easily as the wind in the trees. What he said he meant and he would do everything in his power to make a promise come true. He believed his words and so should she. The question was whether he could make this grand intention real. And could she convince him that the needs of all the other living creatures, plant, animal, insect, and sea were the same as those he espoused.

There was something about this woman Jaxson couldn't figure out. Shit, there were probably a million things he'd never figure out but this was more otherworldly. The way she said 'humans' and 'camp' gave the impression she was either from another place or time. Now he had to wonder if he had stepped into Ian's bizarro world or was just imagining things. Lotta pot under the bridge.

Meanwhile Back In Mobile

The Crescent Calls

After two days of recess and recreation in Mobile, a beautiful city with many activities to recommend, especially the beach close by, it was time to be moving through the increasing humidity and heat. Mobile to New Orlean wasn't very far on the map but reality has a way of stretching when discomfort plays a major role.

She had called Henry to apprise him of their whereabouts and plans. He was delighted to hear all and promised a joyful reunion in the Big Easy. He suggested the Hotel St. Pierre. It was an ancient place with courtyards, fine people, close to Armstrong Park, within walking distance of the Quarter and waterfront, and all activities New Orleans. Once they checked in, he would Taxi down and meet up with them. At his age, he explained, there was no need to drive, not with so many modes of transport in the Crescent City.

Aron figured with traffic, timing, prayers, and luck they would be safely ensconced in the air-conditioned luxury of the Hotel within a couple hours. They had parking at the hotel for a nominal fee—about what a mid-priced hotel in a small town would run—would accept Oscar and had rooms. Perfect.

The Hotel St. Pierre might not have been the most luxurious and opulent hotel they would occupy on this run across the southern tier but it was definitely New Orleans in every way. Just what, literally, the doctor ordered. They arrived close to Aron's ETA by virtue of Goggle maps and light traffic flowing in as opposed to the parking lot flowing nowhere out.

Still, Carrie was ebullient to set her suitcase and sundry bags inside her room and lay on the bed. For a young woman who had never traveled further than the beaches of Oregon a hundred yards distant from her home, she had now traveled the length and breadth of this massive continent. She was jiggered and bone weary. Though, upon further consideration and a glance at the map on the wall, she realized she had hardly scratched the surface.

Good to his word Henry showed up in an SUV sized taxi to take all down to Frenchmen street for a light lunch and some music. When asked why they didn't head to the much closer Bourbon Street he patiently explained that was where the tourists went, he wished to avoid the better part of touristique! Most had not yet discovered Frenchmen so the music was more authentic, the food more homestyle, the people more forgiving of errors of etiquette.

Carrie had done her level best to prepare Barbara, Aron, and the girls about Henry. He was not your everyday octogenarian. "First off," Carrie ticked off the reasons on the fingers of her right hand, "He has decades of living under his belt, and I do mean 'living'." She air quoted. "He's a doctor, jazz pianist and loves every second of every day. But his skin is as smooth as a teenager's. The only give away is the pure white ring of hair that has his bald head surrounded and his pure white eyebrows. He also has the attitude and temperament of that same teenager. His eyes overflow with mischief and moxie, his step light, fluid and quick, his laughter contagious. He is, as they say throughout the Midwest, a hoot and half. He is the essence and embodiment of life." The tinkle of laughter that escaped her lips told of her excitement at seeing one of her closest and most endearing ties to other great love of her life.

Henry had loved Kim like his most beloved child and his heart had shattered with Carrie's at Kim's passing. Carrie only knew the man through those too brief interactions but she had made a deep connection of love and loss with him.

So, it was with reckless abandon that Carrie and Henry hugged and kissed each other as the reunion unfolded in the middle of Burgundy Street. He picked her up and twirled her while Oscar barked and danced awaiting his own love. The others stood on the sidewalk not wishing to be run over by the passing vehicles, tooting horns, hollering, and laughing at the joyous scene taking place in the midst of the busy thoroughfare.

At long last Carrie seemed to remember her 'family'. Introductions were made and everyone climbed into the, now, tightly packed, but cozy SUV. The girls sat one each on Barbara and Aron's laps. He was now the official big brother and loved the designation. Oscar lay in the back.

Henry explained, as they made the short ride down to Frenchmen Street, that with the girls and Oscar in tow they would not be permitted into the music clubs, but they could grab some sandwiches at Frenchmen All Day and saunter down the avenue where they could listen to the different afternoon bands while they munched. They might even find an outdoor table frontside of one of the clubs or a patio where all could sit for a drink and listen. It sounded delightful.

It was warm and muggy, even for New Orleans, but not oppressive as they made their way down the street with a couple Cuban sandwiches for the uninitiated, plus a roast turkey sandwich and a chicken salad for the less adventurous. He'd added a container of red beans and rice and crawfish etouffee for the more wandering palates. To satisfy thirst, assorted soft drinks, sweet tea and beers for the adults. Not every club had live music wafting out of their open doors but enough did they could make a short afternoon into evening of the exercise.

And after several days cramped inside vehicles exercise was welcome. As they strolled Carrie and Henry talked quietly of Kim. A few memories leaked down cheeks and hugs were shared. Barbara, Aron, and the girls kept back out of earshot to give the two some privacy while they compared love. Oscar, dutifully, at Carrie's side.

As they crossed the street and headed back north. from whence they had come, Carrie decided they had kept to themselves quite long enough. Pulling all back into a tighter orbit she began to explain to Henry what she wanted to do with all the finances she had inherited through death and suffering. Her wish was to alleviate some of the same in other people.

She wished to go back to something she had attempted before she met Kim. A safe zone, as it were, for women, children, and lost souls searching for themselves. A place off the streets for hundreds, if not thousands of flotsam floating in the human current until collecting on the west coast. All this without making the same mistakes and pitfalls she had before.

One thing she wanted not to do was set up right in the center of temptation. She had mistakenly thought this would attract those with problems and bring them to her. Oh, it had, in its way, but what it also had drawn were those with the basest wants. Those who would prey on the innocents she was attempting to lift up. Drug dealers, pedophiles, human traffickers, the underground of perversion. She expected the police to keep such away from her door, but they didn't have the manpower or wherewithal to control the quantity she was fighting. She'd lost.

She'd lost the respect of the professionals. She'd lost support from churches and juvenile services, professional drug rehab and alcohol recovery services, all of it. She wanted to begin anew with help from professionals from the start. Good intentions were fine, but not without support of those who knew.

This time she would bring in health professionals, psychological professionals, counselors, and here she nudged Barbara and Henry took note, a clean place for a clean start. She had her eye on an abandoned hotel complex just south of where her place was in Newport. It had more than a hundred rooms, outbuildings for meeting halls and recreation. A separate building they could convert into a simple clinic or infirmary. As she explained it, all her enthusiasm rose with the complexity of what she was attempting. No religion, no forced belief except in oneself. To allow them the freedom to become what they dreamed, because hope and worth were what they desired most. To rise from the ashes of a life set on fire far too early. To see the promise, become the promise and pass the promise of a better life on.

Henry loved her passion but could see where this could go off the rails in an instant if she didn't rein in some of that fervor with practicality. Yes, she was going to need help, the question was, was he the one to help? And was she even asking him or just asking advice.

"How long are you going to be in The Crescent?" He asked hoping for a reprieve. Yes, he liked what she was proposing but this would require some time before they could even hammer the first nail. And, he had to ask himself, was there a better course of action?

"A few days, maybe longer if it would help. Though to be honest I am itching to get back to my ocean and settling down. Travel is wonderful but I am a homebody at heart." A crooked grin settled in her eyes and around her lips. She was tired, she needed a break.

"Let's get you all back to the warm embrace of your rooms. Get some rest, walk around my city, take in the sights, and we'll talk again soon." The taxi was waiting for them at Burgundy and Frenchmen.

They had walked the levy, taken a paddleboat ride down the Mississippi and a carriage ride with accompanying humorous recitation. They had eaten six or eight different kinds of gumbo according to what they could remember, etouffee, jambalaya, and heard numerous live bands while walking down Royal Street, Decatur Street and eating beignets.

Kim had always told Carrie she knew in her bones when it was time to move. Carrie understood. She felt that need for motion, to be heading somewhere, anywhere, though that wasn't exactly true either. Her homing instinct was strong, she required the ocean, her ocean.

She had seen the Gulf of Mexico and found it far too tame for her blood. The beaches of the Atlantic too pacific, too smooth and gentle. Her blood raced with the thought of rocky beaches and huge crashing waves, the sound of life.

All the others could sense her unease and were becoming jumpy within her aura. She was about to say the words, 'pack up, time to be rolling', when the sound of her phone playing startled her back to reality. It was, of course, Henry. Timing is, was, and always would be, everything.

A car was coming to pick them up and bring them to a restaurant not far away. Carrie mentioned they could easily walk as it was only a half dozen or so blocks away, but he insisted they use the car as the girls were young and he didn't want to tire them out. It was flimsy but there was more, she could tell by the tone of his voice. He wanted to talk and he wanted to talk now.

When they arrived through the long hallway to the large outdoor courtyard in the center of the restaurant's labyrinth, she saw Henry and another, much younger man sitting at a long table. Just enough chairs for the seven of them with room in case a few more showed up. Looked like Henry wanted a council meet.

He introduced the young man, Ray, with a little background of who he was, where he had come from and where he wanted to be. A doctor. Well, thought Carrie, maybe she was going to meet a new associate.

"I love your passion and I love your plan, but you need an ounce or two of brutal truth," So much for easing into the meat of the matter, "What you plan is a long-range plan and will take several years to bring to fruition. You can't get folks involved in too deep unless they realize this will take time, patience, and a wagon load of hard work. Just the idea of transforming an old, dilapidated hotel into this oasis of salvation you propose will take much planning and doing." Henry's smile said it wasn't disapproval he was preaching but caution and understanding of the scope of the proposal.

"Where we need to begin is with a competent architect. Someone who can look over the property, the existing buildings with your ideas in mind—so you can come up with a more concrete plan than what you've been dreaming. He can then tell you a more realistic estimate of what you are looking at to accomplish your dream." He took in each member with a sharp, piercing eye, gauging their commitment to this outrageous prospect. "Ray has recently set up his own physician's office in his neighborhood to serve his people. He probably can give you some very realistic ideas of what that entailed and what you would need for your own clinic. I assume Barbara can take you by the hand in her own specialty and suggest what might be required to house, treat, support, train, and feasibly set a new course for those who have been so horribly mistreated." He glanced at Ray to see if his protégé might wish to throw in a few cents of advice.

Ray sat thinking of what Henry was trying to get across and an idea rode, hell bent for leather, into this frontal lobe. "You know, there's some kind of musical road show that has been traversing the backroads of America with kind of the same sort of goal. I wonder if they might be of some assistance. I read they are heading west along the southern tier drumming up support and cash for their own outlandish dreams. Might be worth stopping to catch some music. I think, unless my mind is too jumbled with all it's got going on, they are pulling their circus into Memphis after a few more stops." He pulled out his phone and did a little Googling and smiled. "Yep, they are in Birmingham tomorrow night and then Memphis two days later. Maybe we can talk some more if you can stick around 'til then and see if we can't solidify some thoughts a'fore you head up north. If that interests at all," he added.

Carrie took in her little tribe to gauge what they might be thinking. Barbara appeared to be weighing a few more days on the road against joining forces with some folks who had a bit more experience than they. Landing on the side of sensible, she cocked her head in an affirming way. She was in the Memphis camp. Aron shrugged, what the hell was a few more days running around the country. She had come for advice and they were shoveling as fast as they could, why not take a pound or two. Phoebe spoke, "I hear they have real good music there too! Just like down here only different." Aron grinned his pleasure that Phoebe seemed to be opening up and music was the key. Izzy would agree with whatever the majority ruled. Though Carrie wished she would have voiced her own opinion.

Springtime, Time For A
Well-Timed Vacation

Spring might be moving into summer in the lowlands and valleys but the mountains clung to winter like a mother suckling her child. Snow capped the peaks and gathered in pure white piles under trees and in the lea of boulders. The breezes from the north, not wishing to offend, allowed the cold to ride with them as they pushed the warmer air away from the frozen inhabitants of Rock Ridge.

Padon thought he might never feel warm again, the cold had set up an impenetrable fortress deep within his bones. It would take a conflagration of biblical proportion to pry it from the marrow.

He and Maggie had become quite the item in this small town ever since their 'coming out' party crashed headlong into Mr. Carpenter's celebration of immortality. They were inseparable either at work or when trying to enjoy a few moments alone. Padon continued to work at the Café, doing all the chores no one else felt inclined to do as well as learning some of the more intricate details of the restaurant biz.

That was the greatest asset in a small-town café, everyone was part and parcel of the team. What one wouldn't or couldn't do someone else would. It ran like a well-oiled, finely tuned, several century old engine. Steam powered and needing constant attention but well-loved.

Padon had moved out of Doc Caldwell's home and into the apartment above the café with Maggie. It had taken a couple months of getting to know each other, more than a few dates and evenings spent with Janet—Doc Caldwell's friend and exceptional nursing assistant—and Jo-Ann—Doctor Caldwell's secret identity. They would play cards and sip bourbon until the day's activities in the café, and Doctor Caldwell's time with patients, tuckered them out and to bed. It was a quiet, peaceful existence. Padon had to wonder why he had fought so hard to avoid it.

Summer was still a month away in the high altitudes and everyone needed a break. The town was quiet. There would be no visitors from the lowlands, no vacationers getting lost and winding up in their little town. People avoided the mountains this time of year. They required the warmth denied them for the past several months and feared the possibility of spring snowstorms. It would be July and August when the heat of the plains and lower valleys would drive the flatlanders back into the cool recesses of the mountains.

"I think we have earned a little time away from the hustle and bustle of the everyday," Maggie said as she eased her tired bones onto the stool at the lunch counter.

"And do what?" For all his whining and wanting to have this burgh in his rearview mirror the first few months of his internment, now he could think of very few places that held his heart more. He had fallen in love with the people—his friends, true friends—the laidback energy of the mountain ranges, his Thursday nights playing at Merle's with Wally just jamming tunes; some originals, some requests from the neighbors. His deep conversations with Mr. Carpenter, the oldest man on earth, and his mature and growing love of Maggie. My how life had changed.

"I thought we'd hop in my jeep and head south to warm the bones and eat some fat inducing food and drink to excess. I got some old friends down Colorado way, out on the plains just east of the Springs. They have a nice spread and we could lay back, float on the river and hang out for a few days." She lay her head on her crossed arms and smiled at the thought.

"What about the café? People here still got to eat and someone's got to feed 'em." For someone who'd never owned more than a couple guitars and a guilty conscience Padon discovered he liked having a piece of the pie. This place wasn't his, it was hers, but he loved it as if it were.

"Jeannie can handle the slow times just fine. Everybody knows her, everybody likes her, especially the crew. Wally and Ralph got the kitchen and have no desire to go any further than Merle's for a beer and a soda. Harvey will keep the crockery and cutlery clean. And we can get by with a skeleton crew on the floor. We'll cut back on the hours. Everybody could use a little time off. Really, we do it every year." There was something she wasn't saying, something beneath the surface of this offer.

"Why you all a sudden want to get away from your heart?" which was how he thought of the café. She had come here with nothing but two kids and a shattered life. This place had healed her, healed her kids, given all of them a new life, a good life. "These 'friends' of yours, they wouldn't happen to be kin, would they?" The thought struck him like a horse kick to the head. Did she want him to meet one or both of her kids?

Her head shot up off its resting place on her arms. "No! They are not. Just some folks that found themselves up here ten or so years back and we try to cross paths every so often. I thought you'd like to meet them." She stood, glared, and headed to the kitchen.

Well, he had done it again. Padon had this knack of sticking his foot up to the knee in a big pile of cow shit. His mouth was cranking six thousand RPMs while his brain was still trying to find first gear. Time to grovel. Thing was, he didn't mind groveling to this woman. She made him want to be better than he'd been and good enough for her. Never said such, she wouldn't, it was something in his own head, but it was truth.

"When do we leave?" He once again found his famous boyish charm had no effect on the intended. She was impervious. "Oh, come on, I didn't mean nothing by it. I actually would love to meet your kids and anybody else you consider friends. I'll buy the first tank of gas!" He wasn't pleading he was dealing.

"And where are you going to come up with the cash for that?" And she was going to make him haggle for all he was worth. She knew he had started a bank account—his first ever—and had a secret stash, a holdover from his hard drinking, drugging, and philandering days when he would hide money from himself. But he'd hurt her feelings and she wanted her speck of flesh.

"I got a girl who likes me." His crooked grin elicited a crooked reply.

"Are you sure she'll spot you the seed?"

"I was, up until a few minutes ago," sheepish but confident.

She kissed him hard. "Yeah, I want you to meet everybody. Though more important, I want them to meet you!" Another kiss, this one more tender, "We'll head out in a couple days. You better check with your keepers and make sure the medical establishment has no problem with this or can train me quick."

"Look, I'm sorry I jumped in with presumptions but we are still getting to know each other and I just, I guess, I, shit, I don't know. Guess I'm still a bit uptight after my first foray into the long-term relationship pool." His embarrassment colored his neck and ears. Maggie could tell his complete failure as a husband and father still weighed on him and his fear of commitment ran strong through his psyche and bone.

"All I'm saying is we have only shared constant togetherness in a work limited form. I thought we might expand our awareness of each other by getting away for a few days or so and seeing what we are like without the safety of the necessity of shared drudgery." She grinned an evil sensual grin, "Maybe see what we're like when we can concentrate on each other rather than the customer!"

"Yeah, I get it. I'll try to shove my insecurities where they can't get sunburned and close down my doubtful mind. I'm trying, I really am but I'm fighting almost sixty years of me and I'm one tough sonofabitch," he took her hand and tenderly kissed the back of it.

"Yeah, well we both got a trunk full of old baggage that needs to be tossed aside, I'll help you if you help me." She winked conspiratorially. "Ain't you and Wally giggin' at Merle's tonight?"

"Yeah, best get cleaned up. He'll have my head if I'm late."

"He sure does like playing, must've almost killed him to stop." Sad coated the thought.

"It wasn't the stopping playing that almost killed him it was the extracurricular what done him in. Now we just get to play for the fun of it again, that's when it's the purest," he peeked at the clock before turning to head upstairs and claim his own fun.

It Ain't The Road, It's The Repairs

Each crack in the pavement, dip in the road, ravine of a chuckhole, and swerve of motion bit into his shoulder. The pain sharp, deep, and humbling. He would like to voice his discomfit except he'd had the prerogative to remain stationary in a slightly more comfortable hospital bed back in Columbia. Ian had not chosen wisely. He could complain of the pain and suffering but it would fall on deaf ears. Maggie, Jaxson, Dugie, Ben, shit, even Gabby and Joya had admonished him to remain and heal for a few days or a week and catch up with them later on the tour.

A week? They wanted him to lay about for a week? He'd be insane by the time it was over. So, he'd packed his meds, changes of dressing for his healing shoulder, his bad attitude and they'd rolled out early afternoon, only a half day late. There were shows to produce, money and awareness to be raised, decisions to be made and miles to be traveled. This was what Ian lived for. It was his lifeblood.

And probably the reason his shoulder felt numb and wet at the same time. Where was that small nurse? And was she really a nurse? She didn't act or care for him like most nurses he'd ever come in contact with. She wasn't cool to his needs nor quick with a pill or injection. She fell on the holistic side of medicine, preferring comforting and natural poultices

146

to the more sterile methods modern science advocated. He was concerned about her philosophy of therapeutics, though he had to admit her approach was soothing and working. Up until a few minutes ago.

Just as the thought was birthed, she entered the bus from wherever they were stopped for lunch. Her smile warmed him, reassured him. She sat softly on the edge of the bed and pulled back his pajama top to see the wet gauze and began to carefully unwind the covering. The incision was red, raw but healing nicely. She cleaned it with a warm solution before drying it and inspecting.

"Looking very nicely," she said combining two thoughts into one. It was another thing that wasn't quite right about this woman.

She spoke as if from another culture, one where English was not their first language or even their third. Mixing metaphors and colloquialisms as if forcing puzzle pieces into spaces they were not meant to occupy. Yet she didn't have the appearance of someone from a foreign culture, more like someone from First Nation; and he meant very first nation. That was it. She didn't have the characteristics of the Native folks he knew, yet she obviously was. Only more so.

Bingo! She didn't have the stamp on her of First Nation folks of today. People who'd had their genetics diluted by a century or two of mixed-race breeding. She was pure Native. Darker than the Native Americans of today. She had no white in her. Ian didn't know why that was so refreshing but it was.

"My people come from a place not bothered by Europeans," she answered his unasked question. "Both Nash and I, though of different tribes. Believe it or not there are still pockets of pure-bred people on this land."

And there it was again, that halting, searching way of speaking. She didn't like white people, Europeans as she called them still, but she didn't hate them. Or, at least, she didn't hate those she surrounded herself with. She wanted something from them, him, from this gypsy caravan. The question was, what?

If she knew what the mission was and wanted them to help her people all she had to do was ask. But she seemed reticent. As if just by asking he, or they, would turn her away. And then his conversation with Nash at the hospital came back.

"You and Nash are of the same tribe?" he was grasping for concepts in a culture he was too white to understand. Yet he wanted to more than anything at this moment.

"We are of the same People," and he heard the capitalization of the word, "but not of the same, hmm," again seeking the right word, "species." She said it as if it were a question.

"I don't know if I would use the word species, as we're all of the same species, people, that is. More as if you are part of different families." He hoped he was getting this right. "You share beliefs, religion, a way of life, I guess. Though not like us, not a modern way of living, more like the Amish, I guess."

"What are the Amish? Are they people or are they different altogether?"

Well, now he was in it, how do you explain people who had chosen to live in the past rather than avail themselves of all the conveniences of the modern world. How to explain people who chose to be backward in their lifestyles?

As if reading his mind, she brightened with understanding. "They are those who prefer to live with only one thought of how all should live, yes? In the past, yes?" She nodded her head vigorously to show she did understand. "We are not like them. We live our way because it was what we were created for, to watch over all of our children."

This was something Nash had tried to get him to understand back in Columbia. Ian wanted to get it but they were asking him, in their way, to take on a belief he could only comprehend as myth. Stories based in the lore of primitives.

Yes, he knew a decent extent of Indian, Native, he corrected himself, religion, and beliefs. But they were all based in the ignorance of science. Belief in magic, the creation of the universe by some omnipotent, all-knowing, all-seeing god. Wait a minute, his teeny brain ordered. What the hell was so different between what they believed and what every other religion preached? Why was he so quick to condemn one belief while giving the others a pass? He had better sit down and rethink his thinking because his thoughts were completely influenced by others thinking. Thinking that had been born thousands of years ago by people no more evolved, and probably less so, than these. His head swam and he passed out.

Ian stood naked and alone and, to be honest, quite shocked to find himself in the dreamscape. He had always assumed that dreams only came to those asleep, not to those who had lost consciousness, passed out, or in comas. He was not shocked enough to come out of the dream, which he imagined would be the case, and considering he knew this to be dream, that, also, should have brought him out of the REM state. Interesting.

He wandered through the canyons of his mind, exploring what had been and what he thought could be until he realized he was not alone. Someone or something was tracking him. Paranoia struck deep. Could he be debilitated in a dream? He was already injured in real life, could some vestige of his subconscious cause further physical damage while he slept? He had read somewhere in a doctor's or dentist's office about people dying in their sleep with the causation possibly some harm that had come to them while in REM, as no physical cause could be found. Something had found them in the dream world and killed them, his desire to remove himself from this doomed possibility should have brought him back to conscious safety. No such luck.

There was a powerful entity anchoring him to this out-of-body experience. There was movement off to the right, near the brook burbling through a copse of trees. If there had ever been a more restful scene, he didn't think he'd witnessed it, yet it reeked of danger and threat.

Suddenly, a shaking of branches as if something passed through them. Something small, he realized as all the movement was in the lower limbs. Apparently, whatever was coming was not concerned with him knowing it was approaching.

Ian had never been one for study, except contracts, music, production, you know, the important things in life. Biology, zoology, wildology, or forestology had been nap time for the short time he attended high school. When one is promoting bands, playing DJ on the new format of radio, or discovering new bands, songs, and stars, one doesn't have much time for sleep, except during science, civics, and history classes. So, he didn't know what kind of cat came sauntering out of the underbrush though he knew it was large, had long claws, a predatory gleam in its eyes, and long incisors which were on display when the damn thing smiled.

Ian was so caught up in the stare of the huge cat he failed to notice the small animal riding its back. Again, Ian's lack of knowledge of animals in the wild did not serve him well, it was either a weasel, a beaver, no, a skunk? Nope wrong coloring, he may not know much but he could remember black and white. Maybe a rodent of some sort, or possibly—what the hell were they?—some kind of otter.

Whatever it was it rode the cat without fear and that fact seemed to reassured Ian. After all it was just a dream, wasn't it?

As Ian was about to take flight, he thought if this was a dream, he should have the ability to fly away. He turned to see what options presented themselves when he heard the soft voice, "Please don't. We have come to you in the dream world to talk to you, to reason with you here in hopes you will understand our need."

Slowly he turned, step by step, he attempted to back his way out of absurdity. Dreams are our subconscious manifesting our desires, fears, and fantasies. Though Ian could never recall desiring a talking animal or fantasizing about Disney animations come to life. He was a realist. He believed in songwriters, musicians, publicists, artists, creative people, ok, maybe he wasn't rooted in reality but at the end of the day he could hear what had been created. And it sure as shit wasn't this.

"I know you might find this beyond your realm of belief but we are Nash and Suzette. You met us, and know us, in our human manifestations. This is our true selves. We are immortal spirit guides created to oversee our children." The large cat growled, "Our children who are now at the crossroads of extinction. You have been touched by spirits other than what we know. We believe you have been chosen."

The small, brown rodent like animal hopped off the haunches of the mountain lion. Yes, came the thought to Ian. That thing was a mountain lion, he'd seen a picture of one in a book or in a zoo, or something.

"Ian, you know me, I have been caring for you for the past couple days, since Columbia, South Carolina. I'm Suzette," Ian didn't know why but he believed her. Sure, why not? He was having a nightmare nervous breakdown, why shouldn't he believe anything that comes rolling down the pike?

"OK, let's say I believe this sleeping hallucination is reality for the moment. What do you want of me? I don't know shit about spirit guides. Are you here to guide me somehow?" Grasping for answers such are straws in the wilderness.

"You know something of Native lore, yes?" Suzette decided to take baby steps. She'd forgotten how white folks thought about the dream roads. They either loved the salaciousness presented in dream they could not experience in real life or were terrified of what the subconscious revealed.

Ian nodded. He was relatively certain he nodded both in dream and back on the bus. It was heartening.

"We are two of the animal spirits the native people seek to provide guidance, protection, and wisdom. Though we also watch over and try to protect our children as well." She sat back on her haunches for comfort, it would appear she was going to be here for the long haul.

"Your children?" Suzette was not the only life form here requiring baby steps. Ian was struggling to take this all in and understand.

"Yes, each of us watches over certain species. We try to protect them by guiding them to grazing land, or good hunting, plentiful fishing, whatever they need to survive. Over the last few centuries that has become exceedingly difficult as habitat has shrunk, with mankind destroying everything in their path. They destroy habitat which destroys the resources our children need to survive." She knew she didn't have an infinite amount of time so was consolidating facts. "You seek to lift humans from their deplorable conditions, we seek to lift our people from the precipice of extinction. To do that we could work together to make the Mother whole, to heal the scars. We seek to join forces with you and your troop." Well, there it was. The whole reason she and Nash had shown up, helped, and would continue, if only to help their own.

The overwhelming scent of ammonia salts roused Ian from unconscious to semiconscious with a little shake completing the trip. The bus came into focus, Maggie's worried expression was where that focus landed. His heart tripped on his love. He wanted nothing more than to jump up and hold her, to let her know he was alright but the strength of the nurse held him in place.

"Not yet. You need to steady your pins and head before you try to get up." She whispered.

He realized his head was swimming in a whirlpool and she was the only solid object he could grasp. He'd have to wait a minute until the spinning wheels slowed or stopped. He did manage a smile to assure his wife he would live.

Finding Clarity In Picasso

Maggie gently pushed her way past the small brown nurse, excusing herself constantly, but she wanted to be by her husband's side. They were partners in everything and that included pain and suffering. And though with Ian there was always some kind of pain and suffering, this was beyond the pale.

"What the hell is going on?" She was a very small cork on an extremely large ocean and the waves were kicking up threatening to swallow her. Ian was her rock as she was his.

"I...don't...know," his words halting and whispered. He was as lost as she. Though he was drowning, weighed down by more information than he was willing to share, even to save himself, because he wasn't convinced of the veracity.

Sheepishly his eyes wandered past Maggie to take in Suzette. Was it all dream? Reality? Somewhere in between? She certainly was not an otter here, just a very pretty woman who had patiently allowed him to heal. Her methods were very old school, herbs, poultices, natural, holistic, but they were effective. No chemicals, or fancy medications just time and nature. Just like one would imagine a spirit guide from centuries ago would care for native folks.

Returning his attention to the love, the focal point, of his life, he had no words. What could he tell his wife? She was already beside herself with worry. If he told her about the dream, the animals, the talking, the suggestion of working together with animal spirits, she would assume the worst. That either because of age or injury he had lost his mind. He had no desire to keep such important information from her but the better part of valor, and wishing to remain free of the asylum, sealed his lips.

As thoughts flew through the cranium of one Ian Sperling, he caught the face of Nash as he strolled by the parked bus. Were they in Birmingham already? Ian had been in and out of reality so much lately he was having great difficulty determining where they were and whether where was important or could be known. The face of the quiet Native scrutinized Ian for the few seconds their eyes locked. Ostensibly attempting to see the unseeable, unseeable to all except to those who had the ability with the openness of mind, heart, and spirit to see beyond what logic could comprehend.

Ian knew you couldn't trust what was said or done in the dream city but they had been so sure of him being 'touched' by something and 'chosen' for the same purpose. What the absolute fuck did any of that mean?

He had been told he was touched before by many friends and acquaintances but they meant he was not mentally stable; he didn't think Nash had meant the same. And 'chosen'? there were many concepts of chosen. Chosen for good, evil, dinner, as a subject to research and analyze? Chosen as some gods experiment or chosen as a sacrifice to appease one of these animal spirits. He wanted to curl in his mother's arms and hide. Though if he did curl up in her arms no one would find him as she was six feet underground. His meandering confusion was thankfully interrupted by his dear friend.

Jaxson stuck his head around Maggie who was still clutching Ian to her own breast as if that would provide protection from the cruel world that had decided to assault him at every turn. "We're at the hotel. We can drop off unnecessary Gypsies here and move equipment and personnel to the ballpark or we can sit here and hope someone else will do it for us," his grin was mischievous as he taunted his best friend into action. Something Jaxson knew would be as healing as any balm, poultice, or drug this nurse might slap on or in him.

Ian knew he heard Jaxson's voice, could see him peeking around Maggie, that smile, but he couldn't bring it all into clarity. It was as if he watched the scene through a filthy window. His thoughts muddled, he sought words, to answer, to communicate but the whirlwind in his body carried all such inconsequential concerns away. He was lost, alone, and in the background of this play was the sound of drums. Rhythmic, like a heart, the heart of the world or the universe, pounding, vibrating in his head, in his chest, in his soul. What was happening? He had to find a fingerhold and climb out of this before he found he could not return.

Maggie was saying something. There at the periphery of thought, of sound, he heard her voice and seized onto it. He clung to her presence, a life raft in the stormy sea and immediately wished he had a gummy or a pipe nearby. Jesus on a ritz this was wackier than opium. What in the hell was that Suzette putting in the poultices or in his water?

He locked eyes with her and the drumming intensified. He could smell campfire, trees, a stream filled with fish, dead meat searing on the bonfire of his imagination. He wanted to vomit. He was vegetarian, the smell of burning flesh was anathema to everything he held dear.

"Ian!" Maggie's insistent demand for his attention sliced through the hallucination and brought him to the surface. Focus, old man, focus. There was Maggie, with Jaxson's concern over her shoulder, they'd been joined by Ben, Dugie, and Gabby. Suzette sat off to the side watching, taking it all in. It was, it was, shit, it was the final scene of the Wizard of Oz. Only there were too many of them. But he knew Maggie was Dorothy, Jaxson was the Scarecrow, Dugie the Cowardly Lion, Ben the Tin Man, Suzette, he guessed was Toto, since she was some kind of animal anyway. And Gabby must have been the Wizard, though it didn't quite fit. And that's what brought him all the way back like a wet kiss at the end of a hot fist.

"What?" More brilliance from the great puppeteer of the music industry.

Maggie was snapping her fingers right in front of his eyes as if that would kick start the synapses deep in the recesses of his distracted mind. It might have though only because of how irritating it was.

"Stop!" He commanded, though politely. "I'm alright. Just a little off. I've had bit of a rough lifecycle lately. If we could all ease back and let some air into my body, I think I can return to the land of the slightly mentally functioning." He took a very long, slow, cleansing breath, shook himself mentally and physically before opening his eyes, stretching, twisting, and testing his shoulder and, "We leave those here who need some rest and cleansing. We'll come back in a few to pick them up for sound check and rehearsal," he knew Jaxson would love that, "road crew, sound and lights will head over to the venue. I'll call those nominally in charge and let them know we are in town and want to set up. Dugie, Ben, and Gabby will check out all the usual electrical and stage needs, while you and I consider shaking up the lineup for tonight's performance. Let's have some fun!"

From somewhere in the sheets, he produced his ever-present phone and waved them all away, except Maggie and his 'nurse', whom he was still not sure whether she was magical or temporal but he wanted her near in case he required her ministrations; and to keep a close eye on her. To all in attendance Ian appeared sharp, focused, the Ian of old. Though they couldn't see the boiling cauldron of 'what the fuck' inside his head. He clung to what he knew, his job as his second lifeline, in case Maggie had to use the little girl's room.

Everyone left Ian's side and exited the bus, chatting as if all was well with the world. They exhibited a confidence the boss was back, though still physically injured, but back in charge of the circus. Ian knew you could not rise to this level, professionally, in any business without the ability to pretend your boss was sane. Acting is not exclusive to the stage and screen. Some stayed to rest, some rode to setup and work, Ian in their company.

As Ian went about his business, list in hand, Maggie at his side, he couldn't shake the feeling of being watched. It was discomfiting in several ways; One, he didn't like people snooping on him, no matter their reasons. He didn't care if they thought he required constant surveillance due to injury and recuperation or if they didn't feel he was up to snuff. He was a professional and had done this work for over a half century, he could do it on his death bed if needs be. Two, paranoia had taken up residence at the base of his skull and he had an itch that couldn't be reached. The ache in his shoulder gave credence to that paranoia, but he didn't like it, none the less. He had never been insecure of body or mind and he hated that one incident had brought it home to roost. And three, he didn't want this maniac with a rifle to define his life or this tour. He didn't want his people walking around looking over their shoulders afraid they might be next. This tour was about remaining low key, relaxed, smoke a bowl, play some music, and enjoy. They were helping others less fortunate. We can change the world but not from a hidden position, hunkered down behind our fear.

Fear would not have a ticket to this show! He wanted to scream it! Instead, he came to the conclusion the best way to convey that was to be out front, showing no fear, no reticence, only love and confidence to prove they stood on solid ground. Belief becomes reality when lived from the soul. Birmingham, be prepared for one helluva show!

His thoughts were disrupted by a commotion just outside the gates. Ah well, time to be the boss and find out who or what was massacring the good buzz he had worked so hard to create. He popped a gummy in his mouth to mellow the brain and lessen the pain while heading in the direction of the screaming. Something bumped into his good shoulder he glanced over to see Maggie pointing at her open mouth. Yeah, if he needed bucking up, she could use a little bear as well.

There was a well-dressed man, suit, tie, shoes polished to a point you could comb your hair in the reflection—which he had apparently spent some time in the effort—standing at the closed gate, his back to the ballpark, bible in hand, castigating the early arrivals who had camped outside the gate to be first in.

Great, thought the ringmaster, just what I need, some thumper, thumping where no one wished to be thumped. He would've liked to have security toss the thumper to the curb and maybe thump him but Ian was a great believer in the concept of free speech. He had seen enough head banging and Billy clubbing back in the sixties, he would not add to that egregious total.

"The lord will judge you and find you wanting in your sins." His forefinger trembling as it searched to find the souls of these blasphemers. Though what they were blaspheming about was anybody's guess. Ian could only assume the semi-circle of tired, old, long-hairs crowding in, though not too close, to hear the message were curious about which of their sins would be wanting and which would be considered sufficient to allow them entrance to the promised land. Sometimes these sermons were to cleanse the soul, sometimes just marginal entertainment to pass the time until something better, like an all-day festival, came along.

"You blaspheme the lord by filling your bodies with drugs and al-cohol," he began again.

"Didn't Jesus turn water into wine?" asked a truly curious middle-aged hippie while proffering a bola bag towards the well-coiffed man.

Ignoring the allusion to the obvious hypocrisy of his point, he con-tinued, "You spit in the lord's eye as abortionists and worshippers of the flesh!" he was kicking this thing into gear.

"Yer a little late on both counts, deary, by about four decades, but we appreciate the thoughts," laughed a septuagenarian woman while others joined in the gaiety, passing a joint and bottle.

"Laugh at your peril but understand there is a change on the way. The lord is coming to set things right, the way He created all life to be on this world. With women and people of darkness," and here he turned and pointed at Maggie, Suzette, Joya, Gabby, and others before returning his attention back to the assembled in front, "subjugated to their superiors!"

"And whom might those be?" Nash didn't yell, he didn't threaten, he didn't have to.

The 'preacher' took a step back from the large, smiling man. Though to his idiotic credit he didn't back down. "The white man. The race god intended to rule the world."

"Let's see," Nash held the man in place with his stare, "that would be the white human who left nothing but death, disease, and destruction in his path while he was trying to subjugate the rest of the world? Like the embodiment of the four horsemen? Buying and selling other human beings as if they were less than chattel. Those white men? They are the ones who your god wants to rule? " the friendly tone that had begun this tête-à-tête had lost some of its softness and had taken on a harder edge. One born of centuries of memories of Europeans ravaging and clear-cutting his children and native-born humans, believing they could own the Mother. Who, incidentally, would be around long after mankind had been flicked off her beautiful skin like fleas in the mud.

Though late morning, Ian could feel the temperature surrounding them beginning to rise and the last thing he needed right now was a brouhaha right outside the gate. It wouldn't matter to the local constabulary whether the right winger started it or whether the big native did, though he knew who he'd put money on as to who the locals would arrest. He wanted this to stop before anyone got hurt.

Enter Jaxson Grahm. Jax walked in between the two, smiled his most gratuitous smile and sighed. "Here's the deal, I don't know you," he said pointedly to the dapper preacher, "though I've heard your spiel before. I didn't like it then and I like it a lot less now but I'm going to let you spew while we get setup. You folks may listen politely or add a few mocking rebuttals but no violence, threats of violence or shouting down. He will have his say." He held up a hand to stay the burgeoning protests. "In payment for your freedom of speech, when we are done and you are done, you will accompany Nash," he indicated the aforementioned with a quick wave of the hand, "inside and sit, in communion with all these same people while the concert takes place. You will listen to us, musically, verbally explaining what it is we hope to accomplish as opposed to what you say you want. Then you are free to leave and live whatever life you chose. But you cannot leave until the concert has ended. Fair enough?" Jaxson stood back to await the verdict.

All could tell this preacher's mind, small and entrenched as it was, thought itself superior to all who gathered here. He was fighting a mental battle with no weapons and no reserves except a certainty he stood on the righteous path to glory. He had no desire to commune with these heathens, these unwashed sinners, but the chance to speak openly and freely to these pagans was too much to pass up.

Confusion Brings Peace

Ian scratched his head as they walked to the infield. He was as confused as he had ever been and with the way things had been going over the past week or so that was carving new territory.

"I don't quite understand your reasoning," he began as they watched the crew assembling sound and lights simultaneously. He and Maggie had the ends with Jax in the middle. "Why bother with this bigot? Why force people to listen to his racist spiel when no one coming to this show will be swayed by whatever rational he tries to throw at them? Why invite him in when he will bring that hate filled vibe with him?"

"Simple," replied the peacenik and true follower of the love movement, "I know the fans will treat him the way I asked, because they are good people and mostly stoned. I also know one on one it is hard to reason with such as he but take him and submerse him in the vibe of love, music, and message, supported by thousands of people all on the same wavelength and he will either change or leave with the same hate filled heart. Either way we win. The folks out front get to have a little sport with his hypocrisy and we have done what this tour is supposed to be about." He gestured with both hands as if to indicate simple, ain't it?

"But people like that never change," Maggie kicked in as unconvinced as her husband.

"We are about lifting people from poverty. Poverty of hope, poverty of respect, poverty of soul. If there was ever someone who suffers from poverty of humanity, that's the guy. I am willing to bet the rest of my tour salary that more than one of the people waiting to enter has studied that book he carries far more intensely than he has. I know a little about it as it was forced down my throat as a child. He hasn't a leg to stand on if he is using the bible for justification."

"So, why bring him in?" Maggie reiterated.

"We have to try. If we can win over one person like this through our efforts, our message, and our people, then we will know we can win over many more. We will never convince everyone; we just need a plurality." He shrugged the possibility of failure, "But we have to start somewhere. Let's just say he is an experiment in love and music."

"I guess," Ian was not convinced, "but why saddle Nash with him?"

"Well, he's big enough to quell any disturbance before it can take hold. And I think he gives off an energy, an aura if you will, that is palpable. And he has been converted, been moved in some manifest way by the music and I think the depth of his emotion will rub off. At least, that is the theory!" He laughed at his own folly.

As they made their way backstage, they were greeted by a small, Southern-pretty, woman dressed for a rock concert if the rock concert was business causal and she'd had to go buy the outfit.

"They tell me you boys, and the lady," she added quickly taking in Maggie, "are the head honchos of this carnival. Mary Wilson, I'm in charge of this facility," she stuck out a hand in welcome. Her grip was firm, reassuring, as she took each one of theirs and shook it. "Daddy worked the rigs," she explained to their somewhat astounded expressions of her handshake, throwing a thumb in the direction of where they assumed the gulf was located. "He always said people would judge you by your handshake, so make it mean something. Don't be a dead fish, nobody likes to grip a dead fish." Her guffaw was heartfelt and loud. She was the portrait of life brimming over the top.

"As much as anyone can be," Ian laughed, answering her original statement. "Mary Wilson?" he questioned

"Well, not that one," said the zoftig white woman, "Ain't got the voice or the looks. But daddy was a huge fan." She shrugged off the obvious.

Ian understood what she meant when she said she didn't have the looks, she wasn't talking color, she was talking pretty, and he found it unfortunate she thought that way. She was an attractive woman in her own right, though mostly because of her open joy, her love of life, and her welcoming attitude.

"I heard that feller caterwauling' outside the gate when I come in. Noisy SOB ain't he?" She bobbed her head in the direction of the natty preacher. "Want I should call the locals and have him escorted from the property?" She cocked her head in question.

"Nah, we gotta deal with him. He can pontificate until the gates open then he has to come into our church and see which one is a better fit." Jaxson immediately dismissed any further comment on the man.

Mary cocked her head again, kind of like a dog when you say certain things, will do as if trying to understand what you said. Ian thought that gesture was the most endearing thing he'd ever seen. She grinned and let out a loud guffaw as she realized what Jaxson had meant. He didn't mean they had to deal with the man, he meant they had a deal with the man. Funny, these Yankees.

"Well, I guess y'all know what yer up to. I'll leave ya be, if you need anything here's my cell number. I'm only a few minutes away and my man, Herbert, ah, here he comes now, he'll be your go to while I ain't here." A man in his middle to late years sauntered up to introduce himself. He had the look of a man who was maintenance, janitor, handy man, could handle payroll, or any other thing that would come down the pike. Yeah, Ian liked him as soon as he took the man's hand. Firm grip, just like the boss'.

"Everything, good?" he asked nodding toward the stage, meaning everything they had installed, electric, stage position, everything, whatever they might have problems with.

"All looks perfect," said Ben smiling as he joined the group. "'bout as good as anybody could hope for. Thank you." And he meant it with his heart. Any time you can walk into a gig and not have to worry about anything at all is a blessing.

"If it's ok, we'd like to do a bit of a run through in about two hours, once the crews are set and happy," Ian informed Herbert.

"You is the ones running the circus, up to you when the elephants parade in," Herbert tipped the hat he wasn't wearing and made his way to whatever chore was silently beckoning him.

"If you guys can live without me for a while, I'd like to get back to the hotel and meet up with the boys." Jaxson said as he walked toward one of the buses whistling to himself and pleased with his solution for the crazed preacher.

Ian had known Jaxson since they were both young men starting out in the music biz. Ian in radio, Jaxson as a brilliant songwriter and musician. He didn't remember seeing Jax this excited about playing with folks in decades. He had recorded an album with these fellas from over the pond a quarter century previous. Them showing up to aid Jaxson's crusade against inequity in the world had sparked a change in Mr. Grahm's attitude.

Stars play the songs people love to hear because that is why they came. Though after playing some for, literally, decades you can become tired of hearing them, no matter how great a song is, it wears on the ears after hearing it night after night for fifty years. The fans never quite understood the problem. They would come to a concert once a year and want to hear songs they hadn't heard live for as long, not realizing the performer had been playing these songs every night for decades. With the arrival of Flaco, Tino, and Kiko they could play the same songs but with a decided Spanish or Moorish influence thereby keeping the songs fresh for him. He was like a kid just learning favorite tunes.

The best part of the whole change was it gave all the rest of them fresh ideas as well. One night in Columbia, a shot that ricocheted them into giving their all, and a renewed intensity in purpose. All while Ian had lain abed in the hospital and missed it all. To him that was the worst part of the whole incident; not being shot but missing how it affected the show.

Can't live in the past. It was time to concentrate on his wife and the upcoming show. Funny, but Ian was almost as excited about today's concert as Jaxson. He wanted to taste some of what he'd missed by being winged. Sound check could not come soon enough.

The day remained warm, bordering on hot, as all preparations were completed. The road crew were as efficient as Ian could remember; the lighting crew were almost pleasant; he didn't know what it was about lighting crews but they were never satisfied with anything. Placement of mic stands, where the singers were positioned, drumkit should be over here not over by the bass amp, except that was exactly where the damn thing should be, and why does the piano have to be pushed off to the right side requiring its own lighting? Because that was where keys always were, out of the way of traffic!

Around two in the afternoon the players began straggling in through the back gates. The buses would be making trips back and forth to the hotel as groups readied themselves for showtime. They would bring their show clothes with them and change in the provided RV's and tents before going on stage. The dining tent was set up with some fans to keep the performers cool.

Yes, the excitement of another show ran like electricity through all the folks involved. Another of the million reasons Ian loved this job; no matter how many times this crew setup and tore down there was always that optimism, that tingle of excitement when showtime neared.

By three everyone had gotten their chance to hear the stage and were as satisfied as they were going to be until show time. Lighting and sound made final adjustments, as final as they were going to be. That is until everything went to hell once the people were in and the show was in full swing with performers moving and dancing wherever they wanted, not where the lights and sound were. It made Ian smile, his mood rubbing off on the woman at his side. Maggie was not about to let him out of her sight, not after what had happened the last time she'd done that. Ian had warned her she was not to accompany him on the stage; she was the last person who required the admonition. Her fear of the stage and becoming center of attention had been well documented.

Open the gates and let the thundering hordes enter.

Ian stood off to the side of the stage arm in arm with Maggie watching folks hustle—well, hustle as much as people in their sixties to eighties could—to get prime field seating. It was interesting, he thought, that he hadn't noticed how the younger folks held back while the seniors made their way to front center of the stage. They easily could have by-passed the older contingent but they chose to wait and allow their elders first dibs. Respect.

He was about to point that out to his wife when she commented how nice she thought it was that the 'kids' were doing just that. Nothing got by the woman, he smiled. Just then he felt the presence of another human join them. Gabby. With a presence as big and prodigious as his it would have been impossible to ignore. They all watched the gathering multitudes in silence.

Ian noticed the large native, Nash, ambling in with the preacher in tow. It was not that he dragged the man it was more as if he had caught him in his wake and the fella couldn't disengage. Ian noticed that as Nash walked people just naturally got out of his way. They wouldn't even be looking at him but, like Gabby, his presence could be felt. It wasn't fear or threat they felt, more respect. He emanated a certain power, an aura of natural strength of spirit that was as palpable as the wind.

He found his spot and spread out on the lawn. No chair, no blanket, comfortable on the grass. It was his fluidity of motion, the way he would slink, elegant, graceful yet with power, that caught the attention. It was not the way he appeared, long tan hair—though that should have stood out as most natives had black hair, to Ian's recall—blue jeans, flannel shirt, and ankle high moccasins, that made him stand out, it was his quiet resolve. The way he comported himself. A mountain that would not be moved.

The preacher slunk down next to him. Ian had to give the man some points for keeping his word. He could've easily bolted when the gates opened, though Nash probably would have caught him two steps into his escape, but he hadn't. He might not wish to be surrounded by these dirty hippie lefties, but he remained quiet.

Ian had noticed how many of the attendees looked at the man as he passed. He was, apparently, known in this area and not well liked by the expressions on faces. Ian supposed some of these fine citizens had been on the receiving end of his spewage at some time in their lives. A woman in her seventies, Ian guessed, boldly walked up, and set herself down next to the 'man of god'.

She stared at the stage, watching the final preparations but her lips showed she spoke. Ian guessed her intended was the preacher. Yes, this man was known. Her face betrayed no anger or hate, just a woman having a conversation with someone she knew in her heart wouldn't listen, yet she had to try.

"Wouldn't you like to be a mouse sitting in the grass and listening in on that conversation," Maggie posited.

Ian chuckled, "Not sure I'd want to be on the receiving end of whatever's on her mind. Nash is doing a fine job of ignoring, though he certainly doesn't appear uncomfortable sitting that close to the onslaught." Ian felt the barometric pressure increase where he stood.

"She is asking him why he is so filled with hate," his nurse stood next to Maggie and right behind Ian. She had silently joined them. "She wants to know what happened in his life that has made him so dismissive of women. Who filled his head with such idiotic, her words not mine, concepts? How could he possibly believe that the color of one's skin made any difference as to their intelligence, work ethic, or character? All good questions and one he doesn't seem to wish to answer," her voice was even as if reporting on the conversation without judgement or editorializing.

Ian turned his head slightly so he could see her, his face questioning, though the question remained within.

"I can read lips," she answered the unasked. "When you have been alive as long as I, certain things have been learned and become second nature."

Been alive as long as she? Ian thought, the woman couldn't be more than forty! Forty-five tops. He never ceased to be amazed at the arrogance of youth. And, yes, he thought, from where he stood on the road of life, forty or so was youth. He was about to say as much to this woman when she spoke again.

"He is responding in his way with his magic book which seems to mean anything the person holding wants it to mean. It is like the talking stick." She noticed their puzzled expressions. "The talking stick is a stick," she shrugged as if that needed no further explanation, "it is passed from person to person in a circle when they share stories. Whoever holds the stick holds the floor and cannot be interrupted while they have the stick. No one questions the holder; their story is their own. It is the stick that gives them the power to tell what they will. It is just a stick, a piece of fallen tree, yet it means something completely different to each who holds it. Their stories are just as true as the last person who held the stick. Look, now she is asking for the book, it will be her turn to tell her truth with the talking book. I would bet her truth found in this book will be far different than his." She grinned.

"She is speaking to him about his great opposition to abortion. She tells him she wishes there was no need for such but it should be available to those who need. Even the talking book says you are not a living person until birth. What is Genesis 2:7?" she looked to Maggie and Ian who both expressed their ignorance. "Something of Then the LORD God formed a man from the dust of the ground and breathed into his nostrils the breath of life, and the man became a living being. Does this sound familiar?"

Again, nothing from the heathens. These two might be good people but religious they were not. Though Ian felt a sense of pride that one of the fans of this tour, and thereby of the mission they were on, would know this stuff. Silently he cheered her on.

"He seems to be trying to interpret what she has said, but she has the talking book and is reinforcing his own words that the rhetoric contained must not be interpreted but taken as fact. Now she is on him about ownership of others. I salute her efforts. She seems to know this book. She is quoting Acts 17:26 which she tells him says man is of one blood, therefore no one color or ethnicity is any better or worse than any other. We are all one. Mitakuye Oyasin, we are all related, as we say in our culture." She nodded her head in appreciation of the woman and her debate. "The preacher is unconvinced as it doesn't mean what he wants it to mean but she is holding the book and flipping through its pages. She is not done with him." Suzette actually clapped her hands in praise, she was enjoying this as much as Ian had ever seen any human enjoy any sporting event.

They both almost missed the tuning of strings and murmur of the crowd as the quartet took their seats on stage.

Music Hath Charms,

The Savage Is Lacking

Just as the final check of tuning was happening the woman held out the bible to the man of his god and said, "And one or two more words on the sanctity of life in the womb from your book. Please take the time to read these words; God enumerated his punishments for disobedience, including 'cursed shall be the fruit of your womb' and 'you will eat the fruit of your womb,' (Deuteronomy 28:18,53) directly contradicting sanctity-of-life claims or possibly, God will punish the Israelites by destroying their unborn children, who will die at birth, or perish in the womb, or never even be conceived (Hosea 9:10-16) and before the music begins, look at this," and she opened the book exactly where the verse was as if her fingers could feel the words, "read this before you go to sleep tonight, For rebelling against God, Samaria's people will be killed, their babies will be dashed to death against the ground, and their pregnant women will be ripped open with a sword (Hosea 13:16)" She passed the book back to the evangelist before laying back to enjoy the coming glory.

There was something about the woman that rang familiar in Ian's brain, though certain he had never set eyes on her before, there was this feeling that he knew her. And while he stared at her she turned her head and made eye contact with him. Suddenly he was drawn to her, no longer separated by a couple hundred feet but as if he stood nose to nose with her. From the deep well at the base of his skull the name Marie popped in and then flew away on laughter. No, it couldn't be, as she looked nothing like the granddaughter of Marie Laveau. The strains of Mozart took the thoughts even further from consideration.

As the music found its footing Nash, in what was quickly becoming his M.O., stood, tiled his head back, closed his eyes and clasped his hands at his waist. The very portrait of the state of ecstasy. Soon more stood to bathe themselves in the beauty rippling and streaming from the stage, rolling through the crowd, until all stood to accept the offering of perfection.

All with the exception of one. The sky pilot sat with eyes closed, hands clasped in prayer, head bowed in supplication to his deity apparently asking for guidance or understanding. Mozart would not oblige; he would not be unheeded.

As Mozart grudgingly gave way to Felix, the majesty and glory could not be denied. Even the apostle had to stand before magnificence and accept the recognition of fulfillment. Tears flowed from closed eyes, his hands now unclasped and raised in honor to the vast unknowable universe, or so Ian saw it. It was possible there was hope for the awakening of the man's soul.

As the final notes of Mendelsohn wafted away on the slight breeze, the assembled, as if gathered in their own place of worship, sat on grass, blankets, lawn chairs and each other, to await the official commencement of the show. Ian paced for several seconds before taking the stage to introduce the All-Girls' Choir plus One. He had no desire to be on the stage, in the wings, yes, but front and center, not on your life. It had been decided by the overwhelming majority of the gypsy clan that he should welcome the audience by introing the show and the first act. It only seemed fair as he had been so instrumental in forcing Gabby to do the same with the explanation of the reason for the tour.

As peace settled on the mass of humanity and the smoke began to rise Ian slowly paced out to the center mic. A few deep breaths to calm the nerves and he stepped up to the microphone. To his surprise the audience, as one, stood and began to applaud, hoot, whistle, and cheer. He stepped back wondering what might have elicited such a response when he realized the narrative of Columbia had raced them here and won. These folks knew of the attempt on their luminaries and that, according to myth, Ian had stepped in front of the bullet to save his performers. A bit of a stretch of the yarn.

He wished to stop the festive arousal but when he chanced a glance in the direction of Maggie, she vehemently was shaking her head, no. She knew what he wanted to do but also knew it was the wrong thing to do. They were celebrating what this whole tour was about as personified by Ian and his supposed actions; allow them the joy.

He welcomed them all, thanked them for their kind applause, and introed the magnificent harmonies of his favorite choir.

The audience returned to earth though only for a moment. The interweaving of vocal harmonies with subtle but sophisticated beauty of Jesse's fingerpicking and underlying melody on guitar wrapped them in a cocoon of splendor. Joya began her song of hope, *'Look Up'*, and by now, after it had caught on in NYC, all knew where to sing along. The ballpark was bathed in glorious hues of love and harmony. Ian thought he witnessed some deeper emotion slide across the visage of the preacher though it could have been the setting sun.

Each woman had a two-song featured set with the others backing them. When Joya began her second tune the crowd erupted in celebration. She stopped the song, so taken aback by the reaction, it took her completely by surprise, until she noticed the reason why. Joya knew her music was finding a larger audience through the many platforms online, still, they couldn't have elicited this kind of response but the sight of her old friend and mentor, Christopher Shackleton, could. Now, there was someone who had more than earned the reception. She hugged the big man as he doffed his large Stetson to acknowledge the crowd. Whatever song she had about to do was lost in the dust of history as they immediately went into an old tune of his they had recorded together several years back, *'Simfoni ti o dun'*. It hadn't been a major hit but it had been played and some recognized the song.

The round robin returned to traverse the Appalachian hills, Laurel Canyon, the plains of Oklahoma, to a small cabin in Maine. Each singer brought their own life to song and here in the south they accepted and immersed themselves in the wonder of the land. As the last note rang out, Christopher launched into one of his many hits with the help of the band of renown backing him. He played a tight set of hits and old favor-ites, some by him, some recorded by others, as was his want, before thanking the crowd with a wide sweep of his Stetson and walking off the stage to thunderous applause.

Joya was there to greet him and thank him for coming. Tears of happiness and welcome running like mountain streams down her perfect, round, brown face. She hugged him tight telling him how much she missed him, though she had found a home. She thought nothing could bring her more bliss until she turned and saw Christopher's wife, Jenna, beaming at both of them from where she sat on a trap case. Joya ran to the woman and closed with love. This was a woman who had taken Joya in when Christopher had brought her home after hearing her sing, swear-ing he was going to do whatever he could to shine light onto her talent. The two women had become immediate sisters. Now, they were together again.

"How long am I allowed this ecstasy?" Her eyes jumped from Chris to Jenna.

"Well, if y'all will have us we'd like to join the circus." Christopher laughed, "Seems we ain't got us a tour for some time, and ain't much happening up on the farm. So, we thought if Ian and Jaxson wouldn't mind, we'd travel along with y'all fer a spell." Everyone turned to see what Jaxson's response would be.

"What're you looking at?" he grinned, "It's not even a question, we can always use a good guitar tech!"

"Well, I'm just yer guy," Christopher laughed, "I know a little bit about them things." Yeah, it would be a good fit.

James had taken over on stage after Bonnie had come out and done a quick half hour set following Christopher. The music ebbing and flowing. Day eased into night with a gorgeous sunset to paint the back-ground of sound.

Kiko, Flaco, and Tino joined the band onstage for several tunes from across the sea. There was a Spanish song of longing for sailors lost, waited for, found, and some never to return. A north African melody from Morrocco of love lost on the sands of the Sahara and an upbeat rousing flamenco inspired tune of passion complete with dancing and castanets!

Jaxson came out to a standing ovation, he nodded to the masters and introduced each to the audience. He signaled to Lee Starling and

Russel Crunk who took up the intro with Tino filling the percussive needs on *'Finding the East'*. And so began a lovefest of music and rhythms until Jaxson sat at the piano and began, *'The Cannons of Peace'*. Kiko, Tino, and Flaco had only done this once, that being two nights ago in Columbia but they understood, pianissimo.

Gabby hesitantly, as always, stepped onto the stage and the crowd went silent, respect. His stage fright was well chronicled. He stepped to the center stage mic and said, 'Ya-Hey', his way of touching base with his people. And the thumping of the heart began. Softly at first but increasing in strength as every single person in the audience held up one hand in salute and beat their chest with the other in solidarity with the Mayan.

Ian gazed across the vast thousands of humanity who had become one because of a man they never would have met or known his story without this tour. His heart swelled. Everyone stood, even, he noted, the preacher. He didn't have his left arm in the air but he did, tap his chest with his right. Though whether because he felt something or a case of 'when in Rome', but Ian didn't think it mattered. Jaxson, in his ecstatic mood may have done something quite extraordinary and Ian would be overjoyed with that. He locked eyes with the woman standing next to Nash and the sky pilot again, she grinned and nodded in the affirmative. Now, what the hell did that mean?

Jax brought everybody back out on stage for the encores, including road crew, sound engineers and the lighting folks that were close enough and not busy. They closed with Jesse's anthem, *'Love Now'*, sending the assembled home, worn out, tired to the bone, and happy. Ian watched as the preacher shook hands with the woman, then Nash, then received hugs and handshakes from dozens of others as they passed him by on their way out. Ian had no idea if his mind had been moved from its unbudging position but hope springs and Ian had other chores to occupy his mind.

They would move on to Memphis for a show in two days' time then on to Little Rock, OKC, Albuquerque and then, where? He really couldn't remember and didn't care right at this moment. He wanted to share a pipe and some convivial companionship with his wife and friends. Just as soon as the trucks and buses were loaded and back at the hotel.

They had two days to make a one-day drive, a hotel bed would bring joy to his back tonight.

One More Before We Go

Carrie came to the conclusion that by Ray saying they could 'talk some more and come up with some solutions' he meant they could attend a major party at his mother's home, eat and drink until they were comatose and sleep for a half day. She smiled as the miles rolled beneath her.

It had been a really good, scratch that, a great party. Apparently, when Ray's mom, and extended family, found out a friend of Kim's was in town they immediately set in motion the plans for a welcoming committee. The fact it would take place as said company was about to disembark New Orleans made them no nevermind. The idea was to have a party to let Carrie know how much Kim was loved and her memory was kept close to their hearts. So, Ray asked or begged her to stay for another day or two so the family could meet her and say their condolences while sharing their love. Plus, Henry was going to be there.

What a whirlwind. Kim had told her about the welcome she'd had in New Orleans but Carrie had always thought it a bit of an exaggeration. Boy, had she been wrong. If anything, Kim had understated the life, the joie de vive, the energy of these people. As Kim had once mentioned during a conversation out on the chaise lounge of Carrie's beach house, wealth meant nothing without love, friends, family. She had spoken of the almost poverty of Ray's family financially, though mostly of the great wealth they had in love. Kim and Carrie had wrapped each other in their love while Kim waxed poetic about the great web of Ray's kinfolk. Carrie found herself drowning in jealousy at what had been denied her throughout her life. She had consoled herself with the joy and completion Kim had brought.

A wave of grief passed through her body as she realized that had been taken from her as well. She shook herself physically out of this despondency. She had Aron, Oscar, and Barbara with her, for however long that might last, and she would treasure each second. It was a promise she had made to herself and Kim's memory.

And Henry was going to come meet them once they finally made it back to Newport. He would consult with the best minds he could find until then and bring their recommendations as well.

And now they were on their way to a music concert where the music was secondary to the mission. She was pretty sure she understood the objective of the show. To lift people out of hopelessness and poverty of spirit, but she couldn't quite get how music, alone, could do that. She would discover what she needed to know when she arrived.

The slap of the wheels seemed to keep time with the music selection Aron had found on their Pandora. This had been a godsend from the constant commercialization of horrid they had been forced to listen to while they crossed the country with nothing but terrestrial radio. The streaming services offered music without the bombardment of mindless sales pitches. Though she missed the local news and weather.

Local stories occupied the small radio stations across the country, not grand, earth-shattering doom and gloom, but stories of high school sports, births, deaths, celebrations, and weather. In small communities all across the land local weather was what stopped conversations and increased volume. You needed to know if it was going to storm and how violent that storm might be. Would it be a gully washer, a term she found particularly endearing, or did you have to head to the storm cellar.

Carrie was a product of the west coast, born and bred. The ocean was her backyard and play area. If you paid attention, it would never harm you, it was only when you thought yourself smarter or more wily that the great expanse of sea would slap you down. But she would warn you first. Not out here. If the storm was coming it could pass by, drop a few inches of rain, blow down the chicken coup, or tear down everything you held dear. You needed to know minute by minute where it was going and whether it was going to intensify or tire itself out.

They'd had to update some of the electronics on the seventy-year-old pickup to make this marvel of modernity work but it had been worth the shake-up of authenticity. What the hell, she wasn't going to ever sell her love. So, with abandon they tooled down the highway towards Memphis. Some Jaxson Grahm came on and though it was well before her time, she loved his melodies and lyrics. They were much more meaningful and truly expressive than most of what people her age listened to. No bitches, hoes, or bling, just true emotion and honesty.

Yeah, this would be a good side trip, something to occupy the mind while she considered the plenitude of suggestions, needs, and im-possibilities weighing down on her as she planned her retreat for lost souls.

Aron's constant chatter with the girls via cell phone was also a welcome distraction. He had become quite close to the girls, actually had been since they'd met on the side of the road. He was very protective and patient of them and with them, like the best big brother in the world. Her pride in him grew every day, he was coming into who he should have been. No use crying over lost years, he was more than making up for them now.

Speaking of which, she wondered if they could take Aron and the girls to this concert. She hadn't really checked out the line-up, though she didn't remember hearing, or Aron reading anything, about rappers or heavy metal. The girls didn't need to be exposed to that, not yet. She should ask Aron to check specifically for the suitability of the entertain-ment. She didn't think Barbara was a prude but there was outward prud-ishness and 'these are my children' prudishness.

Her cell phone rang startling her out of her reverie. Who the hell? "Hello," she said holding the phone up to her ear with her right hand while the left kept the truck between the lines.

"Girls are getting hungry," Barbara sounded apologetic, though whether because they would have to stop to feed the children or because Carrie would be footing the bill, Carrie couldn't tell; neither was necessary. They had time, she had money. Now, she had family as well.

As Carrie hung up the phone, she noticed Aron was already searching for the best place to feed the girls. He continued speaking to them on speaker but searched as well. The last couple weeks had taught Carrie a few lessons in life, especially one that included two small children.

She'd gotten used to the freedom of travel with just herself and Aron. Aron had, of course, lived homeless for several years and could go without food for long periods of time. Not that he'd had to, she provided him with three squares of healthy dining every day, but if they missed a meal there would be no complaining. However, with two young stomachs growling and grumbling, stops were very necessary. She didn't mind she just had to readjust to the new reality.

She'd made several life altering adjustments over the past year, some were painful, some were normal, getting older kind of things, and some were glorious in their rewards. Barbara, Phoebe, and Izzy were the greatest. And Aron, she amended, chancing a quick peek at the young man to her right.

Aron found a TA about thirty miles ahead which gave him time to give notice to the vehicle in front of them and prepare himself to be hungry now. One thing living on the streets taught him is to be hungry whenever food revealed itself. You couldn't allow your stomach to rule you on the streets, there were no normal times of meals or when they might present themselves, so when they did you had to make yourself hungry even if you just ate five minutes ago.

They were within two hours of Memphis and Carrie, if she had her druthers, would have druther made it into the hotel, unpacked, relaxed for five before heading out to find grub. But children did not understand waiting and she was going to have to live with that slight inconvenience.

"See what you can google that might be halfway healthy," she commanded her copilot and navigator and considering the content available at truck stops.

After a few minutes of googling and starting over and googling and homing in he was ready with his conclusion. "I would say if you want something healthy, the closest exit is in Chicago," he sighed, "Though if time is of the essence, the closet place with any hope is about half hour north in Grenada. It's a mom and pop called Juju's Market. Not sure it will fit the bill but it should fill the stomach." He shrugged and shut down the phone.

"When choice is no choice take the best choice. Phone the fam again and tell them we'll stop fill up the tanks and the children there, instead, before moving into Memphis." Deep breaths and patience.

It was family, laid-back, country, rustic and would do. They at least had something that resembled vegetables along with chicken not delivered by a corporate truck, and the usual southern cuisine, some that was not deep fried. And it was two minutes off the highway. Healthy would wait.

The stop only cost them forty minutes, all told, before they were happily cruising back north toward the big city. About a half hour south of Memphis Carrie's phone rang. It was Barbara, now what?

"Hey, Isabelle is not doing well," Barbara used Izzy full name and that, she knew from stories was not good.

"What's wrong?" Carrie tried to keep the frustration out of her voice and hoped the worry would cover it up.

"She's running a fever and has sharp abdominal pains, I need to find a doctor," her tone conveyed she would brook no argument. This was her child and she required medical attention.

Before she could ask, Aron had his phone out and his fingers flying. "Methodist University Hospital isn't the closest but it has the best ratings and reviews," his words flew with an immediacy Carrie would not have believed. But this was his new little sister.

By the time Carrie, Aron, and Oscar pulled into the parking area by the emergency room the nurses had taken Izzy in for examination. Barbara had gone in with her and Phoebe, brave Phoebe, sat patiently waiting for her extended family to arrive. She saw them pull up, ran out to meet them, hugging, kissing Aron and Oscar the most but refusing to leave Carrie's side.

After a very long half hour Barbara walked into the embrace of her friends. "They think she has some kind of an infection in her gut. They want to keep her overnight and put her on heavy antibiotics." She did her best not to show the terror that ran like a raging river through her body and soul.

Carrie took a breath while considering options. "We will go check into the hotel; Aron says it's not far from here. We'll feed Phoebe and keep her company so she will know everything will be fine. Once we get settled, we'll come back down here to keep you company. And if they feel she needs to be here all night we can take shifts so no one is left here alone." She appeared satisfied with the plan formulated within seconds in her frazzled brain.

"Carrie, you won't be able to meet up with the festival. How can you talk to them, confer, compare, and decide if they want you or you want them? This just isn't fair." If Carrie's brain was flying at a thousand miles a second Barbara's was in hyper speed. "Maybe leave Phoebe with me while you and Aron go check things out." Worry, guilt, a conscience that wouldn't let go of all the good things Carrie had done for them, and here she was, denying Carrie what she most needed right now.

"Right now, the only thing, the only person who matters is Isabelle. And you, of course. Family. All of us. We're a family now and that is number one on the hit parade. Maybe I'm not supposed to meet up with these people. Maybe it's not supposed to happen today or next week, or who knows fucking when!" Carrie closed her eyes to concentrate. The only person she'd had to worry about, think about, since she was fifteen was herself. Emotions threatened to overwhelm as she thought about the little girl in the next room, sick, running a fever, far from what she knew, and all Carrie wanted to do was comfort her. And yet, that was her mother's job. So, Carrie had to comfort Barbara, and Phoebe and Aron and, Christ on a saltine, herself.

"I just don't know how to ever pay you back for all you've done," Barbara was overcome with the weight of her little daughter in a hospital, no home, no money, no future, no, no, no. When Carrie shook her before enfolding her in a huge bear hug to settle nerves. They all had to get a hold of themselves.

"You don't owe me a thing. If you're concerned with paying things back, you'll get your chance once we get settled on the ocean. You have to grasp your training and take care of yourself. You have a little girl who needs you. Let us take care of the rest. We'll get settled, bring you a good meal, and if Iz is up to one, something for her as well. I'll call once I see what vittles are available and you can tell me how things fare. We don't have to make any decisions right now, just take care of Iz, that's it!" She grabbed Phoebe by the hand and turned Aron in the direction of the exit. "Go to your daughter I'll call you in a couple hours."

I'll Follow The Sun

The air was chill, temperature around forty-five degrees but with the promise of sun and warmth. Much more warmth the further down the mountain they traveled. Padon had gotten Doc Caldwell to give him, not a clean bill of health, but her permission to go back to the blacktop as long as he followed Maggie's instructions to the T. He had sworn on all he held dear he would follow her every word as if it were from God, his god, the muse, herself. One last check with the crew at the café and a guarantee to check in no more than once a day, they put the jeep in gear and crept out of town.

They hadn't packed much; they weren't going to be gone for months just a week on the plains. A small suitcase, backpack, and his guitar—Maggie had insisted—so he could keep his callouses and good humor. He had found that since the night of the party he really loved to play again. There was no alternate motivation, no gigs, well, except Merle's with Wally every Thursday night, but that was something laid back. A reason to write new songs to keep them from getting bored. Oh, they'd play the occasional cover tune and some of Wally's favorites from the Forties and Fifties, classic stuff, a little jazz and bebop, but it was all in fun. He didn't have to prove anything to anybody ever again. He had all he could ever have hoped for. He bussed tables, and helped in the kitchen, talked to the customers and kidded with the employees during the day and lay in the arms of a woman he respected and, whew, loved. Yeah, he admitted, it was love. Not teenage infatuation though there was a bit of that, but love of someone he could share anything with. No hiding, no keeping it to yourself, just an open, honest, deep relationship. He grinned.

"Something you'd like to share?" Maggie's tone was playful, not snappy like the ex's would have been. No, she was content, and happy to be traveling with him.

"Just thinking about us. I hope you know how happy, how fulfilled I am that you took me in. Surprised," he tossed in for good measure, "but so grateful." He wanted to add, 'I do so love you,' but those words had yet to be spoken. Oh, they'd been said a thousand different ways but never verbalized. Some day.

"Well, someone had to, god knows, you couldn't take care of yourself," she laughed, a tinkling of silver bells.

It always took him a back that this hard working, strong, remarkable woman, had such a beautiful, sensuous, delicate laugh. It was music. It was his favorite song in his life. "So, just doing community service?" He jived.

"Well, I had to make up for being mean to my employees by being nice to you," she leaned over and kissed his cheek.

Yeah, this was good, this was needed, this would be a week to get to know the other side of each other. There are always at least two sides to every person, the work side and the relaxed nothing-to-do-but - lay-around-and-enjoy-a-lemonade side. These two knew each other's work side. They had, literally, lived it for the past four months. It was now time to find out if they could survive the relaxed side. Intensity versus laziness and lethargy. You could love the way someone worked hard, concentrated on the chore at hand, but could you tolerate that same slug lounging about, swinging on a hammock with a beer in hand and absolutely no inclination to accomplish a damn thing. Those were two separate people. You could love the one and curse the other. It was easy to admire the drive and single-minded passion work required. It was not so easy to admire the goldbricking wastrel. Though both had their upsides, you just had to find them.

They drove the same Mountain two-lane that had almost claimed Padon's life but, like Maggie herself, it had given them new lives, better lives they hoped. Yeah, thought Padon, they didn't have to hope, they knew. They had found a place of peace. A place where their past wasn't waiting on the doorstep every time they left the house. And they had found each other. Broken dolls left on the island of misfit toys, repaired by time, empathy, friendship, love, and community. It was good.

They chit-chatted about the town and her people, the café and her employees, Doc and Janet, and the luxury of small town living when surrounded by truly good people. They hadn't known what they were looking for when they'd stumbled into Rock Ridge, just a safe harbor, they thought. They certainly knew what they had found.

The snow patches became smaller and further apart as the elevation dropped and the temperature rose. By the time they had come to rest on the floor of the western edge of the great plains it was downright balmy. Padon was in his shirt sleeves and Maggie in a t-shirt. Life was definitely on the upswing.

He had driven the first four hours or so, which from where he came from was just a quick trip to the store for milk, but he hadn't been further than the town's edge in half a year. Maggie took over proclaiming she had made this drive a dozen times and knew the way. She even closed her eyes for a quarter mile to prove the point before Padon demanded she open them if she was going to drive.

It would be early evening by the time they made it to her friend's home about a hundred miles south-southeast of Colorado Springs. Padon would be happy when the wheels came to rest. Geez, he used to drive twenty to twenty-four hours on end, running hard from one town to the next. He found cleaning tables, setup, and resetting, sweeping floors, running food to tables was a walk in the park compared to the idiocy he used to run.

They sat out on the back patio after a fine dinner of steak, potatoes, and wine. Off in the distance to the west, they could just make out the outline of the great Rocky Mountains like a mirage against the darkening sky.

It was a beautiful, if mostly non-working, ranch situated on the western edge of the Great Plains. If you stood out front and gazed east, Padon was quite certain you could almost see the borderline of continent and ocean; there was nothing to obstruct the view.

It was interesting, Padon's intellectual bent hypothesized, he had become so acclimated to the confined landscape of the mountain town he now felt a bit agoraphobic with all this wide-open space, devoid of tree, town, or hill. He shook it off, took a sip of the soft, full-bodied merlot and forced his attention back to the conversation quietly taking place around him.

It was the usual chit-chat of small talk that takes place after a wonderful meal among friends who haven't seen each other in a period of time. Catching up on not so new news, of work and happenings involving common acquaintances. It was soothing in a normal lifestyle kind of way. A lifestyle he had previously been unaware of, except as a nebulous concept. Padon found he enjoyed the simplicity of it.

He thought it amusing that on the second glass of after dinner wine the conversation turned to 'how long are you staying?'. Not in a 'don't overstay, fish smells after three days' kind of way but more probing with a purpose in mind.

Padon forced his attention from mountains and oceans to the sharp turn in talk. He made eye contact with Maggie and she shrugged. They hadn't discussed how long they would be gone, just the going and purpose of needing to get to know each other better.

"We hadn't really considered leaving, we just got here," Maggie said in a half joking tone.

"Oh, we're not tired of you yet," replied Marylou, her friend for the past fifteen years, "We just had an idea in mind and thought if you were going to be here it might be fun." Her tone reflecting Maggie's.

Maggie had met Marylou and Robert when they had stumbled on Rock Ridge while lost on a spring journey through the mountains. The usual way folks discovered the town. They found it fit the concept of a laid-back Mountain town that they were seeking and so it had become a yearly stop ever since. They were friends, but really didn't know each other that well, so Maggie was cautious about where this conversation was taking her.

"And what might that be?" Cautious but curious.

"Well, if you two can see your way clear to hang for a few more days there is a concert coming in a week. It's not a huge rock fest as it were, but a midsized music fest featuring Jaxson Grahm, Bonnie Welch, supposedly James Nash is going to be there, and a bunch of others. Kind of an all-day music extravaganza just outside the Springs. They are playing small semi-pro baseball parks. Everyone is very excited they are coming our way." The excitement she felt was contagious, though Padon appeared immune.

"I'm not sure," Maggie began seeking some sign from Padon what his thoughts might be. She knew he was still feeling uneasy about music, concerts, and doing much more than his Thursdays with Wally. Maybe this would be too much for his fragile state of rehab from his former life. She watched him sort through his wide range of emotions and fears. She swore since almost the first day they'd met she could read his every thought as it passed behind his eyes. She patiently waited.

Padon knew what she was doing and he loved her for it. She was allowing him the freedom to decide for them, though he could tell she would really like to go. She also knew how this might affect him and his almost irresistible desire to return to the big stages. She also would not pressure his decision. If he was going to live with the realization he'd discovered on the trip down, that he did, indeed, love her passionately, then there were sacrifices more consuming than hiding in a mountain town away from temptation to be made.

"I would have to check with my boss to see if I can have the time off work for that long, but if she agrees..." He grinned.

"I can call her if you'd like and tell her you broke your arm and will need a couple days to heal," Maggie suggested, playing their game of boss/employee.

"I wouldn't want to lie to her. She's a really good boss and I'd hate to lose the gig." He gave the impression of someone deep in conflicting considerations.

"OK, you two," Robert chuckled, "we already bought the tickets and made hotel reservations so you're going."

If you are going to change your life there will be tests.

Maggie's inner teen jumped for joy at the thought of attending a real rock and roll fest. She hadn't been to anything like that since she was, well, a teenager. Her bastard old man wouldn't let her out of the house without him lording it over her. Once she found her way to freedom, she'd never had the time or extra cash to go to shows. Yeah, she was excited by the idea. Padon was reticent, she could see it in his eyes and feel it like a blast furnace from his bones. But why?

Padon saw how excited Maggie was and couldn't bring himself to bring her down with his fears. His terror that he might be recognized by any of a dozen artists and road crew. How many had he worked with? At least that many. Shit, man, there would be thousands of people at this concert the chance of him being recognized, or even spotted by anyone he hadn't seen in decades was miniscule at best. Relax, he told himself, go, enjoy the music and let her have a day of fun in the sun with great tunes. One thing he knew, there would be fantastic music.

Fame danced and sang around the pool of life, staring so hard at the happenings below, Fate thought she might set the water on fire. Her small breasts bounced in delight, her hair flowing in glee, and her pert derriere puckered with barely contained joy. She clapped her perfect hands and jumped like a child of three with a brand-new puppy.

"Well, your mood seems to have improved," Fate could not hide her own petulance at her friend's bliss.

"Lose one, gain one," sang the goddess of fame. "this one chased and wooed me for decades to the point of almost dying for me. He finally thought he could never have me and so settled for far less. But now, he sees me beckoning in his sunset years and might like a bite of the apple one more time. I think, since he was such a good boy for so long and gave up so much to win my favor, I shall allow him a taste. And if he behaves maybe much more than a taste!" she giggled and danced some more. Fame knew once tasted, even at this advanced age, she could not be denied. This man would give up all he had gained again, once he was in her thrall.

Fate took a quick glance to find who Fame was so intrigued with. Hmmm, the man looked happy enough with what he had found. The woman and friends were more than he could've hoped for, the life was fulfilling and brought contentment. Fate checked her line and felt no tug of remorse for the path set before him, but things could change quickly. She would have to keep an eye on the lifeline for this mortal and reign happenstance in if she thought Fame might steal him away from the serenity that was his course.

All The Way From Memphis

Memphis has a lively music scene ranging from blues to rap to pop to jazz. Ian thought this would be a good place to begin using some of the local, regional acts on the program once again. He and Jaxson sat in the back of the bus running through what they could find of Memphis acts that might mix well with the flow of the other acts, while adding more flavors and texture to tomorrow's show.

The concept of using local had gotten lost somewhere in NY and they both thought it was time to bring it back, the question was who and what. They didn't really want rap as they thought their audience was too 60s to dig the new art form; though, really, it wasn't that new, just uncomfortable to those who couldn't understand the lyrics. Old hippie types dug lyrics and rap might have some great stuff but to those with hearing disorders, even with the help of technology, trying to keep up with the pacing and invention of verbiage was taxing.

They wanted something different, but not so different that the majority of the audience would be lost. They settled on two. Bailey Bigger was more traditionally what they had served up to their audience, she would be a fine fit. But they still wanted to shake it up a bit, just not to the point that when it was opened it would explode. Here is where Charles Pender II came in. A jazz artist of some renown who they thought most in the assembled would dig from the get-go, and others would find it easy to get on board with once they took a toke and settled back. Jazz had meshed well with many back in the hey day and they thought it would again.

Once again, the musical safari was in place. They would see if they had upset the apple cart or if it would roll smoothly. That was the fun of adding and subtracting, one never knew until the end of the show whether the choices had been wise or if they'd require a wrecking crew.

Adding acts meant adding time. They had discussed the concept of an intermission but quickly discarded it. If people wanted a respite there were plenty of opportunities to break away and have a nap, a nosh, or a quickie behind the bleachers. Though with this assemblage of talent neither could think of any act someone would wish to miss.

They brought in Dugie, Ben, Maggie, as Ian trusted her judgement more than any other person in the world except maybe his own, and for some reason Nash and Suzette. He had come to trust these two oddities. There was a sense about them, something beyond mere mortals, that made him believe they operated in a different lane than anyone else. It could be how she had healed him more quickly than he had been told was possible. The doctors had been explicit when explaining it might be weeks or months before he would be himself again and yet, through her ministrations, he believed, he was running on most cylinders within a week. Maybe it was the dreams he'd begun having each night where he would wander another plane of reality with the otter and cat discussing wild concepts and ways to make the Mother heal, if only they all could work together. It felt like he'd been gone for months when he woke up but there he was, in the same time zone, same tour.

And Nash was tranquility itself. There was an assuredness about him, a strength, not just physical but inner. A spiritual power Ian could perceive ten feet away. Serenity and passivity until needed and then that strength, that power gave the impression nothing could stop him. Ian was well aware he had hallucinated in the moment when the bullet took him in the shoulder but he could swear the man ran past him in pursuit of the assailant at a supernatural speed. Imagination, injury, and memory combined to create myth.

He might as well have asked Nash about quantum physics as jazz, he gave the impression they were about the same in his book. Suzette assured him it would not disturb his enjoyment of the show. He trusted her judgement until proven wrong. Everyone else thought both additions were stupendous. They would let Bailey follow the quartet and perform a song with the All-Girls' Choir plus One. A welcome to the show kind of gesture and it would give the choir a slight shake-up which was always welcome. They'd slip the jazz in later in the show. It would be an excellent break in the flow of singer/songwriter/band artists.

The Napoleon hotel was perfectly situated a block from the venue. The buses pulled up out front and all disembarked collecting their few pieces of luggage while Ian went to the front desk to sign the paperwork and assign rooms in the clusters where most felt comfortable. It was always a dance to try and get lights with lights, road crew with road crew, female singers by the band, by the featured artists, by the Ian. Some folks were happiest alone and others liked to room together. He pirouetted and jitterbugged until all the pieces fell into place. Many times, he asked Ben to figure it out but Ian also felt he should take part in the ritual so he could appreciate the amazing job Ben did. Dugie would take care of getting all the needed crew over to the stadium where, hopefully, the equipment would be awaiting unloading and set up.

The hotel staff were accommodating and very pleased this crew had chosen their business. All were aware of what this tour stood for, the sacrifices made in service to others, and appreciated what the music, the artists, the crew were doing for people, in many cases, just like them or their families. People who worked the desks, housekeeping, maintenance, and kept the hospitality industry running were usually from the lower rungs of the economic ladder. And these people, these musicians gave a shit about them, not your customary customer.

There was something happening, some vibe, he guessed, outside the confines of the tour that wasn't disconcerting, Ian thought. More as if there was some metaphysical force sculpting, carving from the massive block of granite that is life, a form not yet recognizable. He thought it would be a beautiful piece of art but it had yet to reveal itself. Something, and there was that nebulous word again, was happening here. The grand question in the grandest bargain was what the fuck was it? Magic swirled, pieces were being fit into place and he had no control. That was a something he didn't like. When he did not have complete control, things had a tendency to go off the rails and crash into the gully a thousand feet below.

Ian flinched with the light brush of a touch on his arm. Maggie tried to see where he had lost himself, though she doubted even he knew. Now she had to wonder if the wound, though healing well, was affecting him. His confidence, his irrational belief in his own immortality, and his belief he could solve any problem that the road could throw at him. Nothing had happened to shake those beliefs, nothing that she'd witnessed, and yet he wasn't quite the Ian of a month ago. Things outside his control were forcing him to rethink reality. She didn't know how she knew, woman's intuition or forty years of sharing a life, but she knew. All she could do was be there for him.

Jennifer Jones, not that one, another one entirely different from the one everyone thinks, was the manager of the ballpark where the concert would take place. Auto Zone park was a pleasant ball yard in downtown Memphis, where a baseball park should be. Ian loved that some towns still honored the idea that baseball should be played where a goodly number of humans could still walk up to purchase a docket and enter the pasture where there is baseball. Too many moved these edifices to the national pastime out on one side of town or another and into the great exurbs of America. It lessened the chances that folks from inside the city could enjoy the beauty of the game. Maybe that was the reason they moved them so far away. Ian felt a touch of despondency roll over his mood when he considered the reasons why people did what people did and who they were attempting to exempt from enjoying.

Maggie shook him as the touch on the arm didn't seem to have accomplished its purpose. She saw him jump, but apparently, she needed more juice to get his attention, to get this engine to turn over. Ian was about to utter an unpleasant retort until he saw who had disturbed his ruminations. And the laminated sheet of paper in her hand.

"You might want this." She handed it to his startled expression, "and soon." She pointed at her watch and the sun at its apex in the sky.

Then she pointed out the woman standing patiently waiting for Ian to notice her.

"I'm sorry, lost in my own thoughts and rambling through the brambles of my mind," which Ian thought was a wonderful turn of phrase and quite poetic. Though the blank expression carved into the woman's features would give some doubt to his conclusion.

"Yes, Jennifer Jones," she held out a soft, well-manicured hand for him to, well, he wasn't certain what to do with this fish. It was too fragile to shake, too prim to hold, too cold to want to. He stared at it before nodding his head. "Just checking to see if you have everything you need as per our agreement." She scanned the sheet of paper in her own hand as if reading it for the first time. Her scrunched-up nose and eyes betraying her lack of understanding what most of the wants and needs might be.

"My crew has not found your venue wanting. Beautiful ballpark," he thought a little flattery might loosen the muscles in the gluteus maximus.

"It suits the purpose," tight as a drum.

"Not a baseball fan?" Oh, why not push against the rock and see if it has the ability to roll.

"My father loved this pit of iniquity. It is not where I would prefer to spend time with cultured friends." Whoa, this horse only seemed to have one piece of anatomy that made sounds and Ian had no desire to be in range longer than necessary. "I find the clientele quite boorish and quite unsophisticated as a whole."

Shit! How could someone own and operate a baseball stadium and not love the game. And what the hell did she mean as a hole? He guessed all holes would be unsophisticated.

"Not a fan of the game," he tried again, keeping his tone light, nonjudgmental, though he knew he lied.

"I think grown men playing a child's game as a career is quite sophomoric. I would sell this structure if there was someone willing to purchase it. And according to my father's will and stipulations, I cannot tear it down or use it for any other purpose. So, I am stuck with this albatross choking me. Though not financially as I am subsidized by the primary organization, so it is not a complete loss. I am hopeful your musical program will instill some measure of savoir vivre within the confines."

"Oh, it will instill some kind of savoir," he mocked, though it was lost on his audience of one. "I hope you enjoy the music."

"Oh, I won't be here to hear," she sniffed the air as if someone had farted not too far from where she stood.

When Al Campanis had demurred and told Ian he would not be in attendance Ian had insisted Al come. He wanted the man to experience the glory of the music. And he had been amply rewarded with Al's reaction. When it came to Ms. Jones, as Ian was quite certain there was no Mr. Jones, he decided the better part of composure was not to have Ms. Anal Repressive attending the festivities.

They had found over the past half year that keeping the bad vibes to a minimum increased the good time to the maximum. He never could understand how certain people could work so hard keeping a good time at bay. Loosen the cheeks, unbutton the hem of your fetters, and loosen up a bit Margaret! But she was one of those who found her joy in the misery of others. She would hate the ecstasy that filled the air.

"Well, it would seem your team has given us everything we need, so there is no need for you to be needed when it's obvious you need to be elsewhere." Ian no longer cared what the woman thought or felt about him or his band of gypsies, she may be excused. They had a contract, 'nuff said.

The last thing Ian wanted was to have this wrinkled prune of morals tsk-tsking every move, every sip, every bare breast or bottom, and toke, to be revealed during the six hour plus afternoon into evening of bacchanalia. This extravaganza was about reminding people they still had time to live and experience, while contributing to the vast underserved and downtrodden.

And so, Ian, with trusty checklist in hand, set off to assure that the world remained steadily gyrating on its off-kilter axis and would continue to do so for another day. He had more than a plentitude of oddities and eccentricity pulling at his reality. What with all his bizarre dreams of people who weren't; dream states that were more solid than the malleable, supposed, representative reality of shootings; lifesaving, and odd feelings that things weren't what they appeared. He needed his rock, his binky of reassurance, his foothold in certainty. He turned and grabbed hold of his wife and went about his business. He had a show to put on.

Feeling Alright?

Soteria sat quietly at the front of the bus, on the step where she could gaze out the front window and not be cajoled into conversation about the road, her life, her past, and banality galore. She couldn't answer questions about events not found in her memory. She didn't know much about life before she ran to save Howie. She couldn't remember how she knew what she knew but she knew it well enough to save the human. And why did she think in those terms? Wasn't she human? She really couldn't answer her own question, which was why she sat down in the stepwell where others couldn't ask her either.

Gabby put an end to that supposition as he sat down on the next step up. The bus bounced gently with the rolling of the road, swaying with the breeze, and settling back into a soothing sameness of motion.

"You, ok?" He didn't push. He wasn't prying, hell he didn't take his eyes from the miles being gobbled by their motion. Just a friend checking in.

"Yeah, why?" Her words were not reproachful, they did not sting.

"Well, you've been awful quiet ever since Columbia. Since Ian got, you know, accidently shot." He took a sidelong glance to try to read her face. Nothing. A stare out the windshield at a place so far away he didn't think this bus could reach it in their lifetimes.

"Just thinking." She gave him a crooked half-smile. "Does that happen often?" She gently maneuvered the conversation away from where it felt like it was moving. She really didn't want him prying open a past she could not recollect.

"What's that?"

"Ian saving someone's life," now she stared hard into his eyes as she moved the conversation back to Asheville. There was something about the head of this pack that rang familiar. She had known people who were in the business of saving lives. Well, she thought she had.

"It's kind of a poorly kept secret, I guess. It's like a facial tic, something he can't seem to control. It happens more by accident, as I understand it, rather than intent. I think he wishes it would go away," Gabby's expression was one of bemused curiosity. "To me it would be the highest calling one could ask for, but to him it seems a hinderance. He doesn't like the attention that comes with it." He shrugged.

"I guess I get it. Too many people wanting to know what makes you tick. What are the reasons for it? To touch the hem of your gown in worship." Her eyes returned to the moving pavement in the windshield, "Too many eyes prying into what you might not want to reveal." Shit, had she phrased that wrong? Would Gabby now know there were things she didn't want him prying into?

Silence wrapped the two interrupted only by the road slap of tire on concrete transitions. The hum of the road, murmured conversations broken only by outbursts of laughter behind them.

"How long until Little Rock?" Gabby queried the driver.

"Aln't stopping in Little Rock," he said as if it was common knowledge, "bit of a fracas over the show. Folks protesting outside the ballpark and such. Others, who want this concert to continue clashing with those trying to stop it. The honchos decided it wasn't worth anybody getting hurt. This thing is about stepping up to assist others, not about getting beat down."

"That don't seem right." Gabby felt his dander kicking up, "We're supposed to be lifting people out of this kind of stupidity. How could anyone be protesting us using music and our own dime to lift and improve the lives of folks beat down?"

"White nationalists," the black driver almost spit, "they against anything that might show people are all equal. They don't want folks doing nothing that could improve the lives of black and brown folks. Or letting women think they actually equal with these bright bulbs. Stupid. But violence ain't what we're chasing." His eyes never left the road but his words traveled different avenues.

"This is bullshit." Gabby was not settling down. He had seen and lived enough running from this kind of vermin. The kind that thought might gave them the right to run other's lives. "Why didn't Jax and Ian ask the rest of us what we thought ought to be done?"

The buses pulled off the highway in Carlisle, Arkansas. Radio traffic had been fast and furious with the crews and bands wanting to stop to talk while the lords of the gypsies wanted to make time through enemy territory. The masses had won on points, it was time for a meet.

They gathered outside the parked buses and trucks as if circling the wagons before those who lands they were about to usurp were coming a calling. There was murmuring and quiet talk while Ian and Jax stood in the center.

"I'm guessing everyone has discovered that Little Rock is canceled," Ian stated the obvious, "and, apparently there is dissension in the ranks. Why?" A simple way to begin the conversation.

"I don't understand why we are running from inferior beings," the strength of Gabby's words were balanced by the soft tone of his voice.

"They are not inferior beings," Jaxson began, "We cannot fight their hatred and ignorance with our own. Then we are the same."

There were nods at the seeming rightness in his argument.

"But we are not the same," Gabby would not back down. These men had instilled a sense of righteous indignation in him and had nurtured it until it had bloomed into a magnificent flower. "What we propose expands human dignity, lifts those who have been held down for too many generations, reveals the possibility that we are all the same. What they offer is some kind of superiority for some while others wallow in degradation. Not the same. If we allow them their way because they threaten us with violence, we show them that violence is the way to keep others from climbing out of poverty of soul. This is not right."

Now there were vigorous nods and the voices took on an edge. These people had spent a half year giving of themselves to make a point as well as to lift others. Should they back down because of a threat?

"First of all," Ian was firm in his rebuttal, "the ballpark has canceled the show. They have to be concerned with safety for all involved and I, for one, agree with their reasoning. There are a lot of people who could be hurt. Whether our fans refuse to leave the premises or not, there cannot be a show without a venue." Ian wanted them to understand that sometimes events were outside their control. This was one of them. Dennis nodded his heartfelt agreement. He seemed satisfied sanity had finally won out.

"So, we can't even get in the ballpark?" asked Joya.

"No." That sounded like the final word from Ian.

"And yet, you tell us that the people who wanted to come to the show continue to camp outside, is that so?" Raj had been silent since returning to the fold but that had come to a close.

"What? You want to go put a show on for the campers?" Jaxson tried levity, though his words betrayed what his heart told him it wanted.

"Why not? They stayed. They didn't run away and hide." Joya's gaze took in the assembled. "We, peacefully, pull up, unload what we need, and play music, like we always do."

"There is a very good chance someone could get hurt," Ian was serious.

"You mean like stepping in front of a bullet? Or jumping into the ocean to save another? Is this the line, then? White power? Christo fascists? They get the final say?" Joya knew Ian had fallen but she also knew he had taken a bullet meant for her. That was what this tour was about, others.

"You'd better call ahead and alert the media. Maybe if there are cameras and reporters there will be less chance of violence." Jaxson had surrendered, Ian would have to capitulate as well.

Soteria felt a pull in her chest, a strange, unfamiliar tug she had never felt before. She could only assume it was something she'd heard mentioned in conversation, pride.

All climbed back aboard their prescribed buses and settled in for the final forty-minute drive. Ian pulled out his phone and began scrolling through numbers and emails. He was not a happy passenger.

"You wanted this." It was a statement of fact and, though he never raised his gaze from his phone, Jaxson knew exactly whom he was aiming the barb at.

"Maybe," he didn't pretend to be contrite.

"This could get ugly." Ian was not giving one millimeter.

"Look someone has got to stand up to these troglodytes," the smirk on his face gave the truth. He was looking forward to the confrontation. "You can't run from bullies."

"Why did we cancel the gig in the first place then?" Ian glared hard at his friend. "Oh my god, you agreed to cancel just to get this reaction out of the crew!" The revelation was stunning in its audacity.

"I knew there was a possibility," Jax began before Ian could stop him.

"This could be very dangerous," Ian shook his head as he hit the call button. Maggie stared at Jaxson and wondered if she ever truly knew her old friend at all.

Ian had put on concerts throughout the United States, Canada, Europe, South America, and Asia over the last half century, he had contacts in every burgh, town, village, and bus stop across the land. His 'friend' at the local rock station in Little Rock was overjoyed to hear from him and even more so with the plan to put on a free concert in the parking lot of the stadium. They would begin to announce it within ten minutes. He would also alert his friends at the local TV news and in the newspapers that still existed. He was an old hippie type himself and the chance to cause a little good trouble was uplifting.

When the buses and trucks pulled into the parking lot there was a scrum of people yelling at each other, nose to nose and utterance to vociferousness. No one had thrown a punch or there would've been blood but several of the white supremacists were holding axe handles and bats, that was not a good sign.

Nash and Suzette seemed fascinated by the calamity. Old, long-haired, tie-dyed, bearded folks trying to reason with hate. It was interesting. They both strolled over to where the disturbance gave the impression it was centered. Nash stood listening to the verbiage being tossed back and forth like a pickleball tournament. He smiled.

"You think this is funny, Geronimo?" Asked one of the more erudite of the troglodytes. Apparently, Geronimo was the only native he could name.

"I think it is very humorous that you believe yourself superior because your ancestors were afraid of the sun," Nash's tone was light but his eyes were deadly.

The hominid tore his eyes away from Nash's commanding gaze. As if that freed him from his stasis the lowlife grabbed his axe handle with both hands, planted his feet and brought it around to take out the large native. Suzette raised her arm as high at the petite woman could reach and caught the handle before it could make contact with Nash's cranium. She smiled as the nazi attempted to pull it back again though he couldn't break her grip.

"Remember, she's the small one," whispered the cat as he took hold of the axe handle, relieving the pressure on Suzette's arm, and snapped the handle in half.

Nash turned at the gentle touch of a hand on his shoulder. Jaxson nodded to him and stepped between the two men. Suzette stepped back into the scurry of activity as roadies and other assorted crew began unloading a few pieces of equipment from the buses and trucks. This would be strictly an acoustic affair. There was no power in the lot, no stage, no place to set up the lighting. This would be a bare bones, no amplifiers concert.

Chistopher Shakleton looked as though he wanted join the scrum but the touch on his arm from his wife stayed the motion. He hung back to help unload and set up, he still remembered how.

As Jaxson sized the backwoods cave dweller up, he heard Dugie's excited voice calling to Ian.

"I'm an idiot," Dugie said as if there was nothing and no one else to contend with, "We have the buses!" He said it as if it were the greatest revelation in the history of music, though all could see the buses as plain as, well, as plain as the huge buses sitting right behind them.

"And that means what, Lieutenant conspicuous?" Ian was not in the mood for games and he had already run dry in patience.

"We watch tv on the bus. Play music on the bus. Cook meals on the bus." He was attempting to drag Ian along by the significance of what he was trying to get across without actually saying the words.

Ian's fried brain had been flipped too many times today and it was becoming rubbery with the cooking. "And that means what, Dugie? And please use small words and concepts so I can climb onboard and ride with you."

"If we can do all those things, it's because we have transformers and shit throughout the buses. Which means we can run a couple extension cords from bus to the place of music and set up a few amplifiers and a small sound system. This is great!" He was so wrapped in his discovery he had forgotten the white supremacists holding the show hostage.

As Dugie came to his exciting conclusion Jax turned back to the dumbfounded hominid standing in front of him. Jaxson was a musician by trade but a peacemaker by choice. He wanted to turn this into something good, but as he gazed into the vacant wasteland behind the heathen's eyes, he began to doubt his course of action, but in for a penny...

"I'm not sure why you believe what you do," He began his unprepared remarks, "and I don't really care. I will tell you that violence solves nothing. It never has and never will. If you follow the course of history for the past few thousand years, you will note, that violence of any kind, of any scale, has only killed millions but solved nothing. Violence only begets more violence. Once the violence has been abated all boundaries, tribes, land acquisitions, everything goes back to what it was. Your threats of violence to stop the progress of the human species will only result in people getting hurt, some might die, but in the end your kind will lose because what you purport to believe is verifiably wrong." He took a deep breath while the primitive mind of his antagonist worked out all the words.

"Look, we are going to put on a bit of a concert right here in the parking lot." He heard more scurrying, more activity, conversation, and the sound of reporters testing their audio. This really wasn't what he wanted. He had hoped to have this minor crises solved and in the books before the news showed their ugly heads. "You like music, don't you?" Keep it simple, appeal to their primitive understanding. "Well, that is what we are going to do. Now if you would like, you could stick around and listen and enjoy. Or you can start shit in front of all these television cameras, reporters and the nation revealing your true selves as ignorant, backwoods, hilljacks, and idiots. Is that how you want to be seen? How you want your families to be seen? Is this how you would like your ancestors to be seen?"

"Don't much care what outsiders think of me and mine. My grandaddy woulda come down here and stove in a few heads of them coloreds and then started in on y'all," he laughed his ignorance like he was proud and the others joined in the church of stupid.

"And how did your grandaddy fair? He's dead and dust with you being all he left on this world. More trash from trash, filled with hate 'cause the rich man tells you to do so. Yeah, your grandaddy used violence to keep people in line but did they stay in line?"

Jaxson stared the hilljack right in the eye. "Well, did they? Oh, your kin might have had the upper hand for a short time but folks rise up sooner or later and when they do, they're gonna bring a whooping with them. Lotta water's been carried and now the toll is due. So, keep the hatred, the violence against those with less than you and sooner or later your kids and grandkids are going to pay the price. Yeah, real bright. Because as the species evolves what you believe will be bred out of mankind and that means at some point in the future your grandchildren and great grandchildren will judge you and find you wanting." Jaxson let some of that filter through the miasma blocking coherent thought from breaking through the sludge with the hope a thought would move into residence.

"You will find the people of color in this brigade to not only be your equal, but superior to you in their enormous talents. Now, be a nice boy, get out of the way and let us get this show on the road." Jaxson turned his back on the man showing he was not afraid and would honor him with trust. As he did so he almost ran into Chistopher Shackleton who had moved into close proximity in case of need, he could only hold himself back for so long, especially when another musician was putting himself on the line.

Chris took one look at the hilljack who blinked and then rubbed his eyes, as if not believing who he was seeing. Chris tipped his large cowboy hat and shook his head as if embarrassed the guy recognized him. Before 'Billie Jack' could join up with his friends someone in the middle chucked a huge rock at the parked buses and smashed a side window. A few of the road crew made to jump these dumb rednecks when Jaxson pointed a finger then shook his head NO! They quickly went back to work.

"That's going to cost you," Jax pointed again, only this time at the boy he had spoken to.

It was then the police showed up in force.

About time, thought Maggie, shit, how long had these idiots been out here mouthin' at these old hippies just trying to hear some memories and making new ones. Jesus on a ritz, she almost screamed, what the fuck was wrong with these people? She felt Ian wrap her in his right arm and steer her away from her fury.

All You Need Is Love,
A Strong Will, And Patience

The cops separated the two groups, though found it much more difficult to control the one rather than the other. The ancients were pissed! They had come to hear music of peace, love, togetherness, living as one, a celebration of all life. Instead, they ran into a bulldozer of stupid hatred based on centuries of being fed horseshit as if it were caviar. These lowlifes had discovered over the years they loved the taste, just so long as there was someone, anyone—though when that someone was different it made it easier to pick them out to hate—was worse off than them.

"Shove your racism, shove your hate, we came to hear what made us great!" not the most clever slogan ever devised by Madison Avenue but it rhymed and that really was all that mattered. Jaxson grabbed James Nash by the arm to see if they could lower the temperature before this pot exploded. Bonnie and some of the women came to join them in the false hope that these Neanderthals wouldn't attack women. They hadn't considered the fact that to hate filled white trash there wasn't any difference between man, woman, child, elderly person or one with physical or mental challenges, just color. Hate was hate, and it was color specific.

This was going to get completely out of hand, just as Ian had predicted. It was then the music began. Ian would not have been surprised if it had been Chrisopher trying to sooth these savages with his well know tunes. Or if The girls had begun to sing one of their gospel numbers, but it wasn't. It was Bach's Cello Suite No. 1, yes it was a bit hackneyed, but it was known and it was beautiful, hence the reason so many knew it. It was magnificent.

One man, one cello, one abbreviated piece. Ten minutes in the other three classical musicians joined him on the Mendelsohn quartet. God help the human who tried to stop this while Nash was listening. Ian could almost feel the temperature dropping as the people's tempers were pulled back. This might be hunky-dory after all.

As the final strains of the melody were carried softly on the afternoon breeze, another took its place. This was more rockin' in an Appalachian-front-porch- down-home-half-a-jar-gone-while-we-was-tuning up, kind of way. Howie, the guy that Soteria had dragged out of the sea, was standing up top of the crew bus fiddling to beat ten bands.

There are many things in the world that a group of redneck hilljacks can resist, culture, a well-cooked steak, a woman who is intelligent, strong, and won't put up with any shit, but a damn good fiddler ain't one of them. Those who hadn't been converted by the Bach and Mendelsohn were now hopping around the parking lot likes toad on fire. Yeah, it looked like this day might just get saved.

Ian felt a touch on his shoulder, he turned to see a middle-aged man in a blue polo shirt, blue jeans and work boots reaching out a hand that looked like it required shaking.

"Having a show in a parking lot?" The man appeared amused that they would be standing across the street from a perfectly good ballpark and here they were setting up on the blacktop.

"Well, we were supposed to be inside the stadium but then these yahoos showed up threatening to start some shit and the owners and we agreed not to put on the show out of concern for safety. But my crew," and here Ian pointed at the beehive of activity as the music continued while the setup worked around them, "were a bit put out that we would allow the threat of hostility to put a halt to the music. They carry their passion for change and for peace on their chests and in old wounds from the sixties. So, we are going to do an abbreviated show for those who came to celebrate diversity, humanity, and raising those considered lesser from the depths of squalor." Ian could not keep the pride from his tone. He knew this could have led to a melee and injury. He was very proud of his hippie army.

"Good people," the man nodded his approval. "when you are willing to put your ideals, your deeply held beliefs ahead of your own safety, especially in service to others. That says much about your troop." He grinned, "Would you like to use the ballpark?"

Just then the apparent chief of the assembled police and troopers joined the conversation, though not with a welcome. He had a stern bearing and a face not made for smiling, this was not a man to be trifled with.

"They tell me you are the man in charge of this traveling show," with a change in tone it might have come across as a jovial welcome. He did not use the change in tone.

"Yes, Trooper," Ian responded recognizing the tone and the bronze cluster on the man's uniform. He also knew, no matter where in the country you went, when it came to Staties, as he knew them back in his day, every single one of them wished to be referred to as 'Trooper', no other designation was wanted.

"If they continue to play without a permit, I will be forced to arrest every single one of you. No exceptions." Why did these guys always have to come across as hard asses rather than your friendly neighborhood cop on the beat Ian had grown up with? Something in the milk.

"I'm afraid the permit I had is probably no longer any good," Ian threw out hoping that the fact he had one would cut some mustard with this guy.

"I'm afraid not," The Trooper grinned. This sonofabitch was enjoying this! "This is private property and we know that your little show was cancelled this morning. So, no show." He stuck his thumbs in his belt, spread his legs apart, and glowered like he was some kind of gunslinger.

Sheesh, thought the ring master, what an asshole!

"Just curious, Trooper," asked the man who'd let his previously asked question drop when the long arm of the law decided to stick its finger wrist deep in this delicious pudding. "What if we could get the owner of the property's permission to use this space for a little show?"

"That would be up to the owner, though I can't let this thing get out of hand either. We would be inviting the whole state to come and drink wine while breaking other laws," he sniffed the air.

Ian wondered if he would try to bust the entire troop, fans, outsiders, and anyone who reeked of skunk. And who was this other guy?

"Well, I happen to have a scrap of paper stating that these folks had a permit to put on their concert. And it seems that, no matter what you were told, according to the law, this can only be canceled by mutual agreement of both parties." He handed the Trooper a document. "Would you like to cancel our agreement?" He asked Ian.

"As a matter of fact, no, I wouldn't," Ian's questioning gaze elicited a crooked grin from the man and the attractive middle-aged woman, Ian had failed to notice, standing next to him.

"This all seems in order, Mr. Spalding," said the severely disappointed Trooper as he handed the papers back to the gentleman. "No funny business." He poked his finger in the general direction of Ian.

"Spalding, is it?" Ian smiled and a chuckle escaped. "Not any relation to?" He didn't finish knowing the answer.

"Nope, he was just a character in a movie, though one of my favorites, both movie and comic actor," Mr. Spalding added. "Eric." Again, the hand and this time it found welcome contact. "My wife, Ilene." He introduced the lovely woman next to him.

"I'm Ian Sperling, grand master and elephant cleanup man for this circus." He turned his head at the snip at his ear, where he found Maggie had stepped up during the altercation with the policeman to see if she needed to dig bail out of the family purse. "My wife and keeper, Maggie." Hands were shaken, pleasantries exchanged and calm settled.

"So, why involve yourself in this? The show had been canceled," Ian reiterated what the other man obviously knew. "Why piss off your local constabulary?"

"For one, my wife and I are fans of most of your troop. We grew up listening to Mr. Grahm, Mr. Nash, Bonnie Welch, and Stephen Gatos, who we were saddened to hear would not be making the stop. We also don't like being told what to do with our own property." He said as if it were the most natural thing in the world. "Question is, would you rather be inside or out?" He pointed at the beautiful stadium across the street.

"Hang on a sec," Ian had Maggie whistle loudly to get the attention of those whom wished to join them. Which, if the whistle was to be believed was pretty much the entire crew. Ian introduced Jaxson, James, Christopher, and some of the others to the verklempt couple. They, apparently, had never met any of their idols. They were shy, embarrassed, awed, and just so pleased. Ian explained the offer to all within earshot before asking what Dugie and Ben thought of actually setting up the staging and what the bands and performers thought of doing the whole show or a reasonable facsimile.

After much discussion and challenge, Dugie and Ben accepted the goad. The musicians and singers were, of course, on board. And the attendees were all for being closer to beverages, food, and bathrooms. The only group that was put out were the local country folk. They had put away their axe handles and bats with the arrival of the fiddles. They wanted to be a part of the music, if nothing else, but had no tickets.

"You can be my guests," offered Jaxson in his usual conciliatory fashion. "If you help carefully unload and do what Mr. Dugan and Mr. Friedman tell you to do. You would be more than welcome." He winked in the general direction of their troop. Ben and Dugie were not enthusiastic. They really had no desire to babysit.

With the assistance of the locals and the pride of the crew they had everything up and running within just over an hour. It would not be perfect but it would be more of a show than trying this in an unlit parking lot.

The quartet took the stage by five kicking into Mendelsohn to the disappointment of those who had loved the Bach in the lot. Nash stood and they all stood with him, Suzette at his side deep in thought. The barbarians at the gate hooted and hollered their approval of every song the All Girls performed even the ones Joya sang. They especially loved when

Gillian led Cinda, Michelle, Jesse in some Appalachian inspired tunes joined by Bonnie on the last so she could make the smooth transition into her own set. It was beautiful, if a little bumpy. Christopher wowed with a set of a selection of his many hits joined in a trio by Joya and his wife. James played a set of his best-known numbers and then to the delight of all, especially the owners of the park, Stephen Gatos had shown up, unannounced, to play a set with the backing of the choir, the band, and several of Jax's Spanish friends.

Everyone was pumped by the time Jaxson took the stage. His set was a magnificent intertwining of old and new, new takes on old songs with help from the boys from across the ocean, and heartfelt memories. When Gabby came out on the stage the crowd went completely silent. One of the country 'gentlemen' hooted something and was immediately shut down by a look from Nash.

As he slowly made his way to the center microphone the heartbeats began until thousands patted their hearts in unison. Even those unfamiliar with the ritual joined in, carried by the energy of the initiated. He began softly as if afraid he might frighten those who came to fight into flight. He spoke his truth. His people's truth. A truth as old as the Mother herself. He told how there were millions, billions who suffered under the whip of bigotry and intolerance. How entire cultures were held as less than cattle or chickens, worth less than a bag of rice. He spoke quietly but with a steel conviction that moved even the coldest heart. He spoke of his own life and meeting Raj, how they had become dear friends. He spoke of the women in this crew, Soteria, Betty, roadies, of the women who worked the lighting, climbing the trusses and handling the heavy lighting cans, of the singers who traveled hard without complaint. And he welcomed those who had come with open hearts, open minds, and open wallets. Laughter. Welcomed his Native friends, his black and brown, and white friends. And he spoke of extinction. Extinction of species all across the world, the decimation of habitat, of starvation in the oceans and mountains. Of extinction of hope, of worth and a reminder that all are pieces of the same puzzle, that all belonged to the family of life. Mitakuye Oyasin! Ya-hey.

The crowd cheered, threw money and pot in the circulating cans, as the rest of the Untouchable tour came onto the stage. This would be an encore to remember!!

As the crowd filed out of the small ballpark, Ian noticed the group of protestors who had almost shut town this performance. They were such a small percentage of the overall crowd and yet had almost derailed a fantastic day and evening out of hate. They didn't seem to be talking to others or amongst themselves as they made their way to the exits. Ian wondered if any minds had shifted. He itched to go ask. The itch would be scratched.

He noted, as he made his way through the crowd to intercept the small body of white supremacists, that they didn't interact with any of the other participants. They pointedly walked by where Nash stood scrutinizing the mass of people to assure no stupidity would be birthed. Not one acknowledged his presence. They appeared to be avoiding contact with any of the black or brown folks in attendance or the obviously liberated females sauntering and swaying with the music remaining in their minds as they danced towards home.

Ian decided he would not engage, instead tried to get close enough to catch whatever words of astuteness might float by. To be honest, he really didn't care what they thought but he had hopes, if for no other reason than to prove Jaxson right. He heard snippets of tense verbiage about the 'colored girl', (she was pretty good, you know for a... he shut out the rest), a comment or two about that big Indian, though whether the reference was to Gabby or Nash, Ian couldn't tell, again, until they mentioned his 'bullshit speech about people being the same'. Ian sighed. Then he heard one fella say, 'I thought they was all pretty good, even the colored ones', and few of the others grudgingly agreed.

Ah well, Rome didn't conquer the barbarians to the north in an afternoon and neither would they. But culture and civilization did wash across the European continent after a few centuries of blood, death, raping, pillaging, rampant disease, and plague. Oh, and couple of devasting wars involving most of the known world, but things had settled down for the past few decades. So, there was always hope. It was hotel time, rest, and get moving west in the morning.

Opportunities Missed, Opportunities Made

They stayed in Memphis for two days. Izzy had remained in the hospital for the first day and half and was weak and tired when released, so they stayed the next night and the better part of the morning. They all agreed getting her strength back and to some modicum of healthy would be their guiding light.

They, obviously, had missed their chance to go to the concert. More importantly, to try to talk to the organizers of this tour about either joining forces or, at the very least, picking their brains for ideas on how Carrie could proceed with her own plans. Carrie had been disappointed, but only just. She'd never had children, never been around children, didn't have any friends back home who had procreated, but she had taken to these two girls like any favored aunt would. Maybe her exposure over the past half year to the teenaged angst of Aron had mellowed her on the concept.

As she considered her time with him, she was surprised at how much she had come to mother him. Only a dozen years separated them chronologically, and yet she was a mother hen with a baby chick in tow.

He had experienced more in his short life than most of the people in this country would in their entire lives. He had grown in so many ways, mentally, physically, and responsibly. His maturity in many aspects of life revealed that, though in so many other aspects he was puerile and innocent as a child. Her pride was evident in the way she handed him more responsibility for their travel plans and the way she relied on him for his judgment.

The trek through Arkansas was quicker than she had anticipated, it not being a large state like many they had traveled. With warm, sunny conditions, Oklahoma looked to be pleasant as well. That was until she noted the gathering of storm clouds to their west. Kim's retelling of her close call with the tornado in Colorado immediately came to mind.

"Do me a favor and check the radar on your phone to see what the hell we are running into up here," she asked Aron not taking her eyes from the blackening skies.

Aron had been lost in thoughts of Izzy's illness. He hadn't noticed what Carrie had and was about to say something he would've regretted until he saw what she had been watching.

"Shit!" the expletive seemed to hurry his finger taps on the phone. "Looks bad. Heavy rain, wind, thunder, and lightning. Big storm." His fingers continued their dance on the screen of the phone as he changed the focus of his search. "Looks to me like there is a town of some size south of the interstate with some decent options. And from what I'm seeing on the radar, it might be the safer option as well. We are heading directly into the storm on 40 here and it looks to be heading directly at us." His concern was evident in his clipped tone.

Just then Carrie's phone came alive with a loud alarm warning followed quickly by a call from the leading car. "Do you see what I see?" asked Barbara trying her best not to sound frantic.

"Yeah, we're going to get off in a few and head south to…" she glanced over at Aron.

"McAlester." His search continuing while he sought safe harbor. God, what if he fucked up and they wound up in worse danger because he read the radar wrong. Maybe he was leading them directly into the path of this monster.

"McAlester," Carrie repeated into her phone. "get off here at Checotah and head south on 69. Aron says it should take us out of the line of fire. We'll get rooms and hunker down until tomorrow. We have time." She hoped.

Carrie thought she had experienced living on the edge when she escaped her perverted uncle and silent aunt's home, but that only was a precursor to what life held in store. Within the last week she had been faced with a very sick child, plans fluctuating at the speed of life, flying by the seat of their own pants, and now a huge thunderstorm was bearing down on her. Her senses were at their peak and she wanted to scream. She couldn't, of course, with Aron relying on her but she sure felt the urge.

They made the Holiday Inn Express with time to spare. It was a solid looking brick building that had the feel of one who could stand against the end of the world. She hoped that would not be tested.

The woman at the front desk was unperturbed by the impending doom and calmly checked them in. They had plenty of rooms available, did Carrie and company have a preference?

"Yes," Carrie replied, the nervous tension of the past half hour evident in the creases about eyes and mouth. "Somewhere on the first floor, away from windows."

"Hmmm," quoth the desk clerk, " we have plenty of rooms on that floor but all have windows. If you would care to join us in the break-fast room it is well situated away from windows and in the center of the building." How could this woman be so complacent when disaster was knock, knock, knocking at her front door?

After, literally, tossing their suitcases in their rooms all six of the newly arrived ran to the center of the building and the breakfast room. The only things Carrie had pulled together were two bottles of wine from her bag and Oscar. If someone thought he was either staying in the room or in the truck they had another several thousand thinks a-coming. Oscar was her closest, dearest friend and where she went, he went.

There were maybe a dozen other occupants in the closed off area. A few gave Oscar a wary stink-eye but no one said a word. Oscar curled up on the floor with both of the girls using him for a pillow and emotional support.

The storm crashed into the building and windows rattled hard while debris flew and swirled in every direction. Carrie hoped that by parking the vehicles on the leeward side of the building that might protect them from major damage. An unseen, but heard, hodgepodge of metal, wood, and natural debris bounced off the brick, a few windows broke, a metal sign died screaming for release from the pole holding it hostage. Then, just as quickly, everything was silent.

Slowly, first the desk clerk, then the maintenance man, and finally several of the guests began to make their way into the lobby before heading out front to assess the damage. Sunlight streamed where darkness had held sway. If it weren't for the scattered detritus of a few folk's lives strewn about, one would've believed it to be a beautiful late spring/early summer day. Carrie, Oscar, and Aron joined the inspection tour while Barbara took the girls to their room to rest. The stress had not been good for either child but had affected Phoebe the hardest. Barbara didn't know why, the child had experienced Nor'easters and left-over hurricanes, this wasn't near as bad. It had lasted but moments and it was gone. Storms on the Atlantic coast could last days, with high winds, rain, snow, sleet and no mail delivery, no matter what they claimed.

There were a few scratches and minor, hardly noticeable dents in each vehicle—probably from hail, one man suggested—but nothing to slow their progress. Just two very tired, worn out, frightened girls, a mother at her wits end, and Carrie and Aron trying to hold the whole thing together.

Damn, this was stressful! It was one thing when it was just her, Aron, and Oscar, she'd always felt they could handle about anything. They were a little tight knit support group, but that was then; this was now. They had the lives of others, a good woman and her children, to consider. Carrie had to take them into her deliberations and slow her ass down. They would stay the night, regroup, and see where tomorrow would lead. And they would keep a much closer eye on the weather and radar!

They brown bagged dinner from one of the fast-food joints up the road. Well, from a couple of them actually, as each girl had a favorite,

Aron had never had a Culver's hamburger, Carrie and Barbara wanted chicken. So, they split up, ferreting out the wants and needs of each. After the events of the day Carrie and Barbara decided each should be allowed anything they wanted; and they wanted some more wine!

The morning was filled with birdsong, the sound of insects buzzing, life. This would be a good day, bet on it. As they loaded up their vehicles, they noted the desk clerk from yesterday was carrying a couple baskets of yummies out to her own car as if heading out for a picnic. Two bottles of wine peeked their heads out of one basket while the scent of roasted chicken wafted from the other.

"Going out to enjoy life?" Asked Carrie with great understanding. Aron looked up from where he was tying down a recently purchased tarp over their possessions in the bed of the truck.

"There's this concert in Oklahoma City later this afternoon that I had been hankering to go to but couldn't get tickets. My sister called after the storm yesterday and said one of their group had bowed out, so I get to go!" She giggled and squealed like a prepubescent child going to hear Donnie Osmond and Justin Bieber, something Carrie had never quite grokked, but to each their own.

"What concert?" asked Aron.

"Bunch of old hippie songwriters and singers. They're raising money and awareness for people who have been shit on for thousands of years and they want to do something to lift them out of depravity." Her grin lit up the parking lot brighter than the morning sun.

Carrie didn't think the woman quite understood what the tour was about but she didn't care. These were the guys they had hoped to run into in Memphis and they each had caught up with each other. It would appear the great hurdle would be in scoring tickets for the show. From what this woman said the show was sold out, had been for some time, tickets would be almost impossible to obtain. All they could do was show up and pray to the great ticket god in the sky and offer stupid amounts of money to get in.

Packed up, loaded and wheels turning they headed back north to the freeway. The sooner they could get into Oklahoma City the better chance they had of attaining entrance.

They were shocked to see the destruction left behind by the storm. According to the weather guys on the local channel there had not been a tornado but there had been powerful straight-line winds causing significant damage. Trees were down, power lines were down, though not where they were. Some homes and businesses were damaged but all in all it had been a minor storm compared to what could have been.

Back out on Interstate 40 traffic was stop and go as people did their best to avoid debris scattered along the road. Carrie, attempting to avoid any kind of fender-bender with the gamboling traffic, failed to notice the wooden planks on her side of the road until it was too late. She ran several over. Hoping against hope turned out to be futile. She could feel the air leaking rapidly out of the two passenger side tires. Shit! She pulled over onto the shoulder to inspect the damage. Barbara paying attention to everything and everyone around her saw Carrie's truck on the shoulder and pulled over fifty yards ahead of her.

Two flats. Two fucking flats. No one carries two spare tires. They were fucked. No way were they going to make it to the show or anywhere for the time being. Shit!

Aron offered to jack the truck up, but Carrie reminded him it would do no good. They required two tires and they only had the one behind the driver's side, between the door and the wheel well. They would just have to sit and wait on AAA to come and rescue them. The day was warm, if a bit humid from the left-over excess of the previous days storm, though not unpleasant.

Most people flew by, traffic picking up as the debris got knocked off the road. She couldn't fault them, they had sat in stopped traffic and slow stop and go for an hour, or so it felt. A couple of good Samaritans pulled over to check on the women and kids marooned on the shoulder but they couldn't do more than offer their condolences and a phone. The group had phones but they appreciated the commiserations. Carrie patiently explained that AAA was on their way but it was going to take some time as they had to bring a truck with a tire machine on the back to change the tires. The chance anyone would have wheels for a '48 Ford pickup were nonexistent. Patience was required, though patience forced does not patience make.

The squatter's attention was drawn to the east where the sound of beeping horns, blasts from air horns, and general commotion could be heard approaching. What the hell? It sounded like a parade was moving at highway speeds in their direction. None had ever heard of a parade progressing at highway paces.

The parade came into view. There were a half dozen buses and a couple small semis surrounded by cars and trucks waving, tooting, screaming, and making fools of themselves while almost causing major devastation. As the first bus passed them, they could see the faces of the occupants staring at their predicament and pointing at the children.

The second bus slowed for a better look. The third bus had several of the husky appearing gents taking pictures of Carrie's truck with their cell phones. The fourth bus had no audience at all and the sixth bus slowed and pulled over in front of Carrie's disabled vehicle.

As the door whooshed open a large exotic appearing gentleman with long tan hair exited and in smooth fluid motion headed over to where the six of them hunkered down in the grass. Oscar growled deep in his throat, not loud, more a warning, yet the man continued to close the distance. He was whispering something none of them could hear though it showed signs of calming Oscar. Interesting, thought Oscar's best friend.

He was followed by a beautiful chocolate brown petite woman of native descent if Carrie was any judge of such things. The man following her and the woman with him were an odd match. He had the look of South America or Mexico or, well, she hadn't a clue, but the woman was attractive in a Mediterranean way.

Well, she may not have recognized the first who disembarked but she certainly knew who Jaxson Grahm was, followed by James Nash, Bonnie Welch, and a late-middle aged guy who smiled their way, though gave off the aura of a man who would rather be moving.

"Broke down?" Asked the tan haired man. Who had tan hair?

"Flat tires," she responded, "there was a ton of debris on the road from the storm yesterday. Guess I ran over some I shouldn't've." She glanced at the flat tires.

He walked over and without a word lifted the back of the truck off the ground with one hand while slowly spinning the tire with his other. Carrie's shocked expression along with the same on four other faces caught the dark woman's eye. She cleared her throat, the man squinted in her direction where she was subtly shaking her head gesturing 'no' and he set the truck back on the ground.

He held up a nail pulled from the tread of her tire so all could see the culprit, ignoring the stunned faces gaping at him.

"Triple A is on their way, though it might be a few before they arrive. I'm told the eastbound traffic is backed up worse than it is here." Carrie sounded apologetic that they had stopped for naught.

"We'll wait with you," the elderly man appeared put out, but his heart didn't care. He was a decent sort or so his wife kept telling him.

Barbara stood by, holding Izzy and Phoebe close to her as she had at first sight of the large native with tan hair. Now she began sobbing for no apparent reason. As the intensity of her break down increased Carrie came over to hold her, no words, no other action, just human to human touch, while the rest of the contingent stood helplessly, powerlessly watching. Until Jaxson came up and wrapped them both in his arms, he being the one most used to this kind of reaction when in close proximity to women.

Finally settling down, Barbara began to apologize profusely and without cease while the assembled assured her it was alright. Carrie explained they had been through so much over the past few weeks or months or years but could not do their travails justice. She needn't have tried. All here had gazed over the edge of madness at some point, they could sense Barbara had slipped a little closer with all that had taken place over the past twenty-four.

"I've got an idea," suggested Maggie, "why don't these folks ride with us on the bus?"

"What about the vehicles?" Asked Aron. "we can't just leave them on the side of the road."

"Dugie! Could you step out of the bus, please?" Ian hollered through the open bus door.

Mr. Dugan had chosen to remain on the bus, as whatever was happening outside had nothing to do with the show or his duty to assure all connected with it were being taken care of. He had been revamping the stage plot and thinking of changing the lineup for Oklahoma City. Always the working man.

"Yeah, Ian, what's up?" Still distracted by his cyphering and chess plotting he seemed groggy but present.

"I want you to drive the vehicle for this nice family while they ride with us in the bus. It will provide you with time alone to think through your pursuit of perfection for the stage without anyone to bother you." He turned to take in Barbara and the kids, "would that be alright with you? We have munchies and soda and such on the bus. Some folks even sing while we drive." He smiled.

"That isn't necessary, but how can we turn you down," Barbara was now completely composed and well within her teen fandom for the pretty Mr. Grahm.

"That leaves us and the truck," Aron was in protection mode for both the truck and Carrie and, of course, Oscar who still kept a wary eye on the large native with the tan hair.

"How's about you and the dog," began Nash.

"Oscar." Aron and Carrie said in unison.

"How about you and Oscar ride on the bus to keep the family company and I'll stay with the woman until the repair person comes. We can then ride into town together." Nash did not take his eyes off the dog or the boy.

Aron was about to protest when Carrie stepped in, "I'm certain I will be quite safe in the company of...?"

"Nash," answered the small brown woman, " and yes, there could be no safer person to place yourself in the protection of than he. He is of unquestioned honor. If he gives his word he will die before breaking that vow."

"Nash, I am Carrie. Do you promise, then, to take care of me and bring me to my friends once the truck is repaired?"

He bowed his head in solemn affirmation.

"Settled, then. We'll see you in Oklahoma City. Where, is the question," Carrie thought she should have a point of reference, a place to meet up.

"How about at Chickasaw Bricktown Ballpark?" Suggested Maggie.

All Good things Come To Those Who Wait, And Wait

They sat on the gate on the back of the bed of the truck. The sound of traffic buzzing by at seventy-five miles an hour droning into background noise, then soon settling into the thrum of nature. She would have thought that nature would be drowned out, instead nature found a way to sooth through the noise of man.

She thought she should engage this quiet overpowering presence in conversation, small talk to pass the time yet every time a question formed in her mind it dissipated like mist beneath a hot sun. She found the silence opened her up to listening to the quiet vibrations of life. Bird song, the buzz of insects, croak of a frog somewhere to their right, the breeze passing through leaf and limb, her own thoughts. It was refreshing and impressive.

Aron had not wanted to leave her here with a complete stranger, no matter he had ridden in with the rest of this eminent company. He was in protect mode which filled her with a love for him that only a 'mom' could experience. She had finally convinced him that Oscar needed him. The big dog was not comfortable around strangers and would be calmer and mellower around these well-known artists if Aron were with him. He had reluctantly agreed. Oscar stared out the window directly at her as the bus pulled away.

Now, here she sat with this large native. Swathed in the beauty of the day and without a hint of threat. He sat like a boulder on the side of a mountain gazing across the rolling hills of Oklahoma. He had a sense of permanence she couldn't quite express. even to herself. She sensed no menace, just peace. It was as if he was not part of this world or not completely. Otherworldly, that was the word, as if inhabiting two planes at once.

Her meandering thoughts were cut short by the arrival of the mechanic with the automotive repair shop on the back of his truck. He was polite, if quiet, though wary of the big Indian. He worked with precision, removing one tire from the truck, laying it on the tire machine, using a flat iron bar to remove the punctured tire then flipping the same bar over to put the new tire on the rim. It was simple but ingenious the way one came off and the other on and the next thing you knew you were riding on all four wheels again. She had never actually watched the process before and neither had Nash, judging by how intently he studied the procedure.

Done, signed, paid, tipped and back on the road. The wind whipped their hair through the open windows as they plowed down the highway in the right lane while those in a greater hurry passed them by. They would meet the others at the ballpark. It struck like a wet fish to the side of her head. They were meeting these musical notables at the ballpark, the ballpark where the concert was taking place. They were going to the show after all and she could possibly get her chance to pick some brains in the course of events. Kismet indeed!

"Have you worked with Ian, Jaxson and them long?" She at long last found her question and her voice.

"I don't work for them or anyone except the Mother and my family." He never took his eyes off the passing landscape as if answering to the wind.

It was an interesting way to phrase his answer, thought Carrie. So, he must work a family business in which his mother was the matriarch. "Nash. Is that your first name or last?" Maybe a small pry bar was required.

"It is just my name. I am named for my people." This was going to a be very long forty-minute drive.

Before she could ask, he explained, "My name is Nashdoitsoh, it is Navajo. To the Cheyenne I am Nanose'hame, my Lakota people call me igmu'watogla. In Ojibwe my name sounds like bagwagi-gaazhag. Humans can never seem to agree on the simplest things. I answer to all." This time he turned his head so she could look into his eyes rather than at his tan ponytail.

Carrie was lost, if only for a moment, in the depths of time and space. She could see the forming of the new age of mammals, millions of years were encased in that look, time meant nothing. She thought she might fall forever into the birthing stars in the sky until she jerked back to reality and the road in front of her.

"You have known much pain, suffering and great joy," his words rode the wind gusting through the windows. "Now you seek to join forces with others to lessen the suffering of others. That is a greathearted gesture. We seek the same." His words were approving though cautious. Was he concerned she thought to horn in on whatever he was attempting to accomplish?

"You wish to join with the tour?" she wanted some kind of clarification.

"We wish to join with their crusade, though to expand it to much more than what they see. We wish to open their eyes to a much grander vision." He took long, slow, cleansing breaths as if he had said more than he intended though he was tired of keeping his own counsel.

Carrie stewed in her silence. She had asked he had answered. Whether she liked the answer was not his concern. It would seem she was not the only one who had the idea of joining forces with this troop of do-gooders. And he had arrived first, he would have first dibs on the asking. She would have to back-off. She could still ask questions and advice, that wouldn't be stepping on toes.

"You keep saying 'we', are you part of a group? Or maybe a movement? Environmentalists? Animal sanctuaries? What?" she knew she was prying but she had to know who else was interested in joining up with this circus to save humanity.

"Yes." He spoke.

"Yes, what?" Confusion made its second entrance in the play.

"All of that and more. It is what the Mother asks or maybe I would just worry about my own, but Mitakuye Oyasin."

"Mita what ya?"

"Mitakuye Oyasin, it means we are all related. You cannot separate one from another, we are all part of the puzzle of life." He watched the exits going by, "I think you want to go down that road." He pointed at the exit sign.

Carrie had a thousand questions bubbling and burbling at the back of her head, they would have to wait. What she had to do right now was pay attention to the signs and the road. She desperately wanted to be reunited with her family, to assure herself that Barbara, the kids, Aron, and Oscar were fine.

They saw the buses, trucks, and Barbara's car in a fenced in area behind the stadium, Carrie made a beeline for the lot figuring someone would have given security a heads up that they were coming.

They had been forgotten; she could tell by the look on the large, overweight man's face as he scowled his way over to her truck. He appeared about to chastise until he glanced at the passenger side and caught Nash's eye. Immediately he backed down and turned to open the gate.

"Someday I would like you to teach me how to do that." She didn't have to say what, his smile told her he knew.

"I don't think you would live long enough to learn," he did not say it to demean. She could learn, but it had taken him centuries and he didn't believe she would last that long. Their kind seldom did.

Carrie thought the response arrogant but let it slide. There was an ethereal quality to this Nash fellow and though she didn't believe in spirits, ghosts, magic, or supernatural mumbo jumbo mojo stuff, he made her question her certainty.

They parked the truck and were greeted by hugs, kisses, a few licks to the face, courtesy of Oscar and a growl for Nash, handshakes, and relief from the overwrought Aron. She assured all they'd had nothing to fret over, as she was in the capable care of Nash.

"Thank you for watching over me and for the gift of pure silence." She couldn't say why but deep down she knew he was responsible. "I would love to speak with you again about what you are attempting to do for your people. Maybe we can all join forces, create something much larger and more encompassing than what one or two can accomplish."

"That would be advisable," he bowed his head in acknowledgement. They would continue their talk.

He turned to go find Suzette and pass on some thoughts he believed should be shared with Bear and company; and soon. His thoughts and motion were interrupted by screams. Something was happening out front, something not especially good.

Nash arrived seconds before Jaxson, Ian, Joya, Maggie, Carrie, and Barbara to see one of the light crew dangling by an ankle from the main truss. He was laughing maniacally and the glazed eyes and vacant expression told Ian everything he needed to know. Howie, he of the rip tide Howie and unsteady gait on the bus, hung by his one good leg from the truss.

Nash made to rush up the support to where Howie dangled thirty feet from the ground but Suzette's hand on his shoulder stayed him where he stood. She pointed to the other support opposite them where Soteria was already several feet from the cross truss. She grabbed the metal skeleton and began swinging hand over hand like Tarzan of the jungle until she had reached where Howie swung upside down, as if he hadn't a care in the world. She used her legs to create momentum until she could swing herself up onto the cross truss and lay along the length providing herself steady purchase while she reached down, grabbed Howie by the safety belt cinched at his waist and, seemingly without effort, pulled him up enough to free his ankle. She then used the safety line to slowly lower him to the stage. With her right hand she lowered herself over the truss where she could again use her legs for momentum and swing herself free, performing a double flip and landing softly on her feet.

She ran over to where Howie was laying on the stage laughing hysterically, his pulse pounding so hard she could see the veins in his forehead dancing. The pupils of his eyes were dilated to the size of dinner plates and he was sweating profusely.

Ian stared at the woman. Shit! Everyone stared at the woman, even Nash. Though his gaze was one of admiration and burgeoning knowledge. This was no ordinary woman; she was no ordinary human. Just as the Ian man was no ordinary human. Yes, they required a meet with Bear and the People soon.

A hush had fallen over the entirety of the crew. Ian was awestruck, befuddled, and quite uncharacteristically speechless. He felt Maggie's arm around his shoulder though whether it had been placed to stop any accidental lifesaving on his part or as a sign of hope that the resurrectional epoch of his life had come to a close, he neither knew nor cared. There was something extraordinary about this woman and he intended to find out what.

Before anyone could find their voice, she straightened up and sheepishly took in every single one of them. "I was a gymnast in high school, placed third at state. Then did a little time with Circus Vargas. We need to get Howie to a doctor," she rushed the statement as if it might erase everything that had been witnessed over the past several minutes.

What had she done? And how had she done it? Again, the missing years. Her body acted of its own volition. A reflexive action taken due to circumstance. The question was, where had she learned to do these things and why didn't she remember? Where did the gymnast story even come from?

Ian understood her reticence to accept recognition or accolades, she didn't give off the feeling she knew what she was doing at the time; just reacting to happenstance. Her eyes were wild with shock at what she had done, again.

"Alright, this show's over and we have another to put on. Let's get up and running. Someone take Howie to his bus and keep an eye on him. I want to know what he's on. Who gave it to him? And why the one main rule for this tour has been shattered. You all know one of the main causes of tours being clusterfucks is drug use. We all agreed pot, alcohol but no hard drugs. Fuck!" His frustration oozed from every pore.

No one said a word, no denials, no protestations of innocence, no excuses, someone had fucked up big time and their tour, this tour of tours, was in jeopardy.

All Ian could think of was, someone or some entity was fucking with his show and he didn't appreciate it. Every single person connected with this show knew how important it was not to bring, do, have any hard narcotics. Most of the crew and many of the performers had had to lift themselves from the depths of an addicted life. He couldn't shake the feeling that Howie had been the victim of a drugging. But why and who? He hated mysteries.

Fame giggled like a schoolgirl.

"What did you do?" Fate was becoming more irritated with each intrusion, each interference on lives Fame put in motion. It was one thing to assist those who asked, it was quite another kettle of beef stew to actively interfere with humans lives when they were innocent or desired none of the offered 'blessings'.

"Oh, nothing he wouldn't have done himself given the opportunity," a coquettish smirk and pretense of innocence. "For Zeus' sake, these people have done enough psychedelics and hard drugs to kill a bull elephant. He can handle it! And look how they now regard their new savior!" Her dismissal of humans as playthings disgusted Fate.

That was not their job as goddesses! They were to love and care for humans, to watch over them, give them blessings, when deserved, and punish only when justified.

"The man had a drug problem for years and you fucked with his sobriety. I will not stand idly by while you destroy a life just to appease your fragile and bruised ego." Fame had had enough. "And why her? She doesn't remember who she is, though now I do, minor though she might be, she is still one of us!" Now Fate's dander was really up. How had Fame brought the girl into her machinations? She had been missing for a century or more and she just shows up? At this moment in time? It was past time she brought Fate a little reminder of who she fucked with.

"And what do you think you can do about it?" This little bitch needed a good comeuppance.

"Nothing I can do. Though I think Nemesis might like to know what you've been up to," Fate knew Fame and Nemesis had walked a very rocky road in the past. Nemesis always had the upper hand.

"OK, point made, no more preemptive meddling." Fame was pouty though Fate knew it wouldn't last long, she would have to keep an eye on her sister. And protect the unaware amnesiac.

Putting Both Feet In The Water

Carrie, Aron, and Barbara were somewhat verklempt at the reaction the lifesaving had evoked. None of them had been to a music festival, or in Barbara's case not in a very long time, but they'd seen highwire acts and such on the tube. This didn't seem that much different, not realizing the acts they had seen on tv were well rehearsed and timed precisely. What they had witnessed was spontaneity. Still, it had been exciting and promised a wonderful show later in the day if this was the precursor, though a more ardent response seemed in order.

The backstage and front of the house, (they were to learn quickly was the term for out there) were hives of activity, as the roadies and specialty crews continued their work. The big stuff, as Aron referred to it, the PA and stage and such had been brought in from local sources so all the tour techies had to do was set up the drum, keys, amplifiers, microphones, lights, monitors, run cables, to the defined 'boards' and make sure every 'i' was dotted and each 't' crossed. Nothing to it.

While all that was taking place Ian, the presumed head of this troop, as he seemed to have no other discernible position—he was not a musician or one who did any of the heavy lifting or hauling of things— walked about inspecting and checking things off a list. Jaxson sat at a table in the commissary area, another term for place to eat, playing guitar and a small portable key board, practicing. Apparently, to limber up fingers and vocal cords. Everyone seemed to have a specific job and they went about it intently.

Carrie wanted to talk to someone to see what they had accomplished thus far and what they hoped to do in the future. She had to determine if her plans might possibly be incorporated or if she should chuck her ideas and come join the band. But everybody was too busy.

At long last the little Indian, from India not here, finished helping the large South/Central American looking fellow setting up amplifiers and came to sit down, loaded with a ream of papers. She found the two an interesting twosome, a Mutt and Jeff, mismatched team. It was possible this man might have some idea of what was and would be taking place with their enterprise. It appeared every single person working here was heavily invested in whatever it was they wished to accomplish, he would be no different. She slid down the bench they both occupied until she could tear his attention away from his papers.

"Excuse me," she cleared her throat to assure his attention was on her not the numbers in front of him.

"Yes," though sounding slightly peeved at the interruption, he almost appeared relieved to have the distraction.

"I am attempting to determine what it is you all are attempting to accomplish here. I mean, I know you are readying a show for the people lined up out front but the purpose, the mission of this tour, I can't quite grasp what it is that you hope to achieve." She was stumbling through whatever question she was trying to verbalize and just butchering it into ground chuck.

"Raj." He held out his hand in greeting though his smile was welcome enough. "You have found yourself the appropriate Untouchable, I am thinking." The capitalization was evident in the intonation. "I am the one who sends out the checks and checks out what he sends."

"Carrie." Hands were shaken and nods were given. "I guess I want understand what it is that you hope to accomplish." She simplified the thought.

"Are accomplishing," Raj corrected with a glimmer of whimsey in his eyes, "We are already accomplishing much. Some of it up on the Pine

Ridge Reservation in partnership with the Lakota people. We supply the money and know how; they supply the ideas and labor. This way we don't just throw money at a problem, we try to also provide the solutions. Such as training in a trade, education in fields that a person is interested in and will translate into a good paying job when they graduate. The idea is to lift people by allowing them to find pride in themselves and worth in their lives." It was a recitation of something he had told many times. He tried not to make it sound like it was by rote but when a phase or explanation has been repeated so many times it is hard not to make it sound so.

"But how does that help them out of despondency, addictions to alcohol or drugs or whatever?" Carrie was trying to take this grand plan and form fit it to her own. "What about those left by the side of a dirt path or tossed aside like garbage. Or those who, through no fault of their own, find themselves lost and alone on the streets and too young to know what they need?" She, of course, was thinking of her own life and that of Aron. "What about those who flee a horrible, dangerous situation and find themselves without funds or any kind of support; financial, emotional, or psychological, only disparaged by a society that wants to define them?" The sheer scope of what she, herself, was attempting caught up to her and threatened to swallow her whole.

"Whoa, whoa." Raj held up both hands as if keeping an attacking enemy at bay, though he knew she wasn't attacking only drowning in her own queries and begging for a life raft. "We ask."

She stared at him as if he had stated something so simple it was brilliant or so dumb she couldn't believe she was bothering to talk to the man.

"It is really quite simple and the brilliant idea of my dear friend and coworker, Gabby." He pointed at the large man whose ethnicity remained a secret to her. "Mayan," he responded to the continually unasked question of Gabby's heritage. People were constantly mystified by his heritage. "We were up in Rapid City and being questioned by some of the Lakota as to our intentions. What we planned on doing with all the money we were raising. Mr. Jaxson," here he pointed at the man Carrie knew to be one of the most brilliant songwriters of past half century, as Dennis had drilled into other head, "Began to explain to the head of the native contingent what they, the musicians, were going to do to help the poor, indigenous people. Yet he had no idea what they might require. That was when Gabby simply asked the man what they needed. You would have thought the sky opened and the brilliance of enlightenment shone down on all of us. To be honest we really hadn't thought quite that far ahead. We thought we knew what was needed. Gabby did. People needed to be asked what they required, not told what we would do." His laughter was delightful and contagious. They sat on the picnic bench laughing for several moments before catching breath.

Jaxson seeing and hearing couldn't help but come over and inquire as to what the joke might be. "I was telling her of our learning to ask what each people required to help themselves."

"Yeah, that was an eye opener," the musician shook his head at his own foolishness, "We thought we would just come in and start building schools or community centers and be done. Boy, were we ever wrong. It was a good learning experience." He had to laugh at the arrogance of the do-gooder class, himself included.

"Did it bother you?" she asked, "That they told you they didn't want what you were offering?"

"Not once I got my ego in check. See, I had to learn that I had no idea what was needed to make their lives better for them. I only knew what I thought they could use. That was a hard pill to swallow. Nobody likes to look in the mirror and have their flaws, warts and boils revealed. Especially when you think you are such a fine example to others, only to find out you are only a fine example to you. We all have ego and arrogance; it is whether you can keep them both in check that counts." Jaxson shrugged at his own impotence and smiled at his education. "Raj helping you out here, is he? He's a very good man." He shook Raj's shoulder as a sign of affection. "Aren't you the one with the truck?" She nodded. "We aren't holding you up by bringing you here, are we? Do you have somewhere you had to be?" Now he was concerned, they were making the same mistakes again, deciding what was best for others.

"Actually, we were on our way here to listen to music, ideas, ways to make life better for others. I guess to meet you, and we have!" she laughed though a few tears found their way past the barrier she had put in place.

"Dugie," here he reached over and grabbed the man who had driven Barbara's car here, "will get you set up with laminates and full access. If you need anything, tell us and we'll do our best to answer questions, get you what you might need, help in anyway." He grinned as he strolled back to his guitar and began singing a lovely song to her.

As the next question she had for Raj arrived at the tip of her tongue and made ready to dive, her thought was interrupted by the Ian guy ambulating through the backstage area and in a loud voice announcing, "Fifteen until show! Fifteen until show! We start on time or we don't start at all. Please be ready for your time slot, schedules are posted every three feet so there is no reason for tardiness. Miss your call, miss your spot." That's the guy she had to talk to.

"Excuse me, may I have a few words," she tugged at his sleeve.

The look in his eyes was darker than the storm gathering in the sky yesterday. An error in judgment had been made. "After the show, on the bus, not now." And he walked toward the stage.

As people scurried gathering instruments and whatall they needed to perform, Carrie was surprised to hear the strains of classical music. At first, she thought she was hearing things, or that someone had a radio on somewhere and was about to get a comeuppance, before she realized it was coming from the stage. It was beautiful.

She made her way around the side of the stage to get a better view and a sound understanding of what her ears delighted in. She eased around the corner of the stage to see four people seated on the stage playing the most beautiful music she had ever heard. Carrie had never heard live classical music, a concert, only having Dennis try to shove it down her throat via recordings. It was so much better live.

And, apparently, she was not the only one affected this way. Most of those assembled were standing, swaying, eyes closed to block out any distractions, heads tilted to the sky as if in prayer. And there, not forty feet from the stage stood the big, tall, tan haired native, Nash, tears running down both cheeks in a state of euphoria unless she was much mistaken. She had so much to learn.

As the music faded to silence the intimacy of the mood was on the threshold of breaking when the most wonderful sound of five voices and an acoustic guitar eased itself into the gap, strengthening and massaging the overall ambiance in the stadium. Carrie thought she might weep.

"Beautiful, isn't it?" Asked Nash from so close she thought he might be touching her. Where had he come from? Had she been so wrapped, so enthralled in the music she was oblivious to her surroundings? Yes.

"It is magnificent." It was all she had.

"We can slip in the back and talk, if you wish. You can still hear the music," he threw her a bone to entice. "My friend would like to meet you."

The very pretty, small, brown woman was sitting on the bench that just a few minutes ago had been occupied by Carrie and Raj. She was either deep in thought, deep in sleep, or deep in the music, no matter which Carrie was uneasy breaking the trance.

She had no need to worry. As she and Nash approached the woman opened her eyes and lit up the already bright day with her welcoming smile.

"I understand we may share common interest." Carrie blurted without preamble, as she petted Oscar's head, who had finally discovered where his best friend had gotten to and was delighted to have found her. Though he was leery of the company she kept.

"So, Nash apprises me," Suzette patted the seat next at the edge of the bench to indicate where Carrie should sit. Nash took the seat across the table. Oscar sat next to his friend. "You wish to heal humans lost, abandoned, hurt, and mistreated, is that right?"

What a weird way to put it, ran through Carrie's mind like a flash of warning? Was this woman saying either she or Nash were not human, which Carrie could obviously see was not true. Or was she saying more needed to be done as far as saving and treating, again, who?

"I guess, yes. There are thousands, if not millions of children thrown away, living on the streets, either because the parents don't like who or what they are sexually, idealistically, or because of addiction. And speaking of addiction there are parents who can't deal with kids because of their own addiction. Women and children beaten by an abusive husband and father, now running for their lives with no safe harbor. So many needs, and very little help, just jail or forced rehab, which doesn't work." Her hand never left the top of Oscar's head, petting and stroking as if for both their comfort.

"You love your dog." It was a statement not a question.

"He is not just a dog, he is my best friend, my confidant. He consoles me, loves me, and is always there for me. Unconditional love is the greatest gift any being can bestow upon another." Carrie stated the evident.

"Would you do for him what you propose to do for humans you have never met?" Suzette was going exactly where she planned, Carrie was following without seeing.

"That and more," proclaimed the closest companion.

"Then we have common cause. I would like to talk more, to plumb the depths of what we can accomplish but it is my, and my friends," and here Carrie felt she was including many more than present company, "belief that we should all work together, to join forces and help each other. We believe stridently that one plus one plus one would equal one billion, four hundred and thirty-two million, six hundred and seventeen thousand five hundred and four in this case. Of course, that is just a guesstimate, I would have to work the numbers to be certain." She smirked.

Was this woman mocking Carrie? She couldn't tell. Though if there was a chance they could assist each other, Carrie would be foolish not to join with them.

The music was increasing in volume which meant they would have had to continue this later anyway. Carrie would have to beg Ian and Jaxson to remain in their tribe for a few days if she was to have any possibility of learning what she didn't know, what they knew, and how to know what there was to know.

There Are, Actually, More Than A Billion Questions

Carrie had had a great meet with the musicians, crew, and Ian after the show. She had sketched out as quickly as she could her vision. She wanted their input. All they wanted was bed after a long hard day of setup, tear down, and concert in between. She told of her life, her love of Kim, their short time together and what she wanted to do with all of her death money. Which was how she continued to think of her wealth. She was well aware she couldn't change the world, not all the cash in the world could change it. She just wanted to make her dent in the inequities and prejudices. She couldn't cure addiction or abandonment, or abusive mates, but she could do something. She laid open her life, her dreams, and her faults before them like a gutted fish.

They knew, to the heart and soul they knew, each and every one of them. They hadn't had her financial good fortune, as they thought of it, but they certainly had had their share of misfortune. Bad homes, bad relationships, stupid decisions, drugs, alcohol, you name it, they brought it. And they knew of her desire now to bring some light into others darkness. Wasn't that exactly what they were attempting to do?

They welcomed her into the pack and promised to listen to her outlandish ideas, then honestly critique or add more outlandishness to the pile. Want to know how to help an addict? Ask one. Want to know how to get away from abuse? Ask someone who had run through the broken glass. It was simple and all credited Gabby with the concept. One that most had never considered.

Jeanette asked if she could write about Carrie and Barbara, the kids, Aron and Kim, with aliases, of course, and no extremely personal information.

The family wanted to have a private clambake where they could discuss among themselves without hurting any feelings. Aron was the most supportive of the idea. If he could share his families name, his sister, his mom, and dad, it would keep them alive if just for a news cycle. He had nothing to be shamed by, he had suffered and survived. He was probably the most balanced and, seemingly, strong, and confident of them all.

As long as no one looked too closely. Aron wanted his past preserved, that was true. He wanted people to know about his home, his life, and how he had fallen through the cracks to a place where only one do-gooder could find him. All those who claimed they stood with the homeless, the forgotten, the down and outers, had failed to notice a kid living next to a dumpster in one of the richest places in the country. Had failed to notice his filthy condition, unless it meant they could judge him and be disgusted by him.

He shook off the anger, the pain. He wanted this and hoped the others would agree. Carrie was on the fence, he could tell. Her life had been almost as horrible as his and could have been worse but for the love and guidance of her angel, Dennis.

Though he had to consider what this would bring to the fore. He had come from, not a good or bad home, one with great troubles, but one with love as well. Through no fault or action of his own he wound up like tumble weed blowing across the land, trying to forget, until he stuck on a rock in Park City.

He might've died there without the intercession of one whacky woman and her dog. She had lifted him from the pile of refuse he had settled into and brought him on an adventure he couldn't have imagined. Traveling across the country, seeing beauty beyond belief, eating food dropped from the heavens and beds like the softest clouds. And look at him now, hanging out with music superstars. Just because he had never heard of most of the performers, well, thousands obviously had. People had come, they had listened, they had found bliss. And so had he. He loved the music and hoped to hear more like it. And it was all being offered on a silver plate.

The fear that crept up his spine and nestled like a frozen lake at the base of skull was, what happens next? Carrie had found others to help with her dream, what did she need with a street urchin? He had no training in any aspect of what her dream was about. He had no schooling, no concept of what others had lived, only what he had. He was a stone around her neck. Holding her back because she had to take care of him. Would she just cast him aside like a worn-out toy?

He hated where his thoughts had wandered, into the brambles and briars of his jungle of insecurities. He couldn't see five feet ahead when his brain fizzled like this. She was his friend; she wouldn't leave him. She had promised. They would all talk and decide together like a family. A real family. One that had been formed from heartache, agony, broken spirits, and need. Yeah, their bond was one of filling each other's holes and patching cracks, and love.

He had two new sisters and where they went, he would go. They had to have someone to watch over them, protect them, let them know it was going to be alright. That's what big bothers do!

Barbara was reticent. This decision was about so much more than her. Don't get her wrong, if it had only been about her she'd've hopped on board while the train was refueling but this was about her children. Could she ask them to continue living a vagabond life while Carrie chased an idea Barbara still wasn't convinced would pan out. It was all pie in the sky. She had to consider what was best for Phoebe and Isabelle.

They'd already missed the last couple weeks of school, no matter what, so that wasn't a consideration, though she wanted to get them settled where they could begin to make friends, settle into a new life, new home, new surroundings. She didn't want to wander for the rest of the summer and then throw them into all that. Traveling with what constituted nothing more than a band of gypsies traipsing across the land. That was not a proper way to raise children. Or was it?

Wasn't part of being a parent to expose your children to new ideas, expand their horizons, and show them the world? Barbara knew some, if not many, of the crew and musical acts smoked marijuana and drank but was that any different than what they'd been exposed to by the behavior of their own father. These people appeared to be decent, well-balanced, well, as balanced as musicians and such could be. They weren't violent, they took care of each other, watched out for each other, like family.

Maybe this would be a good experience for the kids. They could see that people lived different lifestyles but were still just people. There wasn't good or bad, just life. This was a community without judgments of sexuality, who partnered with whom, it was as live and let live as any group of people she could imagine. And if her experiences could help others, let them know they were not alone, wasn't that what her profession was supposed to be about?

If Jeanette, who she had just met but was a decent sort, for a journalist, wanted to tell their story wasn't it her duty to allow that? It was time she stopped living by other's expectations and what other folks thought. It was time to live her own life and show her daughters what a strong, confident woman looked like. She had lived her life by what her parents thought she should be. What her husband thought she should be. What her friends thought she should be. It was time to live her life by what she thought she should be!

She was in.

What could Carrie say? If these two wanted to let Jeanette into their lives, who was she to say no. She wanted to travel with these people, to learn what she could do or not do. To grow, to absorb their knowledge and life experiences, to share. Yeah, WWKD, Kim would be pissed if she didn't live to the fullest.

Besides Ian had mentioned they only had another couple weeks on the road what could possibly happen?

Meanwhile, Back In The Metaphysical

Bear took a long pull on the tightly rolled joint before passing it to Tatanka. The evening was warm, the sun had only just set so there was diffuse light still creeping over the tops of the mountains. They sat in companionable silence enjoying the sounds of the smallest members of the People with the sounds of Rebecca and Alexandra in the house preparing some morsels for all mixing and blending with nature.

Bear had offered, and been sternly rebuked for his effort, to help prepare the vittles. Rebecca knew he wanted time alone with the massive Tatanka. Even in human form the man was grand. Standing nearly seven foot tall, broad as a truck at the shoulders and thick as a tree in the leg. They stared at the sky and mountains, appreciating all that the Great Spirit had gifted them with. Each blowing a plume of smoke with the exhale in thanks to the Mother and the ancestors as well. It was a good evening for silence.

Bear turned his head slightly towards the corner of the house where so many had made their entrance over the years that a permanent path had been worn in the yard. He loved that path; it was the welcome mat to all who would come.

His thoughts rambled around old friends not seen as often as he would like. Sheriff John, now retired yet continuing his rounds out of habit, would stick his head around the corner with a bottle in his hand, smiling a questioning invitation. He didn't partake of the herb very often, some cop habits die hard, but once in a great while he would allow himself some latitude. Bear would take him across the divide and they would hunt and fish for a few weeks spirit time, camping under the canopy of the great pines and drink some bourbon, laugh, and retell stories told so often you could almost see through the lies. Good times.

He'd heard the scrape of shoe leather on grass. Only one of his kind, one of the People, could hear something so soft. He waited. Someone or something was pausing for a breath or two around that corner in no hurry to make an entrance.

Bear thought it best not to press whoever wanted to speak to him. They would come in their own time and time was something they had by the truckload, or so they all hoped.

After a few more well-timed heartbeats Sung made his way into the backyard. He looked tired, wan, like he ain't et in some time. Bear and Tatanka rose from their seating to greet the Wolf. Whatever he had come for he would tell soon enough. One didn't travel this far with that look and not want a meet.

Sung settled on to an upturned log while the other two reclaimed their seats. He gratefully accepted the bottle proffered by the large bison. He drank deep before taking a long pull off the endless joint handed him by Bear.

The sound of a wooden screen door slamming brought all their attention around to where Rebecca and Alex were coming out of the kitchen carrying a platter laden with meats, cheeses, vegetables, bread, and a bottle of wine for themselves.

Their grins widened at the sight of the Wolf, though Bear could see the worry lines around Rebecca's eyes deepen. She hugged the Wolf before telling him to sit back down and eat.

From the way he dug into the offered banquet it had been some time since he had last partaken of sustenance. He sat back rubbing his now distended belly and nodded his thanks.

"Hunting," he said without being asked, "they're hunting my children again." He wanted to scream to the skies and universe, but he didn't have the energy or strength.

Sung didn't need any further explanation. Man had hunted his kind ever since the two crossed paths a hundred and forty thousand years ago. Wolves had roamed free without any predators until man stood up-right and decided he would be king of the Mother!

"I thought they had signed pacts and laws to let your children be?" Alex was both curious and furious. When would mankind leave the natural world alone? Shit, when would mankind abide by his word, written or spoken? It was because they thought they were not part of nature, a verifiably wrong concept. Not only that but they had concluded because of one book written by illiterates and superstitious zealots they had dominion over land, sea, and air and all who dwelt there.

"Their pieces of paper mean less to them than the ones they use to cleanse their asses," had not the women been there Sung would've spit into the grass, "ask the First Nations about their experiences with papers."

All nodded their heads in acceptance of truth with a few 'Ya-heys' thrown in for good measure.

"What have you heard from Otter and Cougar?" Asked Tatanka hoping for a glimmer of light.

"They both agree that these people are sincere in their hearts and they have a good, solid plan." Bear sounded confident though his demeanor spoke otherwise.

"You appear to have grave doubts either about their assessment or the troop," said Rebecca.

"I guess I have doubts about whether we can convince these folks of the connection between their well-being and ours." He took a pull from the bottle while ignoring Rebecca's sniff of disapproval. She had spoken on more than several occasions about the necessity of using glassware but he insisted this was how the People showed their connection to each other. "It is one thing to be committed to helping your own, it is quite another to apply that same empathy where others are concerned."

"Ya-hey," quoth the Bison, "especially where most humans are concerned. Just think how beautiful all of the Mother would be if more would emulate the Red Road of our native children." The natives had hunted his people as they had hunted all the children of the People, though out of necessity and hunger. They did not kill just to kill as others did. And they certainly did not kill to extinction. Old water and many bridges. But it brought him back to the problem at hand. "Can we set up some kind of meet with them? Maybe, once they understand the severity and interconnectedness of all, they will be more willing to join forces and resources." If nothing else Tatanka was an optimist, you had to be when you had come back from the brink of extinction.

Barking, yipping, and nails on a linoleum floor erupted from the kitchen. The commotion woke him out of a deep nap and he was immediately at attention. Something or someone was out back either in the field or hanging in the back yards. Glen looked out the screened back door of his home next to Evan's to see what all the commotion was about. And he saw. Sung was sitting with the Beach's and Tatanka—who had been there when Glen lay down for his usual four-hour afternoon nap to compliment his three-hour morning nap.

He hadn't seen Sung in forever or so his brain told him though truth be told, it might have been yesterday, but it felt like forever. He swung open the door and the cavalcade of a dozen yapping and slobbering dogs of every shape, size and mixed breed bounded in the direction of the Wolf.

The sheer size and number of them was enough to knock Sung off his stool. His laughter rising like the phoenix from the death throes of his heartache. Nothing could lift his spirit like the greeting of a dozen joyous hounds.

Glen finally got all to settle with many head, tummy, and butt rubs, a few pieces of the meat and cheese off the platter didn't hurt. He was as overjoyed as his children to greet the Wolf, though he could contain his bliss; just.

Greetings were passed around like a platter of fresh fixings as Sung continued his lament on the condition and deaths of so many of his children. Glen wept with the telling and held several of his own kin tightly in his arms as if to protect them from the horrors Sung described. How could humans be so cruel they would kill without cause or reason. Maybe a couple cows had been taken, wasn't that what they were for? Wasn't that what the humans bred them, fed them, and raised them for? They were meat, that was the only purpose they had in life. Glen could feel his fury rise from the base of his groin. He wanted nothing more than to bite somebody, though he never would. Well, maybe just on their ass.

Condolences followed the telling and the subsiding anger. What could be done? The question need not be voiced, they all knew the answer, nothing. Man controlled life on the Mother and instead of being a compassionate, charitable manager he was a bloodthirsty greedy one. It made no sense. Life on the Mother was not unlimited, just the opposite, it was precious and should only be taken when necessary for survival.

Mr. Beach—Glen might not be allowed to call him that to his face but it would always be how he thought of the man who had saved his life and shown him his true self—looked to be ready to go on a rampage. Glen was not the only one whose dander was up. Tatanka wept openly though whether it was for Sung's children or the memory of his own dying by the millions due to that same greed, Glen couldn't tell.

The endless joint joined the endless bottle as it made the swift completion of its appointed rounds while the mood of this reunion fell into depths not planned.

The hound at Glen's feet was the first to scent a new guest to this gloomy party, his nose being the most sensitive. He bayed once before recognizing that scent. Jumping to all fours, he ran for the corner of the house, tongue lolling and happy yapping.

He was all over Suzette as she tried to push her way through the, now, dozen overwhelming presences. Though they kept their distance from the towering Nash. Laughing and petting, slowly she made the rounds of saying hello to the welcoming committee before being allowed entrance. She felt the sorrow like heat from an open oven door as soon as she got passed the welcome.

"More bad news?" She asked the assembled.

Sung gave her a brief synopsis of what he had just related to the others, not wishing to have to recite the savagery of mankind.

"It is hoped," Bear said, and here all nodded vigorously in accord, "that maybe you can shed some light on the darkness."

"Maybe I, er, we can." She pulled Nash into the circle so they could share a smoke and a pull in communion before the meet would take place.

"Were your ears burning?" Laughed Evan, Bear, though just, "Your name had only just come up a few moments ago. I was being asked what I had heard from you and here you are, to tell all of us." He grabbed a folding chair and set it next to himself for her to sit. Nash chose a seat slightly away from the group.

They all knew Nash, or of him, and his children. They were voracious eaters when there was game and the game didn't matter. They liked live; they were skilled at the kill. Now, no one could impugn the spirit's children for the act, Sung's did the same. But Nash's were solitary creatures by nature and killed mostly for themselves and their pups. Wolves killed for the family. A miniscule distinction but to Sung, at least, a profound one. Nash was welcome as one of the People, but his natural inclination was as the loner.

"We have traveled with, shared meals with, and lived with these humans for several of their weeks. We," and here she indicated Nash who inclined his head assenting, "believe them to be very committed to their cause. They are as pure of heart and purpose as any human can be."

"That is all well and good but the question is can we find common cause with our purpose of saving all, or as many as possible, of the families outside of man, as the Mother allows." Sung could not keep the vehemence, pain, and need for vengeance out of his voice.

"I believe we can if we have a meet with them. I believe, and Nash concurs, that if we have a contingent of maybe a dozen of the People, not enough to frighten but in numbers sufficient to let them see we are in solidarity with each other. They will have no choice but to acknowledge that it would be in their best interest to join with us. To save all."

Murmurs of approval were passed with the white stick.

"I believe present company should make up the bulk of that contingent with a few more to round out the People." She sat back in the aluminum folding chair. "I will suggest this, if I may?" Bear waved her through, "Glen should be one of the group. There is a young lady with an extended family that has joined the gypsy caravan and I believe, and again I think Nash is in full agreement, there is something about her, a scent, an aura, a power, if you will, that makes her essential. And she has a friend, as close as any human could be to a nonhuman, who is one of Glen's children. It could be the thumb we need on the scale."

Nash cleared his throat wishing to say something though not wishing to force his way. Bear nodded.

"There is magic at play here. Maybe magic is the wrong word, but some kind of power I cannot describe or name it but it is evident when you are near certain members of this tribe. We should proceed with some caution until we know its source." He eyed the platter on the picnic table. His kind, like many of them, knew to eat when food was available because it might be days before one could find game or leftovers. Rebecca passed the plate as Alex went to the kitchen to fetch more.

The Long And Winding Road

The bus bounced, veered, and jostled as the driver attempted to navigate the pockmarked road with the least amount of resistance. How roads that never froze and thawed could be this uneven the driver had no idea, but he did his best to chart the smoothest course. In his windshield rearview mirror, he could see the heads of this hippie enterprise doing their utmost to hold a meeting concerning... who knew what. Certainly not him. Bus drivers drive buses not attend interminable meetings about saving the world. He did think it humorous he had a windshield rearview as there was no need, you couldn't see out of the back of the bus. Half-million-dollar vehicle and nobody thought to shave a few wasted bucks, made him laugh.

Carrie was included in the circle as they wished to pick her brain as much as she wanted to pick theirs. That was one of the first things she noticed about the cadre of gypsies, they respected all opinions and ideas. She sat on one of the couches next to Maggie and Ian, Jaxson occupied the one chair bolted to the floor, Raj sat on the floor with Gabby, they were inseparable partners, Dugie and Ben held onto anything bolted down for dear life while Regis, who had wormed his way in to the convo, stood and moved with the bus like he was born to it. Suzette and Nash had mysteriously disappeared in the night and no one knew their whereabouts. Oscar lay at Carrie's feet where he could be petted by any close enough to touch him. Jeanette found herself reclining in the stairwell, she didn't care, she wanted to be part of this meeting.

Jaxson had made the unilateral decision that Dugie and Ben should find them a couple tow bars so Carrie and Barbara could ride with them while the buses towed the cars. He thought it would save on gas and they would have time to acclimate to life with a rock and roll caravan. Barbara and the girls, along with Aron, their protector and big brother, rode several buses up with the musicians and singers. The singers having taken in the family and were happily mothering all. They loved having the girls on board as they could spoil them at every turn, play mommy and get some time with children. Some of the crew were missing their own kids terribly.

Carrie was concerned about the absence of the two natives as she really wished to pick their brains as well, though no one else seemed troubled. Jaxson explained they had disappeared before yet always found their way to the next show. He was confident they would arrive in Amarillo about the same time the buses did. Carrie prayed they would.

"The thing is," Jaxson was saying to her, "we seem to have the same concept, ours is just on a much larger scale. What I am thinking, because you have to understand none of us, no matter how much money we raise and how good of a job we do with messaging, is going to change the world overnight. We have to be committed to this for the long haul. It will take decades if not centuries to bring this massive ship about. Those with the wherewithal have held those without in check for centuries!" He threw his hands up for emphasis.

"Actually," Raj added, "in my country it has been in effect for more than three thousand years. That is a very long time to ingrain a concept into the psyche of an entire culture. People believe, because they have been repressed for a thousand generations. And no one is in any hurry to change that concept. Those at the top do not wish to lose their advantage or share even the most miniscule amount of power with those they see as lesser than human. We are attempting to educate millions of people so they know they have been lied to for time immemorial. Obviously, those on the higher rungs don't wish to educate those much further down as they would then realize the lie they have been fed for generations. Imagine the anger, the violence that would unleash towards those who knew all along." His tone held three thousand years of shame but he also did not wish to be responsible for so much death and suffering.

"It's the same thing here, in this country with black folks." Regis chimed in, to reiterate what most here knew, "It was illegal to teach them how to read, write, and cypher. Someone who can't read don't know how much better folks everywhere have it than them. If you can't write you can't communicate with anybody further away than your voice. And if you can't cypher you can't tell how bad you being cheated. Ignorant people are much easier to control, to hold down, to lord over than folks who can think, reason, and realize." His words may have been well thought out and reasonable but his timbre was on fire.

"Our idea," Ian turned his attention away from Regis to Carrie, "is to inform folks, especially those who don't want to know and don't want those below them to know. Though the folks who have been left behind, intimidated, dominated, and denied their rights as human beings are the ones most in need of the education. So, we want to train them for the jobs they want, replace drugs and alcohol, which have been used as a way to repress the poor, with hope and the means to make faith in themselves a reality. We want to instill worth in the children and let them know poverty of spirit, of opportunity, and finances is not the road they need travel." Ian expressed the steadfast beliefs of every person associated with the tour of the Untouchables.

"So, do I fit in anywhere in that dream?" Carrie hadn't thought much beyond the concept of her center which now felt so small and inconsequential compared to the grand dreams of these people.

"Actually, yes," responded Raj taking in both Jaxson and Ian for permission to speak. Though his heritage told him he had the right to demand they listen. His newfound awareness of where he fit in to the human race told him to ask. "What we have done, out of necessity, is begin small. The community center on Pine Ridge will contain a clinic, a drug and alcohol rehab center combined with training in the trades and soon a school so folks can get their GED and prepare those who wish for further education. It is one of a couple small projects we have begun as test kitchens. To see what works best and to provide safety nets for those who fall between the cracks. Nothing lifts like knowing someone has your back, it gives you the freedom to fail without dying."

"You would like to use my idea as one of your test kitchens?" Carrie was catching on.

"If we may," Gabby spoke for the first time, "what we have learned is that we need to ask what is needed, what can we do to assist, and if we can be involved. You cannot work with someone by telling them what you are going to do. Partners do not demand, they cooperate."

Carrie cared less for the financial support they might bring than for the vast experience in many of the areas she wished to address that they could supply.

The drive across Oklahoma and into Texas is a good a place to contemplate the past, the future, and all concepts of time and space. It is as close to what it always was as any habitable place in America. It is flat, wide-open, farmland, prairie. It takes very little imagination to see with the mind's eye herds of buffalo, tens of thousands strong grazing, turning the landscape black with their presence. You could visualize First Nation tribes camped out along the meandering rivers and streams, teepees lining the banks for fresh water and campfires burning.

Carrie let the quiet conversations recede into the background of her consciousness as she considered what had been offered. She had her own ideas of what she wanted to build. Where she wanted to build it. And what she hoped to accomplish. If she entered into some kind of compact with these people, would she be giving up her control, her dream?

She had daydreamed for more than a month while they drove of building the retreat, this haven, with Aron, who really wanted to find purpose and direction in his life to pay homage to a family years gone. And what about Barbara? Hadn't she dragged this woman and her children across the whole of the united States with the promise of a fresh start, a new home, safety? What would she tell her, there was no room at the home for her? No, Carrie had to remain committed to the purity of the project. There had to be a place for Barbara, the kids, Aron, all who begged for life, for health, for a home.

"They won't, you know." The voice was soft so no one would hear except her but not so close as to be imposing.

She brought her attention to the here and now, not a perceived future. Gabby's eyes were a pure brown, deep, endless, you could see the birthing of the universe if you stared long enough. His attention was focused completely on her.

"Wh-what?" Stammered out on a breath of confusion.

"They, Ian, Jaxson, these people, won't steal your dream," his face was expressionless as if he didn't want to convey more than the words he was speaking.

"Did I say something, out loud? I was only thinking..." How could this man have read he thoughts so easily? And if it was so crystal clear to him, was it to the others?

"No," he said to her thoughts. "We learn to read the thoughts of others by the change of expression, the tightness of the eyes, puckering of the lips, a tilt of the head, it's a survival trait where I come from. When someone is blowing smoke up your ass with promises, you have to know whether it is a warming fire that produced the smoke or a fire that will burn down your life." His crooked grin and the twinkle left her wondering if he was pulling a fast one or expressing truth. "The second one." He replied. "these are good men and women, they want what's best for those who have been denied too long, the true Untouchables all over the world. They like what you want to accomplish and only wish to have your back. They have learned not to impose what they think is best on others but allow those with the dream to bring it to fruition."

"It's just that I have friends who wish to help, to bring in the right people for what the kind of shelter we hope to create. Architects, builders, designers, medical personnel, psychologists, drug and alcohol counselors, educators, health experts, and dieticians." There were so many different specialists needed it almost overwhelmed her.

"Like what the Lakota are accomplishing at Pine Ridge, only smaller," He laughed, not at her or her vision but at her passion and love for people she had never met. She was a good woman, though very young and very inexperienced in so many ways, but long past her years in empathy. "You might wish to confer with Joseph Standing Bear, the head of the project in South Dakota. You two could share a path and support each other." The idea felt so natural, like laying naked in soft bed of mud while the sun warmed your body, he wondered why no one else had seen the possibilities. "There is much talk required. One person cannot solve all the glitches in our world, we must work together." And with that he moved back to join the lively conversation about the show tomorrow in Amarillo.

If the big Mayan, what the hell that's what everybody else referred to him by, spoke absolute truth about anything at all it was the need to work with others, together, as a team to solve obstacles and move past hindrances. She hadn't considered, though now that her mind had been opened wide, things like permits, city planners, business licenses, hell, she probably needed a separate license to build a kitchen to feed everybody. Yes, they all were right, she would need experts galore and experienced builders to make the dream a reality.

Objects Are Closer Than They Appear

As the day of the concert drew closer Padon found his anxiety growing exponentially with it. He had to get a grasp on the why. Christ on a Premium Saltine, he hadn't seen any of these people in years and he'd only been an opening act on shows for them. The crews he'd worked with only met him as a minor regional performer with a couple songs people knew well enough to sing along to. They'd probably worked with hundreds before him and hundreds after, no one would remember a provincial singer with a drinking, thinking, and ego problem. Or were those the kind of assholes that stuck out in the mind?

How big of an asshole had he been? He didn't think he'd been bad when he was riding high. He'd share what he had with his openers and the crew. Bought dinners for a bunch when he was flush. He didn't become a huge dick until she'd taken the kid and flew the coop. He probably had nothing to worry about. And what the fuck? He wasn't going there to play but to be part of ten or fifteen thousand other fans. He really had to get a grip on this ego.

He settled into the chaise lounge, out beneath the awning facing west, to watch the sunset behind the mountains. Ever since his trip with Joe into the mountains on that cold, frigid, sun spayed day Padon found he loved watching the sunset behind these majestic peaks. The black of the mountains silhouetted against the reds, yellows, blues, and purple hues that ran the spectrum, made his heart sing. A soothing elixir he desperately required. The concert would be wonderful. Maggie wanted it and that should be his only concern. They were here to fall deeper in love and this was just the music to move that along.

"You don't really want to go to the concert, do you?" Maggie had come up behind him and kissed him soft on the forehead. In her heart she knew what was chafing his soul. He was terrified that going to this show would ignite the lust for stage time. He would soon be chomping at the bit to get back on the road and play. He had been healed up in Rock Ridge and she had been foolish enough to believe that the want to had been scabbed over and mended. She saw how much joy he took with Wally on their Thursday nights, just playing off each other and had hoped that would be enough. Shit! Well, the scab was about to be ripped off and she had no one but herself to blame!

"No, really, I think it would be good for us to go, sit, and listen to excellent music. It's been a very long time since I got to be a fan, an audience." He grinned at a memory so far in his past he couldn't be certain it was a real memory or something he'd read about. It didn't matter, it was real enough to him. "When I was a child, my mother took me to some concerts in the park. A small orchestra on a bandstand oompahing out some John Phillip Sousa, old German drinking songs, and a few classics. We'd sit on the grass, sipping milk, and nibbling on cucumber and butter sandwiches. Just the two of us. It was wonderful." He laughed at the image.

"Your dad didn't come along?" She was surprised it wouldn't have been a family outing.

"Nah, he thought it was a complete waste of time. He'd rather stay home and fix something he'd neglected to fix for six months. We'd find him at the local watering hole, Murphy's, on our way home. He'd be half in the bag and berating us for wasting our day," Now the laugh had a bitter edge to it. "I'd rather spend the day with you, sitting in the grass and listening to some fantastic musicians." He held her close knowing she thought she knew his reason for trepidation but not wishing to correct her.

They would hang around the ranch for the rest of the week riding their choice of horses across the open prairie. Padon had never sat a horse in his life but found once you got past the sore ass and aching thigh muscles it was an enjoyable waste of time.

And that was the thing, wasn't it? He enjoyed wasting this time with her, which, of course, made it not a waste of time at all. He thought his father disapproved of his pursuits because it showed he was too much like his mother's family. They had all been artists, musicians, painters, writers, neer-do-wells who died in poverty and yet, not a one of them regretted their choice of profession. His father would never understand, those who create for a living do not choose it, it chose them. And poverty, loneliness, being ostracized by friend and family alike, even to be shunned by society in general would not stop the artist from being what was at his core. You can no more walk away from creating than you can from breathing. It is life. Padon sighed, as it ever was, it ever shall be.

Robert and Marylou brought some wine and snacks out onto the patio. They were more than decent sorts. Middle aged, still in love, kids were grown, and now they could spend time on each other again. That was part of the problem with being in a long-term relationship with kids and a mortgage. Sooner or later the mortgage was paid off, the kids were grown and you had to learn to be a couple again. There were no scream- ing distractions, nothing to pull you together in an us against them way, a sick child, bills due, jobs you hated but needed. Life pulled you into a whirlpool so strong you couldn't concentrate on why you entered it in the first place. Then one day it was all gone, leaving just the two of you staring at an older, more tired stranger who reminded you of someone you used to be totally and completely in love with. Now you had to push through what life had done to both of you to find that person again. They had.

Early summer maintained late spring evening chills; a fire was lit to hold it at bay. All agreed it was too beautiful of an evening to be chased indoors, not yet anyway. Glasses of wine were refreshed, several blankets brought out as backup, small talk and chatter filled in the empty spaces. It was a perfect evening to increase each other's knowledge of the other. That's what quiet evenings are made for.

Maggie told Padon of the summer night that Marylou and Robert came to the café just as they were closing. They were tired and hungry after a day lost in the mountains, something Padon related to only too well, and sought sustenance and knowledge of a place to stay for the night.

Though tired after a long day of schlepping victuals out to those passing through and those who were more permanent, Maggie wanted to tell them they were too late. Then she remembered her own introduction to this burgh and told them to sit at the counter as all the tables had just been wiped down.

They apologized for causing any inconvenience. If they could just get a sandwich and some chips or something, and pointed in the right direction of a bed, they would be most thankful. Maggie went into the kitchen to find Wally and Ralph just shutting down the ovens. Ralph saw the expression on her face and asked what she needed. Maggie explained the situation and grabbed a couple pans while cranking up the oven once more. Within twenty minutes the couple were treated to a Wally and Ralph special of steaks, medium rare, some au gratin potatoes, green beans and pie, apple, warmed and with a side of vanilla ice cream. They were overwhelmed.

Robert had proclaimed that if there was somewhere to find a bottle of wine or other spirits, he would pay whatever premium involved so he could toast his benefactors. Maggie pulled out the bottle hidden under the counter for bad day relief or good day celebrations, and then pulled Wally and Ralph out of the kitchen. Wally declined the offering as he didn't want to slip on his sobriety, Ralph had no such qualms. And a friendship was born that had lasted fifteen years.

It was a lovely story and a quiet stillness enfolded the quartet gazing into the flames in recollection.

Robert broke the silence, "Did Maggie tell us you play some music?" It was nice way to ease into his background.

"Yeah, I have been known to pick a few tunes, " Padon smiled. Normally he would hate to be asked, but there was no chance of that happening. People never asked in these circumstances, as it was too intrusive on the ambiance. This time he was wrong. Robert asked and, for once, Padon didn't mind, he knew Maggie would love it if he played.

K. Adrian Zonneville

Just Another Day Riding Ponies

Amarillo promised a huge turnout as it was situated in the middle of a desert of civilization. There were towns and villages surrounding but it was the largest city between Oklahoma City and Albuquerque. Folks would be coming from hundreds of miles around. The owner of HODGE-TOWN, the official ballpark of the Amarillo Sod Poodles, had begged them for two nights instead of one and they had happily agreed. Anytime they could bed down in the same hotel and get to settle into a town for more than one night was welcome. And the Sod Poodles were on the road for a week visiting other Double-A ball clubs in the region.

The first day was off the charts with people spilling out of the snug Texas ballpark and onto the 'porch' in the outfield. They were ten deep behind the chain link fence. The discomfort in Ian's loins, belly, and back of his head were causing a major distraction while he continued to go through the precheck 'list' of all that had to be accomplished before the gates could open. This was too much like the park in Columbia where the shooting took place.

He knew it was a freak accident that he'd been hit but it wasn't a freak accident that someone had taken the shot. And this was Texas. Didn't every mother's son own a plethora of shootin' irons in Texas? He knew he was being paranoid and relying on stereotypes, but weren't most stereotypes based in fact. There had to be some reason why they'd been born.

So, though his eyes and attention were supposed to be focused on the sheet and the show, his wandering paranoia kept stealing glances at the gathering throng. Shit! And he had two days of this to look forward to.

The soft touch on his shoulder made him jump more than he thought was suitable for a grown man who considered himself, if not macho, certainly grown.

Jeanette seemed startled by his startled reaction. "Sorry, I didn't mean to frighten you," she apologized.

"You didn't frighten me," Ian replied with more vehemence than was necessary or intended. "I was concentrating on preparations for the concert." He wished he hadn't sounded so frightened while expressing he wasn't frightened.

"Maggie thought it would be appropriate for me to shadow you again while you go through your precheck. You know, so I get it right for the book."

Ian had totally forgotten that Jeanette had taken a sabbatical from the *NY Times* so she could write about their cross-country tour raising awareness of Untouchables throughout the world. And now, she apparently was writing two books at once, the original idea and a book about Carrie, Barbara, and those kids. Whew!

He liked Jeanette, she was bright, capable, well-versed in the art of the pen and had become a dyed in the wool convert to the Objective. She had seen how people's lives could be affected positively when they realized they had worth. A trait they had been denied for centuries.

She wanted the story of a plucky tribe of idealistic musical Gypsies and their cohorts who honestly believed they could change the world, if only by millimeters. Once a Massive object is put in motion the energy will build exponentially until it is unstoppable. Physics, she thought.

"You may follow, lead, ask questions, pick my teeny brain or wander this desert in silence, I trust your sense of purpose and values more than most any person I have encountered," he winked so she would know, and she did.

"I know we don't have a bunch of shows left before the end of the tour, so I thought, if it is alright with you, I would shadow you for the next couple weeks. I want your perspective on all the background stuff. I've spoken to most everyone else but you are the big clamato!" She shot him a quirky smirk at her own misappropriation.

"How's it coming along?" Ian had been so busy with all the minutia of keeping the wheels turning he hadn't kept tabs on her work. He hadn't the need, she was an accomplished woman, she did not require nor want his approval or blessing. Though she was also a professional and would not publish without his input.

"I believe I am collecting and collating all pertinent information and only need to tie up some loose ends. The hard part might be incorporating facts and data with personality and story. It is the eternal struggle of balance. Get the point across in an interesting and engaging way." She shrugged. She knew in her heart she would have no problem incorporating the personality of this group with all the dry fact.

Ian realized they'd been standing still while talking and he required motion. He hated standing still when there was work to be done. He would allow interviews, though he hated the attention, preferring they concentrate on his acts instead. The interview would come with the warning he wouldn't sit for the interviewer. If they wanted to talk to him, they had to move with him, so move they did.

Little did these two realize that Soteria was following them, whether because that was where work was taking her or because she wanted to be there in case Ian performed one of his miraculous accidents. She had discovered through small talk and chitchat that Ian was considered the tour's good luck charm. They didn't make a big deal out of his lifesaving as they didn't want to jinx him or the tour, but it wasn't exactly a secret either. They had opened up as she had become more integrated with the crew and had saved Howie twice.

They made their way around the backstage and staging area, Ian checking off each individual item as he assured himself all things were as they should be. Jeanette and Ian shared tidbits about the tour. She asking of things she hadn't been privy to, such as the happenings of the first three months before she hooked up with them, and he filling in details. She, as was her want, had her digital recorder in her hand and running.

Once done with his check list he made his way to the center stage to clear with the rest of the crew they were set and ready. It was a habit born of fifty years of mistakes. Ian did everything in his power to assure there would be no foul-ups during the show. Once assured all was set, he announced to security to open the gates and allow admission to the proletariat.

In minutes the quartet would take the stage for the forty-five minutes submersion into tranquility, serenity, and intellectual freedom. There was something about the music that compelled people to introspection, cognizance, or intellectual intercourse. That was until the Mendelsohn when Nash would stand to allow the melody, the composition to surround his being and enfold him in majesty and the nobility of form. He would weep and those around him, and soon the entire congregation, would stand and be connected by the same.

He stood. A lone Native surrounded by those who had stripped him of his home, whose ancestors had lied, cheated, poisoned the people and land, and massacred the wildlife like a massive scythe purging the continent. Yet, he showed no conscious knowledge of the thousands of hats and boots, just as they showed no conscious knowledge of what their forebearers had done. They didn't know or care. This land was their land now no matter how it had been acquired.

Ian really wanted to know what this man felt. Why this music affected him so thoroughly. He had decided earlier in the day that when the music began, he would go, stand next to the Indian, and listen with his heart, his open mind, his gift, his innate sense of musical balance. The musicians played with passion, as if drawing inspiration from Nash and the assembled as they began to stand. Ian rushed to be there, to feel, to finally understand to the marrow of his bones.

As he rushed to be near or next to Nash he stepped on a bola bag, popping the cork, deflating the bag, and causing Ian to lose his balance. He tried to regain his equilibrium but only succeeded in toppling the man in front of him who in an attempt not to fall grabbed hold of several people surrounding him until a great domino affect came into play. Knocking down and scattering them like a child's game being kicked by a petulant, frustrated, kid.

Nash remained standing while Ian righted the ship of Sperling and attempted once again to be by this rock of a human being. He made it within a foot before tripping on one of the fallen bowling pins of personages and knocked into Nash just as the whistle and whiz of a projectile flew by, just missing the native as the collapsing Indian went down.

Several more shots were fired before silence reclaimed the area. As Ian lay prone on the grass the thought flew like a bolt of lightning through his muddled brain, 'Wasn't Jeanette right behind him?' Fear gripped his loins and intestines. Damn! He should've had the courage to roll over and see if she was alright. He lay still.

A tap on his thigh and whimper of a prayer told him she lived. The question was whether she had been hit. He knew, intimately, that you can be alive and in excruciating pain at the same moment. He lifted his head and saw her pleading expression.

He jumped up as if a jolt of electricity had been shot through his body. He prayed to a god he hadn't ever believed in and quick-stepped the two yards to her side. He saw no blood pooling, no sign of injury but that didn't always mean anything, did it?

He rolled her over to inspect the front of her knowing as he did so he probably shouldn't have but he had to know. No holes leaking red, no tears in the fabric, just a whimper. He did a physical inspection and saw the ankle twisted at an obviously painful angle. Not shot but injured none the less.

Nash was now standing by his side and saw the same. He bent down and gently raised her up, as if lifting a very fragile loved one without jarring the injury, and quick walked her to the back of the stage. Ian, though unencumbered by anything other than a consuming feeling of guilt, had trouble keeping up with the man.

They were greeted backstage by a dozen hugs, kisses, cries of relief, and worried, quiet queries of Jeanette's condition. Ian endeavored to calm distress explaining it appeared she had twisted her ankle in the tumult.

Dennis and his contingent of FBI/roadies came marching in the back with a young man cuffed and disheveled from their scuffle taking him down. He was a child, thought Ian, just a kid filled with hate. Hence the distorted features as he attempted to wrestle free.

"He's just a kid," Ian couldn't stop the words coated in sympathy from exiting the pie hole.

"Yeah, a kid with a rifle and a belly full of venom and spite. Probably instilled since he was born. He wasn't very happy being brought down by Agent Murray." Dennis' smiled was wicked and overflowing with satisfaction. He loved the irony of an agent of Jamaican descent being the one to take the perpetrator down. It's the small victories.

"Is he the only one?" Maggie's voice trembled slightly with fear and relief.

"Yes," sighed Dennis, "It appears he is another lone shooter though I'm willing to bet incited by the same group the Columbia shooter was."

"What about the show?" Jaxson knew he asked the impossible.

"I don't know." Dennis wanted to say it was over. That they couldn't take another chance, but he knew Jaxson, had traveled with the man for a month now. He knew his heart and the why.

"If we cancel, the shooter and his hate win." Jaxson stated the obvious to nods and angry affirmations from the crew, the musicians, the singers and mostly from Jeanette.

"I'll be alright. See if Suzette can wrap it or put one of her magic poultices on it. I'll walk out on the damn stage and challenge the rest of them if you want." This was one tough human being. Ian's cup of respect washed over.

"Nah, you rest, you've had enough excitement for one day, I'll go out."

Dennis stopped Ian as he made for the few stairs leading up to the stage. "I can't guarantee anything. I mean, I am ninety-nine percent sure he is the only one, but that's the problem with lone wolves. We can't know for sure." He really wanted to cancel this thing and he wanted Ian's support.

"Dennis, I'm not afraid of dying, to be honest, I'm afraid of not living. This is what we do, who we are, I should say. If someone is going to attack us for trying to lift people out of the horrors they've been subjected to for centuries, then let them give it a try. I would rather die in the attempt than as an old man lying in bed." He grabbed Dennis' shoulder to give hm some love and reassurance. "But I'd rather not die at all, so, there's that."

Much to the relief of Ian and Dennis, as well as the rest of the tribe, no one took a shot at Ian as he climbed the stairs, made his announcement of continuing the concert and the fact no one had been hurt beyond a twisted ankle, to cheers, tears, and a roar to his proclamation that hate would not rule the day.

Enter one lone Cellist and J. S. Bach.

Once We Take A Beach...

Vilhelm Wilhem caught up with the tour the next night. He found Ian, Jaxson, Maggie, and Ben backstage an hour before gates. After saying his hellos and hearing once again about his style or lack thereof he settled back into a folding chair to hear every detail of all he had missed on this leg of the tour.

"First off," Ian began, "I want to thank you for suggesting and not giving up on the idea of this quartet opening each show. They have gone above and beyond several times, obliterating my concept of classical artists as mamby pamby, weak kneed, sycophants. They have nerves of steel and hearts of iron. You should be very proud of them. They are now, and have been, on the same pay scale as everyone else in this circus."

Vilhelm's shocked expression morphed into one of gratitude. "I cannot tell you how much I appreciate that," he began before Ian shut him down.

"They have more than earned it, as well as the respect and gratitude of every member of the entourage. It is our hope you have not shown up to take them away from us, we would very much like them to complete the tour to the west coast." Ian waited until his words caught up with Vilhelm's deliberations.

His grin showed they had met, shook hands and were in accord. Ian then gave him a brief synopsis of most of what had taken place since NY. His injury, Jeanette's ankle, the additions of Nash and Suzette as uber security and nurse. The kismet of finding Carrie and company by the side of the road and their addition to the commune, the whole enchilada. He related the story of the white power folks in the parking lot in Little Rock. The belief that this whole endeavor was being guided by some hand other than their own, whatever anyone wanted to call it, and the need to continue the tour no matter what.

And then Ian invited the man to travel with them for the rest of the journey. Vilhelm, as well as those seated around the two men, was shocked. After what had happened earlier on the tour, he thought he and Ian would never come to terms. Ian was not one to hold a grudge, especially when that grudge was with his own misguided judgment. They sealed the deal with a handshake and good feelings. It would be good show tonight.

Word had circulated throughout the area of the assault and people had shown up to prove it wasn't them. They were not like the kid with the rifle, which he had obtained legally without any impediment to prevent him. The people spilled out of the stadium; blankets laid out for families all along the fences in the outfield. No one would get closer than a hundred feet to the park unless they fought their way through the love. These Texans would not be defined by the hatred of one.

Vilhelm had expressed his pride with the quartet and told them of the love the rest of the company had for them, which they evidently reciprocated. Their performance that night was even more spirited and extended. Twelve thousand people stood with the Native, held their children close, hugged, joined hands, and allowed the music to embrace them with its beauty and magnificence.

Each act raised the bar higher and higher. The audience responding, cheering them on. The sunset in glory as if in harmony to the sounds. The music soring, skipping, and sailing from the stage. Before anyone was aware it was time for the *'Cannons of Peace'* and Gabby.

Jaxson sat at the electric baby grand and began to play. It was just him, the music and, now the lyric. As usual he sang the first verse and chorus before pianissimo. As he softened his touch to prepare for Gabby to walk on stage, he heard something, something he had not heard previously. He glanced over to where Gabby had taken several steps onto the stage before halting.

On the breeze coming over his right shoulder was the most hauntingly mesmerizing solo violin weaving in and out of his piano. Gabby stood stunned by the splendor. His eyes, tear filled and reflecting the sunset, glanced from the mic to Jaxson, to wherever that wonder was coming from.

Jaxson wanted to stop, to listen to that forsaken, lonely, estranged sound but he couldn't. Gabby took a few more hesitant steps before being buffered by the sound of a cello, another violin and the violist joining in. Now the sound was full, one instrument reinforcing the other, hope, worth, promise, acceptance were all rolled into that sound. Gabby sat on the stage not five feet from his intended goal. He allowed the music to rise and fall, the sound of it pleading with him to stand, to walk those few steps. He was rooted where he sat, tears streaming down his cheeks. The music begged motion of him, but he was stunned.

Nash stood behind him flanked by Suzette and Maggie. Ian watched from the wings as the rest of the cast began to assemble behind the seated Mayan. The crowd didn't know what was happening or what to do, they were as bewildered and confused as Gabby. Then one stood, her partner joining her. The couple next to her joining them. A dozen more stood, in silence, as if in prayer or meditation. Then group by group as the music took on a life of its own, more and more stood until one man, an old man, long white hair streaming down his back, raised a fist before bringing it down to pound on his chest. Within minutes twelve thousand men, women, children, hippies, cowboys and Indians, bankers, borrowers, and tax assessors, mechanics and plumbers, carpenters and college professors were banging their chests.

Startled back to life Gabby looked around and seemed to remember where he was and why he was here. He rose without the aid of his hands standing straight and tall he walked to the mic and began to speak.

"Ya-hey! Mitakuye Oyasin!" He called to the assembled before singing his words from his heart, from his mother's heart, from the heart of the Mother and the Great Spirit. "We are all one, we are all the same, we are all of the blood, none should live in shame." And the words flowed, interweaving with the violins, piano, Cello, and viola. It was the music of mankind, of the earth, of all living things, all braided and entwined with all other life.

And when it all came to an end there was no applause, no cheering. Everyone sat back down on the cool, damp earth, and held each other. Like a crocheted coverlet of many colors and patterns from one infinite ball of yarn. Jaxson competed the evening with several encores accompanied by the entire musical community. They ended the night with a segue of several old timey tunes showcasing Gillian, Cinda, Michelle and one to showcase the talent of Joya joined by Christopher. Let there be light!

It was a hushed though satisfied band of Gypsies that made their way back to the hotel that night. Ian had called ahead arranging for the bar and restaurant to stay open, if only for an hour or so. The restaurant promised appetizers and nothing more, as the chefs were already gone. It would do. They wanted to sit in the lobby and have a few quiet drinks and nibble on crap while letting the evening wash over them.

These were all veterans of hundreds of tours, tens of thousands of miles on the road, and musical miracles, but tonight had been overwhelming in its passion and emotional energy. They were drained physically, emotionally, spiritually. It was good. Even Vilhelm, though his outfit screamed party, his demeanor was of contented gratification. He loved the musicians who comprised this quartet but tonight they had exceeded any expectation he believed possible.

Gillian was the first to break the hush. "Anyone want to maybe get up a little earlier than regular departure to make a run out to the Cadillac Ranch?" She managed to find a grin somewhere at the back of her head.

"What?" Asked a tired Bonnie.

"The Cadillac Ranch," smiled Joya. "You know I grew up not far from here, maybe four hundred miles as the eagle flies," and there were chuckles as those from the east coast would never consider four hundred miles to be 'close to here', "and have traveled through here a hundred times but never took the time to hop off the freeway and go see that."

"What the hell are you two talking about?" Ian perked up, though only just, "Isn't that a song by Springsteen?"

"Yeah, it is," smirked Gillain, "but I don't think he's singing about this place. Some fella back almost fifty years ago decided to bury Cadillacs nose down in the dirt along route 66."

"Wait, I know about this," Lee Starling chimed in, "It wasn't just a guy, it was some billionaire wanted to do something outrageous that would baffle the locals and be like an art project. He imported the cars from somewhere but got a bunch of artsy hippies from San Fran and they put the cars in the ground to show the evolution of the tail fin, or some such bullshit." He laughed, "Fuck yeah, I'm in!"

Soon there was agreement all the way around. Their next stop was up to Colorado Springs and they had two days to get there. Even taking the back roads, as they would have to for at least part of the journey, they could easily make it in plenty of time. This would be a marvelous distraction and could replenish the spent emotion from tonight. They finished off their drinks and the few remaining apps amid chuckles, small talk, and anticipation of what the morrow would bring.

The folks driving the trucks decided the three of them would rather head north than add any more miles to the trip. The bus drivers, on the other hand, were always up for a new adventure. They loved the tour, the country and all her oddities. Most of the time they were running church groups to bible camp or the elderly to Niagara Falls, this was much more fun. Bunch of hippies and neer-do-wells out trying to save the world and wanting to see it in case they failed. Bus drivers loved stories and these folks certainly seemed hell bent for leather to provide grist for the barn.

Carrie and Aron rode in the last bus with Ian, Maggie, Jaxson, James, and Ben. Barbara and the kids rode with the band and singers, who weren't about to give up one minute of time with the girls. Dugie had gone with the trucks. Carrie was surprised, to say the least, by how excited everyone was to be going to view a kitschy roadside tourist trap. You'd think they would've seen a thousand bizarre, offbeat, tourististy crap attractions. But they were beside themselves with glee at the pro-spect.

"Why?" Carrie didn't need to expand on the basic premise of the question.

"You tell her, honey," Ian turned the why over to Maggie, who understood after being married to the road for forty years and having put in her time on it as well.

"They never get to really see much of anything," she began, "See, when they're on the road it is from one place to another without stops. They go from the bus to the hotel, the hotel to the venue, the venue back to the hotel, and from the hotel to the next town. They never get a chance to be tourists. So, when they get a chance like this, to see some strange, arty, goofy, eye candy, out in the middle of nowhere, it's like a field trip in middle school." She guffawed at the image that conjured. A couple dozen middle to late aged hippies on a field trip to see the great peculi-arities of America. "Well, pack a lunch, we're going to have to be bus monitors." Some secret, long ago trip passed between Ian and his wife, maybe they had snuck off somewhere or they'd had to go in search of lost children but it was a pleasant reminder none the less.

They spent almost two hours gazing at the remains of the Caddys pointing into the turf at an odd angle. They hypothesized about the angle, the reasons, and a little sadness that so much damage had been done and pieces taken as souvenirs. It would have been so cool to see these when they were in pristine condition. Still, it was worth the detour. Time to head north-northwest up route 287 to 354 cut over to 87 to interstate 25, they would be to the Springs by early evening.

There's A Meet Down The Road A Piece

Bear had decided on the contingent going to Colorado Springs to speak with the representatives of this traveling show. He wanted People of various species and temperaments. Not just his closest friends, though he wanted them as well, but he had to have dissenting voices who would question not only the motives of these rovers but of him as well. He had made most of the decisions in the past, they had not turned out as he had hoped. Now he wanted dissidents to challenge his thinking.

He wished he could convince the Mother to put in an appearance but she had respectfully declined. It was up to the children to save them-selves. Humans, mammals, birds of the air, denizens of the deep oceans, and the insects that troubled them all. Representatives would have to be found for each.

He rounded up the usual suspects, Tatanka and Elk from the plains, Sung and Nash from the hunters, he had Otter and his family, Owl had a good mind balanced by Finn's knowledge of law. Cynthia would represent the reptiles, Iktomi was surprised he asked her but honored to serve. Chasitity had swum around making a commitment but when swim finally came to crawl had capitulated, as long as there would be comfort-able chairs at the meet.

Mika wanted to tag along but Bear had said unequivocally not. The last thing he needed was Coyote mucking up the works. Besides, he had Glen and Sung to more than represent the canines. In two days, they would make their way to Colorado Springs and the ballpark. Until then they would gather in Bear's backyard and try to come up with a plan of action to assure the children of the land would not be forsaken once again.

Mika was not happy with being left on the sidelines during this very important meet. Hadn't he come through in the past? Hadn't he been there for Bear when he had attempted the same thing before? Yeah, there had been some bumps, scrapes, and wounded feelings but not all had been his fault. He was of the mind that all had been forgiven and he was back in the pack. Bear was being quite unfair. So, Mika felt no remorse as he lay low in the deep grass behind Bear's to listen into these brilliant minds.

As they gathered around a blazing bonfire in Bear's yard the pipe was passed along with the never-ending bottle. This would guarantee shared interest, truth, bonds of unity and friendship. Bear took his eyes from the gathered People to see former Sheriff John peeking around the corner of the house. Shit! The one human he should never forget had been forgotten.

Bear got up from his seat to welcome the sheriff—it was the only way Bear would ever think of the man—and apologized profusely for leaving him out of the meet. Here was the one human Bear would trust with his life and the lives of his most precious, Rebecca and Alex. And he'd slipped from Bear's mind like an inconsequential buzz. He would want to have the man's counsel.

John, of course, forgave his old friend while he traded hellos with all he knew and met those he hadn't before. Bear gave a quick synopsis of what the tour had accomplished, hoped to accomplish, what he hoped their meet would bring together and what each of them would bring to the conclave. All of which ignited an animated debate.

Most were of the mind they didn't want to trust man again. They had attempted that before only to have man decide killing was once again the answer, not living side by side in peace. They all had had enough of death, what they desired most was life, to allow their children to multiply and grow strong. Maybe it would never be as it had been in the long past but they could envision a future for all except man.

"If you think you are going to exterminate man or extinct him in any way you have not been paying attention for the past couple hundred thousand turns of the Mother. Man breeds faster and with greater destruction and hunger than any other animal on the Mother. Unlike most of the People man is never satisfied with what he has, he always feels the need to have more, even to the point of gluttony." Sung wanted to help Bear but he had watched his children being slaughtered every single time they began to recover. Their stomachs growled with hunger while man sat bloated and gorged and wondering where he could find more. Man didn't see the future only the now. What did he care if his children's children would suffer? He wanted everything and more on a gold plate.

"I believe the first thing we have to do is not judge all by the actions of a few," Bear wanted to nip the anger before he had a revolution on his hands.

"A few who destroy everything they touch," murmured someone who sounded very much like Tatanka.

Bear had counted on him being a voice of reason, though if any here had just cause to want his pound of flesh that one was seated across from Bear right now. He chose to ignore the taunt.

"We have a group of bohemian hippy types traveling around the country with one purpose in mind, to raise awareness of the mistreatment of their most vulnerable."

"Yes, of their OWN." Muttered Sung.

"Yes, of their own. If they care that much about humans who have been oppressed, enslaved, beaten, killed without afterthought, and abused as deeply as humans have us, maybe we can convince them we share a common cause. The abuse of one is the same as the abuse of all.

"If we join forces with them and their followers, they will see that benefits all. How one child cannot survive without all other children. Maybe, just maybe, we can put an end to all the massacres." Bear was tired. He had fought this fight for decades. Though even as tired as he was, as tired as his words were, they still carried weight. "I think if we present a unified front, maybe even show some of these decent kind who and what we are and why we fight, maybe they will see the truth and wish for life."

The sound of crickets, buzz of night fliers, the croak of Finn's people from the creek out back mixed with thoughts and considerations. Most here felt the edge of extinction so close their claws were dangling over. They knew they could carry their anger against man until the end of time but what would that bring them? More death? They could sing the death songs until they themselves were no more and man would continue in his way. Hadn't they convinced some back when they had joined forces with Juan Maria Olevares from the United Nations? Maybe they could find those same humans, those who had fought so hard to save the Mother to take up the battle once again, only this time for all.

They would have to convince humans to take a nonviolent approach to ending the destruction of habitat. Owl nodded vigorously. "Yes, we have to convince them it is not only beneficial to our kind, but also very much to theirs." He was thinking of the clear cutting happening throughout the world's forests, taking away the game, the food supplies of small rodents, fish, snakes, frogs, all the good things in life. Just as that took away the filtering of the air.

Cynthia and Finn eyed him suspiciously, though they knew he was only killing to live, not out of greed. They, themselves, killed lesser lives to sustain their kind, he was only reverting to nature. It was as the Mother and Great Spirit had created them. But only what was needed to live!

"Do we wish to remain here and solidify our bonds with each other until we travel?" Chastity eyed the small brook where she had swum up from and sighed. It would keep her wet and her skin moist but it would not be the most comfortable few suns. Sometimes you have to suffer for your art.

"We have food for all," Rebecca announced after getting an eye affirmation from Alex. "I believe we have considered all diets and requirements. You are more than welcome to share what we have. When was the last time we shared company with this many of the People in peace and alliance without animosity?"

"Ya-hey," responded the assembled. "Would there be more of this fine drink and smoke?"

John sat back and marveled at how well these different species could come together for a common purpose and wondered why humans never could. His met Bear's eyes and they both smiled, old friends don't hold grudges. John would be there for whatever Bear required, advice, counsel, or friendship. One more adventure with the myths of the past. Ya-hey indeed.

A Test Of Will Power

The evening had turned out better than Padon could've hoped. It was almost as wonderful as his evening with Dr. Caldwell and Janet, when they tricked him into playing them a couple songs in Dr. Caldwell's dining room. They had decimated him with a deck of cards and he had arrogantly jumped into the trap. He'd had to play.

The great outcome of the beat down and resulting dining room table concert was that he realized he found great joy just playing a couple tunes for friends. It had awakened his love of playing once again. The pure pleasure of sitting around with a dram or two of very fine bourbon and playing songs for people he cared about. It was what the music was created for. Or should have been. He had lost his way years before and had no idea how to come out of the miasma. He'd had to find the reason d'music. He had in the cramped dining room of a seventy some year-old doctor and her more than capable assistant and nurse, Janet.

He had recreated that ambience on a patio at sunset on the Colorado plains. Maggie glowed with pride at the response from her friends. They thought he was just a guy who played songs in bars for background entertainment. A good time bar song slinger. He was far more than they had bargained for. He played a half dozen of his songs that he felt would fit the situation. They shared wine, a warm evening, companionship, and love. Perfect.

Now they were bouncing along a two-lane gravel road to get to a country route which would join up with the state route finally connecting with route 50 to Interstate 25 up to the Springs. They had found rooms at the Hampton Inn almost right across the street from the ballpark. Rooms had come open when the folks who had originally booked them found out there was an invasion of hippies coming on a mission to make everyone equal. So, they canceled their rooms thinking they would re-schedule their religious retreat for another time.

Padon felt himself relaxing as he watched the dust kicking up behind the Dodge Ram. This was wide open country, the country he had traversed for forty years, playing in little towns to people who would've rather heard OP (other people's) songs. Songs they'd heard a thousand times by the artist that wrote them and by every yahoo with enough cash to buy a Sears Silvertone and a songbook. They played to get laid and drunk. They had no desire to create something of their own, just living off the work of others and pretend they were rock stars.

Shove it where the sun don't shine, old man, the thought flew through his condemnation of others. Why did you do what you did? To get laid and get drunk, you just thought you were something special because you wrote the script. He'd lost his way and now wanted to scream at others who'd never had a way to lose. Let them have their fun, isn't that what you are now doing at Merle's on Thursdays with a friend? Yeah.

Maggie and Marylou rode in the jeep about a quarter mile ahead so as not to cover them completely with dust. He and Robert had the pickup. They had made the choice to bring both vehicles and all their gear so they could leave out of the Springs to head back home. No sense driving a hundred miles in the wrong direction to spend a night just to turn around and head back the way they'd come. Better to bring the shit and leave from there.

Home. What a marvelous word. He didn't think he'd ever had one of those. The closest he could remember was when he lived in his van on the old man's property outside of Burlington. Just him, a guitar, dreams of grandeur, peace, and serenity. It had been good but there'd been no future. He'd lost a lot of time since then, chasing phantoms, such is the promise of fame, until a future he had not suspected had found him.

They would get to check into the hotel two days before the show. This would give them a chance to tour Colorado Springs, grab some damn good grub, relax, and enjoy the town. When Padon had been on the road touring he never really got to experience the places he played. He'd show up at a flop house, grab some fast food for five bucks, chow down, take a nap, get to the club to do sound check, play and go back to the flop for a few hours rest or just hop in the car and hit the road to the next stop, usually fifteen or so hours away. Routing was not his strong point, but when it was only you if you got tired there were rest stops every forty miles or so.

They pulled up out front of the hotel leaving baggage in the vehicles until checked in. Padon, explaining you don't take your luggage in until you know where the rooms might be. They could be right around the corner of the lobby or on the other side of the hotel meaning you had to schlepp your shit all the way or load it back in your vehicle and drive it around.

The lobby was clean and well kept, that was always a good sign. If the lobby looked old, worn, or dirty the rooms would be worse. The clerk was pleasant, right at the counter with a ready smile so there was no wait. Again, a check in the positive column. She explained that she would need a credit card and I.D. from whoever was responsible for the rooms at which point Robert pushed his way to the counter. Maggie insisted they pay for their own rooms; this was their vacation and only right. Besides Robert and Marylou had bought the tickets to the concert. He acquiesced.

The clerk, not paying attention to the conversation as she was putting Maggie's information into the computer, explained that if they were staying for more than a night—she took a quick glance at the screen and nodded—they should be warned that it might get a bit noisy in the hotel over the next few days. She had decided in her own mind that seeing the ages of the foursome they deserved to be warned.

"Something happening nearby?" Asked Maggie with a glint of humor in her eye.

"Concert." Spoke the clerk with some measure of repugnance.

"Not your taste?" Asked Padon.

"We have had some problems in the past with rowdyism and people not policing their garbage or actions." Again, the pinched visage of disapproval, "It is off-putting to the other guests and damaging to the furniture and our reputation."

"I think you will find the attendees are not the rowdy types you may have encountered previously," Robert laughed. "This will bring an older, more staid, crowd whose rowdy days are well in the rearview. It's a bunch of older artists and singers," he explained.

"So, you know." they could feel her welcoming demeanor retreating to the safety of other side of the wall of her façade.

All checked in and keys in hand they parked their vehicles by the closest door to their rooms and unloaded. Padon and Maggie each had a backpack and he had his guitar. He, harking back to his days traveling the highways and byways of American selling his soul for some applause, not wishing to carry more than necessary. Travel light, travel quickly.

Robert and Marylou had a suitcase each, an overnight bag, and a cooler on wheels with snacks, wine, chocolate, and sandwiches. Padon chuckled when he had watched them loading all in the bed of the truck.

"Sure you got enough?" He kidded Robert, "We're going to be gone three days."

"You need to be prepared," spoke the former Boy Scout, "there are going to be a lot of people in an area that is not used to having that many in one condensed spot. The stores may not have taken that into account when they stocked their shelves." He was not going to take any guff from the man who looked like a walking toothpick. They both chuckled at the good-natured ribbing.

Their first night in the Springs was very laid back. They found a lovely restaurant about ten minutes away called The Lazy Dog that had something for everyone and decent selection of Beers on tap, the wine was nothing to write home about but, again, decent. Wine lovers are hard to please but Café owners tend to be more forgiving.

Back at the hotel they sat in the lobby where they could all visit to discuss plans for the following day. The show would be the day after so they thought they would tourist themselves around the Springs while they had the chance. Robert and Marylou had been here a couple times but they'd never really wandered aimlessly and that, Padon assured, was the way to see a town.

Morning arrived before the breakfast bar closed but only just. Padon and Maggie had enjoyed the sleeping in portion of their vacation the most. Usually, they would be up and at work before the sun thought about peeking over the peaks, so they could get breakfast up and running for the early birders. They could never quite figure out why people in town were so fixed on being up early. There wasn't much going on until at least nine, but they'd come wandering in around six as if they had real jobs. They'd eat, then sit around for an hour or two just visiting. Maggie realized it wasn't the food, it was the town spending time together before they got too busy.

They emulated their Café guests here in Colorado Springs. It wasn't until almost noon that they headed out to see the town. The clerk from the day before was back but in a more pleasant state of mind or just too busy to be judgmental. She told them they should check out Old Town on the other side of Interstate 25. They could take Pikes Peak through town and it would turn into Colorado Ave. That would take them through Old Colorado City and from there they could jump on route 24 to Pikes Peak itself. That should fill their day.

They thanked her politely and she smiled, though there was no joy nor curtesy, just a job there. Robert asked if they thought they should bring along some of the sandwiches, they declined, preferring to take their chances on the local fare up through the mountains. Maggie was a major supporter of buying local, for obvious reasons.

Old Colorado City was delightful and nicely preserved. Shops and cafes galore, restaurants and bars that looked very inviting. The touristas all deciding they should go to Pikes Peak first and come back through Old Town for food and libations so they would not feel pressured.

It is a long climb to the top of the Peak but the view is well worth the drive. There's a little café, The Glen Cove Inn, about halfway up or down depending. They had to stop to have a ranger check their brake temperature right before they came to the inn while descending. They were riding the brakes all the way down and they would need to cool off anyway, so the Inn it was for a quick nosh.

The eased their way back down the rest of the mountain and back onto 24 where they could find their way to a bar in Old Colorado City. Dinner and a few drinks and they were done in. Time for the pool, a hot shower and bed, tomorrow would be a long day.

None had been to an outdoor concert since, well, since they were kids. They wanted to be rested. Padon was fidgety, still concerned some-one might recognize him from twenty years ago. It was stupid and arro-gant but his concern couldn't be shushed. He sat staring out the window, his fingers moving as if playing. It was his way of comforting himself.

"You could play for a little while," said Maggie noting his nerv-ousness, "I'd like to hear it, it might help me sleep, and it might be the thing to calm you down."

Of course, she had noticed. He'd been slightly jumpy all day, though he did his best to hide it, to keep it to himself. "Shows, huh?" sheepish and repentant.

"A bit," she couldn't hide her own worry. She had waited a long time to feel like this again and she didn't want to lose what had been rediscovered. She'd fight to keep him but knew it would be a losing battle. He had been honest about his love of the road, the stage, the songs, and writing. She hoped, but reality didn't believe in hope.

Though she knew, if he couldn't fight it now, it would come to claim him when she would be in too deep and the losing would hurt that much more. She'd rather know now. She was a strong woman but strength had its limits.

She feared hearing these bands, these musicians, and singers would blow on the fire that had been banked for the past few months. He hadn't even considered that.

"It's not what you think. I'm worried someone might recognize me. I shared stages with a few of these artists back in the day. I just, I don't know, I just don't want them to see, to know..." he ran out of words.

"That you're a busboy in some small, hidden mountain town in the middle of nowhere USA?" Now she understood. Padon may not have been a star but he had played some pretty big shows back when he was younger. He didn't want them to know how far he had fallen. Male pride, ego, and self-realization collided in Colorado Springs.

"Play me some music, rock star, and let's see if you get lucky. You are not some busboy in a village, you are someone loved, respected, and surrounded by friends who love your music. Let them suck on that for a while." She pushed his guitar case over to him where he sat and waited.

Hope Springs In Colorado

The entire crew, even the lighting staff were in excellent spirits as they made their way across rural America. Sometimes it was refreshing to get off the highways and see more of the country. Passing through small towns rather than around them, farmland as far as the eye could see backed up by ranches where the dark spots were herds of cattle grazing on the fresh prairie grasses. They caught sight of a small herd of buffalo in the distance and shared the two sets of binoculars so all could see. It wasn't a wild herd but one that was being raised and multiplied for bison meat. Still, it was exciting to catch the sight of them.

They pulled over in Clayton, Texas for a late lunch, a small rural community at the crossroads of route 87 and 412. It was as American as could possibly be found anywhere in the country. They had to split the troop between three restaurants or wait for several hours to feed all at one. Some went to the 87 Restaurant; some went down to the Local Hive, and then a few strayed over to the Taqueria Dalhart for small town Mexican.

Ian, Maggie, and Dennis shared a small table at the Taqueria for some family style. Each ordered more than they could eat and shared. Ben and Dugie split duty at the other joints as they had the credit cards. Though upon further consideration Ian decided to hand out cash to pay the bills. Even with a crowd this size, the prices were extremely reasonable and places like this preferred cash, not card fees!

As they sat in eating silence Ian could tell Dennis wanted to talk to him about something and he knew if an FBI agent wanted to talk to you, it wasn't small talk about the weather.

"Something eating you while you're eating that Torta?" Might as well dig into the subject while he dug into his veggie burrito, specially made for him.

"Ian we've been lucky so far," Dennis stopped, reminding himself that Ian had taken a bullet in Columbia, "I know there was Columbia, and that dust up in Little Rock, and then the first night in Amarillo but nobody has gotten killed." He wanted Ian to know he wasn't blowing off what had happened just keeping things in perspective. "But these crazy white power fucks ain't going to go away quietly."

"You can't hide from hate." Ian said around a bite.

Maggie wanted to tell him to seal it but knew that tone of voice. Ian had his heals dug in and wasn't going to back down from hate filled stupid. She touched his knee gently under the table. He looked like he might say something until their eyes met and he kept the words buried in his chest. Hear the man out, he heard her silent rejoinder.

"I know you and your band of Gypsies refuse to back down and believe you can stand against these folks but they play dirty and rough." He wanted Ian to fully understand they had not felt the brunt of antipathy these troglodytes felt. This could get ugly in an instant. "They are not going to just walk away. They'll be back and probably in larger numbers. We have to face the reality of that. Now, my agents are going to do everything they can to prevent any harm, including taking one or two for the team," he stared hard into Ian's eyes to convey what that meant, "but you gotta do your part and get your people to be more cautious especially when they're at the venue. They are sitting targets. They wander around as if they don't have a care in the world. I'm just begging you to explain to them, these threats are real, they are increasing, and they mean you and yours harm."

Ian wanted to rail against what Dennis was saying but his anger would be spent on a good man who was just trying to do his job and protect people Ian loved. Dennis was a good man in an impossible situation. "I'll remind them, " Ian promised, "but let's keep this in perspective. We only have another half dozen dates booked after the Springs and most of them are in pretty friendly territory."

"And they know that as well," Dennis retorted, "And the closer you get to completing this the more incentive they have to make one last statement. The threat level doesn't go down it increases exponentially. And remember there is no friendly territory where these thugs are concerned. Just because the incidents happened in the south don't mean they won't try as we head into lefty territory. Hell, they increase because what better way to terrorize than in 'enemy' territory."

Ian shook Dennis' hand to seal the pact, he would try to impart on his crew the danger they faced, though he already knew what their response would be. He excused himself and told Maggie he would meet her on the bus, he was going to talk to each group in each restaurant and see if he could instill a modicum of fear in some hearts.

Ian sauntered down to the 87 to collect the group there, half of whom were milling about in the parking lot waiting for the others to finish. When they had collected all, they headed down across the highway to The Bee Hive where the rest had decided they liked the outdoor seating and laid-back vibe. Kind of like fast food, yet not, as it was homemade, with a picnic feel.

As they walked towards the seating area, he noticed Lee standing straight as an oak and glaring hard into the eyes of the man pointing his finger at Lee's chest and vehemently saying something Lee, visibly, didn't like. Ian hurried his step; he certainly didn't need to lose the damn bass player to some idiot.

As Ian strolled up, he heard the words, 'your kind', and 'back to where they came from' as he pointed at Joya. Ian had enough. He had come to collect his people not put up with some asshole who wasn't smart enough to note he was outnumbered fifteen to one.

"Can I help you?" Not what Ian craved to say but he wasn't going to be the one who started the ruckus.

"Yeah, you can take these dirty hippies and them two," here he pointed at Joya and Agent Murry, the FBI guy of a darker persuasion, "outta my town!" He poked Ian in the chest, not hard just making his point.

Ian scowled at the dirty finger before wiping the stink off his shirt. "Ah, so you own this town, do you?" He settled into pissed but controlled mode. "I'm guessing because you are white, stupid, and somehow believe yourself superior to all because you don't tan." He had his anger in check but was losing fingernails quickly.

"No, I don't own the town but I live close by and I don't like this trash dirtying up white man's turf." Now, he crossed his arms across his chest to appear superior though only accomplished making himself appear more silly.

"Why is it," began the negotiator in Ian, "you somehow believe yourself to be better than another who is far more talented, more intelligent, more understanding and accepting, because of the pigment of your skin? I mean really, how can your skin color make you better or worse than another. Shouldn't your character, your accomplishments, your living by a credo of service to others, lending a hand to those worse off than you, shouldn't those attributes be the determining factors as to your worth?" Ian watched the wheels seize up as this troglodyte attempted to parse what he was saying.

"Are you saying you think these blacks," and he spit the word, "these females, these hippie scum are as good as me? Probably got a Jew or two to boot!" He laughed a nervous titter.

"Not at all," grinned the Jew in Ian, "I would never lower my opinion of them to consider them your equal when they are so recognizably your betters." Before the ignorance could kick into the molasses masquerading as cerebra, Ian continued, "You know, which I'm sure you don't as they don't cover our tour or what it's about on the propaganda you consume, so far on the little romp around 'your' America, I have been shot, watched my friends get shot at, our fans attacked, had a group of your intellectual equals attempt to close down this show because they can't conceive of the concepts they profess to believe or the words of the man in the book they claim to follow. We have been threatened at every turn with violence because we know that all men and women were created equal. People don't become less so until some Neanderthal comes along with antiquated ideas, that have been proven a thousand times a thousand to be false, as proof some are less than others.

"Go away, leave my people be. If you cannot be of service then leave those alone who only wish to raise those you would hold down because you can't conceive of equality. You have allowed those more powerful, those who would control you like marionettes, mindless, willing to dance every time they pull your fear, to turn you against those whom you should be in concert with. I'm done trying to educate morons, attempting to open eyes closed so tight they will never see, and minds just as sealed. Those who will never have ability to think for themselves. Go back to your cave, be gone and do not multiply." Ian turned to show his disrespect for this craven waste of molecules and atoms and to collect his people to get as far away from this thing as quickly as possible.

He felt the whoosh of air as something flew by him. His first thought was the pond slime had taken a shot at him, an action he was tiring of very quickly. He turned to do what even he didn't know, when he saw Nash standing with the guy spread out on the ground unconscious.

"He thought to attack you while your back was turned. Would you like me to extinguish him?" He asked as if suggesting he empty the waste can.

"NO! We do not kill others, no matter how repugnant they might be. Let him cool off under the hot sun, we got miles to make." Ian turned back to move everyone in the direction of the parked buses. He took note of Dennis replacing his sidearm in its holster. Cheeses! The thought bolted through his very tired mind.

"I wouldn't've killed him," Nash smiled as they climbed aboard their prospective rides. "Just making a point for anyone who might've been listening."

"I trusted that was your point, it is my expectation that both our points were heard and understood." Ian was living on wishes and the better angels of others at this juncture of life. He couldn't say for certain who was more harebrained, the haters or the hated.

The rest of the day passed uneventfully with Dennis reporting they had detected no one tailing them from either close or a distance. He had placed one of his agents in the rear of the last bus with a telescopic lens to be certain. Ian just wanted to get everyone to the hotel without further stress.

He knew everyone was doing their utmost to appear confident and poised but he could see the tension in the tightening around the eyes, the rigidity of their posture, and the way they would flinch at any unusual clonk, crack, or snap. It was a tired, weary crew that pulled up out back of the hotel. Ian, Ben and Dugie went in to secure the rooms and get keys.

Everyone was exhausted from the strain of the ride and the hours on the road. Ian suggested a pizza and take out party in the lobby to allow all to settle in and relax together. They ordered a dozen and half pizzas of assorted meats, cheeses and piles of veggies, a huge salad with extra veggies, some cheese raviolis, soup and a partridge in a pear tree. No one would go hungry. And, as it appeared no one else was staying at the hotel—they had pretty much every room as far as Dugie could tell—they would disturb no one by occupying the lobby. Guitars were brought down, songs were sung, tension was lifted and a relaxed vibe permeated the hotel. Even the uptight chick at the desk seemed to be pleasantly surprised and loosened her panties enough to smile.

The band and crew hit the sheets by ten o'clock and were out by 10:05.

The Temperature Drops Precipitously

The foursome had filled their day with beauty, fresh air, sights that went on for miles and miles, decent food and some window shopping combined with a little actual purchasing. They'd headed back to the hotel, happy, satiated, slightly tipsy, except Robert who was driving so had only taken a half gummy.

They were shocked to find so many parking spaces by the front door, especially considering the lateness of the hour—past midnight— but happy to leave the truck close. Padon grabbed the keys to Maggie's jeep and moved it closer to the front door as well. An old habit of keeping your vehicle in the brightest parking spot to avoid break-ins and loss of what little you had.

Back in their room Padon gazed out the front windows where he could see the glow of the lights of where the concert would take place. It was then Maggie had asked him to play while she dreamt of the concert.

He played quietly though loud enough for him to hear and her to sleep. His fingers danced up and down the fret board while he ran through some old Irish reels and songs he hadn't played in many years. Shit, he hadn't played some of these since just before she had left with his daughter. They were nice songs but had lost their meaning with the loss of everything else.

He switched to some happier times. Songs he had written over the past few months during his convalescent time in Rock Ridge. Songs he had written for Dr. Caldwell and Janet, for the majesty of the mountains and wonder of nature. He had written a jaunty tune for Mr. Carpenter and a few songs to express his growing passion for Maggie. He closed his room set with his masterpiece, as he would always think of it. It was funny, it felt empty without the bass parts that Wally had brilliantly added to the song.

He heard movement outside the door and silently put the guitar away not wishing to disturb the few other guests at the hotel. He had learned many years ago that to preserve his welcome depended on him not playing loud enough or late enough to disturb others. He had no desire to get evicted from the hotel in the middle of the night.

Morning arrived a wee bit earlier than the day before but just by a nose. They wandered down to the breakfast bar hoping to find it still stocked, though from what they had seen the night before, the empty parking lot and deserted lobby, that should not be a problem. They were rested but not quite awake as they fixated on the coffee pot. People who have a regular schedule do not adjust well to having their routine interrupted.

Padon set his coffee down on one of unoccupied tables and headed to where he saw a basket of fruit. The breakfast bar was teeming with humanity. Where in all hell had these people come from? Had they been bussed here in the middle of the night? He took a glance out the front window and saw the still empty parking lot. Weird.

There were a dozen old hippiesque woman eating grape nuts and berries, oatmeal and eggs, bearded men nodded to each other as they passed on their way to cinnamon rolls and scrambled eggs. The juice machine was doing a brisk business as was the coffee urn.

As Padon passed a table with several of the hippie girls from the sixties who appeared to be in their fifties he heard one of them say, "I'm telling you I know what I heard. You can ask Bonnie; she was with me. We were going down to the lobby to snag some snacks when we heard this wonderful guitar. Songs neither of us were familiar with. Beautiful melodies, just striking. When we stopped to listen for a sec Bonnie bumped the door and the music stopped, we almost knocked but didn't want to disturb whoever was playing." The others nodded though seemed unconvinced. "The thing is I don't think it was one of our rooms."

He smiled to himself, it was nice he had made these old folks happy, as he quit eavesdropping and made his way to the table with Maggie and the gang. The low murmur of the other breakfast diners was a comfort to the four now coordinating their day. They wanted to get to the ballpark early but not so early they had to spend hours standing in line waiting for the gates to open.

There was a stir of activity as new folks came in proceeded by their dour expressions. The long haired, bearded guy at the fore, who gave the impression he was in control—the tour guide, Padon guessed from his look and deportment—asked everyone to settle down.

"It would seem our detractors have followed us and done some damage to the buses. We're going to have to walk over to the park and set up there." He was not a happy man. He had the weight of this group on his shoulders and now he had a major glitch getting them to the show that they had been promised.

"Some of us have a bit of gear to haul," one of the women spoke up, "I mean, I know it's not far but we got some shit to carry."

Padon guessed with a group like this going to an all-day music fest they would have folding chairs, blankets, coolers, all kinds of necessities for long time concert attendees. He wondered why anyone would bother to mess with the transportation of a bunch of middle-aged hippies out for a lark, but who knew who was PO'd about whose political leanings and just wanted to fuck with somebody. It pissed him off. He made eye contact with Robert and they both shrugged.

"I'll tell you what," Padon jumped in before he could consult Maggie or his brain, "We have a couple vehicles, a Jeep and a big ol' pick-em-up truck, we can't ferry you all in one trip but we can get you over in a few, if that would help." He still had a trunk load of karma on his tail, this might help lessen the load.

"You shitting me?" asked the tour guy. "That would be fantastic. We'd pay you for whatever gas and stuff."

"Nah, it's only a few blocks and we're heading that way anyway. We'll just take a little longer getting into the show. Didn't want to stand in line for half a day to begin with, this will be a nice distraction." If Maggie was going to argue or take him to task for offering, the looks of relief on the faces of those who would now ride rather than walk stayed her comments. She sighed, wasn't that what this feel-good concert was about? Helping others. They were in no hurry and they could do a good turn.

As the cadre of hipsters began returning from their rooms with their 'gear' in hand, Padon had to wonder what they thought they were attending. Some had guitars, changes of clothes, one guy had a cymbal case. He had seen this when he was touring and doing some of these outdoor festivals. People would bring their shit as if there was a chance an act might not show up and they'd need to be put in as relief pitchers. No one who lugged a guitar to a concert ever got brought up on stage. He wasn't even going to carry his over there for fear he would embarrass himself for the doing. But whatever; he'd offered, they'd carry.

"I'll ride along with you for the first trip to show you where to park and drop everyone off, if that's alright," the tour guide suggested.

Padon figured they must have some kind of preferential bus parking. One good thing, they wouldn't have to wait in long vehicle lines each trip!

"Dugie," a couple of the hipster guys came up to the tour guy, "We're just going to walk. It's nice out and we could use some leg work." He nodded.

Now, why did that name sound familiar? Ah well, one less trip they'd have to make. Maggie and Marylou decided they would get their belongings together while the boys made their appointed rounds.

This Dugie instructed them to pull around back and through the gates. They were headed backstage, who the hell were these people? Padon soon found out as Jaxson Grahm himself came up to the vehicles to thank him and Robert profusely for bringing the musicians and singers over. He asked if they could ferry the classical quartet next as they were the first to take the stage. He gave Padon the once over trying to place him before returning to whatever he'd been doing.

The next trip was the quartet, James Nash, Bonnie Welch, and a couple of other women Padon didn't recognize. A tall native looking fellow with long, tan hair—who the hell had tan hair—and a small very, pretty brown woman said they would make their own way. Bonnie gave Padon a curious look as she got in the back seat of the Jeep. She glanced a couple times in the rearview mirror as if trying to place him before grinning. She kept her thoughts to herself.

Padon was sweating, it was one thing to be nameless and faceless in a crowd of thousands but he was in a car with someone he had shared a stage with. Granted it had been decades ago and he certainly didn't look the same, but did he look that much different? Both Bonnie and Jaxson had given him the squint-eye. They had to, at the very least, think his face rang a very distant bell. Nothing for it now.

Three more trips and they were done. The elderly gent who had kept an eye on he and Robert as they dropped the performers off came to thank them for their help.

"Dugie tells me you guys are coming to the show?" He spoke to Robert but his eye kept wandering in Padon's direction. Robert gave an affirmative answer. "Then, I would like you to be my guests." He handed Robert full access passes to get them and the ladies into the backstage and beyond. What could Padon do or say? Robert, Marylou, and Maggie had never had this kind of access to this level of performer, so he couldn't turn them down. He would just keep a low profile and hope.

When they returned to the ballpark with Maggie and Marlou in tow, the two women were astounded they were given passes into the backstage area.

"Who did you two impress?" Asked Maggie.

Robert was beaming, like a kid living a dream. "Those people we helped out earlier?" he waited for nods of assent from both women, "They were the show!" He almost shouted his glee. "We get to hang out with the musicians backstage!"

Bonnie still sported the smirk she had adopted on the ride over. Jaxson couldn't help but notice. "Don't you look like the cat that ate the canary in the coal mine." He loved to mix his metaphors.

"Do you remember a cat from a thousand years ago, Padon McKensie, pretty good songwriter. Did a few tours back in the day?" She attempted to jump start his memory banks.

"Yeah, I do," a strange glint of recognition flew across his face. "He kind of blew up, didn't he? Lost his wife or something, got drunk stayed that way for a decade or two?" Then it hit him.

"Yeah," said Bonnie, "I think he's the one who drove us over here. Too much of resemblance to be coincidence. And I am damn sure that's who I heard playing last night when Gillian and I went to grab snacks in the lobby."

"What the hell is doing here? Think he is trying to get a spot on the show?" Jaxson thought if that was Padon's plan he had a weird way of going about it.

"I don't think so. He was attempting not to be noticed as far as I could tell. I think he and his friends were coming to the show, stayed at our hotel, unknowingly from the way he reacted when he realized who we all were, and just happened to offer to do a good turn for people who could use a hand." Her gaze turned toward the general direction of where they'd been dropped off.

"How was what you heard?" Jaxson had his humanitarian hat on.

"Fantastic! Stuff I never heard before and can only guess it's his stuff," She knew immediately where he was going. "Not sure he'd play unless forced to from what I saw. Maybe talk to his partner, she might be the only road into that forest." Bonnie knew there were more reasons to walk away from the business than there were to want in. And just as many not to want to play again, though from what she'd heard in the hallway this cat had been playing all along, no matter the circumstances.

"Let's see if we can corral her," Jaxson had a plan forming in the crazy part of his brain.

Maggie and Marylou wanted to explore the backstage area as neither had ever been close to having this access. Robert tagged along because he was a good and obedient husband. Padon found a place where he could sit out of the way and, hopefully. where nobody would notice or recognized him. All the while chastising himself for thinking he had made any kind of impression on anyone here let alone one that would remain after decades, ego be still. Well, he thought, you might have made that kind of impression but he prayed no one could recall the why. He'd fought some tough demons and they'd won most of those bouts.

What had been an isolated attack of nerves when he'd gone to his first open mic had become habit over his career and easily slipped into from where he sat. He always showed up well before the show to gauge the crowd. It soothed the savage to see who was in the audience. Were they young, old, black, white, full of energy or sedentary, cute girls or blue collar after work parties? He wanted to know.

So, here he sat out of the way of those readying the stage and lighting. Though if he was to be honest, he was hiding, hiding from those whom he thought recognized an old worn-out former musician. From his perch at the side of the stage amongst the trap cases, road cases for guitars, and the keys, he could watch as people slowly made their way through the stadium and onto the field. They didn't rush or push each other out of the way in order to get prime seating. They helped the older ones carry folding chairs and coolers, letting others moving faster get in front of the slower ones who would then reserve a spot for those they'd just passed. Sometimes grabbing a blanket so when the slower showed up they would have a place to drop.

No, this was not your typical rock and roll show. These were people with empathy for others, for the planet, for all mankind. It filled his heart with a belief, a faith in the future. He smiled and gazed at the clear blue sky. Was it possible there were enough of these to make a difference in the lives of those left behind?

There was parting in the sea of people as the tall, powerful tan haired native began to come through. He did not ask for them to move aside and appeared perplexed and self-conscious they would. He did not pass through but grabbed canvas bagged chairs, coolers, blankets, carrying ten at time while allowing those with too many years on ancient legs and bodies to lean on him to walk. He traded small talk and knowing nods with those who walked in his wake. The small native woman holding up those who required assistance as well. They were the embodiment gentleness and compassion.

As the strong assisted the old and tired, Padon's attention was forced to where a small band of natives made their way over to walk with the two while also chatting with those who paraded into the ballpark. They, like their brother and sister, relieved the tired of their burdens while rebuffing thanks and gratitude, as if the thanks were unseemly and unnecessary. It was their honor to help those in need, especially the elders.

Padon wanted to cry for the pure decency of it. He wanted to jump down from his perch and run onto the field to lend two more hands. But just as he was rising from his seat there was a gentle hand on his shoulder. It was Maggie. There was a sadness laying deep in her eyes that found its way down to the creases of her smile. Possibility and fear.

The Face Of Fear Is To Face Your Fear

They gathered in Bear's backyard; it was time. They would walk the spirit road to Colorado Springs where they could come out backstage and avoid any embarrassing scenes with the ticket takers. Iktomi wondered why they couldn't just walk by, she could! Bear had to remind her that they were much larger than the Spider. Could she imagine trying to sneak Tatanka or Elk past the security? Plus, he wanted them to all to arrive as one. Nash had told them the time frame of the show and they wanted to be there an hour or more before it commenced, white people time. He knew that during and after the show there would be no chance for the meet. He wanted the full attention of all the Gypsies. Nash would assure all would be where they wanted when they wanted.

Bear put Sheriff John in charge of keeping an eye on Glen. He retained a penchant for chasing things he should not, a problem with focus, and thinking everybody wanted to be his friend. He required watching. He hoped everyone else would fit in with the attendees and musicians. That they would not create a great stir by showing up en mass. From what Nash and Suzette had described, the only People who might stand out were Tatanka and Elk, but that was a size issue and could not be changed. It was ragtag group that played and sang as well as came to these shows, they were oddities personified. These were the geeks and freaks of humanity.

Suzette had taken Bear aside when she and Nash had stopped by to remind him how the machine of human society was oiled and why the fans of this tour were so important. Human societies throughout history were run by the supposed strongest, the most virile of the village or kingdom. That was the story of mankind. The most warlike ruled over the others through fear and intimidation, but as humans evolved their societies became increasing more complex. The most physically intimidating humans were not always the most intelligent and, therefore, did not have the capabilities to handle complex social or technological dilemmas. What they required were the geeks and nerds to decipher issues, break them down into simplicities and allow the leaders to take full credit.

The people coming to these concerts were those geeks and nerds who solved the problems set before them by the figureheads. The humans Bear should seek to ally himself with. They would see the danger of their current course and be solution oriented.

Previously, he had misread the human race, thinking to ally himself with the heads of states. Those in power usually were concerned only with holding onto that power; and the wealth and prestige that accompanied it. They hadn't a clue, nor did they care, how to solve mankind's most pressing concerns. And they certainly didn't have the capacity to equate the danger to any one species as a precursor to the demise of their own.

They had to find those who could see, deduce, were enlightened enough to understand the connections between species and willing to do whatever was necessary to save the whole. She and Nash were convinced that the vast majority, though not the whole, of these concert goers were the humans they sought. They took peyote, smoked cannabis and hash in order to expand their consciousness. They took LSD to travel the dream roads, while awake, to observe and learn. They would see connections not observable by those in power and they had the wherewithal to solve. They knew the machines. They loved their computers and all they could accomplish, because they understood them on a molecular level.

Bear grokked what she explained, though he hadn't a clue how the machines worked. He knew they could solve complexities he couldn't begin to imagine. These would be their last hope to save the Mother.

They passed the pipe and shared the smoke with their brothers and sisters, cousins and all the relatives. They blew smoke to the ancients and drank of the endless bottle to cement their love of each other and their place in the universe.

They stood in a circle around the blazing fire where they could look into each other's eyes, into each other's spirit and know they were one. Bear, Alexandra, Rebecca, former Sheriff John of the humans, Tatanka, Lawrence the Elk, Sung and Glen, Owl, Finn of the amphibians, Cynthia of the reptiles, Iktomi, Chastity of the great oceans; family. They would join with Nash and Suzette once they arrived at the venue. Today was a good day to live. Mitakuye Oyasin.

Bear thought it wise to take the spirit road as it removed the concept of time from their travel. They could share each other's company and dreams while they walked the Red Road. It might take them a month on the Red Road but it would only be a few hours in man's world or they could be there in the burbling of a stream and man would have lived a hundred of his years. Once you knew the workings, it served a great purpose. This trip would take them through the mountains and across the prairie, walk the beaches of the Mother and swim her rivers before crossing back over. It would be good to walk among the People, share with each other, and Sheriff John, though they didn't think of him as a man but of the People, for a month.

Bear took John by the arm as they passed through the vale. It took John several breaths, as it always did, to readjust to the beauty, the clarity, the brilliance of the spirit world. He found it hard to breathe it all in. As they began to walk, he felt his heart rate slow, his blood pressure drop, a sense of peace and completion wrapped him in a cocoon as welcoming as a Mother's embrace.

They spent the next four weeks spirit time hunting, fishing, romping through the forests, past the tree lines, to the peaks of the highest mountains, splashing in the oceans and rivers, bathing in the love and light of creation. They filled themselves with that creation, that sense of renewal, rebirth of faith and belonging to all. They sought joining with the Great Spirit and promised the Mother they would not fail her again. They believed they had found the way, the only way, to save all and they committed themselves to that and only that mission.

It was time, they crossed back over. Nash and Suzette stood waiting, knowing exactly where and when they would come.

If Padon thought he had been impressed by the visage of the large, tan-haired Native, all six foot six or seven of him, it was nothing to what he felt as he watched the body native that strolled out from behind one of the equipment trucks. The buses might have been sabotaged but the trucks, luckily, had been parked over behind the stage with plenty of security guarding them. They had learned in Trenton not to leave anything of import where it could be damaged.

There walked two of the largest human beings he had ever seen, they towered over the tan native and made the small woman look like a dwarf. Padon wondered how those two had made it backstage so quickly through the massive crowd.

The group that emerged included an elderly man and his woman, she could only be his woman by the way they looked at each other, and a young girl, woman, he corrected himself, who had to be family by the resemblance. There was an obese woman who moved with a grace he would not have believed, two men who must be cousins, another small woman who had a sideways gait walking with a woman who seemed to glide through the grass, joined by a young man who was as overjoyed being somewhere, anywhere, as any human Padon had ever seen. Lastly, a tall, lean biker fella trying to calm the kid down, all joined by Nash and Suzette. They spoke for several moments before turning and walking in the direction of Jaxson's private practice area. They were accompanied by a medium height and build, grey haired, man Padon had failed to note due to his ordinariness amongst the eccentric collection. He had the bearing of a cop, weird.

Padon felt compelled to follow, though he knew Maggie wanted to speak to him, it would have to wait. She could accompany him. Though before he could take a step, he noticed the ragged, wan man following the group. His eyes furtive, his steps slow, skulking, slinking, as if worried one of them might notice him trailing them. Curiouser and curiouser. Padon stayed back but shadowed the newcomer. Maggie shadowed Padon just as intrigued as he.

Jaxson was deep in concentration, his fingers dancing up and down the fretboard. A bomb could've gone off next to him and it would not have broken that immersion. He was completely oblivious to the small army as they closed in. Gabby was not, he quick-stepped to get Ian, with Maggie and Jeanette in tow. As Dugie caught sight of the four of them heading with intent, he tapped Ben and the group increased by two.

Jaxson continued to concentrate on fingers and chord changes as he was working out a new tune in his head. He hummed with eyes closed then attempted what his muse was trying to impart on the strings of his guitar. Frustrated he opened his eyes to see what was wrong with the damn chord and was shocked to find himself surrounded by more than twenty people, some of whom he recognized. He smiled. It was typical of himself to be so absorbed he wouldn't've noticed the oncoming storm.

"Can I help?" he wasn't certain to whom he directed the question or if he wanted an answer, but manners were manners and it had to be asked.

"We are told you are the man in charge of this entourage," Bear grinned back. Keep it friendly.

"I don't know if these other folks would agree completely but I certainly count as one small piece of the Untouchable pie." It was here he noticed Nash and Suzette integrated within the contingent. He nodded hello and relaxed. He had come to respect and trust these two, he felt no threat.

Suzette took a step forward, checking with a glance at Bear, he inclined his head for her to continue. "These People,"" and Jaxson heard the implied capital P, "Wanted to meet with you, Ian, and all involved to propose the possibility of forming an alliance."

The small legation was now swelling with interested musicians, singers, and crew. Carrie couldn't help but join along with Barbara, the girls, Aron and Oscar, who immediately found Glen. He sniffed and kissed the young man with a joy Carrie was shocked by. Oscar was a friendly sort but this was beyond the pale.

"It looks as though most of those you would want to speak with have arrived," Jax waved at the assembled musicians and roadies. The heart and soul of the Untouchables road Show.

Jaxson was having trouble focusing on the faces and forms of the newcomers. The more he tried to scrutinize this cadre of natives—yes, he realized, they were all of native blood though of differing nations—the more his eyes slipped away from their forms. It was as if something was pushing his attention away from the group. He thought maybe it was because he was so focused on the strings and fretboard, he was having difficulty focusing on people. Yet he could see his friends just fine.

Padon found a spot behind the trap case of Lee's large bass bin. He could see where the raggedy man had hunkered down to listen while observing the rest as well. If the guy tried anything Padon would be ready and he would be on him like Bearnaise on eggs before he could get close to any connected to the show. He wondered, as he sat hidden, Maggie at his side, where Robert and Marylou had got to. Focus, boy, focus.

Jaxson noticed the older guy with the bearing of a cop, he appeared solid enough, Jax pushed his eyes that-a-way. "What it is you would want from us?"

Now the older man that Suzette had deferred to took over. "We represent the rest of the living creatures of the Mother, what we need to know is if you and yours can concede that we are all interrelated. That man cannot live without the rest of us, that we are all significant to the Mother."

Jax gazed over at Ian to see if he was grasping this better than he was. Who the hell are these people that said they represented all living things?

"We know that your hearts are true, but you seem to be considering only your own kind," Suzette took over again. She knew this man, she knew these people, she had to appeal to their better angels. "But there are billions more that live on the Mother who face the danger of starvation, being hunted, decimated by disease and neglect, extinction.

They suffer just as yours do. Humans never consider how their actions affect those who share the world."

Jaxson rubbed his eyes. Was he hallucinating? He could swear he saw her morph from Suzette to an animal, an otter or something, right before him. He noticed others of his camp shaking heads and blinking. What the hell was happening? Maybe someone had put a little mescaline in the coffee this morning.

Everyone's attention was riveted to the scene playing out before them, attempting to separate reality from hallucination, everyone, that is, except Oscar who could not seem to leave the young man alone. Glen petted and rubbed the big dog hoping it would satisfy his longing, but the more he rubbed the more Oscar wanted to play. The tall, thin, biker looking fellow standing next to the young man could not contain his mirth at the situation. Carrie tried to take control of the predicament but Oscar would have none of it. The crew couldn't help but notice and find the humor as well.

"Maybe the three of you could go have a little walk and let Oscar satisfy his curiosity." Suggested the biker with a grin.

There was nothing for it but to take him up on his suggestion. Carrie, Oscar, and Glen moved out further behind the stage where they would not be a distraction. Within a breath the young man and Oscar were wrestling on the ground like two kids. The more they wrestled the harder it was to distinguish between the two. She could swear she saw two dogs, not a dog and young man, rolling on the ground. She was tired.

Meanwhile Jaxson was trying to process what had been said. The man's words indicated he didn't think of himself as human and Suzette aped that attitude. He had run into groups that placed animals equal to or above humans, P.E.T.A. or rescue organizations, save the whales, the elephants, the panthers, leopards, frogs, and any number of specists, but he had never run into ones who thought they were part of or related to the species they were trying to save. These folks might be in need of a psychological assist.

"Are you telling me that you represent animals throughout the world?" Let's see if we couldn't narrow down the psychosis.

Bear stifled a laugh, "Oh, not just animals but reptiles, amphibians," here Jaxson saw a nod from the small man with the professorial bearing, the thin, lithe woman, "birds of the air, and those who swim in the seas." His words were serious, though he retained a jovial demeanor. "We are the representations of those who roam the prairies and hunt the elevations." Each in turn nodded in acquiescence. The time for obfuscation, playing hide and seek with myth and reality was over. If they were to save themselves, their children, life, from extinction they had to lay their cards on the table.

Bear had decided to take an extraordinary risk here. If they showed their true selves the humans would either choose to trust their eyes or they would flip out, presuming they had been drugged or hypnotized. It was one of the reasons John had suggested trying to get as many of the humans of this troop together as possible, which had happened organically as human curiosity is an irresistible force. The more people there were the less likely they would believe it possible to hypnotize them all at once or, John knew, a few of them would have done enough drugs to know the sensations of being drugged and would discount the possibility as there were none of the above.

John stepped forward to stand next to Bear. Padon thought the man looked small compared to the larger fella, but he was solid as stone and just as permanent. "I want you to know you can trust these folks and everything they say, they speak truth." He wanted these people to understand, to know above any and all else the People could be trusted. He reached inside his jacket, then stopped. Forty years as a cop gave him a tingling warning, every single human froze. Angst stayed all motion. The almost imperceptible motion from the clean-cut crew member, who John now realized was NOT a crew member, stayed his hand. The fella had reached behind his back to the gun that John instinctively knew was there. John pulled his hand out of the inside pocket of his jacket while raising his left hand in the air. In his right was a small wallet. He let it open to reveal a shiny, gold badge. The world let out a breath.

"Sorry, wasn't thinking. I guess you folks have had a bit of trouble along the way." He grinned the apology. "I just wanted you to know who I was, my fault. I wanted you to understand who I am so you will know that what these People tell you is true. That, hopefully, you can trust me and them." He allowed his words to sink in until the tension released.

Bear showed himself. The others followed suit until there stood a plethora of species, animal, arachnid, reptile, amphibian, sea mammal, and fowl. It was like a Disney movie come to life in a thriller, these were not the cuddly cartoons Walt would have had drawn. Ian's dreams came to life while he was fully awake.

Before anyone could have a chance to adjust to this new reality there was a disturbance stage right as a dozen Native Americans pushed their way through the two security guys standing guard. Jaxson tore his eyes away from the large creatures to see what was happening and what was coming his way now! The security guys pointed at the contingent of Indians headed Jax's way with a shrug. Security indeed! Apparently, they could not see the wild hallucination Jaxson saw. They only saw First Nation folks talking with Ian, Jaxson and the others, and could only assume these were part of the whole. Jaxson recognized Joseph Standing Bear. Well, why not?

"Ya-hey," he called to Jaxson, waved at Ian, and hugged Maggie. "Interesting company indeed." He said taking in the group standing across from those he'd met in Rapid City. "The compunction to come to you could not be ignored," he said to the entertainers, "Apparently, it was not you who called. I offer my respect and love, grandparents." He nodded to Bear and the others.

"What in all hell is going on?" Ian liked a good practical joke as much as the next promoter, but...

"We have come to read the hearts and minds of these," Bear waved to include all assembled. "What has brought you here?" Bear found humor where others discovered confusion.

"We have had dealings with these people. We confronted them as, I am guessing, you are confronting them now, in Rapid City, our home." He clarified just in case the Spirits weren't sure where Standing Bear and his troop fit in, "They spoke their truth and we found their words to be honest. They have done for us what they promised without asking for anything in return. They have been the mountain and the wind, solid, clear, always there when we needed them." Joseph stood with the Untouchables. "I am guessing we were called to vouch for them."

"That was for their own or whom they perceive as those like them, human. Will they do the same for all the creatures of the world or are they only concerned with humans," it was Tatanka's voice that caused the earth to tremble.

"We have helped our own as that was our mission," Ian began. "that is true. Those who we set out to lift from being forced into hard labor, enslavement, the outcasts of humanity."

He meant to say more but Coyote jumped from his hiding place. He moved far too quickly for Padon to intercede; and probably just as well as he would not have fared well against one of the People. Padon fell flat on his face in his vainglorious attempt.

"Just like humans, mankind only thinks of himself. I could've told you that but you wouldn't listen," Mika gloried in Bear's failure. This would teach the 'great one' to disrespect and not include him. "Humans only care about themselves, they think themselves above and separate from all the rest of life, don't they?"

Carrie, Oscar, and, she now knew, Glen walked up to catch the end of this discussion. Carrie knelt next to Oscar hugging him close. "It is not only other people we treasure," she said the love evident, palpable.

"Russell Means once told the story that when he was a small child his grandparents taught him that if all the green things that grow were taken from the Mother, there wouldn't be life. And if all the four-legged creatures were gone, there wouldn't be life on the earth. If all the winged creatures of the air were taken from the Mother, there couldn't be life. If all the cousins who crawl, swim, and burrow into the Mother were gone, there wouldn't be life. But if you were to remove all the humans from the Mother, life would flourish. Man is insignificant, to save one is to save all." Soteria stood, eyes closed as if in a trance, reciting something she had possibly learned in grade school, except she did not recite from rote but from her heart. "We choose life."

Silence. No one contradicted her. No one said she did not speak for all. They accepted her words as law. The purpose, the mission of the tour had been expanded exponentially. Mitakuye Oyasin.

"It is my considered opinion we have found our brethren in the species of man." Proclaimed Bear with all his great heart. All the assembled species of life reached out to these representatives of man. Hands were clasped in brotherhood, silent promises made. Faith reborn if only just, now to see if hope would be the seed.

A Pact Made Of Trust And Respect

"I know you have to ready yourselves for your show, so we won't hold you any longer, for now. But I do want to have a much longer discussion to include all my cousin's input. They were kind enough to travel here to show solidarity, we should respect them enough to hear their thoughts. They have many ideas that they feel would be of value to you and your musical family. And I am quite certain you have more than a few questions for us." Bear spoke for all.

The Native Spirits returned to a form the humans could feel comfortable being around. White folks found it near impossible to grasp the myths of other folks. If angels had appeared with thunderbolts in each hand to strike down demons rampaging across the land, they would have no problem getting on board. But legends from Native myths of creation, spirits that are immortal acting as protectors for their children and guides for the indigenous folks who use these animal totems as symbols of strength, honor, and the best attributes of clans, this would take some getting used to.

This foray into the gypsy camp was to make contact, let these humans know who they were and what they would expect the tour to help accomplish. More would come.

"I would invite you to ride with us but unfortunately our buses have been sabotaged. We are furiously," and here Jax looked to Ian for confirmation, "attempting to find either repairs or replacements. Not easy when you have such a circus as this."

"Understood. Though we have no need of your transport, I would like a little more time with you and yours. Maybe we can convince you through another demonstration," Bear had an inspiration, an idea he would need to discuss with the others. He was positive they would hate it but in time see the wisdom. Ya-hey he said to the universe, the Great Spirit, and the Mother. Hope is a comfort, though on cold nights it would not keep the chill at bay.

"You are more than welcome to hang out here, enjoy the food and drink, listen to the music and we can retire to the hotel for further discussion if that suits." Jaxson really wanted time to find out if all the others had witnessed the same hallucination as he. Speaking of witnessing and wondering. "Padon, is that really you?" Jaxson was the epitome of innocence.

Padon had done everything he could to blend into the background but had failed miserably. He stood with his dignity in his right hand and Maggie's hand in the other. She grinned, but there was trepidation behind her eyes. Something else had taken place today and he didn't think he was going to like it.

"Yes." Like the toll of doom. He had failed to stop the one called Coyote and had reignited the memory of a man he respected, not just as a songwriter and musician but as a person. Now Jaxson would find out Padon had fallen hard, spent his life as a failure, almost killed himself, and landed in some speck in the mountains hiding from that life.

"I ran into your friend," here Jaxson indicated Maggie, "before all this falderal took place. I had a nice conversation with her and her friends. Your Maggie tells me you have found a home in the mountains. That you are content. Is this true?" He was teasing Padon but only slightly.

"Yes," again Padon felt as though he was walking into a trap, just like when Janet, Dr. Caldwell, and Maggie had set him up to work at the café. Though, truth be told, that had worked out admirably.

"She tells me you do a regular Thursday night with a friend of yours, and that you are now happy playing just for your friends. True?" He was leading somewhere and Padon was certain as death he didn't want to follow, but here he was stuck between rock and a hard case. He felt Maggie's hand tighten on his in apology.

"We were just talking, before all this..." The words, the heart, the guilt, spilled from Maggie. She knew she had betrayed Padon though she wasn't quite certain how, but she knew. And the confession tumbled like rapids in a spring swollen creek, "I mean, I've been a fan since I was old enough to know good music, and here I am just talking with someone I kind of idolized. He said he recognized you from the olden times, and he liked what you used to do, and he'd heard rumors, but here you were and I just couldn't, I just said, I just..." she was beat red and looked about to break down in hysterical tears. Padon pulled her in close and held her, rubbing her back, reassuring her of his total and complete love. There was nothing this woman could do that would shake that love. Though he was also not overjoyed with the turn this was obviously taking.

At that particular moment Robert came huffing up from behind the group, tailed closely by his wife, with a very familiar guitar case in his hand. He looked to Jaxson, then to Ian, then to Padon, then set the case down and slowly backed away. He'd only known this man for a little over a week, but he'd heard the man's music, knew his heart, and also knew others should hear his songs. If he was wrong let him be wrong in doing right.

"You don't have to if you really don't want to," Jaxson assured him, "though Maggie tells me you have written some marvelous and lovely songs. Would you mind playing them for a few thousand friends. I got a slot right after the quartet I'd love to fill."

Padon had been played as neatly, beautifully as Mr. Grahm played the strings of his instrument. He should be furious with him, with her, with them, but when he looked in her eyes, he saw she wanted this. She wanted to see him in his glory in front of ten thousand. To play songs she loved. She was willing to take the chance this would ignite the want, the need, the craving, to see if his love held. He couldn't turn her down. She had put it all on the line for him, now he had to return it in kind.

"If you got any choruses or stuff you could use a little help with, let us know, we're pretty good and we pick shit up quick," smiled Gillian surrounded by the choir, all grinning and nodding their heads like little kids.

"How many," was all he asked.

"Five," said Dugie and Ben simultaneously. It was too many, they knew, but they also knew Jaxson wanted this. It was his altruistic bent as deeply embedded in him as his heart. They still had to keep this show tight and it was loosening its laces as they stood there.

"Let me confer with my agent," he hugged Maggie to take any of the sting out, "and we'll figure out what she wants to hear."

"Maybe you could use a little dance number to kick things off and buy Padon a few extra minutes to prepare hisself," smirked Joseph Standing Bear. "I have a few drummers and dancers here, like back in Rapid, if you remember. Maybe our friends would like to join us. Really kick the vibe in!"

"Sure, why not?" Dugan was rearranging the show in his head as he walked toward the backstage steps.

Joseph spread his arms wide, palms open to the heavens, as he asked if the totems would join them in celebration and dance. This would be one for the books.

"We dance and then would like to stay and hear all of your music. Nash tells me you each bring a uniqueness to your sounds. This I would like to experience," Sung had finally settled the other canines down. Glen, in human form was panting hard, and Oscar, in his natural state, was not.

"What did I see before? What did we all see?" Jaxson asked Sung needing to know, to understand on visceral level what had taken place. Had they witnessed what their eyes told them was true but their brains could not accept? The musicians, singers, crew, Ian, and Maggie leaned in. They had seen whatever it was and were just as curious.

"Truth." said Alexandra, "What you saw has not been revealed to many white men, and certainly not this many white men all at once in history, and believe me, these folks know history. They are the Spirit Guides of those they represent as well as those humans who follow. Myth is born of truth, they are both." How else could you describe such to people who would never truly believe. Though, she may be wrong on that assumption if the reaction she had witnessed was any indication.

While Padon and Maggie went off to discuss many things including a short concert set, Robert and Marylou tried not to be noticed. They didn't want anyone to wonder why these two were back behind the stage and throw them out. Though he had been the one to bring Padon's guitar, maybe he could be mistaken for Padon's personal roadie!

A smallish Indian man did notice and came up to introduce himself. Raj explained he was the one who kept his eye on the finances and the progress of the programs they had begun. Robert's ears perked up as he was intensely interested in just those aspects. He informed Raj he had been a regional administrator of H.U.D. and before that had worked with the Department of the Interior. He wanted to know what they planned and how they planned on going about it. A geek to details and a nerd to learn. Marylou knew he had found a new labor of love in life and she wanted in this time. She'd been a housewife and mother, now she wanted to try another career.

As Joseph made his way to change into his dress buckskins, he passed Gabby and Teri. They shook hands and shared a hug in greeting. "Your woman represented your tribe well today. Just as you did in Rapid City. You complement each other." He said to Gabby in salutation.

"My what?" Gabby was taken aback.

"Your woman spoke well; she spoke truth to all. It was a fitting recitation," Joseph nodded his respect to Teri.

"Oh, you mean Soteria? Yes, she was wonderful but she is not my woman," Gabby blushed.

"Maybe, maybe not, it is possible you should reconsider your own assessment." Joseph nodded to both flustered faces as he turned to prepare to dance.

As people settled into their camp chairs, blankets, or just lying on the grass the quartet took the stage. Four chairs arranged in a small semicircle around one microphone, a quick check of tuning and Mozart began.

Nash somehow materialized at his designated spot center stage about forty feet from the front of the stage. As the String Quartet No. 19 in C Major began to rise so, too, did Nash triggering a reverse domino effect surrounding him. Once again, the crowd, the lovers of music, stood awash in the beauty of a melody centuries old.

Nash closed his eyes, tilted his head back to allow the sun to warm his skin while the quartet warmed his spirit. The crowd, thousands strong, stood in silent testament to the power of music. Like a field of sunflowers their faces followed the melody, their hearts rising and falling with magnificence. It was a sight to behold, and as Padon stood in the stage right wing he did so. He felt the power of the moment. His fingers running through scales to warm up for a show decades in the making. The concert he never thought would happen. And this one was for love.

The string quartet ran through their usual preshow majesty with a brief jazz influenced piece to break up the classical. They had neglected to mention the change when they took the stage. No one complained, thinking it a lovely addition to the ensemble's repertoire.

As the final notes ot Mendelsohn floated off on the late after-noon breeze Padon made ready for his entrance back onto the big stage when he was halted by the rhythms of America. A steady heartbeat of drums marched from the backstage to centerstage. The dancers chant-ing, singing in their tongue a song of nature, healing, a prayer to the Great Spirit for strength, and a promise to work hand in hand with all the crea-tures of the Mother to save her and her children.

The audience was not prepared to be transported to a simpler time when man and the natural world were one. They stood mesmerized, silent, transfixed, hypnotized by sight and sound until one lone voice from the crowd rose in harmony with those stomping the rhythm and calling to the wind. Nash, his voice as clear as a frigid mountain morning called a response. He danced his own steps in the middle of the crowd. The as-sembled cheered until hoarse still standing, joining in steps they had never attempted and singing a song they had never heard, but sing and dance they did. Until silence.

Joseph Standing Bear slow stepped a simple dance to the center mic while chanting just under his breath, a quiet prayer to the grandfa-thers and grandmothers, to the children yet to come, to the trees and the grass, the moon and the stars, and to all people. And then all ceased.

"We call all the people of the Mother to come together as one, to work side by side with, not just other humans, but all the children of the world. The four-leggeds, those who creep and crawl, sail the winds on wing and feather, swim the river, the creeks, and the depths of the oceans. We call to those who roam the prairies and mountains, the desert reptiles and those who slither thought the leaves and underbrush. Join, hand in hand, join in hope and muscle, belief in a better way, to be as one and allow all life. Do not commit genocide of any one species for the greed of a few. Let balance prevail, be grateful for what you have and generous with those who have little or nothing. Thank the Great Spirit, the Mother, and your neighbor for the joy of life. Mitakuye Oyasin. Let us celebrate in dance and song."

The drums spoke loudly, the feet of the dancers answered, the cries of the chant called for life, the concert was well and truly begun.

As the audience sat back down, spent from the emotional, spiritual, physical expense, Jaxson and Bonnie made their way to center-stage. Normally Ian would come out to welcome the people and thank them but these two wanted to share a moment in time when someone very talented lost himself. Someone both had worked with, respected his music, his way with lyric and melody, and his love of his craft. After so many years he had been found and had agreed to play tonight for the first time in many years. They asked that, even though they were certain the audience would not know his name, those assembled give him the honor and respect he so deserved. Padon McKenzie.

Padon was so stupefied that he just stood there with the Gibson hanging down past his waist and his mouth hanging open. What had they just done? Given him a marvelous intro, now it was up to him to ride that wave. He glanced over where Maggie stood with her friends alongside Ian with his Maggie at his side in the wings. He saw the tears, the pride, the smile. He walked out on stage.

And The Music Shall Set You Free

If Padon had lived a perfect life of altruism and philanthropy, if he had only ever written from his heart to benefit starving children, abused women, to lift from the muck and mire those who had been trampled beneath the feet of the uncaring, left to die of neglect, outcasts of humanity, he could not have asked for more than what he experienced in the twenty minutes he played. He began with his song and story of being found almost dead by the side of the road and brought back to life by Doctor Caldwell and Janet Jackson; not that one, the other one. He sang a song he had written for the woman who stole his heart by making him work so hard physically and romantically to win her. He sang of a fantasy town in the mountains filled with good people who cared for each other and a lost musician but gave no name nor co-ordinates. He even sang the old reel he had written of the robber come a-calling and the race for love. When he closed his quick set with his Masterpiece of the mountain sunset, cold, clear, crisp perfection the entirety of the audience sat in stunned silence before rising as one in a roar of approval so loud he was quite certain his people in Rock Ridge had heard it.

He walked off stage and into the embrace of Maggie. She couldn't stop hugging him and telling him how proud she was. She would understand if he chose music and the road, it was who he was. The singers, musicians, the road crew not occupied came to congratulate him on a magnificent performance. Ian was speechless. Jaxson was beaming. It was Padon's command performance. The one he always knew he had in him.

No one can quite explain what the sound of a naked goddess filled with glee dancing through the heavens sounds like, but it was loud, raucous, bright as the sunshine on a cloudy day and all the colors of the rainbow filling the sky. Until that day no person had ever heard laughter in the sky and probably never would again.

"Lose one, gain another. One fish slips off the line and a grander one, who thought he would never catch you, finds the bait!" It wasn't much of a song but Fame had not believed she would need a celebratory anthem. She hadn't believed until the roar of the crowd, the impact on the other musicians and crew, the glory that filled a dry and shriveled heart told her she had, indeed, won this great battle.

Try as he might to run, to hide from her, Padon had succumbed to her wiles. He would worship her with every breath, every beat of his now full heart. He would get up each morning to see how the rest of humanity worshipped him so he could worship her. She had won! She Had won! She had won!!!

Put that in a sammich and eat it, Fate!

Maggie told him, again, through her tears, of the joy she felt for what she had witnessed and her fear of what it had awakened in him, that she knew this was who he was. Padon nodded and kissed her hard before taking a step back and locking eyes with her so she would know. "You are right it is who I was, but I am not anymore. I cannot thank everyone enough for the opportunity but I have a life, a very good life with you and have no desire to lose that." He kissed her again. "This was wonderful and necessary. I guess I would've always wondered 'what if'. I don't have to wonder, now I know. I am complete. And it is you who complete me. You and Thursday nights at Merle's with Walt." He turned and shook Jaxson's hand, then shook Ian's and put his guitar away in her case.

The crack of thunder on a clear evening shook the world. It was like the cracking of the mountains. The cry of victory crushed by reality into a teeny scrap of the dust of defeat. Anger threatened to swallow the earth whole.

Until the sound of mocking laughter snuffed out the stark emptiness. Followed by the stomping of dainty feet on mortal dreams and record, TV, and movie deals being torn up and thrown away. There would be no fame for anyone until Fame recovered her dignity.

The butterfly had flapped its wings once before storing promise in an old worn guitar case.

Jaxson nodded, he wouldn't try to change the man's mind or convince him he should give up what he'd found to go chasing shadows and wraiths. Padon spent a life doing that and had only found pain, now he had something he could hold that would bring happiness. He envied that man.

"I do want to talk to you about your songs. I have an idea I think you might find intriguing." Jaxson grinned, "We'll talk after the show." He shook Padon's hand one more time before heading backstage to ready himself for his own set.

Ian allowed the audience to settle back down before he introduced the All-Girls' Choir plus One. If anyone could follow what had just taken place it was this gifted ensemble of songwriters, singers, and harmonizers.

"Does it seem like the universe is fixating on this particular geographical point?" Carrie laughed at her own question. Didn't it always feel as though the universe was fixating on wherever we stood? Wasn't that our ego telling us we are important. Everyone thinks that they are the central point of universal attention. And, she knew, they most definitely were not. But there certainly was an awful profusion of activity within a very close proximity to where this concert was happening.

She and her newfound family had traveled with these Gypsies for a couple weeks and had sensed the overall vitality, the esprit de corps, the sense of purpose they all had. They were a team working towards a common goal and each piece was as important as the next. It was a steady flowing wave. All the breaks easy to read, the curl holding forever. But now an eddy, a rip tide had formed and she couldn't tell if it was pulling them in different directions or if it was pushing them all together. All they could do was relax and let it pull them where it would. Don't fight it, she thought.

All these new people, new voices, yet they were like separate sections of a choir, singing different parts of the same song. The question was whether the harmonies would hold or create a dissonance. She hadn't a clue what she was trying to say so sat mute and kept further thoughts to herself.

Her meditation was broken as another sat down close to her on the bench. She felt the weight of them but could not hear breathing. They were as still as death. She chanced a glance and saw the elderly man all the Natives seemed to acquiesce to. Bear, she thought she heard someone call him. He was built like a bear.

"When do you sing?" He asked turning towards her.

Carrie laughed, "I don't sing. If I did it would clear the entire crowd from here." She shrugged but didn't seem bothered by her lack of vocal talent.

"Then you play an instrument?" he was searching for where she fit in with this troop of entertainers.

"Nope," she said, "I have no musical talent that anyone has been able to discover."

He looked her over. Though she was not without physical strength he did not think her capable of carrying the heavy speakers and amplifiers. "Where to you fit in?" He was genuinely curious.

"It's a long and boring story," Carrie had no desire to retell her life. And yet.

"We have time. The music is nice, it would be good to hear your words as well." He leaned back into the table, making himself comfortable.

His woman, Rebecca, if Carrie was paying attention, came and sat next to him, their shoulders touching. It reminded her of, well, it did. She found she couldn't stop herself. She wanted so badly to be with Kim right now, that maybe talking about her would make her come back to life. At least in Carrie's mind.

As self-consciously as Carrie had protected most of these memories from others, she now gushed like a broken water main. She unabashedly spoke of the pain she had felt when both her parents were killed. The feeling of being alone in the world, desperately isolated from anyone who might comprehend the soul crushing despondency she fought every second. She couldn't talk about it with friends or family. Hell, the only family she had were her aunt and uncle. He was constantly pawing at her pretending it was comfort and her aunt would turn a blind eye to the constant assault on her niece. Until Carrie finally decided death was the only answer and so had escaped their home to run to the ocean and end the pain. Dennis had found her and rather than take advantage of this innocent child—her worst fear of out of the frying pan—he had saved her, taught her, raised her, and filled her with dignity, pride, and worth.

She spoke of her years of isolation, terrified of allowing anyone too close, anyone to penetrate the great wall of Carrie she had constructed. It was her, the ocean, and loneliness until Oscar taught her about love. At the sound of his name, Oscar ambled to her side and nuzzled between her arm and side, demanding stroking and petting. If she was going to talk about him, she might as well pay attention to him. She hugged him close, kissing his head, his neck, clinging to this life saver.

Then along came Kim. An immediate connection was made, not just with Carrie but with Oscar. The three formed a bond within moments that was stronger today than it had ever been, even though Kim had died. There, she said it. Kim had died and left her alone once again. Carrie wept as she emptied her soul to these people, as more of the First Nation contingent had silently joined the few around the picnic table. They did not comment, make tsking sounds or attempt to comfort, they let her speak her truth without interruption.

Now, Carrie wanted to give back to the memory of the joyous contentment she had found. To open her heart, her home, her purse to those who suffered alone. Those who didn't believe there was any escape for them but the final one. She wanted to rescue humans and animals, thrown away, left to die on their own, or be killed off by the stronger and more wicked and immoral.

A look was shared by the People. They knew. They knew the hopelessness she spoke of, of there being no way out, but they would not surrender to that despair just as she had not. Sung sat down next to her. He did not reach out to her physically, respecting her wall. He instead spoke of his children and their desperate situation. He told of what they, he and Bear, had done in the past to save his family. And what they hoped to accomplish by joining with this band of Gypsies.

The others told her of their own near extinction at the hands of man. Of the need to expand habitat, of the interrelationship with all life. Bear, Rebecca, and now, Alexandra, spoke of Bear saving Alex from the forest fire. How that had precipitated the return of Rebecca from death, and the salvation and resurrection of Bear. With love so strong, was anything impossible? They did not promise her a resurrection of Kim, but a monument of life to her memory that would allow her to live through so many others.

As the final notes of perfect harmony found them, they had made their connection. Carrie could not accept all they said, it was irreconcilable to all the religious superstition shoved down her throat as a child. And yet, was it all that far-fetched? Hadn't the power of the ocean saved her? Hadn't the love she felt for Kim only grown stronger with more purpose and meaning?

Sheriff John stood before her. He was solid as the Rocky's framing him. "I know these stories are impossible to believe. I thought they were feeding me drugs or hypnotizing me but I have come to accept what they say as true. As true as any of our myths, stories, bible learning or fables. The main difference is, I can reach out and touch my friends here. Just know, they offer strength, love, friendship, and more than anything, family. All they ask is life, not for themselves but for all." John was not much of a speaker which was why he had remained quiet for most of the afternoon but Carrie needed human reassurance and he was the only option. He served as he always had.

That was how Barbara, Aron and the kids found her. Surrounded by, enveloped by love. "Auntie Carrie," called Phoebe, now where had that honorific come from? Yet it fit. It had been earned. "You are missing the music!" Phoebe took one arm while Izzy took the other to drag their recalcitrant aunt into the music.

Bear glared at Mika, who stood silent off to the side of the table. He had refused to leave once he had shown himself and exposed that he had followed them.

"I didn't say all humans, just most of them," Coyote was not going to cut loose this bone once he had his teeth in it.

"No, they are not," Bear stated flatly, "most humans have the heart that you just sat and heard. And those hearts are the stones which will build the path to our future." He stood up, then assisted Rebecca and offered a hand to Alex, it was time for all of them to listen to some glory.

Bonnie prepared to take center stage as the four women and Jesse exited. She felt a hand on her shoulder. Jaxson motioned for her to stay put for just a moment.

He walked to the center mic, "Normally," he laughed at the word, "Bonnie Welch would come out and smoothly transition into a beautiful set of her songs. Not tonight." He waited out the sounds of disappointment. "She will be out to perform," he reassured to sooth the discontent, "but the four women you have been listening to decided very early in this tour to form the choir you've been privileged to hear. Each of them is a wonderful talent in their own right, songwriters, singers, players. And I thought why don't we let them show you just how wonderful they truly are. So, if you don't mind here, one at a time, are Joya Olakundo, Michelle Branch, Cinda William, and Gillian Morse." Dugie was prepared, as guitar tech he handed each one their most favored instrument, the band had already taken up position on the stage.

"That will increase the time by forty," Dugie dutifully reported.

"Don't care, there is something happening here, magic, juju, voodoo, I don't know, but I'm going to hitch my wagon to it and ride like there's no tomorrow." Jax grinned. "And it just got longer." He added as he watched the airport limo pull up to the back gate.

Just When You Thought...

Jaxson made his way quickly to the back gate where security was hassling the driver of the van. He had no idea who was being transported from what airport to his show but the way events were rapidly developing in the most interesting ways today, he certainly didn't want them being sent packing without him finding out.

As the driver tired of arguing and the security was intent on not honoring their request to find him, he supposed, he put the transmission in gear. Jaxson banged on the side of the van hollering for them to hold. He grabbed the sliding-door handle and pulled down; the door slid open all the way. Jaxson's smile of greeting split his face. The occupants had not been, in fact, seeking him but Ian. It seemed his friends from across the pond had jumped said pond to have a holiday in the mountains. Or near them.

He grabbed Richard Stainesby's hand to help him exit the cramped van. He was followed closely by Peadar McCarthy, with Steven Gatos hot on his heels. They stood, stretching out the ride and regaining equilibrium.

"Riding coach?" Jaxson kidded though he was slightly astonished to find three of the best-known artists of the past half century riding in an airport van rather than a limousine.

"Was all that availed," Shot back Mr. Stainesby. He did not seem overjoyed at their mode of transport. "We flew a charter into Springs International and they were bereft of anything more suiting." He wasn't put out so much as put upon, though his usual sense of humor served him well.

"We could have arranged something had we known," Jaxson chastised.

"Mr. McCarthy enjoys the marvel of surprise." His glare at his former bandmate was short lived replaced immediately by a grin as Ian's Maggie jumped into his arms in greeting.

It had been a mere month or so since their last get together in NY but he was a favorite of Mrs. Sperling, but only just so. She left his embrace to envelope the other Mersea Beat member.

Peadar was well and truly welcomed when he noticed the man of the house sauntering his way over to bestow his own greetings. Jaxson was busy saying hello and welcome to Steven before Ian and wife could wrestle him away. They had shared his companionship just a week or so back in Little Rock but were just as pleased to have the reunion replicated.

"What? Why?" Ian couldn't formulate a cognizant sentence, his mind reeling with bliss at the presence of those who stood before him.

"We were doing a wee bit of recording together. Our serendipitous meeting in NY, thanks to your little dog and pony," began Peadar, "being the impetus to discussing the possibilities, leading to a collaborative work. No one, of course, knows a thing about it. We didn't want to leak a word for fear it would jinx the project and we would be left with yolk running down the collar." He laughed at the look on Ian's face. Ian couldn't conceive of anything these three could put together that would be anything less than a masterpiece, but Peadar was ever known for his cautious ego. "Well, for the past several weeks we have been secreted in a studio in jolly old until it was no longer jolly just old.

"Steven had jumped ship a few weeks back to bathe in the restorative waters of your campaign and, when returned, suggested a trip to break the monotony of creation was called for. So, we answered the call and here we are. Hoping against hope that we would be welcomed back into the embrace of the Untouchable Gypsy army."

"Without doubt!" exclaimed Maggie and Ian in unison.

"Just visiting or?" Jaxson was thinking and that frightened Ian.

"We thought if you could use a few itinerant musicians, we would be willing to work for a few victuals and something to sooth the nerves. They frown on bringing your own into the country." Peadar's forlorn expression begging forgiveness for begging. Ian slipped him a gummy to tide them over.

"Please do catch us up on the comings and goings and where the state of saving the world stands." Ritchie eyed the table covered in fruits, vegetables, breads, and cheeses. The trip had been long and quickly planned so snacks only were provided, he wished a more substantial repast.

Bonnie was now on stage, as the four women had completed their swift trip into the limelight. They saw the new arrivals gathered at the catering. Their first thought was to leave the stars alone but then Joya couldn't help herself, she ran to give Steven an uncomfortable hug. His religion frowning on the touching, holding, embracing of a female not your wife. Religion! Christopher joined the group hoping for an introduction which Joya happily provided. Fans became friends, soon to become musical brothers and sisters.

Now everyone was chattering at the same time, saying hello, giving and receiving hugs. Then came the question, were these fellas going to play? Well, they would need to use one of the RV's to clean up, rest for a mo or two, then, yes, they could see themselves joining the fray.

Bonnie exited, James Nash taking her place to a thunderous round of applause and cheering for her last song as well as his appearance. Jaxson grinned ear to ear, there was magic in the air. Gabby walked over to check and make certain everything would remain the same and to ask if the quartet was going to accompany the speech. He had not grown up as fans of these gentlemen though he knew their names, but he was not gobsmacked by their presence. Soteria, by his side, seemed completely oblivious as to who they might be. Jaxson introduced each in turn and explained they were musician friends from Britain come to play some songs. She accepted that and asked if they had any special needs. Were they plugging into amps, running direct inputs, did they need guitars mic'ed? She would provide whatever they might need. They explained she should not worry; it would be taken care of by Dugie and Ben. She could just sit back and enjoy the show.

It was time. Jaxson and Gabby made their way to the stage. Jaxson would only play three songs before bringing Gabby on. The show was going long, his fault, but he didn't care. They had to be done by midnight curfew but they had plenty of time. He shook himself trying to settle the events of this evening into a coherent story, there was no way. The stars, literally, were in alignment. The assembled were enthralled with the spells that had been woven and they had no idea of what was about to happen. Some days are just better than the rest.

James was going into his last chorus, though Jaxson knew he wouldn't leave until he had everyone singing along. So, Jaxson stood off in the wings and let the majesty of the moment flow over him. He could see the Rockies to the west and swore he could see very single face of the crowd juxtaposed against them, grinning in ecstasy. They passed coffee cans, boots, empty coolers, anything that would hold money. Unconsciously putting dollar bills, coins, twenties, tens, anything that came to hand. It was a glorious evening as this tour, this music, this night that hit him in the feels. All the money, and more than the money, was the joining together for common cause of tens of thousands of people all across the country. Even people who had not been able to attend a concert sent donations to lift other souls out of desperation. If he never was part of anything ever again, this would fulfill his purpose on Earth.

The light touch of a hand on his shoulder was reassuring rather than insistent. "Would you like to see what could be possible?" The voice soft, offering him a prize of inconceivable value, if only he would gamble, take a plunge into the unknown. He knew that voice, it was the one they called Bear. Didn't every single person on the planet have a friend named Bear, and weren't they the kindest, most trustworthy people you knew. You were always safe in the company of bear, weren't you?

"I have to go on in a minute, he's closing his set," Jaxson's voice sounded distant in his ear as if spoken from another room or in a dream.

And hadn't today been a dream? Yes, the vandalism to the buses had been trying but then out thin air comes someone he hasn't seen in thirty years to ferry the entire cast and crew to the venue, doing his best not to be noticed and then walking out on a stage and playing one of the best sets of songs Jaxson had heard since the sixties.

If that wasn't magic enough, Peadar and Richie show up with Steven Gatos in tow. That would be a dream to every single person sitting out there thinking they were already witnessing a fantastic show. Dream a little dream with me. He looked over to the other side of the stage and saw Flaco, Tino, and Kiko screwing around trying to throw the band off their groove. Impossible, but everyone was smiling and laughing filled with the ecstasy of the day. No one knew what they'd seen but they knew they'd all seen the same thing and it was wild. They waved at him from across the universe. The choir was backing James up and they had the entire crowd on their feet singing and dancing along with one of James oldest hits, *'The Fire in Friends'*.

No, he didn't want to miss one second of this, he didn't want to go anywhere; and yet. There was such promise in what Evan--wasn't that what one of them had called Bear, Evan—asked.

"We'll be back long before he can finish. It will only take a few seconds here." There was mystery in that 'here', a mystery Jaxson could not ignore.

"You promise?" Like a child asking for reassurance from their parent.

The hand that lay so gentle on his shoulder squeezed tenderly and that was all Jax needed. He nodded his head once and the whole of creation was gone.

Replaced by the most magnificent view he had ever witnessed. The mountainscapes jumped with color and texture. Brilliant hues of green, brown, shadow, and light danced as if the colors lived. The blue of the sky so soft and deep he thought if he fell from the earth, it would catch him, cushioning everything he had ever imagined, thought, and daydreamed about, keeping all safe from harm.

He heard the forest, alive with the sounds of birds, insects, frogs croaking, the hiss of life, the growls, and grunts of a hundred different animals. He could smell the earth, the breeze carrying scents of flowers blossoming, honey hidden in trees, fresh water running in streams and creeks down the mountainside. He was overwhelmed, his senses over-loading on life, life lived in harmony. Life, healthy in its balance and vigor.

Tears streamed down his face. He fell to the forest floor and hugged the Mother, thanking Her for every breath he had ever taken, every sight he had seen, every sound, song, love, won and lost, for allow-ing him to be.

At long last he got a grip on his emotions and remembered the show. How long had he been sleeping? How long had he been drifting alone? How long had he been dreaming only to find the dream was real? He must have been here for an hour or two, people were going to be pissed. He turned his head to chastise the man who had brought him here, though he could find no words, especially when he saw the massive bear, sitting on its haunches waiting for him. Or so it seemed.

It was the oddest visage Jaxson had ever seen. A bear, easily ten or twelve foot in height, he thought, though couldn't be certain with the animal sitting like that. It would not have been unthinkable to find he was reading the morning paper waiting for an errant child.

"You haven't missed more than one line of chorus so far. If you would like we can take some time and you can explore a bit," the bear grinned. If there was anything that could have been more disconcerting to this picture, that was it.

And yet, he was here, would it be any more a waste of time if he were to look about, walk around, see what other wonders there might be? He and the bear, who now stood and walked on his two hind legs, conversing about how important all life was and the interweaving of that life. How each piece of the puzzle mattered, like a Rube Goldberg con-traption, if one link failed it all failed. He implored Jaxson to see how his tour's mission was noteworthy but only one link out of thousands. If he could see his way to incorporating his grand plan into THE grand plan, it would be grand.

They stopped by the side of a brook to take a sip of fresh clean mountain water. He sat on a rock and absorbed the panorama, the spectacle of life laid out before him. Jaxson shook his head in amazement, but it was time to get back for his set.

No more had the thought passed through brain than they were standing, once again, in the wings. His friends across the stage appeared puzzled and then smiled when they saw him again. They would have questions. Hell, he had questions but James was wrapping up, saying his thanks and introducing the star of the show.

Jaxson pulled the strap of his guitar over his head and walked on the stage. The realization struck that in all his years of performing there had never been a single time that he was as relaxed, as content, as completely at peace with who he was and what lay ahead. He knew, in his heart, in his soul, to the pit of his being that he followed the Red Path and it was good.

He thanked James, and all the other acts who had been kind enough to play, then asked for another round of applause for his 'old friend' Padon. He ripped through three of his best-known tunes before explaining that he'd been ill with a sore throat and couldn't play all he wanted to but he would bring on Gabby to do his speech. Before anyone could protest his absence and cutting the show short, he explained he had another friend who had shown up and would play a few tunes after Gabby had finished. People began to protest, as they had come to hear him, until some of them thought of the guests who had shown up on other stops. Could they be in for something special?

Jaxson went to the piano to play *'Cannons of Peace'* and Gabby strolled out to the center mic with Soteria by his side, soon joined by Joseph Standing Bear. Interesting, thought the song master, as he began the first verse. At the chorus, once again the violin, plaintive and wishing entered the song, followed by the viola, cello, and other violin. As Jaxson made his way through the second verse, he watched the 'Choir' return to the stage to join him on the second chorus. He brought the whole production down so Gabby could speak.

As Gabby spoke, Soteria translated his words into Spanish, then, without missing a beat, into Ute. Joseph Standing Bear then translated as best he could into Lakota. Enough to make the head spin yet the cadence on each fit perfectly with the song Jaxson played in the background along with the harmonies of the singers and strings. Then Gabby took a bit of a detour, he spoke to the interconnectivity of all life. That if we are to have empathy for the downtrodden, the subjugated, demoralized, bankrupt of hope, worth, and value then we should care and have empathy for those on the brink of extinction, those who suffer from dehydration and near starvation, hunted for sport, to satisfy ego and avarice not hunger or need. If we profess to love one, then should we not love all. The sun setting behind the mountains only added the exclamation point to what was being said.

The crowd screamed their approval but screamed louder when Jaxson introduced Steven Gatos and his friends from over the pond.

With A Little Help From My Friends

Ian could sense the presence at his side, it wasn't Maggie, though she was there as well, no, it was the cop, Sheriff John, they all called him. Ian could tell John wanted to speak to him but Steven, Peadar, and Ritchie had just taken the stage. Anything that needed to be said could be said in a little while. He just wanted to listen to his old friends.

A woman of middling years had pushed her way up near the front of the stage on Ian's side and was attempting to get his attention. He was attempting to preserve it. He just wanted to listen to his old friends.

She was shouting something but the music was drowning her out. She smiled. He thought she resembled someone he knew or had met or passed on the street but the smile was wrong. Her face was not made for smiling, a scowl would have been much more at home. She wanted him to know something important, like she was having the time of her sad, middle-aged, life, or she remembered seeing these guys just before they broke up or she required a rest room. He smiled and waved at her. Now he knew who she was as her face registered frustration. The front desk clerk from when they had checked in.

She bore a slight resemblance to a person enjoying themselves so he had to assume it wasn't acting and she was just telling him how much she loved what they had brought to her town. He mimed playing music and smiled, rapture on his face and clapping, she frowned. She screamed something into the headwind of guitars, drums, bass, and lyric, then gave an extremely emphatic 'OK' sign with thumb, forefinger and the three lesser-known fingers raised. He nodded and gave it back to her so she would know he understood. He just wanted to listen to his old friends.

The concert ended with Jaxson bringing the entire ensemble onto the small stage, some spilling over into the wings, to sing one last song, inserting a fork into a magnificent cake. The band was spent, the singers were overwhelmed with ecstasy, the guest performers were beaming, the Spirits were satisfied, the gods and godlings had danced the light fantastic. The crowd was exhausted, resting against each other, cuddled in the arms of the nearest aficionado like lovers post coitus after an extreme night of lovemaking. If they weren't satisfied now, they could not be satisfied.

It was time for band, singers, and crew to come down from the heights, back to where mortal man resided. It was not a place most of them wanted to come back to, yet each night there it was, staring them in the face. Normal. Until the next show they would be everyday ordinary people. That's when the lonely, kicked in. The cost of being allowed to play pretend for a few hours several nights a week. The landing was hard. They would be there for each other because no one else knew how large the payment was.

They'd go back to their empty hotel rooms, while Ian, Ben, and Dugie figured out what to do to get the busses up and running, tires replaced, and whatever else might have been done to them, so they could get to the next stop. Nights like tonight made all the travel, the depression, the lonely worth it. Yeah, they'd had one helluva show, they could ride that for a few hours, maybe.

As Padon and Robert began the process of shuttling the band, performers, and crew back to the hotel they were surprised to find several wreckers in the hotel parking lot accompanied by a box truck and mobile tool shed. There were halogen lights to bring daytime lighting in the middle of the night and several mechanics crawling underneath the vandalized behemoths. Padon dropped off Bonnie, Michelle, Gillian, and

Joya at the front door while Robert drove around back with Jaxson, Ian, Marylou and the two Maggie's. It was tight but they managed.

Robert had been explaining to Jaxson and Ian he was a former upper manager with both the Interior Department and HUD. He thought that he, with some egging on by his wife, Marylou, could be of assistance on their crusade. They were planning on implementing programs he had dreamed about when with the government but could never get authorization. Both were intrigued with the offer but now distracted by the activity in the parking lot.

The dour front desk clerk from the day before, who had attempted to get Ian's attention at the show, stood, arms crossed, and smirking in satisfaction as she discussed something with a hefty beefcake of a man by one of the wreckers. As Ian got out of the pickup she waved. He walked over towards her while taking in the scene before him.

"This was what I was trying to tell you at the show!" She raised her voice over the clamor of mechanics as work. "I called my cousin," whom Ian could only assume was the sizable gent to her right. "He runs the truck stop south on 25. He brought up his crew so you folks can be on the road tomorrow, if it suits."

Ian couldn't tell if she had done this out of some good Samaritan act or just wanted to be rid of the dirty hippies stinking up her place of employ. Either way he was pleased and thankful for the assist.

"Well, I don't have the words to thank you, all of you," he said taking in this massive undertaking. This was going to cost a small king's ransom but they would make all dates.

"He promised he wouldn't gouge you," she said noticing the look on Ian's face.

"Gouge away," smiled the producer, "We will turn it all over to the insurance company. Though we'll pay you first and then we'll fight with them." Ian didn't want them thinking that, after their good deed they would have to wait for years while a faceless, soulless insurance company fucked them around.

"We can get all but one of the busses up and running. Someone really knew what they was doing when the fucked up the other'n," apologized the head mechanic and cousin, "some things just can't be fixed overnight, or probably ever." He took off his baseball cap and scratched his head. "I got a guy over Limon way could probably hump one o' his big RV's over this way. Might not be as fancy but it'd do in a pinch. And this appears to be a pinch!" He chuckled at his funny.

Ian glanced over at Jaxson whose mind was noticeably far, far away. They might be having a miniscule catastrophe here but he was pleasantly residing elsewhere. It would be Ian's decision. He made it.

"I would greatly appreciate it. You are going to have to let me do something to show our appreciation," though he wasn't sure exactly what he could do. Ian reached in his pocket pulled out several hundred dollars in medium bills. "I'll tell you what, breakfast is on my crew and once your crew gets rested and caught up, so is a party at a place of your choosing." He handed the man—shit, he never go the fellas name—the wad of bills.

"Bill," he said as if reading Ian's bad manners graciously, before counting the bounty in his hand, "And this is more than we could ever eat or drink."

"Then have two parties," Ian shook Bill's hand before grabbing his friend to take the distracted songwriter inside the hotel.

They settled into the two stuffed armchairs in the lobby as Padon and Robert dropped off another load of Gypsies. It would be a process that would take some little time. While they made the runs, those dropped off went to their rooms and grabbed bottles, pipes, and gummies. There would be a celebration tonight. Though pipes would be smoked out back—away from the mechanics, of course.

Jaxson sat across from Ian, they were eye to eye though his eyes were unfocused or focused on something so far away Ian couldn't have found it with James Webb. He endeavored to find Jaxson with conversation.

"I think we should take that friend of Padon's up on his offer. He is an organizer and has worked with large projects in conjunction with communities and the government," Jax stared at something on another plane. "He doesn't want money, says he's got enough, and his wife is just as gung-ho as he. They'd make a good edition to the organizational side of things." Nothing.

"Are you alright?" Now his tone was insistent. He had known Jax since they were young men and he recognized when his oldest friend had slipped into writer mode. That was when Jaxson immersed himself into words, thoughts, concepts that blocked out all other in creation. "I feel like I'm carrying this all by myself and I'm tired." He meant the conversation; Jaxson woke up from a different reality.

"If you had seen, could see, experience, what I did just before playing tonight you'd gladly carry this on your back until the end of time just for the promise. I can't even begin to describe what happened, what I felt, sensed, encountered, but I know it was real. If you," now his eyes focused on the reality afforded him. He saw his friends, his band, his crew gathered around, he grinned. "If I could take you, show you, let you feel like I do. Let you walk in the pristine, pure, beautiful, untouched plane I had..." the words failed and dissipated like mist in the forest.

"Interesting concept," said a voice not present but clear as the moonshine coming through the front windows. "Let me put it before the council." Before it too, dissolved.

Time passes at differing rates for different people. Ian thought it had been an hour since they had returned, Jaxson thought it about five minutes, those standing around watching the two guessed somewhere around eternity. Until the food was brought in, the bottles of wine were opened, someone mentioned the work crews out back seemed to be wrapping up and several chanced slipping out to have a toke. Time caught up to everyone when Robert and Padon completed their appointed rounds and announced the equipment trucks would be joining them soon.

It was Padon's appearance and his girlfriend's greeting that stirred Jaxson into cognizance.

"How would you like to spend the next ten days on the road? Be part of the show?" He thought Padon would jump at the chance. He had no idea what the man had been through, but if he was just playing one night a week at some bar in a tiny dot of a town in the mountains, well, this would be better.

If Maggie thought the same, she kept it to herself. This was Padon's choice. It was the opportunity he had waited for his entire life. She knew he couldn't resist and she wasn't going to stand in his, "No, thanks." She never got to finish her thought. "We gotta get back to the café. Our team has been holding down the fort for the past ten days, we don't want to take advantage of their good will." His arm found Maggie's shoulders and he pulled her in close.

Jaxson nodded before the biggest grin found its way to his eyes and mouth. "About those songs, though," he began, "I really would like to shop them around. I think I know some folks who would love to add them to their next project."

"Yeah, like me." Came a female voice. "And me." Added another claiming her foothold on this land. "Wait, I might want in on this," James spoke softly but carried a big reputation.

Padon laughed, "I have more," he said. "You can have what you like. I am happy in my little corner of the world with very dear, and I do mean dear, friends. My touring days almost killed me, literally, and I found life. Thank you, you do me a great honor, but I'm going home."

"Can he come meet us in LA?" Jaxson asked Maggie. "You too, of course. It's the last show and I'd really love to have him on it. Maybe I can pick and choose who gets what songs by then. Could mean some decent mailbox money." The carrot dangled, the rabbit bit.

"I'd love that." He peeked at his love, "We'd love that, but then it's back to busboy for me." Maggie wasn't sure what mailbox money was but she had already started a list in her head.

Bear stuck his head in the entrance and caught Jaxson's eyes. He motioned for him to grab Ian and few others and meet him outside.

At the same time, Carrie came down from her room. She had locked out the rest of the world while she considered her options. There was no doubting it, running with the band was fun. They were great people, played wonderful music, and were a hoot, but she now had responsibilities. She had Ray and Henry, coming soon with whoever they had convinced to tag along, to look into her planned retreat. She hadn't talked to either since they had left New Orleans and she knew they were waiting on a call from her.

They would want to know if the musical community traversing the country had any new ideas for her or whether they could incorporate what she envisioned into their own. She didn't know. There were so many people here with disparate ideas of what they hoped to accomplish, but she couldn't grasp the entirety of what some saw. What Bear and his group wished for. His seemed to possess the most comprehensive vision, though she had to wonder, did that make it the most impossible to achieve?

Oscar had no counsel, or if he did, he kept it close to the vest. Still, his presence was the most solid thing in her life right now. Aron had Barbara and the kids, his new family, that needed him as much as he needed them. And none of them actually needed her. And that was the problem, no one actually needed her.

It was a discouraged young lady who came into the ruckus of the lobby. She could sense the excitement, the frenzy, the buzz of life in over-drive, the thrum of conversations, as passionate as they were electric, whirring and bouncing off walls and each other. As Glen entered from the back door, Oscar's ears perked up and he made a beeline to his new best friend. Carrie had no idea what the young man possessed that aroused such excitement in Oscar but, by God, he was Oscar's obsession. She had-n't witnessed the transformation backstage only the interplay between young man and dog.

All conversation paused for a heartbeat at her entrance until eve-ryone realized she was one of their own and rejoined whatever had set this group a buzzing.

"What's the deal?" She asked Regis, the first roadie she came to.

"Not sure I can explain it," he replied, scratching his head, "might want to wait for the wigs to return and inform the peons."

She didn't have long to wait. Jaxson, Ian, Bear, Rebecca, Tonka, Sung and some others re-entered the lobby. Well, she knew whatever these folks wanted to impart she wanted to know.

Before everyone could settle down, that songwriter who had stumbled into the show, the one everyone was chirping about came in with his wife, and their friends. She hadn't come down here for a meet-ing, she'd come to grab a candy bar and soda, but it appeared that would have to wait. She now thought a sip of bourbon might settle her nerves. Ask and ye shall, the bottle magically appeared in a hand before her.

Something in the vibrations of the air told her whatever these folks wanted would affect the rest of her life.

Decisions

Aron stared out the window at the buses and trucks parked in the back lot of the hotel. It was late, he had no idea how late, but well past when he usually was asleep. But sleep was a slippery pig and he was wallowing in the mud. For someone so very young his life had been turned topsy-turvy so many times he felt like a man of ninety.

When he was a child life had been easy; play, eat, school, help around wherever they were living. There were no worries. He loved canned pork and beans, white bread with lard slathered on it, all the foods of a poor family, and he had his family. Then a tornado took them all away. He got lost. Lost in his mind, lost in the world, lost to any and all who had meant anything to him. Landing in an alleyway in Park City where some of the richest people in the world could ignore the street urchin. He lived off of scraps found in dumpsters, a few dollars thrown at him from those who wished to do for others but not have to get too close to do it. He'd made a 'home' in a cave just outside of town where he could hide from the law and the do-gooders who wanted to institutionalize him. He just wanted to be left alone in his grief.

Then she had come along. She and her dog, who sniffed him out. She fed him, didn't stay away from him though he knew he smelled like the garbage he slept in. She wouldn't give up. She didn't want to put him in a home for orphans and destitute children, she actually wanted to help him. She cleaned him up, let him sleep in clean sheets on a cloud of a bed. She taught him, cared for him—really cared for him—and took him to places he never could have imagined. She was his big sister and Oscar was his constant companion. They were a family.

And then came Barbara, Izzy, and Phoebe. Those who reminded him of all he had lost. Of a family blown away by wind and dust. Ashes to ashes, dust to dust, spoke the preacher, well, he was half right. Now he had a version of them back. They were the best version a boy could ask. He got to be a big brother. A person, a person the girls looked up to, relied on, respected. He had never known respect, not that Carrie didn't respect his learning, his way of knowing how to use technology she didn't, but the girls looked to him for guidance, to watch over them. They were his responsibility.

That did not ease the feeling of treason he was experiencing. He had to tell Carrie he was leaving. He was going with his family to the new home in Oregon. Barbara had hinted around that she couldn't stay on the road with the tour. The girls needed stability and this was anything but. Carrie had told her there was a place in Newport waiting for her and the girls, where they could settle in, start a new life, find constancy and a sense of permanence.

Aron had decided he couldn't let her go it alone, he would accompany them so he could watch over the girls. He was terrified if he left them alone, as he had his first sister, they would come to harm. Yes, he'd only been just down the road at a schoolmate's house but he'd left her where she could be hurt, and she had been. Not again, his brain told him. So, he had to go where the girls did. Carrie would be hurt, but she would understand, wouldn't she?

Barbara sat on her bed. The girls were asleep in the other queen-sized bed. They were her greatest treasure and she smiled. Maybe, once they got established in a new home, in a new town, on the other side of the world from him, they could move on with their lives without the fear, the fighting, the screaming and crying. They could become normal. She couldn't say with absolute certainty but she thought the girls might be suffering from early PTSD. She should have left sooner.

Now, she wouldn't wait. It was time to take Carrie up on her offer of a place for her and the girls. She hated the idea of leaving Carrie without friends or family but she appeared to be enjoying the musical life. And she had Oscar and Aron. She'd survive.

There was light tap at the door. Who could it be this late in the evening? She cracked the door and saw Aron surreptitiously standing in the hallway close to the door. She silently opened the door wide enough he could slip in.

"I just want you to know that I know you are thinking about leaving and heading to Oregon," he began. Barbara was slightly stupefied that he had discerned her intent and even more so that he would bring his knowledge to her. "I want you to know that when you make the final decision as to when, I am going with you and the girls."

She was shocked and it must have shown like a brilliant neon sign in the middle of the desert because he immediately followed it up with, "unless you don't want me to."

He hung his head. This had not been in the realm of possibilities he had considered. He had assumed she would be pleased he wanted to go, to help, to be the big brother.

"Have you told Carrie?" Was all that jumped from her lips.

"Not yet I thought I should run it by you first." He took a deep breath, "Look, if you don't want me, let me know now." His low self-esteem came slamming back into the absence of confidence. He had been dropped to his knees so often he expected it when he woke up in the morning.

"No, it's not that, I just hadn't considered, hadn't thought to ask, hadn't the courage to ask, but what about Carrie?" Twice around the roundabout had brought her to the proper off ramp. Carrie had come to rely on the street urchin, what would she do now? She would be alright. It was only another week or so and she would join up with them in Newport.

And that was how Barbara intended to frame it when she explained the whole thing to Carrie. They weren't abandoning her, they were giving her freedom to do what she needed and then she would come join them, once again, in Newport. Right? Oh, shit.

Breakfast was a festive affair. The buses running like champs, the new RV having arrived around seven a.m. Ian was not happy about being awoken at seven a.m. to learn how to operate the monstrosity, becoming dizzy with information that meant nothing to him. He woke the driver who thought he was going to have the opportunity to sleep in and now was pissy for having that hope dashed. Yes, Jaxson couldn't have asked for a better morning.

He dug into a large bowl of fruit and sipped his tea. He had residual joy from his experience with Evan yesterday. Evan, the Bear. Wow! He wanted to scream. He wished he could share that exquisite experience with every single one in the troop, but he didn't think there was any way possible. If Bear had to show each one, individually, what he had shown to Jaxson, they would be three days getting to Salt Lake City, even with the time shifting. Though it might be possible if Bear had convinced the rest of his tribe to try what he had suggested to them last night.

He had no more thought of the big man than he walked through the door with others in tow. The huge fella named Tonka, Lawrence, who was damn near as large, the little women and the two with the sober, serious look of the academic. Jaxson thought it impossible to think them as representations of animals. Maybe it was all a dream.

"We have discussed the concept of bringing all of you over at one time and think if we go to a place where the Mother holds sway, a place of power, it might work. We think our best chance is to come through Medicine Bow-Routt. It is a National park so there will be places to park your conveyances. It will involve a bit of walking but nothing too strenuous. We have to get you off the beaten path and into the sacred."

The little froggy appearing man gazed into the morning sky as if reading a map only he could visualize. "Take your interstate 25 north to the 287 exit. Follow 287 to Laramie. There should be plenty of hotels available this time of year. You are between the winter adventurers and the summer tourists. We'll meet you there and guide you to the Brown's

Peak Loop. It will be good, but if you have some who do not want this or don't believe they can handle this much truth, have them take a bus around the park and meet you in Walcott. See you tomorrow." And with that the group was gone as quietly as they had entered.

Ian and Maggie made their way to the breakfast bar just behind Ben, Dugie, Gabby and Soteria. Lee, Russel, Kiko, Tino, Flaco, though before Peadar, Ritchie, and Steven. Quickly followed by the bum's rush of Bonnie, Joya, Gillian, Michele, Cinda and James. Jesse had said he would join them after he eased into the day. The truck drivers had eaten and were checking tires, suspension, locks, latches, and gas. They would fill up once they got to Wyoming as the petrol was much cheaper than Colorado. Roadies were huddled in the corners of the breakfast nook having been up since first light to triple check their loads and run over to the ballpark for one last run through to be certain nothing was left behind.

This should be an easy day, maybe four hours on the road to Cheyenne. They had plenty of time to get to Salt Lake and they didn't want anything to disturb the rhythm. Once everyone had their fill and were just hanging, waiting for the wheels to start turning, Jaxson called for a meeting. He asked Dugie to collect all the roadies and lighting folks, he even asked Regis to call in the drivers, bus and truck, as this would be a meet of all involved.

Once everyone had settled into the lobby Jaxson stood up to ask for their attention. "I don't know if you all are aware but the reason we get keep to our schedule, the reason we are allowed to get tires on blacktop today is because of that women behind the counter. The same woman who checked you in, took care of our needs and wants, also called in a huge favor to get the buses repaired. Remember that when you are checking out." Everyone turned toward the front desk where the middle-aged woman appeared quite beside herself at the attention. They stood as one and cheered, applauded, and thanked her en masse!

"Secondly," he cleared his throat to assure close attention. "you have been afforded what I am guessing is an exceptional and singular honor. And I mean singular, as I don't believe this has ever been offered to anyone, especially white anyone's, in history." Now the murmuring began and ended in seconds. "As I was preparing to walk on the stage last evening a very bizarre and wondrous thing happened." He shook his head as if to clear what might have been from what possibly could have been to what he hoped had been. "I don't think I can put the experience into words but it was the greatest, most magnificent experience of my life, bar none. It was life altering in a very magical, eyepopping way. And it has been offered to you." Now the excited murmuring became a cacophony.

Questions flew. What would be expected? Would drugs be involved? What kind? How much? When?

"Settle down." He begged, "We would have to make Laramie today, only another hour further than planned, and then get up tomorrow early to get out of civilization and let those who are doing the taking do the telling. The only thing I can promise you is, if you ever had any doubt about our cause, our mission and the mission of others, this will erase every single doubt or worry. It will also allay any doubts, any reassurance you might need, any fear you may hold about this life or the next." Boom, a figurative mic drop, not a literal, not when you knew the cost of a single microphone, but the point had been made.

"Think about what I have told you, what I might be leaving out and whether you wish to participate in this 'experiment'. If you have any trepidation or don't wish to chance losing some beliefs you have harbored no one will think lesser of you for not going. We will have a separate bus take you around where we are headed and we will meet up with you on the other side." He grinned at his little turn of the phrase.

He turned to go to his room and retrieve his bag when he almost ran Carrie and crew down. "Is this only for your crew or can others come along?" Carrie wasn't sure about anything at this point but she didn't think she wanted to pass up this opportunity. Barbara and Aron were less than sold on the idea. "And what about the girls?"

Suzette, who had been standing off to the side behind a pillar stepped up. "The invitation is open to all of you. If it would reassure, I, personally, will take care of the children and Nash will take care of you." Carrie and Barbara knew both of these folks, had traveled with them and knew, if they and the kids were in their hands there was nothing to worry about. And yet, the girls were Barbara's only reason for living, and they were her duty, her obligation, her utmost important responsibility. Could she take the chance?

They had a day to figure out all those questions, though Carrie believed she had to go; it was what Kim would expect of her. She would not try to influence Aron or Barbara, they would make their own decisions

Fantasia

The trip from Colorado Springs north to Laramie had been uneventful, if windy. The wind loved to play on the eastern slopes of the great Rockies, sliding unimpeded down the mighty slopes then dancing across the great plains with nothing but wheat, oats, and corn to wave at its passing. They had hopped off the interstate to take federal route 287 into Laramie, cutting out Cheyenne and its traffic.

They had passed a large steakhouse as they closed in on Laramie called the Cavalryman. It looked to have plenty of room for buses and trucks if need be. A quick Google explained it sat on the former sight of Fort Sanders. It had great promise for a large meal. Ian put in the call to see if they could feed another army at 7 pm.

They'd had to split up between two hotels that were close to each other, visitation would involve bipedal locomotion as the bus drivers wished to remain out of their seats for as long as was permissible. It would be a laid-back evening, in any event, as tomorrow would start early.

Everyone, including Carrie, Barbara, the kids, Aron, and Oscar, would meet up with the band of natives lead by Evan and his family to go into the Medicine Bow-Rout National Forest. They would head to the Brown's Peak Loop where they could park the buses. The bus drivers would hang with the buses as security. Though, from whom was up in the air. This was a fairly desolate part of Wyoming, therefore an extremely desolate area of the continent, but the drivers had decided they had no desire to go traipsing in the woods anyway. The truckdrivers agreed thinking they weren't sure about running around in the forests with a bunch of hippie musicians. It was one thing to share a cup of coffee or tiny little tea leaves in the lobby of civilization, quite another to get lost in the hinterlands. They would go directly to the ballpark in Salt Lake City.

Ben and Dugie were caught in a dilemma of whether to ride with the trucks filled with equipment, lighting, and sundry other needs or to partake in whatever Jaxson wanted all of them to experience. Curiosity is an irresistible force. Dugie remembered the sixties, or what substituted for memories of drug induced hallucinations, but they'd do, and Ben was just a curious sort by nature. When on the road, if opportunity knocks, throw the door wide open and let that baby in!

So, it was with mild apprehension and charged, sparking synapses that they road to the park. Evan had been explicit of where to meet and what to bring. Just themselves. No electronics, gear, manmade items except clothing, no phones, no jewelry, the only possession they would require was an open mind, a nonjudgmental attitude, and the love in their hearts.

As the buses came to a stop the buzz of excitement shot through the line. There before them lay the open mountains. Rocky, scree covered, dotted with copses of pine and lakes. It looked as barren as any place on earth. They were completely alone out here, not another vehicle in sight. Worried glances were exchanged until Lee mentioned they were less than an hour from Laramie, where they had just been, and a half hour or so from the interstate, where they were going. It might look like the face of desolation but they were still in the middle of civilization; or could touch it from here. And besides, he continued, look who is here.

Off to the side of the side road, by a small copse of pine, stood a cluster of people maybe twenty strong. They recognized Evan, his wife and child, grandchild someone corrected, the man Sung, Tonka and Lawrence, the two women, Cynthia and Tomi, accompanied by several others, the apprehensive Mika, Finn and Oscar, the professors as they had come to be known to the musicians. They waved hello and bid the musicians and crew to join them.

They reacquainted themselves, greeting Nash and Suzette, and embraced the band of Gypsies. Tension dissipated like morning mist as familiarity replaced it. Everything would be alright; they had met two days before and a solid connection had been made.

Jaxson had a momentary bout of regret that Padon and Maggie would miss this experience but then thought, maybe they didn't need it. Padon was so deeply content in his new life and Maggie, it was possible he had what was being offered. They were going to have to have a very long conversation when all met up again in LA.

But first, the man, Sheriff John as everyone called him was explaining what was about to happen. He related his experience with stepping through the veil, as he called it. He was a man steeped in law enforcement, one who put his life on the line for facts, evidence, something he could hold in his hand and weigh. What they were about to encounter was miles away from that. They had to leave their beliefs behind them and prepare themselves for a change in scenery, including who they thought they were standing with.

"These People," he hesitated, thinking but forewarned is forearmed, "These People are not who you think you see. You will be shocked at first but understand when you see them, they are still the same souls you see before you. They are more than whom you glimpsed backstage the other night. I don't know if I can explain it any better than that. But what you are about to experience is the most wondrous, magnificent, sorry, I am not a man of words, lifechanging event you will ever be exposed to, and I do not overstate this."

Evan took over, "What we want to do is pair up two or three of you with one of us. It is going to take great concentration and strength to realize what we hope to do. You need to be touching your guide, as that is who and what we are, guides. This has never been tried before and believe me when I tell you we know about the time frame of never." He shared a knowing grin with all of his people.

"If you have any fears or phobias about certain animals, spiders, snakes, wolves, amphibians, whatever let us know," Sung added, thinking it best to separate humans from their worst fears.

Several of the road crew chuckled as they offered themselves as sacrifices to the snakes and spiders. They had crawled through dark, spider and snake infested storage areas under stages, to run power at outdoor venues. They didn't just not fear them they actually liked them. Tomi and Cynthia applauded their embracing of species that terrified most humans. They would take these folks.

Evan took Ian, Maggie, and Jaxson, as he had already been across it would ease the experience. Gabby and Soteria joined up with Joya as partners to Alexandra. Gillian, Cinda, Michelle, always together stepped up to Tonka, he bowed respectfully. Nash and Suzette took Carrie, Barbara, Aron, and the girls, as promised. James, Raj, and Bonnie hooked up with Finn. Oscar, the owl, took Howie, the drum tech who'd had a slight incident but been allowed to remain, as well as Lee and Russel, the two oldest and most experienced in alternate realities. Lawrence guided Peadar, Ritchie, and Steven. Robert and Marylou were paired with Mika, with a warning glance from Evan. Sheriff John joined a couple of the sound guys and gals with the pretty woman Doerean. The rest of the road crew found willing guides and Glen took Oscar, the dog. He thought he could explain it better than most to the German Shepard.

All the humans took a breath as they noticed the shimmer of the veil. They detected nothing physically; no tingling, burning, perceptible touch of any kind, just the shimmer and then the world exploded in colors, life, scent. You could taste the freshness of the air as if had just been made. Hear each sound of insect, amphibian, birdsong, rustle of paw on leaf, the sound of borrowing under the soft soil. Sounds and sights they could never have imagined before this moment, engulfing every sense.

Carrie and her group fell to their knees, as if in prayer. Their legs shaking with the overwhelming intensity of light and life. They sat on the cool grass under the canopy of a massive oak absorbing the magnificence of nature unspoiled. How clear the air, how sweet the scent of nature reborn, fresh, unsullied. The sun, the sky brilliant, clean, the lack of pollutants allowing every hue its glory.

"How is this possible?" The words just whispers on gossamer afraid she would shatter the beauty with thought. Barbara's eyes wide, not with terror but with awe. The girls giggling and laughing with the wonder of it all.

Aron sat, alone, gazing out across the vast wide-open valley, though where others saw beauty, he saw a nightmare of lost souls. Wandering in desolation, living hand to mouth from the refuse of society. Shivering under cardboard tents, eyes empty, devoid of hope, bereft of self-worth. He wanted to scream to say it didn't have to be this way, to show them the path out of this but he found neither the words nor the will.

Nash walked over and gently took hold of Aron's shoulders to turn him away from the vision he was having. He tried to get Bear's attention to ask how this was possible, that this horror would find its way past the veil, to despoil what lay beyond, but Bear was too busy with Ian, Maggie, Jaxson, and now, Raj. Nash was in unknown territory; he had never known any misery or atrocity to find its way through. Did this mean the veil between man and nature was breaking down?

The half dozen roadies who had crossed the shimmering barrier with Cynthia and Tomi stood in astonished amazement. If they thought themselves incapable of being shocked or surprised by anything at their experienced point in life, they discovered they had been vastly in error. They stood motionless as they gaped at the coiled snake staring them directly in the eyes. If that wasn't enough the other three found their stare outnumbered by the eight eyes of the enormous spider smiling at them, apparently thinking the grin would alleviate any discomfort. Iktomi discovered her attempt to be misguided.

Amazingly no one, not the young girls, their mother, the wan Raj, the skittish Herbie, Regis, not anyone, feared where they had landed through the looking glass. These were seasoned professional roadies, light techs, band members who thought they had seen it all and when faced with the inexplicable rolled with the punches. They seemed pleased to be proven wrong and delighted to find another plane of discovery.

Lee and Russel sat on a medium sized boulder overlooking all of creation laid out before them. The hues and shades mind blowing, the sharp delineation between black and white, the shading of shadow, the blending of morning to night just validated everything they had witnessed in the sixties through the early eighties. They had seen this all before but had never consider it might exist beyond a small amount of liquid on a pill or piece of paper and swallowed.

Lee muttered, "I knew it. I knew it. I knew it," over and over like a mantra. His grin one of ecstasy as if everything he had believed possible had just been validated in the flip of a switch.

The Gypsies wandered, in the company of their guides, their animal spirit guides, their impossible dream guides, through what? What was? What could be? What could only exist on a spirit plane separate from man?

Phoebe and Izzy could not get over the Otter that played with them as they rolled and danced in this magic land. She sounded just like Suzette but she sure didn't look like her.

Aron was apparently the only one who saw reality, the reality of the other side. Nash really had to talk to Bear, and now! He turned to holler for a little help here when the air shimmered as another presence materialized. A woman of such stunning beauty it was hard to gaze at her directly stood before them all, grinning at Bear's audacity.

She walked over to where Bear stood and placed her hand on his massive, furred shoulder. Before she could say anything, Alex had broken away from her small group with a question of her own for Bear when she saw Gaia. She ran into the embrace of someone who had meant much to her a few decades ago.

As Nash walked over to where the two, the Mother and the young Bear, were standing deep in conversation, he caught the last of what Alex said, "...doesn't' seem to belong to any group. She's human but not all, spirit but not one of us. Add to that she is very confused by where we are, more so than anyone else, and can't seem to hold together metaphysically or corporeally. I fear for her and for him," She gestured to where Gabby was holding Teri in his arms as they lay on the grass. "I think I should return them to the park." Alex had no idea what she should do. All she could grasp onto was rebooting Teri's psyche, like with a computer.

Sheriff John made his way over to where the two lay in the grass. He had worked more than his share of automobile accidents, killer storms, and tornadoes, it came with the turf. He knew how to comfort, to check for emotional trauma and signs of PTSD.

He always remembered the child he'd come across after his entire family had been taken from him in a tornado. There was no coming back from that trauma. John was called to the devastation left in neighboring Kansas, one of those all points come to the aid of those in desperate need. He'd gone. He'd been the one to find the kid and try to console him. There is nothing you can do or say to console a child that has suffered through something like that.

John had tried to keep tabs on the kid but lost him along the way. They'd put the kid in psychiatric care, tried to foster him out, done everything according to the book and some things well outside it. It hadn't helped. The kid was a runner, someone who couldn't stay where the death of his life lived. Every time they would find him and bring him back, he'd be gone again within a week. John assumed he had a death wish, wanting to join his family. Maybe he made it. He'd run away one last time and never been found. It had happened maybe a decade before but to John it would always be yesterday.

He knelt down next to the couple and began speaking to her, and him, softly, slowly, reassuring and comforting. Her breathing was hard gasps, like a fish laying on the bank of creek. She couldn't catch it and the big guy holding her was lost as well. Something had to be done quickly or they were going to lose both. He shook her gently, trying to rouse her. He forced her eyes open to see if they could focus and almost lost himself. He had no idea what or who this woman was but her eyes held eternity and he was falling into it without a net. The hand on his back pulled him from the precipice.

Not All That Glitters

John fell back onto the grass once contact with eternity was broken. He lay on the soft, moist grass staring at the wide-open sky. Shouldn't there be trees? What had happened to all the pine trees? All he saw was blue, no clouds, no streaks of light just blue as far as...Bear's face filled his vision. The smile was reassuring, even on a twelve-foot-tall bear, when that bear was a life-long friend. John had lost his family to his job, his drinking, their drinking, and separation by disconnect. Bear and his family had adopted the Sheriff. They had sustained him. Bear's face concentrated his world to that happy reminder, his focus narrowed and he came back into himself.

Carrie saw Aron topple where he sat. He lay in a fetal position, eyes open, unfocused, seeing something she couldn't. Nash was talking to the stunning woman who nodded knowingly as he explained what he had observed and deduced. Carrie couldn't wait. She ran to Aron's side, knelt down, and lifted his head so he could see her. Maybe she could bring him back through sheer will.

"Aron. Aron. Aron." She didn't know what it was about saying something three time but thought it held some kind of magic or power that would break through. She shouldn't believe everything she had ever read on the internet. "Are you alright?" He wasn't, but you ask.

Oscar saw Carrie running over to Aron, saw them both on the ground and broke off his rolling and tumbling with this mixed breed mutt. It was fun but his best friend needed him. He ran to her side with the Heinz 57 dog close on his heels.

Lee and Russel had been in a deep, hushed conversation with the large frog, though broke it off as things began to move in a frantic direction. It was time to bring some cohesiveness to the party.

The stunning woman softly requested all to come to her. Carrie called Barbara over to help carry Aron, Gabby picked up the semiconscious form of Soteria, though she didn't feel completely solid, as if his arms were sinking deeply into her body. He rushed her to where the woman stood.

Somewhere in Aron's soul he knew that Soteria was in trouble. She struggled with a deeply embedded inner turmoil. She couldn't adjust to this reality; it had taken her completely out of the sum total of her every human experiences. And that was it! She was human yet she wasn't, well, not completely, not exactly human. Aron knew, sensed, she was a person here but not always, there was more, much more. He couldn't put into words what, or how he knew but he thought the others should see or feel the wrongness of her. Not wrong technically, just as if she was more, that was the only way he could describe it to himself. He had to help her, the others couldn't see or sense her torment.

But what could he do? He had no special knowledge, no magic, no power over heaven and earth. He was just some homeless kid picked up by a Samaritan and dragged all over the country. Yet, she needed him. There was some deep agony that had to be released.

Everyone ceased their exploring both of territory and mind. The needs of the few now outweighing the wants of the many. When the needs of the few were neglected by the many what value did the many truly possess.

Ian and Maggie had been shadowing Bear, so continued. Ben and Dugie, though shocked to find they were in the company of a Manatee, found her to be a delightful guide who knew more than they would expect about the dry world, made their way to the conclave. All were now present as the woman smiled a beatific welcome. Though they had scattered like leaves in a storm, they soon were gathered as one.

"Your friends will be fine in a few moments, sometimes it is a matter of balance, equilibrium between the human dominated plane and mine." She shrugged apologetically as if this might be her fault. "It would appear our Aron has seen his fear. The fear that many others will suffer his fate."

"Yes," came the whisper that terror had birthed. "I saw hundreds, thousands of homeless children being trafficked for sex or slave labor. I saw children living on the streets being ignored or, worse yet, being judged as less than human, deserving fate's censure. They had done nothing to deserve hunger, worthlessness, to be considered garbage, nothing but be born only to be thrown away." His words failed him. He dissolved into a wail of angst thar reverberated throughout the forest.

It was a wail of pain and suffering, not of his own, but of the thousands who had lost the love of family, of hope, a cry for all the agony and sorrow dumped on these least of these by an unjust world. It was the shriek of someone who had lost every iota of love promised, but left unfulfilled by circumstance and that same fate, fickle and uncaring. It was a bawl begging for sustenance or nourishment for the soul. It was a cry for Soteria for all she could not save. For salvation and preservation of who and what she was.

John covered his ears; he had heard that sound once before but it would be impossible for it to be coming from the same source. At long last it stopped. Cleansed of the suffering and healed by love. John opened eyes tightly closed against the onslaught to see the astonishment on Gabby's face.

The girl in his arms, the girl who had been fading into insubstantiality, was as solid as the earth. It was as if the shriek of need had brought her back from the brink of annihilation. Her breathing slowed becoming regular, you could no longer see her heartbeat pounding in her neck, she would be alright. Though something screamed at him that she was not normal, whatever that was.

There was a drama playing out in front of the assembled musicians, crew, singers, and Spirit guides yet no one could figure out what it was and who was involved. It would appear the lead players were Aron, Soteria, Gabby, and possibly John but they couldn't be certain. If this was a Greek tragedy then they would be the chorus though they had not been told their part.

The human element had no idea who the stunning woman might be, the native contingent knew exactly who she was. It was Izzy who burst the ignorance bubble.

"Gaia." One word, one name that explained everything. "we just learned about her in school before we left. Mother Earth," she said to Carrie and her mother's blank expressions.

Gaia ceased her examination of Aron to bow slightly to the young girl. "You know me?" she smiled.

"Our teacher had been telling us about spring and how in ancient times the tribes of people would send sacrifices to you. I don't believe they knew how beautiful you are, how kind. I can see it in your eyes. Mother says you can tell a lot about someone by their eyes. You're a nice person," she giggled though with a touch of blushing. "Can you fix Aron?"

There was the sound of nervous tittering from some of the less mature in the crowd.

"There is nothing to fix. He is perfect just how he is. Though he has seen something that frightens him or causes him much angst." The creases around her eyes showed concern though slight. "He will be fine in a few minutes after he has had a chance to think about what he saw and what it means." She turned to where Teri lay staring through closed eyes at the sky. "I think we need to awaken the young lady." There was something in the way she said 'young lady' that Gabby found disconcerting.

Gabby was not the only one who heard the way Gaia had pronounced the words. John was riveted to what was taking place, he had heard it as well. His head was spinning as he tried to concentrate on what was taking place in front of him yet something had taken place earlier that caught his attention and wouldn't let it go; and now, he couldn't remember what that was. Events were moving far too fast. It was like watching a professional con happening so fast you couldn't keep your eyes on where the ball was.

Soteria's eyes popped open as she screamed, "Zeus!" and regained her composure. That broke the spell! The entirety of the magic forest let out a long breath.

It was Dugie who was the first to laugh as a massive wave of relief washed over the forest. Whatever had been about to go wrong had been righted and the crew was back. Bear gaped at Gaia who shrugged as if to say, 'I'm not really certain what happened but it seems to be over.'

He thought for a moment about sending everyone back to the other side of the veil yet all appeared content, back in awe, and wanting to complete their exploring. Why not?

As Aron stood, unsteadily at first then gaining confidence, Carrie asked if he was sure he could walk, he nodded. She then asked what he had seen and what did it mean. He gestured he wasn't certain and he had no idea what it meant, yet

Aron was mesmerized by the surroundings, as all had been previously. He was appreciating it for the first time. He found it hard to breathe surrounded by this magnificence. Finding his breath at last he said, "I can't talk about it right now but I believe I was shown something that will be the most significant event of my life. Please let me clear my mind of those images and fill it with this." His tone was even, there was none of the usual teen petulance or animus, he was calm, collected and wanted time. What could she say? They walked around the clearing and into the forest with Nash and Suzette. Barbara was vigilant, the girls were in heaven, literally.

Bear called all back to the clearing after a few hours, it was time to get the caravan moving. A half hour would've passed on the outside but in here time meant nothing.

"What you have been shown is the purity of a world without man or, at least, one where man has controlled his baser instincts. This can be your world but only if you see the connections of all life. And if you can convince others this is the only way to save the Mother and yourselves. Mankind, through greed and avarice, is destroying the planet and all the children living here. We offer you a collaboration. We would join forces. You continue to do the work you began to lift the downtrodden of your species and train them to understand the necessity of all. To see, to know the interconnectivity of every life on the Mother. To understand viscerally how important each and every animal, insect, mammal, reptile, denizen of the seas, the birds that fill the skies, and those creatures that burrow under the ground, are. Extinction for one will mean the extinction for all, yourselves included.

"You have good hearts, good intentions, we wish to expand on all that you can accomplish. We brought you here so you could see, feel, hear, touch, know what life can be on earth, let us work together."

Life Will Find A Way

Barbara had been quiet as they hiked back to the parked buses. It was not an extraordinary state of mind, most of the cast and crew of the Untouchable Tour were in their own heads on the hike. Those who did speak spoke softly to one and other in an attempt to not distract those who required time to ruminate on the events of the past few hours, as well as trying to grasp the idea that only a half hour had passed here.

When one faces life shattering changes of all things you thought you knew, it is wise to take a few moments to reconsider all the things you still held close to the heart. Maybe Alice wasn't that far off the mark when she decided to step through the looking glass. It was quite possible that, even with the generous use of hallucinogens, mind altering substances, and recreational pharmaceuticals they had failed to notice what lay right before their eyes. It was also possible they had suffered a mass hallucination brought about by months of hard touring on old, worn bodies and brains with an assist by suggestion of a well-practiced and very clever con man.

But for what? No one had asked them to rampage through society destroying and maiming all things holy. Just the opposite. They had been invited to join forces with people, spirits, entities trying to save the world. An impossible task but wasn't life about impossible tasks?

So, Barbara's quiet demeanor was not out of the ordinary. The thoughts raging through her head, on the other hand, were. She was tired, that was a given. She had led a fairly sedentary life, well, as far as physical activity, though not concerning mental assault and abuse. Still, she had not traveled far and wide until her run in with Carrie. Carrie was a force of nature and Barbara had gotten caught up in her wake. Now, she wanted out.

She wished only to sit in one space for more than a night or two, to have a place to call her own. To settle the girls and herself in boredom and normality. To go to work and come home, to have dinner at six and breakfast with the girls before school. Not to live in a fantasy world of talking bears, professorial frogs and owls, and people who weren't quite people; magic and music. She wanted to stop the madness these past months had brought.

She was not a rock and roll girl. Oh, she enjoyed the music, the musicians and crew were wonderful people, but they weren't normal. They did not lead normal lives. They stayed up late and got up when their eyes opened. They ran hard, worked themselves to exhaustion and thought that was fun. She didn't think it was fun. It was strenuous, stressful, and would kill them all someday.

But that was life, wasn't it? Something you pushed on through even when it felt overwhelming. You knew in your heart someday it would all slack off, you'd get chance to relax, to sit and watch time flow by. And then you'd be just as dead as those who were living hard!

Fuck! She wanted to shout it, to scream it to the heavens and all who resided there. Yes, this was insane and no way to live but had her life previously been any less so? Being kept in fear every day, every second of those days, that at any moment he would let the monster out of its cage and it would attack. Mentally, physically, her body, her psyche, her sanity. What would kill her quicker—that or running with crazy people and magical spirits on a mission to stop what she had endured, only on a mass scale. If she died on a great quest to save others wasn't that far better thing than she had ever done? She just wanted to sit in an over-stuffed chair with her feet up and watch some mindless TV.

"You OK?" Carrie had made every effort not to interrupt Barbara's thoughts. She was running around her own roundabout in her own head and couldn't find a way to exit the circle, so she was pretty certain she knew what was happening in Barbara's.

"What do think is on the tube tonight?" Well, if Carrie had thought she knew what circulated in Barbara's head, she had been sorely mistaken.

"What?"

"I was thinking it would be nice to just sit somewhere, anywhere, and watch a soap opera or maybe a game show where you don't have to think. No one is going to take you to a place where magic and fantasy thrive. Where time doesn't exist. Where Mother fucking Nature pops in to say hello. Where you're surrounded by bears and wolves, frogs and owls, buffalo and spiders the size of horses like some bizarro, twisted Disney movie." She sighed. "Just a normal day on the road to save the world." She got on the bus and plopped down on the sofa next to the girl who had gone from solid to partial ethereal to a solid person again. "How are you feeling? Solid?" She giggled at her own little twist on the colloquialism.

Christ, she's losing it, thought Carrie, and she was not alone.

Aron kept his own counsel as he struggled to square what he had seen when they first arrived wherever they had arrived and what had been shown to him once his mind settled down. Two conflicting aspects of the same apple. If this was knowledge as proscribed by the Bible then he could understand why God had kept it from man. Whatever truth or reality might be, he was positive it was now his mission to do everything in his meager power to change the first vision. He had lived it, he knew viscerally what that entailed, and now it would be his personal mission to save as many others from that life as he could.

"I'll say one thing for you, my old skirt," Ritchie chided Ian, "life with you is never a yawn!" He laughed and slapped Ian on the back. "Peadar what say you?"

"I have to admit, since our chum has reentered the orbit, it has certainly increased the pithy quotient," he laughed but it was a cautious sound not joyful.

"Not by choice," replied Ian sullenly. If they thought they were being worn down by events they should try to be the focal point.

"Someone didn't happen to spike the fruit loops this morn, did they?" Richard said it in jest, but only just. He, like the rest was seeking some rational explanation for what they had all witnessed. Drugs seemed the most likely culprit.

"No, no one did anything but go into the mountains where we all crossed, apparently, into another plane of existence. We were given a gift. The gift of knowledge, of opportunity. We were shown, I believe, what could be rather than what has been or is. I don't think we should try to tell others what we saw, as it would only confirm their suspicions that we WERE on drugs. That would allow them to discount anything we said or endeavored to accomplish. This should stay with us, meaning those who were actually there." Ian's sincerity evident, he prayed they would see it his way and was gratified when they both nodded. Steven sat silent lost in his own contemplations.

The band bus was a buzz with questions, theories, conspiracies, and just plain stupid. When a large group of people are subjected to phenomenon outside their sphere of comfort, they begin immediately to find justifications no matter how far afield that might take them; or the enormity of the task and the impossibility of accomplishing any of it. They had known from the start how hard it would be to lift the untouchables of the world, to educate, train millions, if not billions, of people. To instill a sense of worth, pride, and honor when so many would do everything within their power to stop them.

Lee, as elder statesman, once again put things in perspective. "I have experienced many weird and wonderful things in my time on this marble. People have been as generous of spirit as they have been of good humor, of emotional support and of the financial kind. Been down on my luck and taken in by near strangers until I could get enough gigs to pull it together. Been broke down by love and circumstance and had good people sit up with me for days to keep me from slipping over the edge. I have seen the sunrise when I thought I had seen my last and the sunset over mountains that had tried to kill me with ice and snow and been grateful beyond words for the happening. But I ain't never seen nor done nothing that's ever come close to what just happened out there." He stopped took a breath, wiped a tear of joy that just couldn't hold itself back. "And if I die tomorrow, it will be as a man fulfilled and a spirit renewed. I'm joining up with whoever wants to walk beside the healers. Shit man, did you see the pure ecstasy on the faces of those little girls? It was like they done died went to heaven and found out it had been made just for them. Just amazing, who don't want that? And not just for yourself but for every living thing on this Mother!"

Like any good church there was an amen from the congregation and a few high fives and back slaps.

"He's right, man, no matter how many shows we are part of, how many great songs written and fell in love to, memories made and some hurt eased, it is such a miniscule number compared to what we could be doing." Regis was on board. "I thought we was working miracles when we wanted to lift those who'd been shoved down in the dirt but this, this is so much bigger, more ridiculous and impossible, we just got to die trying." Like any good band you couldn't travel without a roadie or two in your bus, just in case.

Unfortunately, that meant one or two soured apples as well, especially when you weren't going to be bunking down on the ride. Lance, the lighting tech who always was the sourest sonofabitch on the tour, well, now that Jake was caught and sent to an institution, couldn't help himself.

"What in the hell are they even doing on this tour? They don't add nothing," he hadn't liked having the girls around in the first place as it cramped his style trying to corral a groupie or two into his room. Some chicks didn't care if you were in the band, sang, were known or just swept up after the elephants, they just wanted to smell the peanuts and taste the cotton candy. He was there to pick up the leavings.

"They're here 'cause the bosses decided to allow them to stay. Ain't up to you who rides and who walks," Herbie liked having the family around as it made him miss his own a little less.

"I just think they ought to be in school or playing with their friends that's all. That woman shouldn't be dragging them all over the country just 'cause she can't get along with her husband." Obviously landing in the nation of chauvinism.

"Yeah, she ought to be kowtowing to him until something final gives and one of them ends up dead or in the hospital," muttered Regis almost under his breath but wanting to be sure Lance heard him. Let's see if he wanted to stand up next to equality.

"What's that supposed to mean?" Lance wanted it to come out more forceful but the words sounded forced from somewhere weak.

"I mean the woman went running for her life, and the lives of those two little girls. Her man was a piece of shit."

"How do you know? She probably was just making shit up so we'd feel for her, take her in, and it worked." This guy really was some kind of tool.

"I know 'cause I happened to walk in on her when she was in the wrong RV changing. Luckily, she had her back to me and was about done buttoning up but I saw the bruise, big one," he held up his hands with thumbs and forefingers to show the area of the bruise, "and a welt that you'd still be crying about." He threw that at Lance just to shut him up. "She don't complain. She don't let on. That woman is stronger than you could ever hope to be and she puts up with all this," he waved his hand to indicate all the insanity that was involved in their lifestyle, "Just for them kids."

"She could've just divorced him, found an apartment, moved on. Kids could've still got to see their daddy and he could've been a part of their lives as well." There was more motivating Lance than hypotheticals but Regis didn't care.

"Yeah, I seen women do that in my neighborhood, they wind up black and blue, broke arms, cowering at every little creak of floorboard. Man strutting around like he's the cock of the walk 'cause he got her under his thumb. Soon or late, someone going to have enough and gonna try to take the other out or die trying. Then it's jail time and their kids got no mother, no father, just nightmares. That your prescription for what ails, doctor?" Regis was talking about his own situation as a child though they didn't need to know that either.

"Point." Chimed in Russel, "We decided we wanted to help people. To lift them out of pain and suffering, be our brothers' and sisters' keepers. Do what Ian did with that guy who was tormenting him, forgive and not forget, but to actually help him heal. Well, we are supposed to be the children of the sixties, the ones who wanted to heal the scars and wounds man had inflicted on the earth. Like Lee said, we seen what could be. We might be a little tardy to the party but we're here. We can't change it all by ourselves, we knew that going in, but now we got allies to lend a little muscle and grease. Maybe, just maybe we can get this moving in the right direction. Sometimes that's the hardest part, getting the damn thing moving from stasis." He glanced around the bus and saw his bandmates with their thinking caps on, considering the whole of their mission. "Someone to lube the skids. Maybe us taking in these people, standing by them, giving them kids a safe place, helping where we can is the first of a billion steps."

"I don't know what I believe anymore. I don't know or care if them folks is native spirit guides, talking bear and antelopes, or just a hallucination, I know they make sense. I know all living things are connected. I know they can do better without us than we can without them in this world. I'm in." Drummers were not known for eloquence and he'd about used up his supply.

What Does It All Mean?

"So, what exactly are you saying," Jaxson spoke the words only because Ian had been dazed by what Peadar had said and sat mum.

"Simple," Peadar grinned as he got the nod from Steven, "our project is finished. Oh, there is some mixing and mastering yet to be done, but I am tired of listening to myself. I have been making records and listening to my own voice for over sixty years. I need to feel needed." He sat back on the couch to let this all sink in, not just for Jaxson and Ian and company but himself. When was the last time he had done a tour like this? When he was much, much younger, the old man sitting on his shoulder grumped. He brushed at his shoulder to rid himself of doubt. "And, after all, you've only another week or so, I think even ancient musicians such as we can handle the rigors of the road for that long.

Ian was gobsmacked. He sat dumbfounded, staring from one Mersea Beat member to the other and then on to the crazed Muslim musician sitting next to them. "But, why, b-but, I don't know what to say." Dumb but they were the first words to fall from his muddled brain onto his tongue.

"Besides, when was the last time you saved a life?" It was Ritchie with his usual humor. "Methinks you are overdue and I wish to witness the savior in action."

"Yes, I as well," Steven eagerly jumped in, "I have heard so much about the contortions you go through to save another and I wish to see it with my own eyes." He was like a young child extracting a promise from a stubborn parent.

Maggie couldn't help herself, she let out a long, loud laugh that might have shaken the bus. Either that or they were riding on a gravel road. Once she started laughing, she couldn't seem to stop herself. She thought of the times Ian had saved people in the past when she was witness and how impossible the whole series of events was. The saving was interesting in and of itself, but the Goldberg machinations were outrageous. She knew in her heart and soul how Ian felt about the whole thing and she loved him as deeply and fully as any human could love another, but, by god, she would like to see another as well. And the convulsions of hilarity intensified until she couldn't breathe. Shit! He might have to save her! Which only made her laugh the louder and harder.

"If that is your wish," Jaxson said while Ian attempted to restore Maggie's sanity, "I'm going to say yes, please, of course, you're in, sign on the dotted line!"

"You know," and now Jaxson's brain was fully engaged, "We had a pleasant surprise in Colorado Springs the other night. A songwriter we knew from the old days," he glanced at Bonnie who had caught up to his thought quicker than anyone else, "happened to be at the show. We begged him to go up and sing a couple songs, just for old times' sake. Well, it turns out he has been hiding out in some dot on the map up in the mountains and writing while falling in love and working at a café." A brief synopsis but all that was required. "The songs are marvelous. Lyrics, melody, everything just incredible. You have a publishing company, don't you?" and Jaxson's next project was under way.

The ride back to Rock Ridge was uneventful and quiet. Padon thought of the show, how well his songs had been received and the reaction of all the musicians and singers. It was nice, he appreciated their kind words, but it didn't change a thing. He knew that Maggie was concerned he would get the fever again and take off like he always had. The thing was, he had never had a Maggie before. He had never had a town like this before. He had never known true friends before, just bandmates, club owners, bartenders, and hangers-on. They were good people but they treated him like every other itinerate musician. They weren't people you could bring your troubles to, who would listen with knowledge of who or what you were and had been. There was no history nor future, just ships passing in the river.

He had so much more now, more than songs, applause, and ac-claim could ever be worth. He had the mountains, their crystal-clear air and brilliant colors, sunshine that warmed from the inside out, friends that when they asked how you were, meant it, it wasn't just an empty greeting. He had all he desired musically every Thursday night with Wally. And Doc Caldwell and Janet.

Maggie was lost in her own thoughts. She knew how much she and the rest of town loved Padon's music but she hadn't realized until she heard the roar of approval of ten thousand people how good he was. Then to have all these famous musicians and songwriters so flabber-gasted by his talent was, well, how could she in good conscience hold him back. She had found love after so many years and now she had to let it go. She couldn't tie him to their little burgh in the mountains. He was destined for great things.

"That was pretty impressive," she stuck a toe in, "I guess I didn't know just how talented my man was." Why did she have to make it sound so possessive? She chastised herself. She didn't own him, his music did.

"Yeah, it was nice," was all he said. He should say more but he didn't want to give her the impression that the accolades had turned his pretty little head.

"Those people were losing their minds over you! Didn't that make you want more?" She said vehemently. She didn't know if he was playing with her or denying what he had to be feeling.

"I chased that dream for forty years. It almost cost me my life, if you remember." He took a deep breath, he had to be completely honest with this woman if for no other reason than to try and make up for all the times he hadn't been with anyone before. "Yes. It was great, it always is when it's like that, but it ain't always like that. And then there's the constant travel, the loneliness, the time in your head when you don't know who you are. I chased fame, almost caught her until I got in my own way. I got what I got out of the show and that's enough. It was enough to know I wanted more out of life. I wanted a stake in something, someone," here he reached across the console to take her hand, "to know what is truly important and worthwhile in life."

"So, do you not want to go to LA for the big final show?" She sounded indignant and petulant but couldn't help herself. He had this fantastic performance and was blowing it off as if it was nothing. How could he just dismiss what she had seen and heard?

"No, I think it would be fun. I'm just not staying. We'll go do the show, have some fun, hang out for a day then come home." Why was she being so touchy? Did she want him to walk away? Was she trying to tell him to move on? Well, he wasn't going nowhere, he had found something worth fighting for and he was going to fight for it. "I love you more than I could ever love the music or the rest." There, he'd said it, out loud and final. "And I love our life, our friends, our stability. I want nothing more. Fame can shove it." He didn't want to argue with her, certainly not about this. "Fame would kill everything I want in life. I could never settle down in Rock Ridge because people would come, they would inundate the town. It would change everything for everybody I care about, can't you see that?"

Maggie was about to say something she would regret. But his words stopped her dead in her tracks. Did he say he loved her? Right out loud? She had to consider everything he said in that light. Wow! He was right, though. Right about all of it. They had a good life and if he were to become famous that would end. People would come. They would come to see him, to see her, to see their quaint town and it would kill it.

"Let's go home."

Fame stomped through the forest surrounding the pond where they spent so many hours watching, plotting, and directing lives. Now she was just pissed. Was she losing her touch? What the fuck was wrong with these humans who would turn their backs on her?

Fate turned her beautiful face to the west so the angry goddess in the east wouldn't see the smirk and the silent laughter. This was one time she was glad the other woman was a goddess of fame rather than the god of war or the sky. Right now, there would be death and destruction or thunder and lightning, instead there was hilarity.

Fate almost felt sorry for her sister but she couldn't. The bitch thought the cosmos twirled around her every whim. Fate was lucky, she set out the course of human endeavor and they could follow it or jump back on the free will train. She didn't much care, either way she could adjust. It was fun for her when humans decided they would not leave their lives in fates hands but would wrestle it away and make their own way in the world. Sooner or later, she would take control again, it was always just a matter of time. Something she had in spades.

Fame on the other hand was a 'get it while it's hot' commodity. Most people who dabbled in the chase would tire of it after a decade or two and succumb to normalcy. They outgrew their need or want of her affections. Yeah, Fame was fit to be tied and Fate knew where to find the bow!

"Hey, Dugie," Regis sat down on the floor next to where Dugan lay sprawled out. Sometimes you had to stretch out on the bus, take the kinks out of legs and back, but Regis had come for his own reasons.

"Yeah, what's up, Reg?" Dugan was trying, like everyone else, to process what he'd experienced. He'd had a very large Bear tell him they stood a better chance of accomplishing what they set out to do if they joined forces and tried to save the whole pie. Kevin had had some very weird trips and tangential run-ins with reality but when a bear makes more sense than almost every single person you'd ever met, well, you should probably take that into consideration.

"You done a bunch of drugs back in the sixties, right?" The stories of Dugie and his friends on the road were legend, though many attributed the fantastical nature of the stories to the amount of drug usage.

"My share, and maybe a little bit more," he shrugged it off with a laugh.

"What the fuck happened back there? I mean, I know what I saw, or thought I saw, what it all felt like, not just on the outside but in here," Regis tapped his temple, "but I just can't come to terms with what it all means. Was that like tripping?" Regis had never done anything more potent than hashish. He wasn't strait laced or a prude, he smoked pot and drank a bit, but this was a long, strange trip indeed.

"I can tell you I done a shit ton of acid, mescaline, peyote and ain't never seen nor experienced anything so close to the bone as what we did back there." He looked Regis right in the eyes, "but there was truth there. Truth I would never believe that came from a bear and his woodland friends." Now Dugie let go a huge, hearty, freeing laugh. "But I gotta believe it's all possible. Maybe we should join forces with the other creatures of the world if we are serious about saving one corner, we should get serious about the whole house."

Several busloads of tired minds, exhausted possibilities, and rabbit holes pulled up in front of the Little America Hotel. No one had rested on the seven-hour ride over. They were tired, cranky, and just wanted some quick grub and a night's rest. They would get the grub but the rest would have to wait.

Jaxson hoped the addition of the Mersea Beat boys and Steven would bolster the temperament of the troops. It would be quite beneficial if the trucks had arrived without incident and they were ready to unload and get set up. Jaxson knew a very important fact about road crews, they could be running on fumes but when load in came they were ready to go.

Ian, Jaxson, Ben, Dugie, and Maggie made their way over to the ballpark to check on the status of equipment. They were met at the gate by a string bean of a human decked out in Salt Lake Bees polo shirt, tan slacks with the Bees logo on the pockets, and Bees sneakers. This guy was all in! They introduced themselves and asked to see how unloading was progressing. He didn't say much but led them into the bowels of the ballpark.

The stage was set up right behind Homeplate. The infield and outfield had been cordoned off to keep everyone, and they did mean everyone, off the grass. The trucks were parked along the warning track on the third base side with the drivers sitting and waiting. Ian walked over to the lead guy, Frank, to ask what the holdup was. Why weren't they parked behind the stage with doors open and ready to fly.

"Ask that guy." His tone said he was no happier about the situation than Ian was about to be.

"Yeah, we can't have anyone on the grass, we just had it replaced and reseeded last year and it cost a fortune, so the deal is no one can be on it. You will have to set down wood walkways for your people to use. Sorry." Though he didn't sound the least bit sorry, more smug.

"We have a contract," Ian glared, "and in that contract it says the stage is set in the outfield and people can sit on the infield up to the stage in the outfield." He was tired, unsure of anything that had transpired in the last twenty-four and didn't need this horseshit right now. He had a busload of roadies on their way over to get this show set up.

"If you move anything or break any of the rules including no smoking, of anything," his smug grin told them what he meant, "no drinking, no drugs. And you have an eleven o'clock curfew."

"And if we don't like your rules, which we don't?"

"Then you can leave." He turned and walked away.

"Alright boys, you heard the man," and he spit the word onto the field, "Turn them around and let's go get a good night's rest."

"You have to play or, or, uh, or we'll sue!" Ian knew the type, wanted to be big shots but could never handle the hard stuff. They had just enough power to make them an annoyance.

Ian reached into his valise and pulled out a ream of papers. "These are the contracts and riders your people signed. You want to sue, have at it but remember the countersuit will change the name of this ballpark to closed." He shook the papers at the receding milksop. "We have put this concert on at two dozen ballparks, nobody complained about a goddamn thing. You want to fuck with me, little man, you won't like the outcome."

"Wait a minute," like it was written for TV.

Ian turned and glared into the pipsqueak's eyes. "You got fifteen minutes to move that stage, take down the barriers, and change your attitude. My guys will be here ready to work." Ian had more than enough by a half, he was done negotiating with stupid.

Yer Killing My Buzz, Reprise

Ian hated playing the heavy but sometimes it was warranted. They had the stage moved, the field open and the guys hustling gear within a half hour. Which was good because they were at least an hour behind with all the dicking around with this guy. He did everything within his power, breathing exercises, walking meditation, concentrating on details, to calm his demeanor. He didn't want his ill temper to rub off on any aspect of the show.

Some people, when they got cranked, would blow off the show, do just enough to satisfy the contract and then skedaddle. Not Ian or those who he worked with. If some promoter or venue pissed them off, they would give the show of their lives, a show like none had ever seen. Then, while getting paid and the asshole was gushing about how great it all was and when could they come through again, Ian would calmly tell them they would never see this act or that ever again. Let the guy know he'd screwed the wrong pooch and next time he wouldn't be such an ass to any act. It was Ian's law.

Ian had seen shows and he had seen SHOWS, but Salt Lake would stick out like a brilliant star on a pitch-black night in his memory until his last breath. He couldn't tell if it was because all the performers were picking up on his vibe or if the audience was jacked because they were getting to be so close or if the stars were aligned and the muse was in an exceptional mood that afternoon, and he didn't care. This would be a show that people would talk about for the rest of their lives as well.

There would be no after show, no celebration of the day, no congratulations on a job well done nor talk of the standing ovation accorded Gabby for his new speech incorporating all the creatures of earth. A tale he wove with such love and respect Ian felt the tears flowing by the time he was done. Add in Peadar, Ritchie, Steven, and the massive pile of talent of the others and, well, what could you say. Mr. Pissy Bees would rue the day, and then Ian laughed. He laughed hard, he laughed loud, he laughed until there was nothing left, and then he slept.

Next up was Las Vegas. It is many things to many people, gambling, entertainment, sex, wild, wide-open abandon to let your ya-yas out. To Ian it had always been a place to avoid. None of his acts fit the Vegas vibe and he had no desire to find any. There was nothing wrong with what happened in Vegas he was just happy it stayed in Vegas.

They had made the troop an outrageous offer to come. Ian had explained what they were about, what the tour was about, and how he didn't think it would fit with what Vegas was about. The promoters explained they were, once again, reinventing Las Vegas as a place of all kinds of entertainment, even hippies could come here. Ian wasn't sold on the idea but they had promised barrels of cash up front and he had just the rickhouse to put them.

Ian had asked that they find a hotel off the strip to lessen the distractions but the promoters wanted them to know they were big time so were set on one of the flashy hotel/casinos on the strip. Ian had argued it was too far away and they would prefer something more laid back and closer. Ian had won out and the Best Western had benefited. Of course, it helped that one of the heavy hitters was also an investor in the Best Western.

The Las Vegas Ballpark is continuously voted as one of the best, if not the best, triple A parks in the country. So, you would have to pardon Ians' trepidation after the skirmish in Salt Lake. The last thing he needed on the penultimate show was more stress. He just wanted to land safely and he already knew LA was going to be LA, especially as they were going to complete this tour with two nights at the Greek Theater. He didn't need anyone getting lost on the Strip, having a gambling addiction kick in, a drinking addiction kick in, an overload on Vegas addiction kicking in or a sexual addiction addicting.

The trip down was without remark as everyone mostly slept where and for as long as they could. It is one thing to try and sleep on a moving conveyance when traveling for pleasure or as a few times a year sortie for work, and that one thing is you never rest. For those who travel constantly, such as those in the music biz, you can sleep while riding the back of a donkey with a bad foreleg and a tendency to kick out with the left hind. You will be rested and sharp when you land wherever it is you land. It is your life, you have survived this way for decades, it might kill you in the end but, while you are deep in it, you live it to the fullest.

They checked into the hotel, dropped carry-ons and backpacks in rooms and loaded up to check out the show digs.

Las Vegas Ballpark is a palace of a triple A facility. It has a pool in the outfield, pristine bathrooms, clean and modern bars, loges, and pretty lights, it is Vegas personified. It is sleek, elegant, and too pretty a place to play ball. One look and you feel the need to remove your spikes before daring to tread upon the manicured lawn. You wonder how they put up with all that dirt running down the baselines and are terrified you might have to slide into any base for fear someone will be up in your face about how long it took to comb and brush that area. Fear settled like an iceberg before the Titanic of Ian's heart.

And yet, there it was, as pretty as the ballpark itself. A massive stage placed gently on the immaculate lawn out in center. Speakers and board had been brought in and put perfectly in place. Trusses set where the lighting would be perfectly aligned with the acts on stage. He should not have been surprised, this was Vegas, they knew about show biz.

The GM came out to meet them as they waited to walk out to that stage, not wishing to step wrong or put foot where it might damage a blade of grass. He was pleasant with a business-friendly attitude, which was fine with Ian as he was not seeking a new friend just someone easy to work with. Don, the man in charge, showed them around and assured

Ian that the fans would have plenty of space to lay out blankets, certain chairs—ones that would not dig into the filed or leave massive holes to be tripped in—coolers, and wine. It was Vegas and everything goes. Including a little pot, though he asked they not promote the harder drugs. Ian was happy to oblige.

The tour was back on the rails and running smoothly. The promoter, the GM, the band, the crew, were all happy again. Rest, recuperation, the time to recharge and re-up into the movement to save all life lifted spirits and focus.

Tour trucks pulled up behind the stage, the trailer doors slid open, the amps, trap cases, and life rolled out and kicked in. They could load in, set up at a relaxed pace. The show wasn't until tomorrow. Nothing but time awaited them both today and tomorrow. They'd be set, the sound check would come late morning, the lights would be fine-tuned. This was the way a penultimate show should happen.

Early evening came with a beautiful, brilliant, red, orange, purple, yellow, sunset over the desert. Everyone ventured out, away from the hotel and town to watch. A few joints were passed around and gentle settled on all assembled.

"Been a weird one," chuckled Lance. He could be a sonofabitch when he was under pressure or freaked out but when nights like tonight came along, he was as normal as anyone in the troop.

"Sad to say it's coming to a close," Russel took a toke and blew the smoke up to the sky.

"Think they'll do another?" Lance asked the sky.

"Maybe," Russel was in a talkative mood this evening. "Once the dust settles, the money is counted, and they see what needs doing next." He had spent what he had; the fumes were burned. Silence consumed the evening.

Show day arrived right on time. Mid-morning and cast and crew were up and at 'em. Everyone was cheery and more than ready to perform at this beautiful ballpark. The management was welcoming, the show sold out, the weather, oh yeah, the weather. It was ten o'clock in the morning and eighty-five degrees. It was going to be a scorcher. Ian grabbed his phone, a cup of tea and headed into the lobby for some privacy while he attempted the impossible.

They would need fans and misters for the stage. They would have to be as silent as they could find so as not to ruin the music. They would need another half dozen behind the stage to cool down performers and road crew alike. He had not one clue how he could control the crowd. His only hope was that since they lived in these temperatures all year, they would have solutions to baking in them for an afternoon.

This was Las Vegas, of course they had businesses that specialized in fans and misters. They'd be at the ballpark within the hour. This would be a good day, a hot day, but a good one. Since they had a plethora of stars on the stage no one would be required to perform longer than twenty minutes. They'd work up a sweat but Ian shouldn't see anyone passing out from the heat. He'd done all he could.

The buzz of excitement backstage was electric. The mood was that of a first show, not one that had been performed all over the country for the past five months. On any tour of decent length by the time you get to the last few shows everyone is looking forward to going home, sleeping in their own bed, waking up in the same room for more than a day or two. This group was pumped for another show and actually saddened that it was coming to a close. The family knew their time together was limited and could feel it pushing at their backs. Every minute of the next few days would be precious beyond worth.

Gates in fifteen. Time to make last rounds, dot some i's cross some t's, sound check was perfect. Jaxson sat at the piano for a few more songs before the people arrived. Magic was in the air and some good would be done in the name of life.

It was now in the lower nineties and threatened one hundred by late afternoon. Not a breeze or whisper of wind could be felt. It was going to be sweltering inside the park.

Ian turned to check backstage, make certain everyone knew the new order, try to relax for an hour before officially kicking off the show. He hated being on stage as much as Maggie did, but he also loved this show, the people on it, and the purpose. It was, truly, his raison d'etre.

Lost in that thought he almost ran over the short, colorfully dress woman standing right behind him.

"Marie!" he exclaimed.

The great granddaughter of Marie Leveau scowled his way for the briefest moment before smiling and embracing him. "Good to see you, too." She chortled at her funny for almost bring run over by he who had not seen her.

"What brings you back into our orbit?" He was not displeased to find the Cajun woman. He just had not expected such a pleasant surprise.

"I have to tell you what I have seen. This show, today, this show right here, is very important," she searched for words that would not alarm but warn.

"All the shows are important when one is attempting to save the planet," Ian kidded.

"This Is not a humorous matter. Fate, your fate and the fate of all you have worked for is on the line. And I know fate." She stared him down until he understood the severity of what she was about to impart. "There is danger here for you. I don't know what, exactly," she threw at him before he could ask. "I just know there is danger and all indications point to you. I had to get here to warn you, since Fate," she grinned, "has decided to tie our fortunes together. I do not wish you to come to harm, please be careful."

"That's pretty vague." He wanted to give her warning credence but when one is given a warning with little or no details, or what to watch for, it is hard to take it seriously. It is just so much hoodoo and voodoo. But, then again, wasn't that the woman's stock in trade?

"It's all I have for now. I intend to stay and watch and see if I can discern what that threat might be, hopefully before you come to harm." She nodded to herself satisfied she had done what she could and would hang to reinforce that warning. With that she was gone, Ian didn't see where she'd gone, she was here, then no longer present.

Ian stood, alone, in the right wing of the stage, watching as people began filtering in. He loved to watch folks coming in, getting settled, meeting the neighbors. It gave him a sense of community. It gave him a first impression as to how show might go. He could gage the level of excitement, the energy, see the condition of the early birds. He wanted to see music fans who were pumped but not inebriated. People who were already hammered would always be a problem unless they passed out. Then they were only a problem when they came to.

Here everyone came in with as few possessions as they could comfortably afford. No chairs or huge coolers, no armloads of blankets or tarps in case it rained. Few belongings, scant clothing, lots of handheld fans.

It was fifteen minutes until time for the Quartet. He saw Nash making his way through the throng of people to his customary place center stage a few dozen yards back from the lip of the stage. The infield and most of the outfield were covered by bodies, sweating, sweltering bodies. He turned to look at the flag hanging limp in the still air. What he wouldn't give for a breeze.

It was then he saw the loner, a kid, though who wasn't a kid when the observer was in his early sixties, maybe late teens, early twenties. Not unusual for this show anymore but he was wearing a long coat and a blank expression. Ian's mind flashed back to Miami, to where this all began. It couldn't be happening again.

He should have called security. He should have notified Ben and Dugie. He should have pressed 911 on his phone with his thumb on send. He should have done a lot of things. What he shouldn't have done was go down the backstairs of the stage and calmly walk out into the crowd. This was something that was his M.O., to the casual observer this would have appeared normal. Just Ian doing a quick walk through the crowd, waiting for the quartet to begin so he could check the sound. Yet he was making a steady direct path to where the kid had sat on the grass.

The kid noticed Ian as he neared within a few yards. He stood. Ian made eye contact. There was nothing there, no emotion, no anger, hate, revenge, religious fervor, nothing. Nothing to indicate he was going to do anything but enjoy the music in a hot coat, on a hot day, in Vegas.

Ian saw the long gun as it came up from inside the coat. No one screamed, no one yelled, no one moved. It was as if time stopped and all actions slowed to half time. Ian gazed down the barrel into the blackness of eternity. He was going to die. The realization slammed hard into the frontal cortex which suggested he should either try running fast or drop to the ground. He stood, stock still, as death stared him down.

He locked eyes with the kid and found, nothing. An empty space where humanity should reside. There was something about the lack of any compassion, any empathy, that filled him with sorrow. He knew he should be terrified; he was seconds from death, but the futility, the stupidity of this action was heartbreaking.

It was funny, not ha-ha but peculiar, how your preconceived notions will arrive at the most curious times of life. He had always thought that death would be dressed in a black hooded cape with a scythe and skeletal features. Not some young fresh-faced boy with a semi-automatic.

Ian sighed. He thought of how this was going to affect Maggie and he wanted to cry for her, but his emotions wouldn't kick in. He thought of a son and daughter, full grown and living happily on either coast, this would come as quite a shock to both of them. Sadness filled his being. Not for himself but for all those who loved him. Jaxson would probably cancel the show. He wanted to tell someone sitting here to beg Jaxson to do the show for Ian. But he couldn't find the strength or will. He could see the muscles in the boy's finger begin to tighten.

Soteria watched in horror from the stage. She wanted to jump down, race to where Ian stood frozen, she guessed, by fear. To grab the gun, to stop this insanity. She saw Nash rise from his seated position as he knew the music was about to begin. He saw her face. She had to get to him and they had to stop this together. But there were too many people, too much distance, there was no way. Her need, the urge, the helplessness she felt, couldn't overcome the impossibility. And then she was standing next to Nash. How the hell? She didn't have time to consider. Nash began pushing his way through the hundreds of people who seemed to have no idea of what was taking place

Maggie had been searching for Ian, she didn't know why, but she had this sudden craving to be by his side, but she couldn't find him. She went to his spot in the wings and saw. This could not be happening. He had saved so many others, could he accidentally save himself, again? He had in NY. No, this time would be the last time. The gun was pointed right at Ian's heart and there was no one close enough to stop this.

As Ian thought of all those who would be saddened by his death, his senseless, meaningless death, his heart broke. As his heart shattered it jumpstarted his frontal cortex and his arm, voluntarily or not, spasmed, and he grabbed the barrel of the semi-automatic. The kid was so astonished by the move, so stunned by how quickly Ian had acted he lost his grip.

Ian wanted to throw the disgusting thing away, to heave-ho it into space. What he didn't want was to hurt anyone so he handed it to Nash, who had appeared as if by magic, who, then, broke the weapon across his knee. He knew what these weapons had done to his people and hated them. He looked to want to do the same to the kid, but Ian stayed him with a hand on his shoulder, which he had to reach up to grab.

As if woken from a deep sleep all the fans seated around this passion play became aware of what had just taken place. They began to clap, then cheer, then scream and slap Ian on the back. Well, that was the last straw. He began to walk slowly back towards the stage. People stood and, as if sensing his reluctance for any kind of recognition, remained silent as he passed until the entirety of the audience stood in quiet reverence. Respect was one thing; he couldn't accept fame, certainly not for saving his own life and preventing the sorrow of friends.

Ian was tired.

WTAF? Could I Just Have A Minute Or Two?

Ian sat hard on a folding metal chair. He was tired to the marrow. Jaxson ran up to him and hugged him with all his might only to be torn away by Maggie who would never let go again. Ian thought about the perfect black of the inside of the muzzle. It had represented eternity, his eternity. He had lost himself in that oblivion. Something had pulled him back. The sound of his heart shattering with the thought of his great loves in such pain at his passing.

"I'm sorry," was all he had. He whispered it over and over and over into her hair, her ear, her soul.

"Don't you ever do anything that stupid again, I swear I would never forgive you." Her tears burned deep into his body and soul.

"I have to go start the show."

As he walked through the misting machines toward center stage, he felt the sun pounding onto his face and the stage, the entire crowd once again came to their feet. They didn't cheer, or applaud, they just stood in silence.

"What we have just witnessed was hate. I don't know why he came to visit us, I don't care, what we give you is love, and love conquers all. Welcome." It was all he had left. The quartet passing him on their way to center stage tapped their instruments with their bows in homage. Let love win.

Ian sat wrapped in the quiet of his confusion. What had happened? Why had he done what he had done? Maggie was right about one thing; it was stupid to the nth degree.

"Excuse me," the soft, almost apologetic voice said. Ian tore his gaze from the green grass to the face of Don, the GM of the ballpark. "That was either the dumbest thing I have ever seen or the most heroic. I have a great respect for the insane. That being said, you have about twelve thousand very hot elderly people out on my field. I have tarps under the bleachers. I'm thinking we can grab some of the conduit we keep on hand just in case and try to set up as much shade around the field as what I have will cover. Also, if you want to spend a little cash, we could run down to one of home improvement stores and grab more tarp, fans and conduit."

Stupid, stupid, stupid, ran through Ian's exhausted brain. He was so caught up in his own little one act play he had forgotten about the needs of those here to listen to the music. "Yes, Yes, whatever we can do. And maybe let's hand out water. Yeah, thank you. Don you're a better man than I." Ian roused himself from where he sat to go find what else could be done for those who baked in the hot sun. You've got a job to do, boy, he chastised himself. Take care of the patrons.

It took almost an hour to buy and transport more of the 'shading' but once people realized what was happening, they all joined in to help set up the cooling stations. Community effort to aid the community members. Old hippies do old hippie things.

The rest of the show went off without a hitch, in fact it was brilliant. After what Ian had done, and what the fans had done, both people and mechanical, plenty of water—donated by the ballpark free of charge—the performers turned in what would be the performance of the tour.

The coolest part for Ian was when Bear, his wife and granddaughter popped in with some of the other Animal Spirits. Yeah, that was cool, Ian chuckled. They'd come to discuss some of the finer points of saving habitat and millions of lives. Bear shook hands with Ian before pulling a joint out of his coat. "Word on the wind is you have had an interesting day here in Las Vegas." He didn't expound, just a grin of appreciation.

"Just another town along the road," Ian was thankful Bear left it where it hung. "It's all about the show."

Looking out on the overheated mass of humanity Bear began to sing. It was a native song from a thousand years previous. Ian couldn't understand the lyrics but he could feel the intent. It was probably coincidence but as Bear finished his song a breeze began to journey down from the surrounding mountains bringing a slight cooling with it. It wasn't a major drop in the temperature but it soothed the assembled. Ian glanced over at the big man who just smiled. They, apparently, had decided to ride along with the gypsy clan to continue the discussion of habitat, needs, hunting, and living. It would be good.

It was an exhausted but satisfied group of Gypsies that filed into the hotel late that night. There was quiet talk of a celebration which quickly died out like embers left in the ashes. They were heading to their last couple of shows at the Greek and melancholy was settling in next to reality.

What had begun as a lark of a tour, a reason to get back on the road and just play some music with friends, had evolved into so much more. And none knew that better than their glorious leader. Ian had been put through the ringer from the beginning. He had wanted to hide from the fame that had latched onto him for saving a roomful of young concert goers. He'd fled to England only to reacquaint with old friends and meet new. He had run into his oldest and dearest friend, Jaxson, in New Orleans, and they had decided to have a little fun on the road. Gabby had convinced them all to try and save the world through their talents and hearts. It had been marvelous. Even with the craziness of finding out Jake was Doug from his youth, who had attempted to kill him when they were kids, holding his grudge close to his warped heart until he could strike at Ian once again. Insanity, real insanity.

And now here they were, one more night, one more hotel bed, one more drive, and the road ahead. LA called and he had to answer, then they could rest, for a bit. Speaking of which, Ian pulled out his phone just to check.

Yup, about a dozen missed calls of which eleven were from the same number, an LA exchange. It would have to wait until tomorrow, it was too late in the evening to return phone calls even to LA.

Barbara had changed her mind about leaving once they broke camp in Salt Lake, mostly because her daughters begged to stay on the tour. They had become close with several of the singers as well as Lee, Gabby, and Soteria. Carrie was grateful as she treasured Barbara's presence, her advice, and her children. Aron wasn't sure about any of this, he wanted to get settled and begin his new life figuring out how to help the multitudes lost on the road of life. Carrie counseled him to be patient as they would have to take the time to work out plans, coordinate with others, and get to work building the new facility. Patience was not Aron's forte, but he listened and tried his best.

It was mid-morning when everyone began finding their way down to the breakfast bar and a brand-new day. Everyone was still pumped about the show, compliments were being exchanged on the lighting, the sound, the harmonies, musicality, and the beauty of the day/evening. How all involved worked as one entity to make it a great show. How impressed they all were that the venue would go to such lengths to ensure the comfort and safety of all their guests. All in all, it had been a major triumph. No one mentioned the 'incident' as if afraid to tempt the fates and bring utter destruction down on their heads.

Ian and Maggie were the last ones down. Everyone assuming they required the extra rest and time to prepare for today. Peadar, Ritchie, Steven, and Jaxson sat at one table exchanging road stories of the past six decades. Gabby, Soteria, Suzette, Nash—who continually snuck glances at Soteria as if he suspected something but wasn't certain of what—sat with Raj, who looked as though he had been up all-night counting. After the incident in NY, he had become even more anal about counting beans and assuring himself all was rectified.

Ian noticed some of the lighting people had made inroads into the roadie class and some of the roadies had made common cause with the bus and truck drivers. Maybe there was hope for this world after all.

Carrie, Barbara, Aron, Phoebe, and Izzy shared a table with the Bear clan and were head-to-head in deep discussion of the utmost importance. Dugan and Ben were in their own little world of planning for the Greek. Ian assumed the rest of the Natives were either outside or wandering the earth taking care of their people. He didn't know what he believed about any of this but it didn't matter.

Ian cleared his throat, not loudly but loud enough to focus atten-tion. It took a few moments but the Gypsies settled down to hear what Ian had to say. No one doubted his commitment to them, the tour, or life.

"When I returned to the hotel last night, I noticed I had a plethora of missed calls, most from the same number. That number turned out to be the manager of the Greek. He has been inundated with requests for tickets, far more than he could ever handle. We would have to play there for ten weeks to handle the crowds." He allowed that to sink in. When all had quieted down once again, "He had a suggestion and that's what I want to put before you this morning. He had a call yesterday from Chavez Ravine and they were offering their ballpark, as they heard we like ball-parks and their team is out of town for two weeks." He sat down.

"Wait," Ben said as realization dawned, "are you asking if we want to play Dodger Stadium?" Now the thrum of realization coursed through the entire troop.

"Yes, and they are letting us use it for free, but they need to know so they can arrange a stage, sound, tickets, food, beverages, all the ne-cessities. They figure we can comfortably fit seventy thousand between seats and 'campers'." Ian sat down and awaited the questions.

"Shit!" Jaxson fully understood the implications, "We could reach a lot of souls in one day and if they spread the word, we could accomplish some real change."

"Any chance we could come up with a pamphlet or one page to explain exactly what we hope to achieve and how they all can help?" Raj was back thinking outside of boxes.

"That might be a wonderful idea," Barbara was back on board, her worries could wait, this was big. "We could put together some photos of the species most at risk, mention hunting, fishing nets, habitat, and link it all together, raising the downtrodden with saving the interrelated species. You could easily put all that in language everyone would understand in less than a thousand words."

"And I know just the thousand words," smiled Jeanette.

"Problem is," Lee put in, "where you going to get that printed and delivered in…" he glanced over at Ian.

"Three days."

"I got a guy," Regis was excited, "and I think he would do it for cost and a little profit." He looked at Ian, Jaxson, and Raj. "I can call him right now, if you'd like." He held up his phone.

Everybody was on board; Ian would make the call.

"I like that you ask all," Evan had sidled up next to Ian.

"We learned that is the best way to find what people need, whether it is to improve their lives, their conditions, or their attitudes, people like to be asked, not told." He shrugged, "Gabby taught us that." Credit where credit is due.

"Good man," Evan remarked approvingly. "Speaking of good men, our good sheriff, now retired, was wondering if the young ladies could use a handy man like him for their project. He has taken quite a shine, I think it the appropriate term, to the children, especially the boy. There is some connection there, though he won't say what." He stared off into the distance seeing through the walls of the lobby. "I would appreciate you suggesting it to both the women. He is a very good man, he misses family." Bear smiled; he had done for his friend what he could.

"I will talk to them all. I think the children should be included," they grabbed forearms to complete the deal.

Ian had given everyone the same offer, they could room at home if they lived within a reasonable distance to Dodger Stadium, they could hang with friends, if they lived within reasonable distance of Dodger Stadium or they could stay at the hotel being offered by the higher ups at Dodger Stadium.

Everyone decided they would stay together for the final lap of the tour. They could hang as friends for a couple days, as there was now only one show instead of two, so they had an extra day off to just be tourists in their own town. Even the Mersea Beat boys decided to hang at the hotel. They had become favored special guests and part of the tour.

Wives would be flown over the pond for the gathering, their children were offered the same. All would come. This would be a family outing.

Many of the road crew, lighting folks, band members and singers decided this was a wonderful idea and so offered their spouses and offspring the same deal. Padon and his Maggie would be flying in tomorrow morning so all could have one day just as fellow travelers. The mood was jovial.

Carrie received a phone call from Henry. He and Ray had been keeping up with the happenings of the tour and since they were scheduled to come out to the west coast at the end the week anyway, they thought they might like to come for the show, that is, if there were tickets available. Carrie assured him she had an in and they would be most welcome. As a matter of fact, if they wanted to bring any of the others involved, the architect, the lawyer, the designer, they would be also welcome. This would be a celebration.

If news spread fast when there was a pony express, it was lightning by virtue of the interwebby thingy. People had been keeping tabs on this tour as it had marched across the country. Those who not only loved the music but were engaged with the conditions around the world could not wait to share their empathy with tens of thousands of like-minded people.

Once it had been announced that the venue change was in place and tens of thousands of seats and blanket space had become available fans began to flock in from around the country; many who had attended the show along the dusty trail

It wouldn't be Woodstock but it certainly wouldn't be Altamont. This would be a coming together of ecological warriors, animal rights activists, socially conscious and human altruists, and just folks who cared. Ian thought this would either be the beginning of something great that could accomplish wonderful things or the biggest clusterfuck in human history.

He knew many of these people had their own agendas and they thought their agenda was far more important than anyone else's agenda. The problem with the left is they had few real organizational skills and didn't want to abide by yours. They had their own way to save whatever it was they were trying to save and if you didn't agree then get the fuck out of their way. They were not so much joiners as they were single issue organizers. This could be a battle. He and Jaxson would use the next couple days to try and coordinate with Bear and his people, Carrie and her small cadre, Raj and Gabby and their loose organization of groups working directly with or covertly with tribes, villages, and untouchables throughout the world. These were the people who had sacrificed for this tour and they were not going to be pushed to the side now.

This final show would be theirs; they had earned it. Ian just had to figure out a way to keep people happy while understanding this wasn't their train. They might have a ticket to ride but they were passengers on an already chugging choo-choo. No signs, placards, demonstrations, no taking over a movement whose mission was to improve the lives of all; all people, all animals, avians, reptiles, insects, fish, sea mammals, crustaceans, vertebrate and invertebrate alike. No one was going to be more important, no life more precious, no way lived more valuable. It was to be all for one and one for all. We all learn to live together or we die alone.

The Final Prayer For Peace

"There can be no violence," Ian spoke softly though his words carried great weight. He had stood looking down the barrel of violence and had not resorted to such. If there was one person they had to listen to on the subject, he was speaking. "I just want everyone to be on the lookout for any sign of trouble. Anyone setting up an area to coax people to listen to them about whatever their beef might be. We are one with one purpose in mind. Peaceful coexistence on the Mother." He had adopted the term the 'Native Spirits' used because he like it. He didn't have to believe the literal.

"We will work with your security as extra eyes and ears," Tonka assured. "We abhor violence just as you do, we want peace so that all may prosper."

"From your lips," Maggie said under her breath.

"I am seeing nothing to indicate any significant disruption in the energy. Fate seems to be on your side for this show." Marie grinned as if she knew something the others didn't. "I admire your restraint when it comes to fame," she slightly bowed her head in respect to Ian, "Most would be chasing television cameras, newspaper reporters, and any other media that they could catch. Why is it you are so averse to fame?" She was curious.

Ian chuckled. He looked around the room at friends who had achieved great fame and moderate fame.

Gathered here were those who had enough to satisfy them the rest of their lives. He thought of many more who would sell their souls for another microgram. His eyes lit on Padon. Now there was a prime example. That guy had chased fame for thirty years until it almost killed him. Best thing that ever happened to the man, he had found what was far more important and she stood next to him.

"Not everybody wants fame. Oh, most everybody thinks they do but if they were to see the price she extracts, they might have a change of mind. Fame takes more than she gives. She takes your life, your intimacy, your small moments with friends, family, children. You can't take a shit in a public restroom, pee in a gas station, eat a burger with condiments dripping down your hands, swim naked in the ocean, lay on the beach with your lover, play with your kids in a park. Fame doesn't allow such things; she is a jealous and furious lover." His thoughts ran through the rolodex of close friends destroyed by their fame, now dead and gone.

"I am lucky, wait, let me rephrase that, these people you see before you are the lucky ones. They have taken only as much as they wanted then wanted no more. They have enough fame to draw a crowd for a concert but not enough to destroy their privacy." A quiet laugh escaped between his lips, "Well, most of them, that is." He took in Ritchie, Peadar, Steven all whose lives had been nearly destroyed by their fame. They were the lucky ones who had been able to adjust and pull back with time.

"No, I have no want, no need for fame, let her land on someone else's ego. And I am the luckiest man alive because my wife doesn't want anything to do with her, either! That and the people, the fans of these fantastically talented artists, respect me enough not to shower me with such a burden."

Bear pulled out a pipe and a bottle, though from where no one could see, and passed each around. Ian refused the bottle, he had for several decades, but the pipe was sacred and the pot smelled primo. They all took their toke, even Padon and Maggie, and Ian was shocked, Carrie, Barbara, Gabby, Raj, Regis, no surprise there, Teri, all, until everyone who wished had shared in the prayer. It was a good day, thought Ian, let's dance.

As they dispersed to their appointed positions Nash grabbed Soteria by her arm and silently asked her to follow him. Gabby right behind. He had a question and he had to ask or it would drive him nuts for the next millennium.

"I have to know..."

"I don't know." She whispered as if ashamed, "I knew I had to get to you, that we had to save Ian. I remember thinking there was no way I could, but the need was great. The next thing I knew I was standing next to you." There was nothing more to say.

"You are a special person. There is something powerful about you, something I can feel but I don't know what or from where," he searched for the why.

"I'm sorry, I don't know either. I have no memory before I joined this circus. I know I felt I had a purpose but if it was to watch over Ian I failed." There it was, guilt, remorse, failure all wrapped in a few words.

"You saved others," he offered absolution.

"Without thinking, without consideration," she would not receive the kindness.

"Isn't that the best kind? He meant nothing to you, little sister, and little to others, but he must have meant something to someone. You gave selflessly, that is a gift." Nash reached out to hold her close. Gabby took her in his arms when they separated.

Carrie's day was made when Henry, Ray, Carl, the architect, Daniel, the designer, and Joe Ray, the lawyer all arrived from New Orleans. Having them near was the bulwark she required. She could bounce ideas off them, ask them anything, and they could just hang. Barbara appeared happy to be reacquainted with Ray and Henry, she had never met the others, and knowing they would all drive up the coast together to get her to her new home added to her contented state of mind. Their being here meant the journey was coming to an end, she would soon be ensconced in a new life. She could, at long last, see her new home, her new neighborhood, where the school for the girls was, and how close the supermarket might be. Normalcy showed her pretty little head and she was most welcome.

The backstage area was beginning to fill with the hangers-on and the LA heavyweights, the movie stars, record people, musicians not on the show, television personalities, all the rich and famous that LA could provide. Word had leaked out about Peadar, Ritchie, Steven, James, Bonnie, the Choir, and a surprise guest songwriter 'you just had to hear'.

Folks milled about munching on the catering, whether they were part of the show or not. The one thing you can count on is that the rich and famous will always scarf a free meal when it is within reach. Several complained there was no booze, beer, or wine for the consuming and Jaxson explained it had been that way since the beginning of the tour. No alcohol before the show and if you're going to have a toke do it well away from the kids. Shit! Who had noticed the kids? But there they were.

Gates would open for the lesser mortals in ten, so, if the famous didn't want to be seen and possibly bothered by the hoi polloi, they should scatter to the safety of the buses. Most did, leaving plenty of room for those working or preparing to hit the stage. They had time before the show but most liked to spend that time considering their performance, any changes to arrangements—yes, this was the last performance but there was always room for change—envisioning the way they wanted the show to go. Some just sat around noodling on their instruments in nervous anticipation.

They had all played large shows, hell, they had just completed a five-month tour of the country, but this was LA, there were seventy thousand people soon to fill every nook and cranny, and most of the media of the world was on hand. They would be just as pleased to write about all the setbacks, headaches, mishaps and missed cues as they would brilliance. That was the beauty of the literati and critics, they enjoyed disaster as much, if not more, than success. Jeanette promised to try and corral them, to focus their attention and writing on the purpose and what had been accomplished thus far.

Ian projected an air of nothing but confidence and if the guy who had saved so many lives, as well as his own, felt good they all should. The astounding revelation was that no one in the media seemed to know a thing about what had taken place on the road. Not one reporter asked about Ian and his proclivity to lifesaving, or where the new girl, Soteria, had come from and whether she was the heir apparent life saver.

It shouldn't have been much of a surprise. In LA, just as in NY, if an incident didn't happen within several yards of the Los Angeles county line, then, it didn't happen. Everyone connected with the show was happy to leave it that way.

Carrie walked her crew around the backstage area showing them how RVs were used as dressing rooms, the catering areas for dining, the little hideaways where the musicians and singers could run through songs away from the hubbub of activity. She noticed the Native brigade deep in conversation with some of the road crew and several of the musicians. She didn't want to disturb the meeting but she wanted Ray and, especially, Henry to meet these entities. She couldn't think of any other way to consider them, not after Laramie.

"I'm sorry," she eased her way into the circle of tables and chairs, "but I was hoping you could take a moment to meet some dear friends of mine." Her gaze took in Evan, his wife and granddaughter, the big man, Tonka, Finn, Oscar, Cynthia and Tomi.

Henry stared at Evan for several seconds, then his wife and the young woman. He turned scrutinizing each person as he did. He seemed reassured by the musicians but confused by the others. "Interesting group of friends you have here." He smiled directly at Bear before noticing the late middle-aged man sitting next to him. He had the bearing of a military man or a cop, though relaxed. Yes, this was an extraordinary collection of folks.

"Black people are far more observant, more open to possibility, than white folks," Bear said, his grin approving of the old man's discretion. "White people consider themselves far too civilized to accept myth and fairy tales."

He would've said more but the stocky, brightly attired woman staring at him caused him to hesitate.

"Bear," she said to herself, "Hmm. Three? Interesting. Frog, Snake, Iktomi? Ha-ha-ha, who would've thought. And the Spirit of the largest, quite a meet," she mumbled as she continued her walk, "Quite a meet." She turned back for a second, "If you need me, I'm around." And she walked away.

Bear couldn't help himself, the loudest laugh, joyful, free, and without reservation. "This company continues to amaze."

It was time. Nash was out front; security was in place. They had taken placards from several people explaining this was a concert for all and none would be placed above any others. They were here to celebrate all living things, all people, all animals, all trees, and life. If someone didn't like that all-inclusive concept they could leave.

The quartet came on stage and seated themselves in order. Before they began Ian walked out. The people up front stood, those directly behind stood, then like wheat knocked down by strong wind coming back to life, people began to stand throughout the ballpark. Maybe his lifesaving exploits hadn't made the news but the respect had filled computers and phones with what this man had done and his aversion to fame. Seventy thousand stood in silent recognition of the man who symbolized all this concert, this tour, these people represented.

"Thank you all for coming," Ian began. He glanced over to where Maggie stood proudly watching him. "Our wish is that we can all build a movement that celebrates all people, all life. To provide some information about how many stand on the precipice of extinction." To his complete surprise and amazement, a large black wolf padded out on the stage. "Every piece of the puzzle is needed to complete the picture. You take out one or two or three pieces and it all falls apart." The intake of breath from seventy thousand caused him to turn his head. Three bears trod onto the stage and stood next to the wolf, a frog on the shoulder of the smallest bear. The large owl flew down and landed on the front stack of speakers. Soon the stage was covered with every species of animal one could imagine until, finally, Tatonka with Lawrence by his side strode out to stand next to Ian. Now, all the musicians, singers, road crew, Carrie, Barbara, the kids, Padon, both Maggie's, and Suzette stood facing the crowd. "Mitakuye Oyasin." Ian yelled and the entirety of those on stage responded immediately followed by the assembled. It was a roar of solidarity for all living things.

The quartet played the cast off the stage before beginning Mozart. Yes, this was a good day to live.

The concert was a blur for all the performers. There were too many highlights for anyone to remember, though they all could remember Padon's songs, the Choir, Peadar and Ritchie singing songs from the collective youth of the crowd. The encore would be played over and over again as everyone made their own phone, digital, and audio recording.

The A&R guy tried to corner Padon but Maggie would have none of it, explaining that he would have to discuss anything with Padon's manager, Ian. As they were going back to their small town on the next tide. And, no, they would not tell him where that town might be.

Padon had never played in front of that many people, hell, he'd never played in front of a quarter of that many people. He thought he might shit his pants, but he'd done just fine. And now, he'd never have to do it again. He'd never have to wonder, never have to dream about it, never feel as though he'd missed some high point in his career. His only regret was he wished Wally could've been there. Though he didn't think Wally would've cared.

Now it was all over, Padon and Maggie would go back to Rock Ridge and live a good life. Carrie, Barbara, Aron, and the girls would head up the coast for a couple days and settle in Newport. Ray had rented an SUV for him, Henry, Carl, Daniel, and Joe Ray. They'd try to follow Carrie's lead but if they fell behind, they'd catch up. Aron had never seen where Carrie lived and she hadn't said much besides it was on the ocean. Aron had seen the Atlantic, how much different could the Pacific be? Barbara and the girls just wanted to plant their flag somewhere permanent and get settled. All would be quite happy with the digs once they got there.

Gabby decided to give up the roadie lifestyle and give his all to the cause. He'd asked Jaxson about that and Jaxson was as happy as Gabby had ever seen him. Jaxson was hoping Gabor would take the role of spokesperson for the Untouchable mission now that he had the experience of speaking in front of so many people. He would be the face of the group. The great benefit was he could be partnered with Raj who, though he had enjoyed his time on the road, was just happy to be back in civilization. Soteria decided she would watch over Gabby and the best way for her to accomplish that was to marry the man. She didn't know her past, where she had come from, who she was, but she knew her future lay with him.

Bear and his group would continue to care for their children and keep an eye out for hotspots around the world where the Nonprofit could send in assistance. They would do everything from buying up land for habitat, showing the farmers and ranchers a better way to raise their cattle and crops without destroying habitat. They would also pass along information on villages, towns, and regions that were crushing the spirit and worth of those downtrodden humans. All would work together to alleviate what suffering they could.

Jaxson and Ian would continue on raising money and awareness, most of the musicians and all the choir said they'd love to continue their part as well. After a nice long rest. Maggie told Ian the idea of a nice long rest appealed to her in a way that, if he knew what was good for him, he would agree to.

Marie Laveau the third grinned at the two who had come seeking a path and found a wonderful one. She was pleased they had come to her, though they would never know why.

"You boys done good. It would seem fate pulled us together." They shrugged but could offer no rebuttal. "Sometimes you should just listen to Fate and let Fame take a walk."

And in that moment, she smiled.

Cast of Characters

***Sequel: An Ian Sperling Saga* melds together, with a common cause, a cast of characters from several of my previous books. Following is the cast of characters by the books in which they originally appeared.**

American Stories/Carrie Come to Me Smiling

Carrie-surfer girl who was Kim's great love. Traveled the country searching for purpose in life, finds Aron.

Aron-Teen street urchin Carrie and Oscar find in Park City Utah. Lost family in a tornado in Kansas when he was just a child. Lost and alone he hooks up with Carrie and her travels

Oscar-Large German Shepard Carrie's best friend.

Barbara-woman running from an abusive marriage with her two young daughters. Carrie and Aron rescue the family from a broken-down car by the side of the highway. Two daughters-Phoebe and Isabell (Izzy)

Henry-Ancient Doctor and piano player in New Orleans who friended Kim and now has taken Carrie under his wing.

Ray-Henry's protégé, large family, Kim helped set him up in practice though he never knew.

Great Things, A Novel

Padon McKensie-Singer/songwriter who almost died driving through the mountains in winter. Saved by a town of decent people he has found love late in life and contentment.

Maggie-Padon's love interest who owns a café in the town of Rock Ridge where Padon is now employed. She loves him too.

Doctor JoAnn Caldwell-the town doctor who saves Padon's life when he is found mostly dead by the side of the road.

Janet Jackson-Doctor Caldwell's intrepid nurse and closest friend who coaxed Padon back ot life in concert with the doctor.

To Dance Among The Stars/To Sail A Barren Sea

Suzette-Native American Spirit Otter

Nashdoitsoh (Nash)- Native American Spirit Cougar

Evan-Native American Spirit Bear

Rebecca-Bear's wife who passed away only to come back to Save their granddaughter from the great forest conflagration. She has become im-mortal as a spirit of Bear

Alexandra-Evan and Rebecca's granddaughter who is also immortal and spirit of the Bear

Lawrence-Native American Spirit Elk

Tatanka or Tonka-Native American spirit Buffalo

Oscar-Native American Spirit Owl

Sung-Native American Spirit Wolf

Mika-Native American Spirit Coyote

Finn-Native American Spirit Frog

Chastity-Native American Spirit Manatee

Iktomi-Naïve American Spirit Arachnid

Cynthia-Native American Spirit Snake

Doerean-Native American Spirit Deer

Glen-Native American Spirit Dog

Sheriff John-retired sheriff of Fort, Colorado, friend of Bear

The Sperling Chronicles

Ian Sperling-Personal Manger to many, has a knack for music, mixing, hearing and discovering hit music, has a gift for saving lives by accident.

Maggie Sperling- Ian's wife, confidant, greatest love, and best friend. His other half.

Jaxson Grahm-Brilliant songwriter and musician, ecological warrior, peace activist, belief in all mankind except the stupid and greedy

Gabor (Gabby)- Mayan, roadie, large, strong man who loves his mother and his people.

Lee Starling-Bassist extraordinaire, older musician has played on literally ten thousand albums. Wise beyond his drug filled 60s exterior

Russel Crunk-Drummer extraordinaire, played on almost as many albums as Lee.

James Nash-singer/songwriter of great renown, many hits if the late 60s-early 70s, friend to Jaxson.

Bonnie Welch-Singer/musician, several big hits in the 70s, respected among all in the industry.

Gillian Morse-gifted songwriter and singer, from the hills of North Carolina

Cinda Wilson-Texas based hard Americana songwriter, musician, singer

Michelle Branch-Nashville based singer, beautiful voice, nice person

Joya Olakundo-New Mexico based songwriter/singer via Nigeria where her parents hail from. Fantastic songwriter

Dennis Moore-FBI, decent fellow for FBI

Flacco Rodrigez-Flamenco guitarist and friend to Jaxson

Kiko Veneno-Percussionist

Tino de Sanchez-Percussionist

Jesse Collins-musician and singer from the 60s, guitarist, songwriter, well-known

Vilhelm Wilhelm-promoter and A&R guy for the Classical quartet

Jeanette Serling-Newspaper Reporter and friend to Maggie

Soteria (Teri)-mystery woman, roadie joined the tour in NY or maybe just happened to show up when needed in Ocean City

Chris Shakleton-well-known country/Americana artist, friend to Joya husband of Jenn

Paeder McCarthy- bassist and singer from the 60s, guitarist, songwriter, well-known from the groundbreaking supergroup The Mersea Beats

Ritchie Stainesbury- drummer and singer from the 60s, drummer, song-writer, well-known from the groundbreaking supergroup The Mersea Beats

Steven Gatos- musician and singer from the 60s, guitarist, songwriter, well-known

New to Sequel: An Ian Sperling Saga

Robert-friend of Padon and Maggie

MaryLou-friend of Padon and Maggie

K. Adrian Zonneville

Author's Bio

∞

Mr. Zonneville has spent the last fifty years as a professional comedian, singer and songwriter. He has written nine books previous, six novels, *American Stories, Carey Come To Me Smiling, Great Things, A Novel, To Dance among The Stars, To Sail the Barren Sea* and *The Sperling Chronicles*; a biography of his father, *Z*; a rock and roll memoir of *David Spero, A Life in The Wings*, and a children's book about one of their rescue dogs, Greta. Harper's is in the works. He has performed throughout the United States, Canada, Ireland, and Holland. He loves his two adult daughters, to travel, write, read, and be married to his most beloved.